DANCING DAYS

Ana: a little girl intently dressing up in her old friend Celia's jewels ... a young woman walking alone to church in her bridal gown ... a loving wife who suffers tragic loss but survives to travel to Africa and fall in love ... an aging woman who still has an eye for form and likes to take a risk, ride pillion on a motor-bike, sing in a woodland glade with a handsome gardener... Ana: who always depends on life's unexpectedness... When such a woman at last comes to retire, do we believe for a moment that her dancing days are over?

DANCING DAYS

DANCING DAYS

by

Anne Marie Forrest

Magna Large Print Books
Long Preston, North Yorkshire,
BD23 4ND, England.

British Library Cataloguing in Publication Data.

Forrest, Anne Marie
Dancing days.

A catalogue record of this book is available from the British Library

ISBN 0-7505-2195-3

First published in Great Britain by Poolbeg Press Ltd., 2001

Published in Large Print 2004 by arrangement with Poolbeg Group Services

Magna Large Print is an imprint of Library Magna Books Ltd.

Printed and bound in Great Britain by
T.J. (International) Ltd., Cornwall, PL28 8RW

The publisher gratefully acknowledges the use to reproduce extracts from the following:

'Little Gidding' from Four Quarters
by T.S. Eliot
Faber and Faber Ltd.

'The Love Song of J. Alfred Prufrock'
by T.S. Eliot
Faber and Faber Ltd.

'Twelve Songs IX' *by W.H. Auden*
Faber and Faber Ltd.

'Warning' *by Jenny Joseph*
Bloodaxe

'The Road Not Taken' *by Robert Frost*
Archive & Library Random House

'A Song' *by Yeats*
A.P. Watt Ltd on behalf of Michael B. Yeats

To Darragh Plant

Acknowledgements

Heartfelt thanks to the following –

Deirdre, John and Louise in Australia who proved to be even better friends when needed.

My parents John and Claire and my parents-in-law Helen and Bob for everything.

Monica and Con who were much appreciated surrogates.

My sister Louise for being there.

And special thanks to my husband Robert.

Also thanks to everyone at Poolbeg, in particular Gaye, Paula, Lucy and Suzanne.

Grow old along with me!
The best is yet to be,
from *Rabbi Ben Ezra* by Robert Browning

1942

CHAPTER 1

We wove a web in childhood,
A web of sunny air...
from *We Wove a Web in Childhood* by
Charlotte Brontë

At the foot of the stairs, eight-year-old Ana stood quiet and still – listening. From behind the closed door at the far end of the dim hallway came muted sounds distinguishable only to someone as familiar with them as she – this only child of the big old house. She knew these predictable mid-morning sounds by heart; those of her mother – periodic weary sighs and the clink of after-breakfast washing-up; and those of her father – the rustle of newspaper and fingers drumming the kitchen table, absent-mindedly. There was no talk between mother and father but, that being the norm, Ana didn't notice the lack of it.

Satisfied that her parents were where she expected them to be, Ana crept up the first flight of stairs, turned on the landing and continued on up the second flight, turned again and on up the third. Then, along the narrow top corridor she skipped and happy that she was out of earshot now she began to hum to herself – one of those tunes she was in the habit of making up, a habit like so many of her habits which really got on her mother's nerves. On reaching the end door she paused, left off humming and with head cocked to one side listened intently to the music playing on the gramophone within and then, when a break came, she knocked.

'Enter,' a refined voice commanded in response and in Ana went, head now bobbing in time as the music started up again.

Unlike the windows in the rest of the house, with their layer of grime, their dense, yellowed net curtains, and their bulky, never more than half-opened fusty velvet drapes, the windows in this room actually let light in and now warm July sun flooded it. And sitting there serenely was Celia, on her rocking-chair, open book on lap. In the sunlight, her wrinkles – as delicate as a spider's web, crisscrossing the pale, baby-soft skin of her face – were accentuated and her head of smooth, silver-grey hair knotted in a neat bun, shone more silver than grey.

Celia was smiling now as Ana came skipping over to her.

'Morning, Celia,' said Ana and after kissing Celia on the cheek, she immediately proceeded to climb clumsily up onto her lap, seemingly deaf to her old friend's protests – half-hearted in any case since, at the same time, she removed the book from her lap and shifted her position to accommodate the girl.

'You know we're both getting too old for this, Anastasia,' chided Celia.

'For what?' asked Ana, settling herself down.

'For a great big girl like you to be sitting on this old lady's lap.'

Ana paid her no heed but brought her face in close to Celia's, enjoying the feel of her skin against her own.

'What's this song called again?' she asked after a while.

'"The Chorus of the Hebrew Slaves",' Celia told her. 'Do you like it?'

Ana listened for a few moments, then she nodded.

'Yeah, especially the bits where they all join in and it gets really, really loud.'

'Yes, well,' said Celia, stroking the child's blonde-white hair, 'somehow I didn't think it would be the quiet bits you'd find appealing.'

Falling silent, they listened to the music and the room returned to the stillness which had preceded Ana's entrance. Still, that is, but for Ana's legs for, with laces hanging untied and socks midway down strong, tanned calves, they dangled out over Celia's own, swinging to the music just that little bit too vigorously for Celia's comfort. But then, as soon as the chorus came to an end, Ana promptly hopped down from Celia's lap and raced over to the gramophone.

'Can I put that song on again?' she asked.

'Ah Ana, can you not let a record play out just for once? Why is that you always want to hear the same pieces over and over again?'

'Because I like them. Because they're the best bits.'

'But how can you know if you don't give the rest a chance?'

'Ah Celia, please,' Ana pleaded, looking over her shoulder at Celia but with her hand still hovering over the needle. 'Please.'

'Oh alright. Just once more and it's loud enough so please don't turn it…'

But the end of her sentence was drowned out for within a split second Ana had managed to reset the needle and to turn the volume to high.

And now, restless child that she was, she was looking around the room, wondering what there was for her to do. Her roving eye came to Celia's dressing-table and rested there for a moment as she weighed up its potential to amuse.

'Hmmm,' she murmured, considering its possibilities and then, deciding they were considerable indeed, she made a beeline for it.

'You're going to trip over those laces, you know,' Celia cautioned over the music but

Ana just glanced down, shrugged, and carried on across the room. 'So why aren't you at school today?' Celia called over, watching Ana as she now surveyed the contents of the dressing-table, the concentration on her little face belying the fact that she was already very familiar with every single string of precious beads, with every bottle of expensive perfume.

'Summer holidays have started. Don't you remember? I know I told you.'

'Oh yes, of course. And tell me, what are you going to do with all that time off?'

'Don't know,' answered a preoccupied Ana picking up this, then that – a mirror, a brooch, a stick of lipstick – only to carelessly discard them again after a cursory examination.

'Did Adrian get his holidays as well today?' asked Celia, referring to the boy next door, two years younger than Ana but her very best friend – apart from Celia. (Adrian however maintained that *he* really was since you couldn't be best friends with an old lady. 'Says who?' Ana had demanded furiously when he'd informed her as much but Adrian didn't know, he just knew that you couldn't; that it was a stupid thing to say.)

'Yep,' answered Ana now. 'But he's gone into town with his mother. He has to get his eyes tested.' Then she sighed. 'Again!' she added, throwing her own eyes up to heaven. 'You know, he'll be killed from all those tests,' she said, mimicking the world-weary tone of her mother. She picked up a bottle of perfume, sniffed it, made a face, put it back down again and then went on. 'Adrian's mother says that he's got a lazy eye or something and that he might have to wear a patch over it.' Finding the next perfume more to her liking she daubed some behind her ears and on her wrists. 'But they'll be back soon,' she said. Then, changing the subject completely she asked, 'Celia, can I dress up today?'

'Ah Ana,' groaned Celia, thinking of the chaos Ana always left in her wake.

Ana ran back over to her and began to plead somewhat dramatically.

'Please, please, please Celia, I beg of you.' She grabbed one of Celia's hands in her own and brought it close to her chest. 'Please, Celia, please.'

'Oh go on, I suppose you can. Seeing that it *is* the first day of your holidays.'

Ana ran back across the room and immediately pulled open every single drawer in the dressing-table. Then she stood for a few moments surveying their contents before setting to work. Well practised at this particular ritual, her little hands worked rapidly and expertly extracting all she needed: a pair of purple evening gloves, an evening shawl – purple too but edged with silver tassels, and a much larger second shawl which was coloured pink. This pink shawl she put on first, wrapping it around her body to serve her as a dress, next she draped the purple shawl over her shoulders and finally, she put on the gloves which were much too big so she rolled them down to her elbows. And then to the jewellery. After opening each and every box on the dressing-table, she stood there for a while, her eyes shining, her glance darting from one box to another and then, magpie-like, she greedily reached out and selected the most glittery, the gaudiest, the very biggest pieces. First, the huge ruby brooch which she used to secure the pink shawl around her body; next, a triple string of pearls and several of Celia's heaviest gold necklaces which she piled on around her neck; and lastly, several gold bracelets, bangles and enough rings with precious stones for each of her fingers. Then she cast her eyes over the boxes one last time to check if there was anything she cared to add – there wasn't, and so she turned to the wardrobe's full-length mirror and considered her reflection.

'There's something missing,' she said, staring at herself critically. 'Hmmm,' she sighed contemplatively as she pretended to think although Celia already knew precisely what it was she was after. 'I know what it is,' she finally announced. 'I need a hat.' But it wasn't just any old hat she was after. 'Celia, do you think I could wear your Ladies' Day hat?' she asked, just exactly as Celia had anticipated.

'Ah Ana,' Celia sighed. 'You know it's far too big for you.'

'Please, please Celia,' pleaded Ana. 'Please. It *is* the first day of my holidays.'

Knowing from experience that it was easier to give in straight off, Celia got up, went over and opened the wardrobe, then reached up to the top shelf and brought down one of several hatboxes. From this she took out a great concoction of a thing, her own handiwork from the days when she'd worked as a milliner. Deep red and decorated with gigantic fabric roses, it had won her first prize on Ladies' Day at the Horseshow in the RDS years ago and the ensuing publicity had done wonders for her then fledgling business, had really been the cause of it taking off and, as a consequence, she had enormous sentimental attachment to it. She turned around now to see Ana looking covetously up at the hat so she dropped it onto her head and, sizes too big, it covered the little girl's face down as far as her chin.

'Bloody hell,' came her muffled voice.

Celia removed the hat and looked down at Ana crossly.

'What did you say?' she demanded.

'I said ... I said it doesn't fit very well,' answered Ana.

Celia stared at her disbelievingly.

'You're a little liar, do you know that?' she asked but despite herself she was smiling. 'What do you think your mother would say if she heard you using language like that?'

Ana shrugged, smirked, then answered, 'She'd bloody well eat me.'

Celia let out a loud laugh causing Ana to look up at her in surprise.

'You shouldn't be laughing,' she scolded. 'Mother will say that you're encouraging me.'

'You're a ticket, Anastasia Moore, you really are.'

'A bloody ticket?'

Celia shook her head.

'No, not funny any more, Ana. Now you're trying too hard.'

Spotting a pillowcase in the bundle of clean laundry on the bed nearby, Celia picked it up and stuffed it inside the hat then put the hat back on Ana's head.

'That's better,' said Ana looking approvingly at her reflection.

Then, keeping her head absolutely steady, for the hat was balancing precariously, she opened the wardrobe, carefully knelt down in front of it and, holding the hat in place with one hand, began pulling out Celia's shoes with the other, being careful not to lose the too-loose rings and bracelets.

'There's nothing suitable here,' she said in disgust as she considered and tossed aside shoe after shoe. 'Boring, boring, boring,' she muttered. 'How come you don't have any nice ones, Celia? Nice purple ones or red ones?'

'What do you think I am? A lady of the night?'

'What's that?'

'What about that black pair with the buckles?' asked Celia, ignoring the question. 'Wouldn't they be nice on you?'

'What's a lady of the night?'

'I said, won't that black pair do you?'

'Aha, they're the ones I always end up wearing,' whined Ana. 'But what's a lady of the...'

'Pity about you,' interrupted Celia. Then she noticed a length of purple cloth hanging from one of the drawers that Ana had been rummaging through. 'Bring that over to me,' she said, pointing to it. 'And my sewing basket.'

'What for?'

'Just once, Ana, can't you do what I ask without bombarding me with questions?'

'Humph,' sighed Ana but she obeyed her all the same.

'Now up onto the bed with you,' Celia ordered, taking the cloth and the sewing basket from her. 'And take off your shoes and socks.'

'Why?'

'Just do it.'

'But why?'

'Alright, don't bother so,' said Celia and she picked up her book again.

'All right, all right, I'm just doing it,' muttered Ana. She took off her shoes and socks and then climbed up onto the bed.

Celia set to work. She slit the cloth in half, wrapped a piece around each of Ana's feet and got her to hold them in place while she threaded the needle. Then she began to sew. Within ten minutes she'd transformed the cloth into two little slippers, each prettily decorated with a flower bud and a bow and a sprinkling of sequins. As she was coming to a finish she could hardly keep Ana still and, as soon as she broke off the last thread, the fidgety child wriggled down from the bed, ran to the centre of the room and pirouetted in front of the wardrobe mirror.

Celia picked up her book and began to read once again whilst Ana entertained herself with make-believe games.

'How do you do, Mrs Montgomery?' she asked her reflection. 'I must say, you're looking absolutely marvellous. Tell me, are you enjoying this evening's...' she broke off. 'Celia,' she asked, 'what's the name again for a party held in the evening time?'

'Soiree,' answered Celia.

'Are you enjoying this evening's soiree, Mrs Montgomery?' Ana asked her reflection.

'You don't say evening's soiree, you just say soiree,' Celia informed her.

'Ha?'

'Not "ha"? Say "pardon".'

'What?' demanded Ana.

'Not "what" either. That's rude.'

'Why?'

Before Celia had a chance to explain, they heard Ana's mother at the foot of the stairs.

'Anastasia! Anastasia!' she shouted crossly. 'Are you up there?'

Both Celia and Ana looked at one another. Neither answered.

'Anastasia!' called her mother again.

'She's up here, Mrs Moore. I'll send her down to you,' Celia called out.

Feeling betrayed, Ana stared at her sulkily.

'She'd have come looking for you,' Celia explained in her own defence. 'Now quick, out of those clothes. She'll have a heart attack if she sees you dressed like that.'

Ana took off her finery and then went downstairs, to the kitchen.

'Yes, mother?' she asked from where she stood at the doorway.

'Run up to the butcher's and collect the meat I ordered earlier,' said Mrs Moore who was too preoccupied with the task of peeling potatoes at the kitchen sink to turn around.

'Now?' asked Ana.

As she waited for her mother to answer, she idly considered her father who was sitting at the kitchen table, hunched over his newspaper. She sometimes found it impossible to tell whether he was reading or whether he was just pretending to while he took a nap. Now, for instance, he seemed to be reading but, then again, he was very still. He was probably asleep, she decided.

A sudden whack across the head put an end to her ruminations.

'Of course *now*, you fool of a child,' her mother screamed at her. 'When did you think I meant – next week?'

Ana ran out of their front gate, ran past Adrian Lloyd's house next door and then down past the rest of the terrace of old Georgian redbrick houses, so typical of Dublin's old inner suburbs. As she was turning the corner onto the main road, she suddenly noticed that she was still wearing the purple slippers. That they'd escaped her mother's notice so far was nothing short of a miracle in Ana's eyes but now she wondered how she'd manage to avoid having her see them when she arrived back with the meat. Such nonsense, as her mother would consider them no doubt, drove her crazy and that Ana had been found in Celia's room meant that she was in trouble enough as it was. Her mother was forever telling her not to be bothering their paying guests, an ever-changing miscellany of people who filled the rooms of their vault of a house, all there on sufferance, welcome only for the rent they paid. But Ana knew she wasn't bothering Celia. They were very pretty though, she thought, slowing down to a trot to admire the slippers but then, remembering that her mother was waiting, she picked up speed again.

Seconds later, her foot went down on a sliver of glass carelessly discarded on the footpath and it sliced through the purple cloth and through the skin of her foot. Screaming in pain, Ana stumbled to the ground.

Mrs Moore answered the urgent knocking on the door to find her neighbour Mrs Lloyd standing there with Ana in her arms and a worried-looking Adrian at her side. She looked at her daughter first, at the ribbon-slippers and at the blood dripping from one foot and then she looked at Adrian who was keeping a comforting tight hold of one of Ana's hands. To Mrs Moore he appeared positively ill, for fear of her and concern for Ana was making his wan face even more wan and his habitually runny nose runnier still. Noticing the fresh patch covering his left eye underneath the glasses she was somewhat puzzled by it.

'What the ... the ... the ... blazes?' she began, stuttering with surprise. 'Mrs Lloyd, what's going on? What's happened to the pair of them?' she demanded, looking in confusion from one to the other then back again. 'What are those things on your feet, Ana? Where's the blood coming from? And what in the name of God is the matter with the young fella?' She stared down at Adrian. 'Did he lose an eye or what?'

Mrs Lloyd was no great fan of Ana's mother and now she roughly shoved past her and carried on down the hallway with Ana in her arms and Adrian following closely, struggling to maintain his grip on Ana's hand.

'She cut her foot on some glass,' shouted back Mrs Lloyd. 'We found her just as we were getting off the bus. Tell me, is your husband here? If he is then send him for a doctor – quick now.'

'A doctor? Are you sure they need a doctor?' asked Mrs Moore, feeling real alarm for the first time, at the thought of the expense. Then, noticing that Mrs Lloyd was on her way into the good room, she shouted after her. 'No, no, not in there, you'll get blood all over the place. Here, bring her into the kitchen. Jimmy,' she shouted as she followed Mrs Lloyd into the kitchen, 'Jimmy, go fetch the doctor!'

Alerted to the commotion, Celia had come downstairs.

'And what are you gawking at?' Mrs Moore demanded, seeing her at the kitchen door. 'Haven't you done enough damage? Don't think that I don't recognise your handiwork. And what are you doing in here anyway? Can we have no privacy at all? Might I remind you that you pay for the room and not for the run of the house?'

Easter Sunday, early morning...

'Oh Jaysus,' Ana groaned as she got down on her knees, bent down low and peered under the bed. 'So that's where you are,' she muttered, spotting her missing shoe, and with the tip of her walking-stick she began nudging it towards her. 'Come out, you bugger,' she muttered as she brought it nearer. 'Come out.' Catching hold of the shoe, she lined it up beside its twin then slowly got back up off her knees and sat herself down on the bed. She paused a moment then began to ease her feet into the shoes. First her left foot, then her right – but with more difficulty for it had never been the same, not since she'd cut it on glass as a child. All these years later and it was still acting up. That foot, as she always thought of it (as if it was a separate entity entirely and one of which she'd no desire to claim ownership) was the reason why, a couple of months previously, the doctor had cautiously recommended that she might start using a walking-stick. Not as a necessity, he'd hastened to add, hoping to ward off the volley of abuse he knew would follow once she'd succeeded in arranging the individual features of her face into the look of outrage they were struggling towards but, as he'd explained, just as a convenience. But despite her need for 'that blasted stick', vanity usually prevented her from using it publicly and she only succumbed when the pain was at its most intense. Still, it had its uses and retrieving lost shoes was only one of them. In the mornings for example, she'd developed the knack of pushing the curtains apart with the stick so that she knew what kind of day it was before ever leaving the bed and, ever since she'd lost the remote control for the telly, she kept it close at hand and used it to change channels or to turn the 'damn thing' off which saved her the bother of having to get up from the couch. But it was probably best employed as a weapon to fend off the amorous advances of Colonel Jackson – a vigorous wave of the stick in his direction was far more effective than all the threatening words even she could muster.

She got to her feet now, to her soft, leather, midnight-blue-clad feet, which she looked down at with pleasure. She loved these shoes

– the turn of the heel, the double gold-coloured buckle, the way they emphasised her still, even if she said so herself, well-shaped ankles. The very sight of them put her in good form. Old Celia would have turned in her grave if she could see her collection of shoes, Ana reflected now, not seeing the irony in the fact that she, who was no longer exactly a spring chicken herself, still thought of her friend of long ago as *old* Celia. A collection fit for a lady of the night, as Celia might have delicately put it – all reds and blues and purples. But then, Ana had never been a friend of subtle dress and as she grew older she became even more of a stranger to it. It seemed to her that a woman of her advancing years was almost compelled to choose between the two 'old lady uniforms' as she called them; the first being the traditional uniform of sensible skirt, blouse and cardigan in colours that ranged from brown and navy to ... to darker brown and navy; the second being the more contemporary uniform of shiny, fluorescent, brightly-coloured leisurewear. But nothing, absolutely nothing, would compel her to wear either and instead she preferred to give full rein to her own rather distinctive style.

Looking at herself in the mirror now, she was happy with what she saw. The green and cerise chiffon dress she had on was one of her favourites. She loved its layers, the way it fell in ripples to just above those well-shaped ankles. The midnight-blue shoes probably didn't go with it, possibly even clashed but still, the whole ensemble was pleasing to the eye. Well, to her eye at any rate, which was all that really mattered. A technicoloured Barbara Cartland, some man or other had called her once and although she couldn't be sure that he'd intended it as a compliment, the image had pleased her. The dress did little to hide her plumpness she saw, turning this way and that and studying her figure. Plump she was, no two ways about it, but no matter – more than one man had been glad of something other than skin and bones to hold on to. Old-looking – yes – that too, but what could she expect? She *was* old for goodness sake and besides, she'd never resort to tucks and lifts and nips, it gave her the willies – interfering with nature like that. In contradiction however, she wasn't opposed to complimenting nature with a subtle hint of paint and powder as she put it, though it was quite a lot more than a hint and there was nothing subtle in the shades of bright pink lipstick and baby-blue eye-shadow she favoured. She looked at her hair now and decided that it was definitely time to make an appointment with Belinda the hairdresser who came each week to the retirement village. Just for a wash and blow-dry.

She'd given up dyeing it years ago and was in fact rather proud of her grand head of thick, white hair.

'Not bad for an old one,' she said, taking one last look at herself. Then, turning from the mirror, she picked up her handbag from where it lay on the bed and, after checking to see that she had everything she needed, she headed out.

'Hello, Elizabeth,' Ana called out, noticing Elizabeth Daly coming out of her own bungalow two doors down.

Ana usually found herself towering over other women. Ellen for example, who lived in the bungalow between Ana and Elizabeth's, made her feel positively gigantic. But Elizabeth was one of the few woman compared to whom Ana felt almost petite for although she was only slightly taller than Ana she was a good deal broader and was very, very strong. She was a powerful woman, as they say. So much so that Colonel Jackson (almost a head shorter than her himself) had dared to ask her on one occasion what it had felt like to come face to face with Hulk Hogan in the ring and, on another, to enquire as to what the going rates for female wrestlers were these days. Only her ensuing apoplexy had ensured his safe getaway.

As Ana and Elizabeth drew near to one

another, it suddenly struck Ana that there was something different about Elizabeth's appearance today but it took her a few seconds to figure out that it was her hair. Always suspiciously dark it was now pitch-black. On a much younger woman, an oriental woman perhaps, it just might have looked natural but on Elizabeth it looked, well, it looked distinctly odd.

'Ana, what wonderful shoes!' Elizabeth exclaimed in her grand Dublin Four accent. 'Where on earth did you manage to find such treasures?'

'I can't remember, Elizabeth,' answered Ana evasively, aware that the other woman was far from being sincere.

Since she'd moved to Rathdowne Retirement Village two months ago, Ana had learned quite a few things about Elizabeth: that she rarely had a kind word to say about anyone apart from her family, that she was partial to a good moan, that she was a dreadful gossip, that she was incredibly nosy and that she was an out-and-out snob – to mention a few. But despite all that, Ana couldn't say she actually disliked Elizabeth and though she wouldn't go so far as to say she'd become fond of her, she had grown used to her. There wasn't any real harm in her and because there was a lonesomeness about her, and discontentedness, Ana was probably more willing to excuse her foibles than she might otherwise have been. Elizabeth could, Ana thought, be best described as silly. Besides, she amused Ana for she was as transparent as cling-film and, even now, Ana knew from experience that Elizabeth would almost certainly mock the very shoes she'd just complimented when she was next talking to Penny or Ellen or one of the other women.

'Do you know that Joan Collins was photographed wearing a very similar pair in this week's issue of *Hello?*' Elizabeth went on.

'Really?' asked Ana politely. A peculiarity of Elizabeth's was the interest she took in the lives of the rich and famous and she was only too happy to demonstrate her considerable knowledge in this area to any interested – or, as was more often the case – uninterested listener. She practically learned the contents of every issue of *Hello* off by heart. 'With a pale blue outfit,' she went on. 'Silk. Very straight. Subtle. Not at all like the outfits she used to wear in *Dynasty*. Her sister Jackie, you know the one who writes the...'

'I see you've had your hair done,' Ana interrupted, realising that if she didn't Elizabeth was likely to go on all morning. Noticing that the scalp showing through Elizabeth's thin hair appeared to have been dyed pitch-black as well, Ana decided it was lucky indeed that she'd never trusted

Belinda with anything more than a wash and blow-dry.

'Do you like it?' asked Elizabeth, patting the back of the bowl-shaped hair-do. 'Janet, my daughter-in-law, insisted on treating me. "Elizabeth," she said to me. "Listen now, there's no need for you to be going to that Belinda woman – God only knows if she's ever even been trained. No, she won't do at all, I simply must take you to Alain's." You see, Ana, he's just opened a new salon off Grafton Street and apparently it's the in-place at the moment. Even Sarah Ferguson goes to him when she's in Ireland. She said so a few weeks ago in an interview in *Hello*. She called him her good friend Alain or something like that. Of course he *is* very expensive. But then Janet can afford it, Harry is doing so well. Did I tell you that he's just expanded into a second premises in Ballsbridge?'

'Who? Alain?' asked Ana being deliberately obtuse.

'Ah no, no. Harry of course.'

'Oh yes, you may have mentioned it.' At least half a dozen times she might have added.

'And did I tell you that the rent per square metre is more than any other building in Dublin outside the city centre?'

'Yes, I remember you saying something like that and I've been meaning to ask you, how on earth did he get conned into renting somewhere so expensive? I mean, an accountant of all people? Do you know if there's any way he can get out of it?'

'Hah? Ah no, no, no, Ana. You misunderstand me. No, it's a prestige thing. You see, in business it's very important to be seen to be successful, so Harry tells me. Especially when you think big like Harry does. God no, I can tell you he's anything but foolish when it comes to money. No, he was always terribly cautious. You know, I remember years and years ago, on the day of his Holy Communion, I wanted to take him into town so that he could buy himself a toy or something with the money he'd received from neighbours and relations. But oh no, that wasn't to his liking at all.' Her face now softened as she wistfully remembered and then she laughed fondly. 'I can just picture him, togged out in his little suit, a right little man he was, standing there looking up at me – his face all serious. "I'll come into town," I remember him saying, "but on one condition. On condition that I can go to the GPO. and open up an account for my money for I have no interest in buying toys." Can you credit that? And he barely six years of age.'

She paused and stood there for a moment, smiling fondly at the memory. Ana couldn't really think of anything to say. He sounded like a very peculiar child to her and not a particularly pleasant one either, an opinion Elizabeth was unlikely to appreciate.

'The money's probably still in there, knowing Harry,' laughed Elizabeth. 'He isn't normally what you'd call a big spender. As he says himself, that's the one sure way you're not going to get rich. No, he's careful with his money alright. That trip to Alain's salon was just a special treat for my birthday, Ana.'

'Oh was it your birthday lately, Elizabeth? I didn't know that – what day was it?'

'Well it was actually some time ago, Ana, probably before you arrived. But with the children and everything Janet couldn't really manage to take me until this weekend. You know how a young family takes up every waking moment.' Then, bringing the conversation around as casually as she could, she went on. 'I can't remember, Ana, but did you say you had a family yourself?'

Ana sighed in annoyance. Within minutes of their very first meeting, Elizabeth had bombarded her with so many questions that Ana, who was reticent about her private life in any case, had resolved not to tell her a single thing. She might have relented in due course except that Elizabeth was so obvious in her continued attempts to wrangle personal information and, though she knew it was childish, it had become a game with

Ana to count the number of probing questions Elizabeth dropped into every conversation they had and to manage to avoid ever giving her a straight answer.

'No, no, I didn't say.'

'So you don't have any family?'

'No, no, I didn't say that either. Anyway, Elizabeth, I'd better get a move on, otherwise I'll never get anything done today.'

And, not giving Elizabeth any opportunity for further questioning, Ana quickly took her leave and headed off in the direction of the main house. Rathdowne House was a magnificent place built in the 1820s by an old Anglo-Irish family and, until 1980, successive generations of this family had lived in the house but the last generation, down on its luck, had been forced to sell the house and the lands. For the following ten years the estate had passed from one developer to another, all hopeful of getting the sixty acres of garden zoned for high-density housing but each had failed. Finally, Zanzibar Holdings, the last company to acquire it, had settled for developing it as a retirement village and for this purpose they'd erected forty bungalows in the grounds and converted the main house to accommodate ancillary services such as a nursing facility to cater for the more minor ailments of the residents, a dining-room, a recreational room, a laundry and overnight accommodation for the residents' guests – all currently run under the beady eye of the formidable director, a Mrs Reynolds. All any potential resident had to bring with them, as Colonel Jackson was fond of saying, was a lorry-load of money and perfect health. Woe betide anyone who fell seriously ill for they were shipped up to Loughlinstown Hospital in the dead of night, under the cover of darkness, never to be seen again – as he exaggeratedly put it.

As Ana rounded the corner of the main house she sighed with pleasure. When she'd first come down to look around some months previously, she'd been deaf to Mrs Reynolds' verbose explanations as to why Rathdowne Retirement Village was so superior but had just stood there, gazing over the superbly landscaped acres. It really was a truly magnificent garden. It even included a lawn-bowling area left over from former times, as well as a maze, a walled-in orchard and a small lake. As Mrs Reynolds had rambled on about how Rathdowne really had to be the top choice for any discerning, well-to-do, mature person, Ana made mental calculations as to whether or not she could afford to live here. Purchasing the bungalow wasn't the problem – she'd made enough on the sale of her house in Brighton to cover the asking price. It was the hefty monthly service charges that worried her. But Rathdowne was so beautiful and she was so desperate to move out of that miserable flat in Dublin that she'd made up her mind to go for it deciding that she'd worry about money if, and when, the time came.

There was a chill in the March air and, walking briskly, Ana soon caught up with Colonel Jackson who was strolling along at a more leisurely pace.

'You were talking to Lizzy I noticed,' he said, glancing across at her as she came abreast of him.

'You didn't exactly come rushing over to join us,' she answered. 'I saw you, skulking along the footpath, terrified that she might spot you.'

'Ah Ana, you know how it is. You really have to be in the mood for that Lizzy.'

'Colonel,' scolded Ana, 'I don't know how many times I've heard her telling you that you're not to go calling her Lizzy.'

'Ah sure, I only do it to rile her. But tell me something, Ana – are there auditions going on for *Madame Butterfly* or what?'

'What are you talking about?' asked Ana, completely lost.

'Her hair? What happened to Lizzy's hair? It's very odd-looking. What on earth did she do to it?'

'Janet took her to some fancy hairdresser's in Dublin, so she tells me.'

'Well, I hope she sues. She should, you know. It's a disgrace what some of those cowboys get away with. So, Ana, did she have any other news concerning the world's most exciting family to impart?'

'Well, you know, just the usual kind of thing. That Harry has just moved into the most expensive office ever to come on-stream and that...'

Suddenly the Colonel caught a hold of Ana's arm and began guiding her towards a nearby bench.

'Ah Colonel,' she protested, trying to pull away. 'Not now, I haven't time. I'm just about to go into Kilmurray.'

Taking no notice, he sat her down dead-centre of the bench, checked that she was sitting upright, moved her chin so that she was looking straight ahead and then, in the officious voice of a quizmaster, he began,

'And now we have Mrs Anastasia Dunne whose specialised subject tonight is Elizabeth Daly and family.' He coughed, raised his voice a notch, then went on. 'Question one. Janet and Harry Daly recently dined at the house of a well-known personality who happens to be a client of Harry's. For twenty points, Mrs Dunne, can you please name that well-known person?'

'Jeffery McGovern,' Ana answered promptly. 'Ireland's second richest man.' Though she had yet to meet any of

Elizabeth's family, Ana, like everyone at Rathdowne, knew far more about the minutiae of the Dalys' lives than she particularly wanted to. Recounting Janet and Harry's account of that dinner at Jeffrey McGovern's had kept Elizabeth going for days. If asked, though it was unlikely since people weren't keen to encourage her, she could have described every plate of food served that evening, every detail of Jeffrey McGovern's house and what each of the guests were wearing.

'Correct,' proclaimed the Colonel. 'Next question, what are Janet and Harry's wishes for their oldest son Tim?'

'That he'll settle down now that they've finally got him into a new school; that he'll turn up for his grinds and study hard enough so that he too can become an accountant; and, that one day, he'll join his father's firm.'

'Correct. And now for your final question. And I might remind you, Mrs Dunne, that there is a lot resting on this. If you answer correctly, then you will be in with a chance of next week's jackpot. So, if you're ready, I'll begin.' He coughed to clear his throat. 'Mrs Dunne, can you please tell me what is currently Harry and Elizabeth Daly's greatest concern?'

'Well...' began Ana, but before she got a chance to go any further, the Colonel interrupted.

'I'm afraid the clock *is* ticking,' he said sternly.

'Wait, wait,' said Ana, acting all flustered.

'Mrs Dunne, I need an answer.'

'That their daughter Sophie won't listen to a word Janet says,' tried Ana.

The Colonel considered her answer for a few moments but then solemnly shook his head.

'I know, I know,' she tried again. 'That the petrol station near Kilmurray once charged Harry ten pence more per litre than he usually pays in Dublin and when he complained to the owner he was told where to go in no uncertain terms.'

But the Colonel shook his head again.

'Mrs Dunne, I'm afraid...'

'That ... that ... the family who've moved in next door to them are bringing down the tone of their neighbourhood because they've a caravan parked in the driveway, their washing-line is clearly visible from the public road and the woman once called Janet a snobby cow to her face when she went around to complain about something.'

'Correct!' proclaimed the Colonel.

'You are mad,' she laughed as he sat down beside her. 'But I take it you know that.'

'Just mad for you, Ana,' he said taking her hand in his.

'Oh God,' she sighed, taking her hand back again. 'Why do you always have to start this nonsense?'

She got to her feet but he quickly followed suit.

'So,' he said, attempting to link her arm. 'Where are we off to?'

'*We're* off to nowhere,' she said, keeping her arm in tight by her side.

'Ah Ana, how can you deny me the pleasure of your company? When I saw you talking to Lizzy earlier I thought to myself, as indeed I often do, that you really are by far the best-looking woman in this place. And, I might add, that includes all the staff as well, all those young ones. Mind you, that new nurse isn't bad, no, not bad at all. Now she's the kind Mrs Reynolds should be employing here instead of the likes of that Nurse Boo. You know, I saw him driving out of here yesterday and God, he looked like he'd hardly survive through the night, he looked absolutely dreadful. I mean, it's hardly a good advertisement for this place to have the carers looking like they're at death's door. No, she should get rid of him and take on another few young ones.' He fell silent for a moment. 'Of course,' he continued, his thoughts once again on the young female nurse, 'she does have the advantage of a nurse's uniform. Tell me Ana, you weren't a nurse in your day by any chance?' And, ignoring her look of disgust he went on, 'Yes, I can imagine you now. Hmm, hmm,' he added, obviously conjuring up some pleasing mental image which Ana preferred not to think about. 'Maybe, we should go towards the lake, Ana, what do you think?'

'*We're* going nowhere, Colonel,' said Ana.

'Ah Ana, where's the joy in going for a walk by yourself?'

'A lot more than having to listen to the rubbish you come out with.'

The Colonel took no notice.

'Laurence!' he called out, seeing his friend coming along the path. 'Laurence! Will you try explaining to this silly woman that there's little point in going for a walk on one's own.'

'What's that, Colonel?' asked Laurence, coming over.

Laurence was the gardener at Rathdowne and solely responsible for the beautiful state of the gardens. When Ana had first moved into her bungalow in Rathdowne he'd just gone on holidays and, aside from a few polite and brief exchanges between them since his return (she complimenting his handiwork, he modestly accepting such compliments) she'd had little to do with him. He seemed a quiet sort to Ana and the little she did know about him she'd learned through the Colonel. The Colonel's highest authority on any matter appeared to be Laurence; he was forever quoting him on all kinds of subjects and they appeared to get on tremendously well even though to her they seemed to be complete opposites. Even physically, thought Ana glancing from one to the other now, they couldn't have been more different and their present proximity served to dramatically highlight these differences. Dressed in grubby overalls, Laurence made the Colonel in his natty blazer look even more of a dandy. Laurence, with his sharp cheekbones and jaw and his lean, wiry build, was all angles whereas the Colonel had a rotund figure with a face to match and his complexion looked even more pink and soft when contrasted with Laurence's leathery one. Even Laurence's head of slate-grey hair made the Colonel's few remaining wisps of straw-coloured hair, combed carefully over his shiny pink crown, appear even more sadly lacking than usual.

'Laurence,' repeated the Colonel. 'Will you try telling this woman here that there's no point in going for a walk on one's own.'

'I suppose the Colonel has a point, Mrs Dunne. It's always nice to have company on a walk.'

'But Laurence I'd prefer my own company than the company of this ... this...'

'See that!' said the Colonel to Laurence. 'See that! Speechless! I always have that affect on women. You know, you could learn a thing or two by watching me in action, Laurence.'

'This ... leech,' finished Ana, causing Laurence to burst out laughing. Then she turned to the Colonel. 'At times, Colonel, I really believe you are truly the most obnoxious man I've ever come across.'

'Don't listen to a word she says, Laurence,' said the Colonel, not in the least bit put out. 'It's all hot air. You see, underneath it all I do believe she has quite a thing for me.'

'Oh please,' said Ana in exasperation. 'Laurence, will you tell your friend here to wake up to reality? A thing for him!' She began walking off but before she'd taken more than a few steps, she turned around again. 'Colonel,' she called back warningly, 'don't you even think of following me.'

The two men stood there, looking after her – Laurence smirking, still amused by the exchange, and the Colonel with a look of admiration on his face.

'Feisty, I'll give her that,' said the Colonel. 'Still, no harm in that now, is there, Laurence?'

1955

CHAPTER 2

What we call a beginning is often the end
And to make an end is to make a beginning...
from *Four Quartets 'Little Gidding'*
by TS Eliot

On hearing Celia call 'Enter,' in response to her knock, Ana came into the room.

'I'm ready,' she called to Celia who was sitting in the rocking-chair in her usual spot by the window, warming her old bones in the autumn sun.

As she crossed the room, Ana noticed how Celia's eyes, blind these last few years, followed the sound of her footsteps and where once her hands had been forever busy – either sewing, knitting, writing, turning the pages of a book – always busy with something, they were still now and resting on her lap. Bending down, Ana kissed Celia on the cheek and in response the old woman's hand went up to Ana's hair and touched it softly.

'So, Anastasia, tell me, what are you like?' Celia asked, her face and voice full of excitement.

'Beautiful, Celia,' teased Ana. 'Absolutely

beautiful. If you could see I'd do a show-off pirouette for you.'

'Like you used to when you were young, vain little madam that you were. Now, Anastasia, describe the dress to me.'

'Well, the skirt is gold-coloured and the bodice is red,' Ana lied, watching Celia's face fall as she did. 'And...'

'Ah Ana,' interrupted Celia crossly. 'After all your promises. You promised me you'd wear white on your wedding day. You promised.'

Ana laughed. 'Listen to you,' she said. 'You sound more like a petulant child than an eighty-year-old woman.'

'Eighty-year-old woman? The cheek of you!'

'Alright then, eighty-two-year-old woman,' said Ana.

'Eighty-two? Eighty-two?' stammered Celia in outrage, though Ana was still a couple of years short. 'You hussy, you!'

'Calm down. You'll give yourself a heart attack,' Ana laughed. 'And I don't want you popping off and ruining my day.'

'It would serve you right. Gold and red! Gold and red indeed! Who ever heard the like? I'm disgusted with you, Ana, I really am.'

'Celia, I was only teasing. The dress is white. White silk. Here, feel.' She took Celia's hand and brought it up to the dress.

'Ah lovely,' muttered Celia, stroking the material. 'So soft.' But then a look of concern crossed her face. 'Are you sure it's white, Anastasia? You're not just taking advantage of a woman's blindness and fooling her.'

'Celia! As if I would.'

'Alright, alright,' she said placated. 'Now, Anastasia, describe the style of it for me.'

'Well, the skirt is straight and stops just short of the ankle,' Ana began, guiding the old lady's hand over it. 'And there's a wide band – white too – around the waist which is quite high.'

'Empire-line,' Celia said, nodding knowledgeably. 'And the neck, Anastasia?'

'Boat-shaped,' answered Ana, bringing the old lady's hand up to it.

'Very flattering, I imagine. Veil?'

'As far as my waist.'

'Yes, that would be nice on you alright. And shoes, Ana?'

'Covered in the same material,' Ana told her, taking one of them off and placing it in Celia's hands.

Eyes staring blindly ahead, Celia ran her fingers over it.

'Nice shape,' she remarked and handed it back to Ana. Then she turned towards the table beside her and felt along it until she found what she was searching for – a velvet blue jewellery box somewhat the worst for wear, faded and worn through years of handling, as much by Ana as by herself.

'I suppose you know what's in this, Anastasia?' she asked.

'Of course I do, Celia.'

'And what was it you were forever saying as a child?'

'That I'd wear them on my wedding day,' Ana answered, referring to the diamond necklace and earrings set she knew the box contained.

'Stoop down to me so and let me put them on for you.'

Taking the jewellery from the box, Celia lay the earrings on the table and while Ana held still she placed the necklace around her neck and, though it took some time, she managed to do up the clasp with her arthritic hands. Then she felt along the table for the earrings. Suddenly, the sight of those hands, with their too-loose skin, their lack of colour save for a few age spots and the way they blindly tap-tapped along the table caused Ana to do what she swore she wouldn't.

'I hope that's not a muffled sob I hear,' Celia said sternly.

Ana didn't answer. She couldn't.

'Anastasia Moore! You're the most contrary creature I've ever come across! What on earth have you to sniffle about? Look at you! Barely twenty, looking only gorgeous – I've no doubt – marrying the man of your dreams and being swept off to London. And, what's more, you've just been given a gift of the very pieces of jewellery you've had your eye on since you were the size of a grasshopper and...'

'Celia! I had not!'

'Don't interrupt, of course you had. Now let me finish. And, spread out before you is the most glorious future any girl could wish for. And what are you doing? Crying! Your husband-to-be is sure to be delighted when he sees his bride arriving at the altar, all puffy-eyed and red-nosed.'

'But, Celia, I'm going to miss you.'

'Of course you are, that's only natural. I'd be sorely put out if you didn't.'

'But...'

'But nothing. What do you want, me to come along on your honeymoon?'

'That's not a bad idea,' said Ana, only half-jokingly.

'I'm not so old that I don't remember what a honeymoon is for and to know that old women have no business tagging along. Ana, don't be feeling sorry for me. I have my own memories to keep me entertained. Of course you're sad to be leaving me. And I'm sad to see you go. But, Ana, you'd be a strange girl indeed if you decided to stay here to keep an old woman company instead of going off to live in London with that handsome man of yours. And I'd be stranger still if I let you.'

'But, Celia...'

'But Celia nothing! You'll be home at Christmas, won't you?'

'Yes – but, Celia, I wish you could co–'

'Now, Ana, be careful what you wish for,' warned Celia. 'Wouldn't you get the shock of your life if you happened to glance down from a window of that new home of yours to see me standing there, suitcase in hand, waving up at you? And anyway, you never know, maybe one day I might decide that I've had enough of listening to that whiney old voice of your mother's and I might just take a notion to follow you over on the boat.'

'Well, you know you're welcome to come and live with us.'

'Ah have sense, Ana. Did you ever hear of a woman my age emigrating to London? Next you'll be setting me up with a job on the sites.' She reached out for Ana's hand, took it and, patting it gently, continued, 'Anastasia, I'm well taken care of here. With your mother's sights set firmly on what she thinks is my fortune, she'll do nothing to jeopardise her chances. So go on now. Enjoy the day. And don't forget to give that handsome husband of yours a fine big kiss from me. And you make sure to tell him that I said he's to take good care of you, that he's a lucky man to be getting you.'

'He knows how biased you are,' Ana half-laughed, half-cried. Then she bent down and kissed Celia. 'You know I love you, you cranky old thing.'

'Less of the old, if you don't mind. And cranky. Now, go on. Don't be trying to drive an old lady to tears. I won't have it. Go on. Go on.'

'Goodbye so, Celia.'

But Ana stayed standing by the door, looking at Celia who was staring straight ahead. She wanted to say more.

'Are you still there?' snapped Celia.

Ana turned and left the room.

Slowly she walked down the three flights of stairs and into the kitchen where her mother and father were sitting at the table. Neither of them looked up as she came in, her father went on reading his newspaper and her mother suddenly seemed to find the back page, the sports page as it happened, extremely interesting.

'So Mother, who's it going to be for the finals then?' asked Ana, noting the headline of the article her mother appeared to be reading.

'Ha?'

'Who's favourite to win? Isn't that what you're reading about?'

'Ah, it's all rubbish,' snarled her mother. 'A lot I care.'

'Well,' said Ana, 'I'm going down to the church now. But there's still time to change your mind.'

For five minutes Ana stood there, looking down at them, willing them to look up, to say something to her. But they stayed as still and as silent as statues.

'Julie has gone on ahead,' she said eventually, referring to her best friend and bridesmaid for the day who'd left earlier to give Ana time to make a final plea to her parents.

The kitchen clock loudly ticked the time by.

'Well, I'm going to go now,' said Ana finally. 'But, as I said, there's still time for you to change your minds.'

They didn't move a muscle.

'Right,' said Ana. 'Goodbye then.'

She left the house and walked the couple of hundred yards to the church.

Waiting outside was Julie.

'They're not coming, are they?' she asked as Ana came towards her.

Ana shook her head.

'No,' she said. 'I guess you're going to have to give me away, Julie. A bit unconventional, but what can we do? So, are you ready?'

Knowing how Ana must be feeling, Julie took her hand and gave it a squeeze.

'You look lovely, Ana,' she told her. 'And Mark is looking even more handsome than usual – if that's possible. But, before we go in, I want you to know that if, by any chance, you feel like changing your mind then you can count on me to come to the rescue. As your bridesmaid I'm even prepared to stand in for you if needs be for I'd hate to see the poor man left at the altar especially since he's travelled this far and besides, it would be a pity to see someone like him go to waste. No, I was working it all out as I was waiting for you. You see, I can put your veil down over my face and keep my head bent so he won't be able to tell the difference until it's too late. We're about the same height and you know what men are like, he won't even notice who's wearing white and who's wearing yellow, he'll probably be so nervous in any case.'

Ana laughed. She appreciated Julie's attempt at cheering her up.

Then Julie went on, serious again.

'Ana, you're doing the right thing, you know. Not that you need me to tell you that. So come on, are you ready?'

Ana nodded.

Together they walked into the church. At the back stood a few of the neighbours who'd turned up for the ceremony – good coats covering a multitude – who smiled and, heads to one side, sighed in admiration as she walked slowly past. Amongst them she caught sight of Mrs Lloyd with Adrian and she gave them a little wave. And then, on up the long, long aisle, flanked on either side by empty seat after empty seat she walked; on up to the front where a handful of people were gathered in the first few pews. On the groom's side – Mark's family over from England, a tidy-sized English family with just the one of everything – mother, father, sister, aunt, uncle, all looking assured in these strange Irish Catholic surroundings although feeling somewhat piqued that the family into which their darling Mark was marrying (and on whom, despite their reservations, they'd decided to bestow their presence) was nowhere to be seen. On the bride's side – her school friends and a few of the girls from the restaurant she'd worked in, all dolled up to the nines and full of girlish excitement, giving her little waves and smiles as she came towards them at this, the first wedding of their group, and such an incredibly romantic one at that. It had all the necessary elements – whirlwind romance, parental disapproval, cross-religious coupling, a bride so beautiful she could have stepped straight off the pages of a magazine and an incredibly handsome foreign stranger.

And at the altar stood the incredibly handsome foreign stranger – her beaming, soon-to-be-husband Mark Harrison wearing his heart on his sleeve. And everywhere else.

Easter Sunday, coming up to noon...

After she'd left the Colonel and Laurence, Ana walked the half mile to Kilmurray, a one-shop, one-pub, one-public-telephone class of a village where she bought the Sunday papers. Then, on her return to Rathdowne, she headed into the sunroom in the main house and there, ensconced in her favourite seat by a window overlooking the gardens, she culled out all those sections of the newspapers which held no interest for her and settled down to peruse the still weighty selection of news and gossip.

When she'd first arrived in, the room had been empty but gradually it had filled up and now Ana stopped off reading, sat back and looked around. Most of the residents preferred to entertain their family and other visitors in the sunroom, in part because the bungalows were quite small and the sunroom itself was so pleasant but, primarily, Ana thought, so that they could show their visitors off to each other. Probably because it was the Easter weekend there seemed to be more people than usual here this Sunday and dotted around the room were little clusters of people composed mainly, but with exceptions, of a single elderly person (predominately female, given that gender's habit of outliving the other) surrounded by their children, their children's spouses and their grandchildren.

To her right sat tiny Ellen Madden who Ana knew to be single and she now studied the group gathered around Ellen and speculated on their relationship. The man sitting alongside Ellen was in his late sixties and had the same frail, bird-like appearance as Ellen and, like her, he too appeared to be a gentle, quiet soul. Ana guessed he was the brother Ellen often talked about and who, from what she said, she was both extremely fond of but very bitter towards. The rather fierce, sullen, and much, much younger-looking blonde woman sitting opposite him must be his wife, whom Ellen hated with a vehemence that was somewhat alarming in one so generally mild-mannered. That she'd 'ended up' in Rathdowne Ellen maintained was the Blondie Trollop's fault, as she invariably (and quite uncharacteristically really) referred to her sister-in-law. Before the Blondie Trollop's arrival, Ellen and her brother had lived together quite contentedly on the farm left to him by their parents but that soon changed when Blondie came on the scene and, in no time at all, Ellen found herself being packed off to Rathdowne. Her brother didn't look the kind who'd force his sister to leave their home but, equally so, it was hard to imagine him standing up to his wife on any matter and Ana could well believe that Ellen's sister-in-law was the main instigator in her involuntary change of abode. Ana remembered Ellen saying that her brother had been nearly sixty when he'd married four years ago and, judging by the number of children now in tow – five in all and every one of them as sullen-looking as their mother – he'd obviously made up for lost time. She was curious as to what this group were saying to one another but, what little they did say was spoken in strong country accents, in low, self-conscious tones, making it impossible for her to hear.

Just then, Ana was distracted when the gathering on the other side of her suddenly erupted into raucous laughter and she looked over to see five freckle-faced, red-haired women, all dressed in brightly coloured shell-suits and all with their heads flung back and mouths wide open as they laughed unrestrainedly. It was Penny Plunkett, another of the residents, surrounded by what could only be her daughters, so strong was the resemblance between them all.

Though an unlikely pair, Penny Plunkett and Ellen Madden were the best of friends. Penny was as loud as Ellen was quiet. She was as inner-city Dublin as Ellen was back-of-beyond country and she was as quick as Ellen was, well, was not so quick. To an onlooker like Ana, it seemed that Penny was constantly bullying and teasing Ellen but

Ellen didn't notice or, if she did, she certainly didn't seem to mind. The pair of them were practically inseparable and on the rare occasions Ana met one or other of them on their own she was invariably asked if she'd seen Ellen, or Penny (depending on which of them was doing the asking) before she'd even got a chance to say hello.

Today there wasn't a sign of a husband amongst the Plunkett women though their numerous offspring were scattered around the room creating havoc, much to the annoyance of the other residents and guests. Only their mothers and grandmother were oblivious to their antics for they were all so busy talking and laughing at the one time, all loudly competing with one another to be heard. Suddenly, Penny and her daughters erupted into even louder gales of laughter and standing between them, Ana saw, was the source of their amusement – one of the granddaughters, red-haired and freckled too, a miniature version of the women.

'And wait until you hear this,' said one of Penny's daughters, wiping away tears of laughter. 'Hush, you lot,' she ordered in her raspy smoker's voice just like Penny's own and then turned to the young girl. 'Lorna,' she urged, 'tell them what you said to your teacher the other day.'

'I don't know, Mammy,' said the young girl, who looked slightly bemused but not entirely uncomfortable at suddenly finding herself the centre of attention.

'Aha, of course you do, Lorna love! Go on, tell them. What did you say when Mr Dunne asked you what happened when Our Lord drove Adam and Eve out of the Garden of Eden?'

'Mam, I heard Mr Dunne telling you, so can't you tell them?' Lorna demanded sulkily for she was beginning to suspect that she was being made a fool of now.

'Because they want to hear it from you. Especially Granny. Don't you, Granny? Go on, what did they say to him when he drove them out of Eden?'

The girl threw her eyes to heaven at her mother's foolishness, sighed, then reluctantly answered,

'I said they got out of the car and thanked him for the spin.'

The women sat in silence for a second, thinking, then they all burst out laughing.

'You're a right ticket, Lorna,' bellowed her grandmother. But, noticing that the girl looked as if she might cry at any moment, she caught a hold of her. 'Ah come here, pet, till I give you an old hug.' The girl hiccuped back a tear. 'Ah Lorna, stop that now,' chided Penny. 'We were only having a laugh,' she said, drawing her granddaughter in close to her and, noticing a streak of dirt on Lorna's face, she licked the tip of her finger and wiped it off.

Sometimes, out of the blue, lonesomeness hit Ana like a ton of bricks. One of those sometimes was now. It was time for her to go she decided and, as she hurriedly gathered up the various sections of the newspapers lying scattered on the table before her, she asked herself what was she, of all people, doing here in the middle of happy family time. She should have stayed away as she usually did instead of sitting here, so conspicuously on her own, so out of place.

When she had the newspapers gathered up and was about to leave, she happened to catch a glimpse of Elizabeth and her family crossing the front lawn. Although Elizabeth talked about her family a lot, Ana didn't think they visited very often; at least she'd never seen them in Rathdowne before and, when she noticed that they were heading for the sunroom, downright nosiness begged her to change her mind and stay to see them up close and in the flesh. It didn't have to beg very hard.

And what a lot of flesh there was. In single file she watched them troop in through the French windows, then across the room looking for all the world, Ana decided, like a rugby team coming on to play. For a second she thought she could feel the floor vibrating and well it might, for their collective bulk was considerable. Every one of them – grandmother, son, daughter-in-law, grandson No.1, grandson No.2 and grandson No.3 – was big-boned and strong-looking and each walked across the room with the same slow, deliberate gait, with solid thigh knocking against solid thigh and solid arms held awkwardly at a distance from their barrel-like torsos. They were all, Ana noticed, weirdly similar in appearance, from Granny Elizabeth who was leading the way across the room, down to grandson No.3 in his early teens who was bringing up the rear. Apart from build, they even shared the same pasty complexion and the same dark hair cut in an upturned-bowl style, though only daughter-in-law Janet's was quite as dark as Elizabeth's – courtesy, Ana presumed, of Alain, Celebrated Hairdresser-to-the-Rich-and-Famous (though in actual fact – mostly to people who went to him because they believed him to be Celebrated Hairdresser-to-the-Rich-and-Famous). Come to think of it, it was very odd how similar mother and daughter-in-law were; Janet looked just like a middle-aged version of Elizabeth.

Finding a free corner, they all sat down, their massive bulks making the seats beneath them look like kiddies' chairs in a junior infant classroom. Over the many conversations going on in the room, Ana caught snippets of what they were saying in their loud grating voices and what quickly became apparent was that they weren't quite the happy family in the rosy 'Brady Bunch' picture Elizabeth liked to think she was painting. Now, all of them seemed to be talking, or bickering rather, at the one time, Elizabeth included.

'Wasn't I waiting half the morning for you to arrive? I'm sure you said you'd be here by twelve.'

'He's an absolute maniac, Elizabeth. You should see the way he took those bad bends coming into Ashford.'

'Sitting there in the passenger's seat, Mom, like the Queen herself. At it non-stop she was. "Watch out, Harry! Slow down, Harry! Didn't you see that man crossing, Harry?" She'd me driven demented.'

'When are we leaving? Will we be back in time for my match?'

'Mom, Sophie's gone missing again. Why do I have to sit here if she doesn't?'

'I'm starving, Mom. And I'm bored. Can I turn on the telly?'

'Why don't you drive yourself so? And where has that bloody girl got to?'

'And why should I drive, Harry? Don't I do everything else? Benjy, stop whining and go look for your sister.'

'Why do I have to? Can't Tim or Ned look for her?'

Sometimes, out of the blue, lonesomeness

hit Ana like a ton of bricks. Other times, such as now, she was just thankful that at least she hadn't a family like this. God, she was beginning to get a headache from them.

'Speak of the devil,' Ana heard Janet say and she looked to up see a young girl, the missing Sophie presumably, arriving in. Watching her as she walked over to her family, Ana saw that she too had the characteristic heavy build and dark hair (though she'd grown it beyond the bowl-shape stage) but, in contrast to the rest of the family, she had a lovely face – very pretty, thought Ana, and there was something very pleasant, something very cheerful in her expression. She looked a year or so older than the eldest of the boys – seventeen, or eighteen at most. Ana was almost certain she'd seen her before, but she couldn't think where.

'Hello, Gran,' said Sophie, kissing the cheek her grandmother proffered.

'Well, Mom, what do you think of Sophie's rig-out then?' asked her father, before Sophie had even sat down.

Going by her brothers' reactions, their father's question was just about the funniest thing these boys had ever heard. So uncontrollable was their laughter that they'd difficulty remaining upright on their seats.

'Dad, please,' muttered the girl, blushing. She cast the boys a dirty look then sat down.

'Thirty pounds she paid for that scrap of material!' her father went on loudly. 'Thirty pounds! Sure there isn't enough there to blow your nose on, let alone cover your essentials.'

'Especially hers,' commented one of the boys, nudging the brother beside him which started all three of them off again.

'Thirty pounds! She must think I'm made of money!'

'Dad, please, stop going on about it. And anyway, I paid for it myself.'

'First it was make-up, tons of the stuff,' her mother joined in. 'Then mini-skirts up to ... well, up to you-know-where. And it's all parties and raves and whatnot with her, out every night of the week she is. And you should see the oddballs who turn up on the doorstep looking for her. Right beauties, they are. From that music school she goes to on Saturdays, so she tells us, but they're nothing but dirty hobos if you ask me and you can be sure, Elizabeth, that it's not her piano-playing they're interested in either, no matter what she might like to think. We're only living in hope that she doesn't arrive home some day soon and announce she's...'

'Mom please,' interrupted Sophie pleadingly, having heard this tirade so many times before.

'...and announce she's pregnant,' her mother finished.

'Mom, will you stop going on like that?'
But her mother was not to be discouraged. She was only warming up.

'I wouldn't be surprised if half those weirdos she hangs around with are on drugs, they certainly look as if they are,' she went on at the top of her voice.

'How many times do I have to tell you they're not?'

'As for our lassie here, well, for all we know she could be smoking pot and whatnot every night of the week. I wouldn't put it past her. I'm telling you, Elizabeth, it's only a matter of time before...'

Sophie glanced around and to her obvious mortification she noticed that every single person in the room was silent now and staring over.

'Mom, everyone is listening. Please, will you just shut up?'

Without warning her mother suddenly reached out and whacked her across the cheek.

'How dare you tell me to shut up!' she shouted.

Sophie looked at her, stunned. Then, without a word, she got up and ran from the room.

For a few seconds the silence in the room was absolute.

'She's out of control, Elizabeth,' said Janet loudly, breaking the silence and explaining her actions to the room at large more than just to Elizabeth. 'She won't listen to a word either of us say. You know that.'

Ana decided that she'd had her fill of the Dalys and got up but, as she was crossing the room, Elizabeth called out,

'Ana! Ana! Come over here and let me introduce you.'

Feeling that she had little choice, Ana went over. As Elizabeth did the introductions, Ana couldn't help but notice that the boys didn't so much as glance at her, they just carried on laughing amongst themselves. Harry didn't appear too interested either. He was looking over at Penny and her family with undisguised disgust as if he thought they were just about the trashiest people he'd ever come across in his life; not that they were worried, if they even noticed.

'You'd wonder how that common-looking woman over there could afford a place like this?' she heard him asking as she walked away.

As she was crossing the front lawn, it suddenly dawned on Ana who Janet reminded her of. From the first moment she'd seen her she'd thought there was something very familiar about her, more than just her similarity to Elizabeth. Now, Ana realised that it was her own mother she resembled. Just around the mouth. Her lips were just like her mother's had been – pursed, narrow, as if she was permanently sucking on something bitter. Suddenly, hearing a girl's laugh, Ana looked over and was surprised to see the Colonel and Sophie sitting on a bench together. Sophie was laughing loudly at something the Colonel was saying. Dirty old man, thought Ana, probably delighted with himself at having a young one sitting there, listening to him. But, to give him his due, at least he'd managed to cheer her up. Curious as to what they could be talking about, she walked over.

'Ah Ana, woman of my dreams,' called out the Colonel as she came near. 'Young lady,' he said, addressing Sophie. 'Move up there in the bed and give the lovely Anastasia a bit of room to sit down.'

'Stay where you are, Sophie, I'd feel safer if you were between us,' said Ana. 'Though, on second thoughts, maybe it would be better if I did sit in between the pair of you. He might look old and harmless but looks can be very deceiving.'

'Ana! How dare you! Don't mind her, Sophie. To tell you the truth,' he said winking at the young girl conspiratorially, 'and just between you and me, I'm beginning to suspect that her stern countenance is just a cover-up. You see, I do believe that though she might not be ready to admit it yet my charm is beginning to have the intended effect. Believe me, any day now she'll have no choice but to give in to her powerful feelings for me.'

'In your dreams, Colonel!'

'Indeed you are, Ana. Every night.'

Ana turned to Sophie and raised her eyes to heaven. 'Honestly, you just can't win with some people, can you?'

'Oh but Ana, I do intend to win with you,' replied the Colonel.

'Did you ever meet his like?' Ana asked Sophie. 'Isn't he just insufferable? Do you know what I call him?'

'Ah Ana,' warned the Colonel. 'Stop now, there's no need for that.'

'I call him Colonel Mustard – you know, after the character in that board-game. Don't you think it suits him?'

'Yes, it does,' Sophie laughed.

'Ah Sophie. I'm disappointed in you. You should be on my side.'

'I'm sorry, Colonel ... Mustard,' she said laughing.

'That's alright so. Now I know who my friends are. And I was just going to tell Ana what an outstanding pianist you are and ask her to come and listen to you some day. But I don't think I'll bother now.'

Suddenly Sophie groaned aloud and Ana looked up to see the Daly family heading in their direction. Elizabeth and Janet were leading the pack and as they drew nearer Ana realised that she was the topic of their conversation.

'Widowed, I think,' she heard Elizabeth say.

'And children?' enquired Janet.

'I don't think so,' came Elizabeth's answer. 'Though I couldn't be sure. She's a very private person, very mysterious. If she does have any family then they never come to see her.'

'Ah, the poor woman,' said Janet looking over at Ana sympathetically, causing Ana to wonder if she thought all old people were stone deaf or plain simple, just because her own mother-in-law might be. They were only metres from her – how could Janet think she wasn't able to hear her? She told herself not to get annoyed, but she could feel her face getting red with anger.

'Maybe she had a falling-out with them, it's often the way,' she heard Janet say authoritatively.

'Four,' she suddenly shouted out much to her own surprise, but there was no going back now. 'Great children, each and every one of them. Though they have their problems, the poor lambs. There's Séamus on the crack, terrible thing that crack, and there's Bertie the Hare Krishna and then there's the poor twins – they're stuck inside you see, one for manslaughter and the other for GBH, though they're innocent I needn't tell you. So you see, between one thing and the other, they don't get much of a chance to visit.'

As everyone gaped at her with mouths wide open, Ana turned to Sophie, grinned and gave her a quick wink and, copping-on to the fact that Ana was having her mother on, Sophie burst out laughing.

'Sophie! Really! Stop that this instance! I'm terribly sorry for my daughter's insensitivity, Mrs ... Mrs...' Janet stammered, in her shock forgetting the earlier introductions.

Might as well be hung for a sheep as a lamb, thought Ana.

'Mrs Dunne, Mrs Smith, Mrs Jones,' she volunteered. 'Any of them will do. Never got around to actually marrying but I've used the names of all my children's fathers from time to time, you know how it is. I suppose the Mrs is what you'd call a courtesy title.'

'Well, yes. Anyway, it's time to go. Sophie, come along,' said Janet and catching a firm hold of her daughter's arm, she hauled her up off the bench and began quickly walking away dragging Sophie with her. 'Tim, Ned, Benjy, come along, boys!' she shouted back. 'Harry!'

Gradually each of them closed their foolishly gaping mouths, managed to uproot themselves from the spot and followed after her.

The Colonel and Ana sat in silence for a few seconds. Out of the corner of her eye, Ana could see him staring at her critically.

'What? What?' she asked, finally turning to him. 'Whatever it is you have to say, just spit it out,' she demanded.

'Ah Ana, whatever possessed you to come out with all that rubbish?' But then a worried look crossed his face. 'None of it is true, is it?'

'Of course it isn't.'

'So why did you say it then?'

'Oh I don't know,' she said crossly.

'You're going to have to explain to Lizzy that you made it all up, or else I will.'

Ana sighed.

'Oh I just get so sick of the way she's forever ferreting around for information. If she wasn't so ridiculously nosy I'd have told her everything she wanted to know long ago.'

'I don't know about that. Haven't you us all intrigued?'

'What on earth do you mean?'

'Just that I never saw anyone as good as you at avoiding questions.'

'That's rubbish.'

'No, it's not. It happens to be true, Ana.'

'Oh for God's sake. I've no desire to sit around listening to your critical analysis of my character. I thought you were supposed to be my friend. I'm leaving.'

She stood up and began walking away.

'See! You're doing it again,' the Colonel shouted after her. 'Walking away in case, God forbid, you might have to answer something personal.'

'Since when did you become a psychologist, Colonel Mustard?' she shouted back.

Crossing the carpark she stopped when she saw Elizabeth standing there waving at the departing Volvo, so heavily laden that its floor practically scraped along the gravel as it made its way through the main gates. Long after it had disappeared from view and its occupants had most likely forgotten all about their visit, Ana watched Elizabeth staring out at the road. Suddenly she felt very sorry for her. She looked so terribly lonesome. Regardless of how dreadful Elizabeth's family was (with the exception of Sophie), Elizabeth was clearly very fond of them. It had been wrong of her to behave so badly. It wasn't fair on Elizabeth. What had got into her? Downright jealousy maybe?

Finally Elizabeth turned away and noticed Ana standing there.

'Ana,' she asked, 'whatever made you come out with all that nonsense? I know it can't be true.'

'I don't know, Elizabeth, honest to God. Sometimes I find myself saying the queerest of things. Maybe it's old age. Maybe I'm going senile.'

'Yes, well, that's what I told them.'

'Thanks very much.'

'It was what they were thinking themselves.'

Then Elizabeth looked back towards the road again.

'Poor Harry. Isn't it all go-go with the young nowadays? They get so little time. There he is, having to rush back to Dublin to beat the heavy traffic. Doesn't even have time to have a proper Sunday lunch.'

In response, Ana thought of several things she might say; that the traffic back to Dublin didn't really get busy until late afternoon and it was only now just gone one. Or that presumably since Harry and family would at some point have some lunch they could have eaten here with Elizabeth or, even better, invited her to join them in one of the many fine restaurants rural Wicklow was noted for. Or, she might have asked her if Harry was aware that Elizabeth never left the grounds on her own.

But there was little point.

'Do you want to come for a walk, Elizabeth?' she asked instead.

Elizabeth shook her head.

'No, Ana, but thanks for asking. I think I might just go and have a lie-down and a bit of a read of this week's *Hello* if I can find it. You didn't see it around by any chance?'

'No, I didn't, Elizabeth.'

‘I thought I left it in the sunroom yesterday. Honestly, I’m beginning to think someone’s pinching them on me. They’re forever going missing.’

1963

CHAPTER 3

To have lived light in the spring,
To have loved, to have thought, to have done...
from *Empedocles on Etna*
by Matthew Arnold

Ana awoke to the feel of her six-year-old son clambering into the bed, clumsily climbing in over her, a knee in her ribs, an elbow in her face and, as he shuffled around in the bed finding space between herself and Mark, she lay still, not wanting him to know she was awake. Then, he too was still but not settled yet and Ana sensed him kneeling up in the bed beside her, staring down, willing her to wake up, but she kept her eyes shut hoping he'd lie down and go to sleep soon. But Pierce obviously had other ideas and, deciding that direct measures were called for, he began to gently blow on her face – but she didn't stir. He blew a little harder – no response. He blew with all his might – but she remained resolute. Then he became quiet again. All was still. But Ana held her breath. And waited. Anticipating another attack. Wondering what tactic he'd next employ. The seconds ticked slowly by. And then it came – an old favourite of his – the trusty tickle under the chin of which he was a master. But long-time exposure had trained her to withstand it and she managed not to give in – she didn't laugh and she kept her eyes closed tight. Until that is, little hands moved from chin to eyes and tried to prise one of them open.

'What?' she snapped, opening both eyes to see his face just inches from her own, peering down at her.

'So you're awake too, Mommy,' he whispered. Mission accomplished, he lay down and cuddled into her. 'I've been awake for ages as well. Ages and ages. But I didn't come into your bed because I know I'm not meant to, sure I'm not, Mommy? But then I thought *you* might be scared.' On and on he whispered in the dark, not in the least bit deterred by her discouraging monosyllabic answers. 'Don't you like it here either, Mommy? Is that why you're awake as well? When are we going back to our own home?' On and on, whispering himself back to sleep.

Leaving her wide-awake. But he was right. She didn't like it here. She found no comfort at being back in her own childhood bed; in this dreary, depressing bedroom she'd grown up in. With its cumbersome mahogany furniture and overpowering wallpaper it had never felt like her own room and even less so now having been the temporary home of several boarders in the intervening years since she'd left. And, like Pierce, she too wished she was back in their nice comfortable home in London.

Propping herself up on her elbow now, she studied the faces of Mark and Pierce. Despite the squash she was glad to have their presence in the bed with her. In the first light of early morning, their sleeping faces were a study in perfection and she wondered, as she often did, how she'd been so lucky. The pair of them, uncannily alike, really were beautiful and she knew that she wasn't just a biased wife and mother; the admiring looks they invariably drew from strangers told her that. Pierce was almost once hundred percent Mark – there was little of her in him. Both had the same head of blond hair, the same sallow skin, the same clear blue eyes, and the same long, athletic limbs. Even the way they were lying now, flat on their backs, was identical. They both even had the exact same contented expression on their faces, as if they were sharing the one pleasant dream. She reached over and stroked her husband's cheek and he sighed contentedly and moved his face towards her touch. She did the same to Pierce and he reacted in copycat fashion. Contrary to her expectations that one day her love for the pair of them would reach a plateau, it never did, it just went on increasing. Sometimes, such as now, she thought she'd burst with love and she could feel a lump rising in her throat so immense were her feelings.

'Ana, what are you thinking about?' whispered Mark, startling her.

'Sorry, Mark, I didn't mean to wake you. Nothing really.'

'Nothing? If I said that you'd kill me.' He looked down at Pierce. 'When did he get in? I'm afraid there's nothing for it, we're just going to have to start setting traps,' he joked. 'This is getting to be too much of a habit.' Then, reaching across him, he took hold of Ana's hand. 'Tell me, Ana, what's on your mind? You look so serious. Are you thinking about Celia?'

'No, not right now.'

'Good, you've done enough crying for one day. You're not still thinking about that letter, are you?'

She shook her head.

'No,' she answered.

The previous morning, when they'd arrived at her parents' house, sadly back in Dublin for Celia's funeral, a letter had been waiting for her. This letter had been full of nonsense – of declarations of undying love for her and of disparaging remarks about Mark. It, like its predecessors – for it wasn't the first of its kind, though it was the first in quite some time – had been unsigned and, already in a fragile state, feeling terribly upset by Celia's death, it had affected her far more than the earlier ones had.

'No,' she went on. 'In fact, I was thinking pleasant thoughts. Of how much I love you.' She stroked his hand. 'I do love you very much, Mark,' she said solemnly.

'Really?' he asked, feigning embarrassed surprise. 'Oh no, I don't know what to say. If only I felt the same way about you.'

'Ah stop joking. We are very happy together, aren't we?'

'Well, Ana, I'm afraid we're not. In fact I was thinking of leaving you but I wasn't sure how to say it.'

'Stop it. I'm not in the mood for jokes right now.'

'No, I suppose you're not, I'm sorry.' He paused for a while. 'Do you know what I think?' he asked. 'I think it's that creepy neighbour of yours, that fellow who was skulking around at the removal tonight.'

'What are you talking about?'

'I think he's the one who writes those letters.'

'Who?' she asked, mystified.

'That bloke with the watery eyes and the runny nose. You know, what's-his-name? Looks like a startled rabbit who's been caught in the beam of car headlights.'

'Adrian Lloyd?' she asked in surprise.

'That's the one. He gives me the creeps. More than once I caught him looking over at you with sheep's eyes.'

'Don't be ridiculous.'

Pierce stirred in the bed between them and they both stayed silent knowing that if he found them awake he'd be so excited that there'd be no shutting him up and that would be the end of sleep for all of them.

'It's not even six o' clock, Ana,' whispered Mark once Pierce had settled down again. 'Try to get another couple of hours sleep. You need it. And I love you too, as well you know. But remember, I'll always have that ten-minute start.'

She laughed, immediately understanding what he meant. Ana always maintained that the moment she'd asked, 'Can I take your order please, sir?' and looked down to see Mark smiling up at her, was the moment she'd fallen in love with him. But Mark argued that her love would never be able to catch up on his since he'd fallen for her ten minutes earlier when he'd first walked into Delaney's Restaurant in Ranelagh and saw her serving at another table.

Soon Mark fell back to sleep and Ana, trying not to let her mind dwell on sad thoughts, lay there listening to the sound of their breathing, her son's short, sharp breaths, two for every one of her husband's longer whistling ones, until finally she drifted off to sleep. But some noise soon caused her to wake again. At first she wasn't sure what. Pierce, she thought initially, but she looked over and saw that he was sound to the world and it was then she heard what sounded like heavy footsteps crossing Celia's room overhead. She sat up in alarm and listened closely but she couldn't hear anything now and, deciding that the sounds were simply the product of an overwrought imagination, she lay back down. But soon the footsteps started again and now there was the additional sound of something heavy being slowly dragged across the floor.

Quickly she got out of the bed, pulled a jumper on over her nightdress and ran upstairs and into Celia's room.

'Mother!' she shouted when she saw her mother struggling across the room, dragging one of the huge drawers from Celia's chest which was still full of clothes. 'Leave that down – it's too heavy for you. You'll do your back in.'

'I can manage,' snapped her mother, continuing to struggle with the drawer.

Ana came over and took it from her, 'Where do you want this?' she asked.

'There, on the bed,' her mother replied.

With difficulty Ana managed to lift the drawer over and up onto the bed. Then she looked around Celia's room. It was in chaos. The doors of her wardrobe were wide open revealing a completely empty interior. The drawers of the chest and dressing-table were on the bed and their contents, together with the contents of the wardrobe, were scattered around the room in bundles or piled high in cardboard boxes. Her mother came over to the bed now, pushed Ana to one side and began examining the contents of the drawer Ana had put there.

'Mother, what in God's name are you doing?' asked Ana, staring at her.

'You were always one for the stupid questions, Ana,' her mother answered, catching up a pile of Celia's clothes and throwing them into a cardboard box. 'What does it look like I'm doing? I'm clearing the room out.'

'But Celia has only been dead a couple of days. For crying out loud, she hasn't even been buried yet.'

'I need to get the room ready. It's the best one in the house and I don't want to leave it idle but I can't rent it out until I get rid of her rubbish.'

'Mother! Surely all this can wait?'

'Would you mind moving out of the way, Ana?'

'Mother, come on downstairs. I'll make us some breakfast. I can do all this later, after the funeral.'

'Anxious to get your hands on her things, I suppose.'

'What?' asked Ana, wondering if she'd misheard.

'Now is as good a time as any to get rid of all this junk,' her mother went on, ignoring Ana's question.

'Junk? These are Celia's things! And look, it's not even six o'clock in the morning. This is absolutely crazy. Mother, why don't you go back to bed for a couple of hours?'

'Don't be coming back here and telling me what to do, Ana. Why don't you go back to bed yourself and mind your own business?'

'That you're up at the crack of dawn acting like some mad thing surely is my business.'

Suddenly her mother swung around.

'Acting like some mad thing, am I? Well, thank you for your opinion but I'd prefer if you kept it to yourself. And no, it's not any of your business. The day you went off to London with that Protestant, that ... that ... that ... English Protestant and had his brat was the day that anything I did stopped being your business.'

Ana stared at her, thrown by the bitterness in her voice and the hatred in her face. If her mother had been talking about a serial murdering rapist she couldn't have managed to sound or look more disgusted. Since arriving home it had been obvious that her mother, for reasons unknown to Ana, was in an even worse mood than usual and Ana had cautiously tiptoed around her, careful not to say or do anything to upset her, knowing from experience that it took very little to set her off.

'Mother,' she said now, despite her resolutions not to get into a conflict. 'That's my husband and son you're talking about. Your own grandson and son-in-law.'

'Ah, they're nothing to do with me.'

'Your own grandson?'

'Grandson?' she snorted. 'And the only reason that lump of a husband of yours is here now is to see if there's any money in it for the pair of you.'

'How dare you!'

'How many times has he ever even set foot in this house before today?'

'You've always made it perfectly clear that you never wanted him here.'

'Not a penny to his name. A teacher in a second-rate school squandering the pittance he earns gallivanting off around the world for months on end and dragging the pair of you with him.'

'He doesn't drag us with him. I like going. And, as I've told you before, he doesn't like teaching. He wants to be a travel-photographer.'

'Wants to be a travel-photographer! Bah! Did you ever hear the like? What is he, a boy of twenty? It's time he grew up and accepted the fact that he's a schoolteacher and no longer in the first flush of youth either, with a wife and child to support. Not that he can even support you – there you are, having to take in other people's brats for a few extra bob. And living in that squalid little house. What kind of life is that for a child?'

'More than he deserves judging by the way you go on. And there is nothing squalid about our house which you'd know if you ever bothered to come and visit.'

'If it wasn't for him you'd have married Adrian Lloyd and you'd be living here in Dublin where you belong. In a house with a garden and not in that dreadful terrace in London.'

'Adrian Lloyd? Mother, are you off your head altogether? Adrian Lloyd? What in God's name has he got to do with anything?'

'That's who you should have married and not that Protestant. Adrian adores the ground you walk on and always has, ever since you were children. You and him were always very close.'

'Of course we were close – we were the only two children on the street. But Adrian never had any interest in me. We were just friends.'

'Indeed he had. Still does. Isn't he forever asking me how you're getting on, every single time I meet him?'

'That's just the way Adrian is – polite. But we'd no interest in one another. And you'd no interest in him as a son-in-law either until you found out that you were going to get Mark as one. Before that you couldn't see him without remarking on what an odd-looking weasel of a fellow he was. A string of misery, you used to call him.'

'Indeed I did not! As if I'd call a neighbour's child anything of the sort! And I've noticed that you've hardly said a word to him since you've come home. Too grand, I suppose. Too full of yourself.'

'What? Like when? At Celia's removal? You know I wasn't exactly in the mood for catching up on old times.'

'All I know is that if that husband of yours, as you call him–'

'Call him?' Ana interrupted her. 'That's what he is!'

'As you call him, hadn't come waltzing over here from England on his holidays and set his sights on you, you'd now be happily married to Adrian Lloyd.'

'You're being ridiculous!'

'Ridiculous is it now? Well, if you find me so ridiculous, why don't you take yourself and your good-for-nothing husband and go on back to London?'

'Her good-for-nothing husband would be glad to go, Mrs Moore,' said Mark from the doorway where he'd been standing, listening to the last part of their conversation.

'Go on then, off with you,' shouted Mrs

Moore, waving him away.

'I'm afraid that much as you'd like me to go, Mrs Moore, and I'd like to go myself, we're not leaving for a few days yet,' said Mark. 'We're home for a funeral but we'd be happy to stay elsewhere if you'd prefer.'

'Home for a funeral! Home to get your sweaty paws on Celia's money more like.'

'Mother! How dare you!'

Suddenly Mrs Moore slumped down on the bed.

'Every penny she left you,' she said bitterly. 'Every bloody penny. After all the years I wasted slaving away, looking after the cantankerous old bitch morning, noon and night.'

Without warning, she caught up one of Celia's shoes on the bed beside her and flung it across the room at Mark. He dodged to avoid it but didn't see the second one coming and the heel of it got him square on the forehead. Encouraged by her direct hit she began grabbing anything heavy or hard that lay on the bed – shoes, handbags, toiletries – and hurling them at him.

'Mother, stop!' screamed Ana, rushing at her, and with considerable effort she managed to grab her mother's two hands in her own but the older woman struggled fiercely to free herself from her daughter's grip. But, just when Ana was sure she wouldn't be able to hold her any longer, the fight left her and she suddenly slumped forward like a rag doll. Sitting down beside her, Ana held her as she moaned softly to herself, rocking herself back and forth and then, after a few minutes, her head came to rest on Ana's lap. And for five long minutes Ana and Mark listened to her muffled moans, looking at one another across the room with expressions that were a mirror of each other's – a mixture of concern and bewilderment.

'Mother, are you all right?' asked Ana, but her mother just went on and on moaning and moaning.

'Mrs Moore, are you okay?'

Without raising her head from Ana's lap, Mrs Moore turned her head sideways and stared across the room at Mark.

'So Mr Travel-photographer,' she hissed at him, 'you'll be glad to know that you'll never have to work a day in your life again, not with your wife sitting pretty on a fortune.'

Easter Sunday, just before midnight...

All the walking Ana had done during the day, around the grounds and to and from Kilmurray for the Sunday papers, hadn't done her foot any good and, by nine o' clock that evening, she was feeling so washed out that she'd taken herself off to bed and had promptly fallen asleep. But, just short of midnight, she woke again and instinctively she stretched her hand across the bed searching for a body beside her but, finding no one there, she felt a familiar twinge of sadness. She'd once imagined that the passing of time would resign her to sleeping alone but it hadn't.

Usually Ana slept soundly, a pattern that age hadn't interfered with, and now she lay in the dark wondering what had disturbed her. She soon found out for, almost immediately, there came a loud knock on the front door and then she heard her name being called in a terribly noisy stage whisper.

'Damn,' she muttered to herself, recognising the Colonel's voice.

'Ana,' she heard him whisper again.

She lay there determined to ignore him but on and on he kept knocking until finally, realising that he was going to wake everyone else up if he hadn't already, she eased herself out of bed. 'What have I done to deserve this?' she grumbled, reaching for her dressing-gown. She put it on and made her way down the hallway to the front door and was about to open it but then changed her mind.

'What?' she called out instead.

'Ana, open the door. It's me,' came the reply from the other side.

'Who's me?' she demanded, determined not to give an inch.

'Me, Ana.'

'No, no – me Ana. Who you?'

'What?' he asked sounding confused. 'Ah Ana, stop fooling around,' he said crossly. 'Come on, open the door. Let me in. It's me, Colonel Jackson. Come on, Ana, it's chilly out here.' Ana wondered what had possessed him to come calling at this late hour and almost immediately, as if in response, he whispered, 'I brought some Scotch with me, Ana. Let me in. We can have a drink together. And I've brought some peanuts,' he added by way of further inducement.

'It's a retirement village we're in, not a bloody boarding-school,' she snapped. 'And I'm a bit long in the tooth now to be excited by the prospect of a midnight feast.'

'Ah Ana, where's your spirit?'

The bungalows were packed closely together and, in this community of old people, insomniacs by and large, very little happened which wasn't observed by someone regardless of what time of the day or night it was. Ana assumed that right now eyes peered from the dark interior of at least one of the nearby bungalows, attentively recording every detail of this nocturnal visit. And, if she was foolish enough to open the door, then news of her brazenness, she'd no doubt, wouldn't be long doing the rounds tomorrow. Which is what finally convinced her to let him in. The thought of the scandal she'd create amused her; so little happened in this place that she thought she might as well give them something to talk about and, if they interpreted a late-night drink as something else – well, that was hardly her fault.

She opened the door. On the step he stood, a thankful, eager smile on his face, the bottle of Scotch in one hand and the family-sized packet of peanuts in the other. She looked him up and down and thought, not for the first time, that he really was an absurd figure. He always reminded her of the red-faced, roly-poly Colonels found in English novels, in Agatha Christie mysteries maybe. The way he talked – all 'jolly this' and 'darned that' – made him sound as if he'd been born and raised in the English Home Counties when, as far as she knew, he was from Greystones. And really, his mode of dress was almost a caricature of the way one might imagine a retired Colonel would dress. During the day he was always impeccably turned out in a smart blazer or tweed jacket, a crisp shirt, a perfectly constructed bow tie with a matching triangle of handkerchief peeping from his breast pocket and shoes that were always highly polished. And she saw now that he was equally particular when it came to his night attire. He was wearing cream-coloured silk pyjamas under a black and red striped dressing-gown, a matching silk cravat at his neck and, on his feet, tartan slippers with little gold crests.

Or rather, she realised somewhat puzzled, one crested, tartan slipper and one highly-polished shoe.

'Trying to start a new trend, Colonel?' she asked, looking down at this mismatch.

'What?' His eyes followed her gaze and then he too stared at his feet for a few moments. He seemed to be as puzzled as she was. 'Yes,' he answered finally. 'Yes. Do you think it will take off?'

'Well...'

'Actually, Ana,' he said as she stood aside to let him in, 'I've a rather nasty infection on my foot so I need to wear the slipper for comfort.'

'And have you had it looked at?'

'By who? Nurse Boo? Oh no, no, I wouldn't let him within a hundred yards of it. God only knows what he'd do – I'd probably end up having to get it amputated.'

Ana followed after him into the kitchen. There he took two glasses from a press and immediately headed back out and, without so much as a backward glance, he toddled off down the hallway.

'Are you coming, Ana?' he called back.

From the kitchen doorway she stared after him, flabbergasted.

'Colonel, where the hell do you think

you're off to?' she shouted, watching as he disappeared into her bedroom. There was no answer. 'Colonel Mustard,' she shouted, 'where do you think you're going?'

'I thought we'd be more comfortable in the bed, Ana,' he called out. 'They really don't heat these little bungalows well enough at all.'

'Well, you'll be in there on your own, Colonel.'

She went back into the kitchen, sat down at the table and waited, knowing that eventually he'd get fed up of being in there on his own.

'Why don't you put on some of that music you're so fond of, Ana?' she heard him call out. 'You know, something to set the mood.'

She ignored him and thought, not for the first time, that he really was an infuriating character. This whole situation was just so ridiculous – she, sitting here in the kitchen in the middle of the night and he, waiting for her in her bedroom. But then, despite herself, she smiled and a wave of affection for him passed over her as she imagined him at this very moment. She could just picture him – propped up in the bed, sipping from his glass of Scotch, and looking expectantly towards the door. Sure he annoyed her, more than anyone else in Rathdowne, and his flirting just drove her mad but, although she didn't care to admit it, she found the attention a little flattering and in spite of it she'd grown quite fond of him. For all his faults he was never boring which made up for a lot with Ana. All in all, she conceded, she was fonder of him than she was of anyone else in Rathdowne – not that she'd dream of saying anything of the sort to him.

'Ana, did you hear me? I said, why don't you put on some of that music you're always listening to? Some of that opera?'

She stayed silent.

'Ana, can you bring some ice for the Scotch with you when you're coming in?'

Five minutes passed.

'Tell me, Ana, is there a dimmer-switch for the lights in here?'

And another five minutes.

And another.

Finally, admitting defeat, the Colonel reluctantly re-emerged from the bedroom and came back up to the kitchen. He sat down opposite her, giving her a sour look, then poured them both some Scotch and begrudgingly handed her a glass.

'Ana, would we not be more comfortable in the bed?' he asked giving it one last shot. 'Your feet must be freezing.'

'My feet are fine, Colonel.'

'I'll go and get you some slippers.'

He got up and Ana smiled as she watched his stocky little figure heading back out again.

'Shall I put them on for you, Cinderella?' he asked, arriving back with the slippers.

'I'll manage. God knows, you'd never be able to straighten yourself up again.'

Having sat back down, he raised his glass to her.

'Well, cheers, Ana,' he said.

'Cheers,' she responded, raising hers.

'A fine Scotch, isn't it?' he said, swilling it around in his glass, admiring it. 'But then I'd only give you the best. Do you know who I got this bottle from?' And, seeing her shake her head, he went on. 'From the President herself,' he proudly announced, watching her reaction to see if she was suitably impressed.

'The President of what?' she asked though she knew perfectly well who he meant for the Colonel took every opportunity to *casually* mention his friendship with the President of Ireland.

'The President of Ireland of course.'

'Of course.'

'Oh yes. I'm not sure if I've ever mentioned it to you but she's a great friend of mine; a great friend of the whole family. She absolutely adores Wicklow, you know, tries to spend time down here whenever she can although, with all her commitments, she doesn't get the chance very often. Did I tell you about the last time I met her, oh it must have been almost a year ago now?'

'No,' answered Ana with a sinking feeling, knowing that she was in for one of the Colonel's stories. Normally she enjoyed listening to them since they were always so fantastic but at this hour of the night she really wasn't in the mood. They were usually to do with the Colonel's most extraordinary family or their equally extraordinary friends. From what he told her, it seemed that his family tree contained more villains, heroes and titled personages than one would expect to feature in even the most convoluted historical television drama and they appeared to suffer a fate every bit as complicated. Amongst their friends they seemed to count every well-known person in Ireland; they owned land all over Leinster; had fingers in all sorts of pies; declared themselves bankrupt and amassed fortunes with amazing regularity; and they married, adulterated and separated with remarkable frequency.

Most of the Colonel's tales were so implausible that Ana was inclined to think they just had to be true for, in every other respect, he'd never struck her as the imaginative type and, if he were lying, then he'd surely try to make them sound a little less outlandish. But, even if she did suspect them to be true, she always let on that she didn't believe a word he uttered; she didn't want to give him the satisfaction. He was so very pompous that she enjoyed annoying him sometimes and, besides, she felt it paid him back for the outrageously politically incorrect comments which invariably coloured his narration.

'A most intelligent woman,' the Colonel was saying now. 'And surprisingly good business acumen too – for a woman. Did I ever tell you that my family own land down by Two Mile Waters? Well, I came up with this plan to set up a golf course on part of the land, together with other facilities centred around the village. It was going to be a top class place altogether, I can tell you, Ana. Jack Nicklaus who's a great friend of my brother's had even agreed to advise on the design of the course. And we'd considered putting in other attractions – a polo-pitch, tennis courts, possibly even an Olympic-sized swimming-pool. Now, I remember on that occasion when I met her last, I discussed it with the President and she thought it an excellent idea. Yes, we were even going to have a very up-market hotel where the golfers could come and stay with their wives.'

'Wouldn't the wives have been allowed to play, Colonel?'

'Oh yes of course, but only during off-peak hours. Men are really the golfers. And, as you know, golfers often like to have a drink after their game so, instead of risking the drive home they could stay overnight at this hotel and drink all they wanted in a club-like atmosphere, like one of those gentlemen clubs which used to be so popular before those women libbers ruined the show. And, as for the wives, there'd be other things laid on for them – a hair salon, a manicurist, that sort of thing.'

He poured himself another drink, then got up and went to the fridge to add some ice.

'Sounds delightful,' she remarked sarcastically. 'And tell me, why didn't you ever go through with it?'

'With what?' he asked, sitting back down again.

'With the golf course?'

He looked at her blankly.

'The golf course,' she repeated.

'What golf course?'

'The one up in Two Mile Waters.' But he didn't appear to know what she was talking about. 'Colonel, I'm beginning to think that you began hitting the Scotch quite early this evening.'

'Ana, how can you say that? This is only my second.'

Suddenly something struck her. When she'd earlier commented on his mismatching footwear the Colonel had explained that he was wearing the slipper to protect a sore foot. But now it struck her that that didn't make any sense – it had been the shoe, not the slipper that had been oddly out of place.

'Your second what, Colonel? Bottle?'

'No, no, my second glass. Really, Ana!'

'Humph,' she snorted, sure he was lying. 'Anyway, Colonel, tell me, why didn't you go through with the golf course up at Two Mile Water, the one the President thought was such a great idea?'

'Oh right,' he said, now recalling what he had been talking about. 'Well, for various reasons really.'

And he was off again. He explained to her that there was too much local opposition to it, that the banks were proving to be uncooperative, and that the land was totally unsuitable. But then, the next minute, he was forecasting that it would go ahead any day now given that all the necessary preparatory work had been completed and that they'd managed to raise the required millions. But, almost immediately, he was backtracking again, telling her that the whole idea had been abandoned since it was no longer considered a sound proposition as the number of hotels and golf clubs on the east coast had already reached saturation level. So, by the end of it all, he had her totally confused and, the more she asked him to clarify matters, the more confused she, and he, became.

After a quarter of an hour, he let the subject go but then, just when she thought he was about to leave, he launched into another topic, which in turn led him into another, which led him into another still. And several times over the course of the next two hours, she told him that she was off to bed, that if he didn't go home soon then she'd leave him sitting there on his own for the night. And several times he'd pooh-poohed such an outlandish notion and just went right on talking until finally she carried out her threat. After telling him where he could find a spare duvet and pillows and that he was welcome to sleep on the couch in the living-room, she left him sitting at the table and headed off to bed.

1971

CHAPTER 4

The stars are not wanted now: put out every one;
Pack up the moon and dismantle the sun...
from *Twelve Songs* by WH Auden

'Pierce!' shouted out Ana, spooning the eggs from the saucepan of boiling water and into the eggcups lined up on the counter. 'Come on down, Pierce. Breakfast is ready.'

She turned down the radio and listened for a moment. Upstairs seemed suspiciously quiet.

'Pierce!' she shouted again, louder this time.

But not a peep. Her son's earlier assurances that, 'Yeah, yeah, I'm up. Just brushing my teeth,' were, she suspected, most likely uttered from the comfort of his bed and she sighed in annoyance; it was the same story every morning. 'Damn him anyway,' she muttered and, setting the eggs down on the table, she went out into the hall, stood at the bottom of the stairs and listened for signs of life. Absolute silence.

'*Pierce!*' she shouted. No answer. '*Pierce, are you still in bed?*' she roared at the top of her voice.

'No, no, I'm up,' came his response but there was a false heartiness about it, like that of the just-awake trying desperately to give the impression that they'd been up for ages now, why practically since the crack of dawn. 'I'll be down in a tic, Mom,' he called out. 'I'm ... I'm just brushing my teeth.'

'What? Still? Who do you think you are? One of the Osmonds?'

She heard a loud thump as his feet hit the floor and then the sound of scurried movement overhead as he rushed about getting dressed and, almost as soon as she'd gone back into the kitchen, he came pounding down the stairs and came rushing in. Going directly to the table, he grabbed one of the eggs and, juggling it to prevent his hands from burning, he managed to peel it and then popped it into his mouth whole.

'Hot, hot,' he puffed, fanning his mouth.

'Good morning to you too,' she said looking up at him for Pierce had really sprouted up lately. Within the space of a few months he'd gone from being inches smaller than her to inches taller. 'Pierce,' she asked now, 'why can't you ever sit down and eat your breakfast like a normal person?'

'No time, Mom, no time,' he mumbled, his mouth still full. Then he swallowed and asked, 'So, where's Dad? Is he up yet?'

'Yes, he's gone for the paper.'

'Is he excited?'

'To put it mildly. I don't think he got a wink of sleep all night.'

'I bet.' He poured himself a glass of milk and emptied it in one long swallow, poured himself another glass and finished that just as quickly and then wiped his mouth with the back of his hand. 'Have you seen my school tie?' he asked.

'No,' answered Ana, sitting down to her own breakfast.

As she began to eat she looked on as Pierce rushed around up-scuttling cushions and newspapers in search of the missing tie. Finally, discovering it stuck underneath the seat of an armchair, he pulled it out and hung it around his neck.

'Aren't you missing something else?' she felt compelled to ask, as she was somewhat puzzled by his appearance.

'Yeah, my sports gear.' He came to the table and poured himself a bowl of Cornflakes. 'Have you seen it?'

'No. And that's not what I'm talking about.'

'You didn't wash my stuff by any chance?'

'No,' she answered and, feeling it necessary to state the obvious, she pointed out, 'Pierce, you're not wearing any trousers.'

His mouth was too full to answer for he'd been shovelling in spoonfuls of Cornflakes at a rate faster than he could swallow.

'Your pants, Pierce, where are your pants?'

she asked.

'Oh yeah,' he answered, having finally swallowed. 'Daniel has them. He's going to drop them in on his way to school.'

For a second she was tempted to ask what his friend was doing with them but then thought better of it for she knew that he'd probably give her some convoluted explanation which would seem perfectly reasonable to him but which would leave her even more bewildered.

'Dad,' he asked as his father came into the kitchen with the morning paper under his arm, 'you didn't see my sports bag?'

'Like where?' Mark asked, looking at his son with a puzzled expression. 'On my way to the shop?'

'What?' asked Pierce, equally puzzled.

'No, Pierce, I didn't see your sports bag. I was at the shop. How would I have seen it?' He pulled out a seat at the table and sat down, then reached for the orange juice and poured himself a glass but, before he took a sip, he smirked to himself and then looked over at his son slyly. 'But I did meet this girl on my way back,' he went on. 'Deborah, I think she said her name was. Nice girl. She was asking for you.'

'Oh God no,' groaned Pierce. 'No, no, no.'

'What on earth's the matter now?' Ana asked, looking at her son in alarm for he'd started banging his forehead repetitively on the kitchen table. ‘What are you carrying on like that for? Who is this Deborah?’

‘His girlfriend, so it seems,’ answered Mark.

‘Most definitely *not* my girlfriend,’ Pierce protested, now exaggeratedly rolling his eyes around.

‘Give over, Pierce, there’s hardly any need for such drama. So tell us, who is she?’ Ana persisted. ‘And how do you know her?’ she asked Mark.

‘Yeah, how do you know her?’ asked Pierce.

‘So she is your girlfriend,’ observed Ana.

‘No she’s not.’

‘But you just said…’

‘I said nothing. I just asked Dad how he knows her.’

‘Well, she stopped me outside the shop, introduced herself, told me that her family had moved into number ten and asked me was I Pierce Harrison’s father.’

‘And what did you tell her?’ demanded Pierce.

‘Well, since I am your father,’ said Mark slowly as if he was dealing with someone who wasn’t quite all there and, in truth, sometimes he was inclined to think that this was the case with his teenage son, ‘I thought I might as well come clean and admit it.’

‘Ah Dad,’ Pierce sighed. ‘You shouldn’t have.’

'And what did you want me to do, Pierce?' asked Mark, exasperated. 'Pretend I'd never heard of you?'

'Yes, yes,' said Pierce shaking his head vigorously. 'The less she knows the better.'

'Of course.' Mark threw his eyes to heaven. 'Stupid me.'

'You'll be sorry, Dad. She'll be chasing after you now for information. Ask Daniel, she has him hounded.'

'So tell us more about her,' Ana asked.

'There *is* nothing to tell.'

'Nothing at all?' Ana persisted.

Pierce shook his head vigorously.

'Nothing.'

Ana looked at Mark. 'Do you believe him?' she asked.

'Hmmm, I'm not so sure. Maybe he's protesting just that little bit too much.'

'So you think he fancies her then?'

'*Me* fancy her?' interrupted Pierce. 'Oh no, you've got it all wrong. It's *she* who fancies me! And stop talking about me as if I wasn't here.'

'So you don't like her at all then?' asked Ana and both his parents looked at him keenly.

'No,' he answered.

'Not even a little?'

'No.'

But for the fact that he was blushing bright red, they might have believed him.

'What? What? You don't believe me?' demanded Pierce, looking from one to the other and catching their smirks.

'Oh yes, of course we believe you,' answered his father.

And both he and Ana burst out laughing.

'I've had enough of this. How can I win with the pair of you ganging up on me? I'm off to school,' said Pierce getting up from the table.

'You'll definitely have trouble fighting her off if you leave the house dressed like that,' said Ana looking down at his boxer shorts and both she and Mark started laughing again.

'Ah for God's sake,' snapped Pierce, 'you're like a couple of children.'

Realising that he had no choice but to wait for Daniel, he sat back down again.

'Seeing as how you're staying,' said Ana, getting up and going to the fridge, 'you might as well give us a hand with this.'

She took out a bottle of champagne and then went to a press and brought out some glasses.

'Champagne! Wow!' said Pierce, instantly forgetting his umbrage. 'I've never had champagne before. Can I pop it?'

'Alright,' said Ana, handing it to him.

Immediately Pierce began shaking it vigorously.

'Pierce! Stop! It will go...' But it was too

late. Pierce popped the cork and lost half the champagne in a spray. 'Here, give it to me,' demanded Ana and she took the bottle from him and poured out three glasses. 'So Mark,' she said, handing him the first glass. 'How do you feel on your last day?'

'Good,' he said, then paused. 'Well, more than good. More like un-bloody-believably good.'

'I'd say,' said Pierce, taking his glass. 'I wish it were my last day.'

'So, let's have a toast,' said Ana. 'Here's to your last day at Burnhill Comprehensive, Mark, and to your new career as a photographer.'

'Cheers,' called Pierce. He took a sip, considered the taste for a second, nodded in approval then drained the rest of the glass in one swallow. Immediately he poured himself out a second glass and quickly knocked that back too. 'And to three months of us travelling through Africa,' he called out – his words coming out just the tiniest bit slurred and sounding a fraction louder than normal. But that didn't stop him reaching for the bottle again.

'Yes, here's to three months of travelling through Africa,' said Ana as she moved the champagne out of his reach.

'They're all dead jealous in school that I'm going to Africa for the summer,' said Pierce now holding his glass out to Ana, thinking that it was worth a try, but she ignored him. 'The most anyone else is doing is going to Blackpool for a fortnight or for a week to their Auntie's in the country.' And, just in case his mother didn't see the glass stuck right under her nose, he added, 'Mom I'll have another drop there, when you're ready.'

Just then the doorbell rang.

'Pierce, that's probably Daniel,' said Ana, taking the glass away from him. 'Go and answer it.'

'So what time are we going out for dinner again?' he asked as he got up and, as steadily as he could, made his way across the kitchen.

'Seven,' answered Ana.

'I'll have time for a game of football after school so. Alright then, see you later. Good luck, Dad.'

'Thanks, Pierce. Oh and by the way,' Mark called after him. 'You can bring Deborah along this evening if you like.'

'Very funny.'

Once Pierce had left, Ana and Mark looked at one another across the table.

'Cheers,' said Ana, holding up her glass.

'Cheers,' said Mark, clinking it with his. He leaned over and kissed Ana, then got up and turned up the radio. 'Come on, Mrs Harrison, what about a celebratory dance?' he asked, grabbing her by the hand and pulling her to her feet.

'But you can't dance,' she protested.

'Nonsense.'

'And I've no shoes on.'

'So?'

She gave in and together they shuffled around in the centre of the kitchen but Ana found it hard to relax and enjoy herself for she was far too aware of the real threat of having her bare feet trampled on by her very awkward husband.

'It is fairly unbelievable though, isn't it?' said Mark after a few moments.

'That you're such a bad dancer?'

'No, no. That I'm finally giving up teaching and, you know, that I'm going to be a photographer.'

'You always were, you just didn't get paid very much. But I know what you mean. Still, I always knew you'd do it. The pity is that you didn't give up teaching years ago.'

'Ah Ana, you know I couldn't.'

'Stubborn as a mule, that's what you are. And far too proud for your own good.'

'Ah Ana.'

'But it's true. I'll never understand why you took my mother's words so much to heart. Celia would have only been delighted to see her money being used to help set you up as a photographer.'

'I know that. But in a way I'm glad that I've managed to do it on my own.'

'Yes, but only after years of double-jobbing.'

'What does it matter? We've had good times travelling around during the school holidays, haven't we?'

'You mean staying in third-rate hotels and grotty bed and breakfasts in the wilds of Scotland and Ire–?' Suddenly she broke off and stared at the weird-looking stranger who'd appeared from nowhere and was now standing at their kitchen doorway watching them. He/she/it, it was impossible to tell, was barely five foot in height, wore star-shaped sunglasses, had a head of wild backcombed hair and was dressed in a long raggedy old sheepskin coat which reached right down to a pair of grubby white platform boots.

'Who are you?' she demanded. 'And what the hell are you doing in our kitchen?'

'It's only me, Mrs Harrison,' the intruder replied.

Between the collar, the hair and the shades, there wasn't much face left to recognise. But the voice was familiar.

'Daniel, is that you?' Ana asked uncertainly, now peering closely.

'Yes, Mrs Harrison. Who did you think it was?'

'What on earth has happened to you?' The last time Ana had seen Daniel – hardly more than a week or two ago it seemed to her, though now she realised it must have been more – he'd looked like a typical teenage schoolboy but, somehow, in the intervening period, he'd managed to transform himself into this – she wasn't exactly sure what he was meant to be – into this hippie she supposed, who was now standing before her. Though his hair had always been on the wild side she couldn't conceive that what she was now looking at could really be his own. It was just so outrageously *big*. There just seemed to be so much of it there.

'Daniel, are you wearing a wig?' she finally asked.

'Course not, Mrs Harrison. Don't be daft.'

'But you look so different.'

'I just decided that it was time I got a proper look for myself. After all, we're growing up, Mrs Harrison, growing up. We're not kids any longer, you know.'

'Daniel,' said Mark, 'I thought Mr Reeves told you at assembly the other morning to tone your dress down.'

'And I have, Mr Harrison. I got rid of the scarf, didn't I?'

'I think he meant–'

'And the clogs.'

'Yes, but...' The blank look on Daniel's face told Mark that it would be a weary and probably a futile exercise to try to explain to him that Mr Reeves had meant a change far more drastic and he decided that it really wasn't worth the effort, not on his last day. 'Anyway, I thought you and Pierce had left for school,' he said, changing the subject.

'Yeah, we had. But Pierce forgot something so we had to come back. He's just gone upstairs so I thought I'd come in and wish you good luck on your last day.'

'Why, thank you, Daniel,' said Mark, touched by such thoughtfulness.

'So good luck, Mr Harrison.'

'Yes, well, thank you, Daniel.'

'May I just say, Mr Harrison,' began Daniel in an oddly ceremonious voice, 'that you'll be very much missed at Burnhill Comprehensive and that it's hard to imagine how they'll ever find a replacement who's even half as good as you were.'

'What?' asked Mark taken aback by such effusiveness and from such an unexpected source. He and Daniel hadn't exactly seen eye to eye in the classroom over the years.

'And I think I speak for all the pupils, Mr Harrison,' Daniel went on.

'Well, thanks, Daniel,' said Mark. 'I'd no idea that you thought so highly of me, especially after all the run-ins we've had.'

'Ah no, Mr Harrison, I understand that you were only doing your job. And, might I say, a most excellent job you did too. Young people need a certain amount of discipline and I think it would be correct to say that you were strict but fair.'

'Why, thank you, Daniel. I must say I'm impressed by such maturity. It seems I've underestimated you. So, I'll see you in school then.'

'Yeah,' said Daniel. But he didn't budge from the doorway.

'Okay then.'

'Yeah.'

'Well, goodbye so, Daniel,' said Mark, dismissing him again for he was anxious to get back to the point where he and Ana had been before they were interrupted. He wanted to savour this last morning, not spend it chatting with one of his pupils.

But Daniel stayed where he was. He didn't appear to have any intention of leaving.

'It must be kind of odd,' he said after a few moments. 'You know, to be starting a new job.'

'Yes, I suppose it is,' agreed Mark.

'But kind of exciting.'

'Well, yes.'

'Even though you're so old and all.'

'Daniel,' said Mark, beginning to realise that if he wanted Daniel to leave he'd have to tell him so in plain words.

'Yes, Mr Harrison?'

'I want you to go upstairs. I want you to get Pierce. I want you and him to leave for school immediately. And I don't want to see you back in the kitchen again, okay?'

'Well, you see,' sighed Daniel, for he too

was beginning to realise that he'd have to be blunt if he was ever going to get what he'd come for, that all this flattery was getting him nowhere, 'you see, Pierce told me that there might be a chance of some champagne if I came in.'

'Did he now?'

'Yes.'

'I see'

'So?'

'So what?'

'Is there any champagne?'

'Daniel, do you see anything wrong with a teacher giving a pupil champagne?'

'No, Mr Harrison. Not really.'

'So you think Mr Reeves wouldn't have a problem with it?'

'Well, I'm won't tell him if you don't. Besides, it's your last day. What can he do, fire you?'

'Daniel, let me spell this out for you. I am not going to give you any champagne.'

'I see. Well ... well, maybe Mrs Harrison could. She's not a teacher.'

'Daniel,' said Mark warningly, in his best teacher's voice.

'Worth a try,' muttered Daniel as he shuffled out.

Once he'd gone, Mark turned back to Ana.

'Where were we again?' he asked.

'I think we were shuffling around the floor

and talking about all the grotty hotels we've stayed in over the years.'

'Ah yes. But they'll probably seem posh compared to what we'll find in Africa. Just think, Ana, of what Africa will be like; think of all the new sights, the new customs, all the new people we'll meet. Imagine, travelling all over, packing up every few days and moving on to another place. The three of us, just like nomads – all summer long.'

Ana looked at his excited face. She loved when he was like this. He was always at his most animated when talking about travel or photography.

'What is he, a boy of twenty?' she asked, now mimicking her mother's words, those scornful words she'd shouted at Ana years before, after Celia had died. They'd become a catch-phrase of hers which she used whenever Mark was getting carried away. 'Wants to be a travel-photographer! Bah!'

'Am a photographer, Ana, am a photographer,' he cockily corrected her.

'And still a boy at thirty-nine.'

'But wasn't it worth it in the end? Just imagine the times we'll have. Do you know what I was thinking when I was coming back with the paper? I was thinking that both *Life* and *National Geographic* have never turned down a single set of shots I've sent them over the years. Do you remember Simon Barton? We met him at that awards ceremony, remember? Well, he thinks it's only a matter of time before *National Geographic* make me a staff photographer.'

'They'd be fools not to. Citation of Excellence in the Overseas Press Club Award. Magazine Photographer of the Year. Of course they'll want to snap you up, pardon the pun.'

'And,' Mark went on, 'even if they don't, I'm getting enough assignments as a contract photographer from them alone to keep me going. They're already talking about a trip to Central America when we come home from Africa. Imagine Central America, Ana, think of actually seeing the old Mayan ruins – you've always wanted to. And then there's the book on Ireland to do.'

'Stop, stop, you're getting carried away, Mark,' interrupted Ana. 'You know I can't go to Central America. Pierce's term-time will have started by then.'

'I talked to Pierce about it last night, Ana, and he wants to come. I think we should take him out of school for a year. It would be such an opportunity for him.'

'We'll see,' she said cagily, already knowing that it would be impossible not to let Pierce go, not now that he'd Mark's tacit agreement.

'Oh God, look at the time,' Mark said suddenly, glancing at his watch. 'I'd better get going.' He gave Ana a kiss. 'Well, wish me luck on my last day.'

'Good luck,' she said, returning his kiss. 'Love you.'

He put on his jacket and picked up his bag.

'Love you too. Bye-bye,' he called as he hurried out the door.

When he'd left, she stayed sitting for a long while at the table, just thinking. All the years of Mark's hard work had been worth it – things were finally working out for him. It was hard to believe that he was actually giving up teaching at last and doing what he'd always wanted to do. She had no doubt but that he was a good teacher but it had never excited him the way photography did. For a second she was tempted to ring her mother just to let her know that Mark was making it as a photographer *and* that he was succeeding in doing so without ever having used a penny of Celia's money. She was proud of him for that. But still, she couldn't help thinking that it was a pity he'd been so adamant in waiting until he was earning enough through assignments before giving up. It seemed such a waste when life was so short. But for her mother's words, Ana felt that he wouldn't have been so stubborn, that he wouldn't have wasted so much time.

Yesterday had been the last day she'd spend minding her neighbour's three children. For a while now, she'd been thinking of finishing up for these once adorable children had grown more and more troublesome as they'd become older. It wasn't as if she and Mark really needed the money and she often wondered why she even bothered. Now, this trip to Africa had presented her with the perfect opportunity to finally make that break. And it was good to have the week before they left free. She really needed it – there was going to be such a lot to do.

But first things first. Her immediate plan was to have herself a very pleasant, very leisurely day in town. In between having her hair, her nails and her face done and going for as many coffees as she saw fit, she was going to celebrate the advent of good times by finding herself something incredibly beautiful and ridiculously expensive to wear that evening. There would be time enough for roughing it when they got to Africa.

She looked at her watch. It was nine twenty now. If she managed to get into Knightsbridge by eleven-thirty, then she'd be doing okay; that would give her loads of time. She got up from where she'd been sitting, cleared away the breakfast things, went upstairs, dressed and then phoned for a taxi. As she waited, she began tidying up the cushions and newspapers Pierce had scattered in his wake as he'd searched for the missing tie but then, the photographs hanging on the wall caught her attention and, with a bundle of old newspapers still in her arms, she wandered over. These were the first photographs of Mark's that *National Geographic* had ever accepted and though she was intimately familiar with their every detail she never got tired of looking at them. Now she went from one to another, considering each in turn. They were taken on the west coast of Ireland and, like all Mark's work, there was nothing gimmicky about them; they were just ordinary, everyday images made extraordinary by his skill as a photographer. She'd been with him when he'd taken most of them and as she looked at one of her favourites – a black and white portrait of an old lady – she smiled, recalling the time he'd taken it. She remembered Mark cajoling this stern old lady out of her initial reluctance to be photographed and the result testified that he'd succeeded admirably for he'd managed to capture just a hint of a flirtatious smile for the camera, or rather for the *fear go hálainn* or the 'lovely man' behind the camera. Ana moved on to another favourite of hers, of an old couple in their eighties – the woman, neat and handsome, the man, as crinkled and tanned as a balled-up brown paper bag. He was grinning toothlessly at the camera but her attention was focused elsewhere – on her husband and her face radiated a magnificent expression of love; her response, Ana remembered, to Mark's enquiry as to what a lovely lady like her was doing with such an old fellow.

His photos of Ireland spanned twenty years and covered every part of it. His landscape shots were as memorable as those of the people and it was easy to see why that publishing company had been anxious to sign him up for a book on Ireland. He'd really managed to capture the textures and shapes of the countryside in a unique way through his skilful use of light and his eye for the unusual. Or something like that – at least that's what the presenter had said when awarding Mark the prize for Magazine Photographer of the Year. She could see what he meant though.

The ringing of the phone interrupted her thoughts and, setting the bundle of newspapers down, she went out to the hall to answer it.

'Julie! Well, this is a surprise!' she exclaimed excitedly, hearing the voice of her old friend on the line from Ireland. 'How are you keeping?' she asked, then listened to the response and the string of questions that followed. 'Yes, yes,' she answered. 'His last day. Yes, very excited, you know what he's like. What? Well, we'll be heading on Wednesday assuming that everything is sorted which is hard to imagine right now. Things are in complete chaos. I've a hundred things to organise.' She listened for a few moments. 'You're what? You're flying over from Dublin? You're joking, Julie! Oh my God, Julie, this is great – I can't believe it! Oh this is fantastic!' She calmed down enough to listen as Julie explained her plans. 'You'll see me here? Are you having me on? No, no, no, I'm coming to the airport. No, Julie,' she interrupted in protest, 'no, *you* listen to me. If you dare turn up here you'll find nobody at home. I'm warning you, you'll be locked out for I'll be out in Heathrow waiting for you. Yes, yes, I know I said I was up to my eyes but I was putting off getting down to things until tomorrow anyway. God, wait until Mark hears you're coming. Oh he'll be so thrilled. Now, we're going to dinner this evening so you'll have to come too. He thinks it's just Pierce and the two of ourselves but I've invited about thirty of our friends along as a surprise. And now you'll be there too! Oh he'll be so delighted. He has such a soft spot for you but only because you flirt with him so much, don't think I don't notice. Oh it's going to be a great night, Julie.' Just then the door bell rang. 'Okay, look Julie, I think a taxi has just pulled up outside for me. Tell me, what time is your flight due in? Four thirty – okay, I'll see you then. Bye-bye.'

She put the receiver down and went to

answer the door.

'Oh hello, Mr Reeves,' she said surprised to see the principal of Mark's school standing there. 'And hello, Jim,' she greeted the second man, Mark's closest friend on the school staff.

'Hello, Ana,' said Jim.

'Hello, Mrs Harrison, may we come in?' asked Mr Reeves.

'Yes, yes, of course,' answered Ana.

She stepped aside and the two men came in and she led them into the kitchen.

'Tea? Coffee?' she asked, wondering what could have brought them here, thinking that it must have something to do with Mark's last day.

'No, Ana, don't mind that,' said Jim. 'Look Ana, why don't you come and sit down?'

'Oh God,' she cried, looking from one grim face to another, suddenly realising that there was something the matter. 'What's wrong? Tell me, is it Pierce? Is he alright?'

'It would be better if you sat down,' said Jim kindly and, taking the bewildered Ana by the arm, he guided her to a seat.

The rest of the day was a blur. Sad-faced people came and went – Jim's wife, neighbours, other friends. Someone had gone to collect Julie at the airport and someone else had brought Pierce home. Pierce – poor, poor Pierce. People hugged her. They cried.

They tried not to cry. They huddled in corners and talked in low voices about how she was doing. They put cups of sweet tea in her hand, patted her shoulder and said, 'There, there'. They answered phone calls from friends who'd rung up to confirm details regarding tonight's dinner only to be told the dreadful news. And again and again they asked her was she doing okay? How could she be doing okay, she'd shouted angrily at someone – she couldn't remember who.

And finally, someone, Julie she thought, had helped her to bed. Not that she slept. She just lay there going over and over what Mr Reeves had told her. It was all just so stupid. Why, oh why, had Mark suddenly decided to take some of his students out onto Burnhill Common? Why, why, why hadn't he just stayed in his classroom? Then none of this would have happened.

She heard her bedroom door open and looked over to see Julie coming in to check on her. Noticing that she was awake, Julie came and sat on the edge of the bed and gently began to stroke her hair.

'Where's Pierce?' Ana asked her after a while.

'In his room. With Daniel and Deborah.'

'Daniel and who?'

'Deborah – that nice girl from down the street. I think she's in his class in school.'

Ana found it hard to believe that it had only been this morning she and Mark had sat at the breakfast table teasing Pierce over this girl Deborah. It seemed liked days ago and now they'd never be all together like that, never, ever again.

'Julie,' she asked, 'were those boys from Burnhill Comprehensive?'

'Yes, I think so.'

'Why did they do it, Julie?'

'Who knows? Because they're mindless thugs, I suppose.'

'But what did they want with those cameras? They weren't worth all that much. They were old. That's why Mark was giving them to the school.'

'Ah Ana, they were just an excuse.'

As Julie continued to stroke her hair, Ana drifted off to sleep.

An hour or two later she woke again to see Julie, still in her clothes, asleep on the bed beside her. What on earth was she doing here, wondered Ana, all befuddled and sleepy. And where was Mark? But her confusion lasted only a split-second and then everything came flooding back.

Everything. All Mr Reeves had told her as he'd held her hand in his, as she'd stared and stared at his fingernails thinking how very dirty they were and had tried to block out what he was saying, but had tried to make sense of it all at the same time.

All the time he'd talked she'd sat staring at those dirty fingernails, with the one ridiculous thought drifting in and out of her head – that really, for a school principal, he was surprisingly badly groomed. She'd stared at those dirty fingernails as he told her about the gang of thugs who'd set upon Mark and his pupils when they were out on Burnhill Common taking photographs; had stared at them as he'd told her how, in their attempt to take Mark's camera from him, they'd knocked him to the ground; and had stared at them as she'd learned how Mark's pupils had tried to fight them off. And she'd stared and stared as he told her how very, very sorry he was, but that Mark had died in the ambulance on the way to the hospital. That he'd died from a single stab wound to the chest.

Easter Monday morning...

Just before eight, Ana was awoken by the sound of the Colonel noisily closing her front door. Then, through her bedroom window she heard him call out heartily, 'Beautiful morning, Ellen! Isn't it great to be alive?' And as she lay there, Ana imagined the scene outside. She could just see Ellen rooted to the spot, gaping after the Colonel, her expression, initially one of puzzlement as she wondered 'Where could *he* be coming from at this hour of the morning?' but gradually changing to eye-popping astonishment as she began to draw certain conclusions. And she could see the Colonel continuing along the path jauntily, with just that little extra bit of bounce in his step. His merry whistle sounded very loud in the quiet morning and it occurred to Ana that, not content with having just the one witness to his early morning departure, he was determined to alert everyone else as well, no doubt hoping that they, like Ellen, would assume he'd been up to no good.

Well, there was little she could do about it, she thought, as she leant out of the bed and reached for her walking-stick which was propped up against the bedside locker and, using this, she pushed apart the curtains and saw that it was indeed a beautiful morning. 'Perfectly suitable,' she said aloud, thinking of her plans for the day ahead. A lucky sign indeed, she decided. She climbed out of bed, turned on the radio, opened her wardrobe and took even longer than usual in selecting an outfit, eventually deciding on a shimmery green dress and complementary shoes and handbag. And hat of course for she didn't hold with this modern decree which confined the wearing of hats to weddings and such occasions – she'd as soon set off on a day's outing without a hat as she would without dress or shoes. She dressed, then sat herself down before her mirror to do her make-up which was an involved task even on an ordinary day but especially so on a day such as this. Fifteen minutes later, when she was finally putting the finishing touches of blue to her eyelids, she suddenly remembered that, at some point in his ramblings the night before, the Colonel had happened to mention that there was a bus strike going on ('Shoot the buggers, I say,'). 'Damn, damn, damn,' she muttered now, wondering how else she was going to get into Bray. She could take a taxi but a round trip would cost her the best part of forty pounds. Just for a second, she considered hitching a lift. It wouldn't be the craziest thing she'd ever done in her life but she'd more sense now and, given that she'd managed to survive to this ripe old age, she wanted to die of natural causes and not at the hands of some psychopath. The best thing to do, she finally decided, was to go up to the main house and see if she could get a lift in with any of the staff. A few of them lived in Bray. Maybe Catherine, the cook who usually worked the breakfast shift, might be heading in at a suitable time.

Catherine was an obliging, outgoing sort and was generally liked by the residents despite the fact that she was absolutely appalling at her job. Even Ellen, the least fussy of eaters and well-known for her habit of polishing off whatever scraps others left behind, found it hard to finish a helping of Catherine's efforts and, as a consequence, when Catherine was on duty many of the residents chose to cook their own meals as Ana did this morning. As soon as she was finished, she tidied away and went back into her bedroom. There she pulled over a chair, climbed up onto it and searched the top of the wardrobe for the bundle of twenty-pound notes she kept hidden there and, having found them, she climbed back down and stuffed them into her handbag. Then she put on her hat, took one last look around to see if she had everything she needed and left the bungalow, intent on going straight to the main house in search of Catherine and the chance of a lift.

But almost immediately she bumped into Penny.

'Before you ask, Penny – no, I haven't seen Ellen,' said Ana pre-empting the other's usual opening question.

'Actually, Ana, I wasn't looking for her.'

'For once.'

Penny, Ana was beginning to realise, was looking at her very strangely, with a sort of sly, half-smirk on her face.

'What?' she demanded. 'What are you smirking at, Penny?'

But Penny ignored the question.

'Well, Ana Dunne,' she said looking at her with open amusement now, 'aren't you the dark horse?'

'What?'

'Oh don't mind playing the innocent with me, Ana. It's far, far, too late for that,' laughed Penny. 'You see, I know all about the carry-on you were up to last night. Yes, a dark horse indeed.'

'Hang on a second now–' began Ana.

'So you and the Colonel,' interrupted Penny, not giving her a chance. 'Well, that's news alright. And what will Nurse Boo have to say about all this? Won't he be sorely put out when he hears? He seems to be rather fond of you himself?'

'Hears what? Listen to me, Penny, there is nothing going on between myself and the Colonel.'

'Go away out of that! Come on, give us the low-down,' demanded Penny, nudging Ana. 'And don't go leaving out any of the juicy bits.'

'There *are* no juicy bits. He came over, had a few drinks, fell asleep and, since I could hardly be expected to lift him back to his own place, I left him in my kitchen where he slept for the night. He only called over for a bit of company, Penny.'

'A bit of company!' Penny hooted. 'Well, that's a new way of putting it alright!'

'You've a dirty mind, Penny Plunkett. God, is there any privacy in this place at all?'

'None. You should know that by now. That

you and the Colonel are–'

'Are what, Penny?' interrupted Ana.

'You know, keeping each other company, as you put it, wink, wink. It's the most exciting thing that's happened here since Frank Byrne, God rest his soul, took a notion to bring Noreen Doyle out for a spin in Catherine's car one Sunday. Like yourself and the Colonel, they were trying to keep things quiet and thought that nobody would notice them sneaking off on their romantic spin. But you see, Frank hadn't driven for a long time and, God help him, didn't the excitement of a day out with Noreen Doyle have him all flustered. By mistake, you see, he set the car into reverse and, before either of them knew what was happening, he'd backed it onto the lawn where it spun around and around and around until suddenly it went careering through Laurence's roses at high speed and didn't stop until it was right in the middle of the lake. And there the two of them were sitting...' Penny was laughing now at the memory '...wondering how they were going to get out of this mess, when they were spotted.'

Just as she was coming to a finish, her eyes suddenly opened wide in alarm for, over Ana's shoulder, she noticed Elizabeth coming their way.

'Ho, ho,' she laughed gleefully. 'There'll be sparks flying now.'

Ana turned, saw Elizabeth approaching and was about to call out hello, but was suddenly taken aback when she noticed that Elizabeth appeared to be glaring menacingly at her.

'Hello, Elizabeth,' called Penny chirpily. 'So, how are you this morning? Any news?'

Elizabeth didn't answer. She walked straight up to Ana, threw her a dirty look, emitted a low, guttural noise like a growl and then marched off again.

Ana stared after her, dumbfounded.

'Penny,' she asked eventually, 'am I imagining things, or did Elizabeth just growl at me?'

'Well, yes, it would seem she did.'

'What in God's name has got into her? Do you know what all that was about?'

'Well,' began Penny watching Elizabeth who had now done an about-turn and was marching back to them, 'I could tell you but it looks like you're just about to find out from herself.'

Elizabeth came to a stop in front of her. 'All I have to say to you, Ana Dunne,' she said, her face like thunder now, 'is that I hope you know what you're doing.'

'What?'

'Toying with the poor man's affections like that.'

'What?'

'Oh don't pretend you don't know what

I'm talking about. I know what you're up to.'

'Elizabeth–'

'Things were just fine here until you showed up and ruined everything.'

'Elizabeth, what are you talking about?' Ana asked. From the corner of her eye she noticed Penny lighting up a cigarette as she got set to enjoy the showdown. 'Why don't you sit down on the bench altogether, Penny?' she snapped. 'You'd be more comfortable.'

'There are names for women like you,' Elizabeth told Ana, prodding her in the chest with her index finger. 'You're nothing but a – a – a – slut!'

'What?' stammered Ana and she was so surprised that all she could do was laugh.

'Laugh away. I suppose you think all this is very funny.'

'Elizabeth, please I–'

'All I have to say to you is this,' interrupted Elizabeth. 'Before you arrived at Rathdowne, things were coming on nicely between myself and the Colonel. He'd grown quite fond of me. Isn't that right, Penny?'

'Oh, no, no,' said Penny shaking her head as she exhaled a cloud of smoke. 'I'm not getting dragged into this.'

'What are you standing there for so?' demanded Ana crossly. 'Why don't you go off about your business?'

'But then,' Elizabeth continued, prodding Ana once again, 'you showed up and ruined everything.'

'Elizabeth, look, you've got it all wrong.'

'You've no right to be fooling around with him.'

'Elizabeth look–'

'Sure she hasn't, Penny?'

'Don't be asking me.'

'Elizabeth I–' began Ana.

'No right whatsoever.'

'Elizabeth, listen to me,' Ana tried again but the sight of Ellen emerging from her bungalow, no doubt anxious to see what the commotion was about, distracted her for a second. 'Look, Elizabeth,' she began again, 'I'm not fooling around with–'

'Oh isn't it easy for the likes of you?' Elizabeth came cutting in.

'What do you mean, isn't it easy for the likes of me?' Ana demanded crossly, beginning to lose her temper now and, noticing that Penny was whispering furiously in Ellen's ear, bringing her up to date most likely, she snapped, 'Make sure you don't leave anything out, Penny.'

'You don't know what it's like to have lived with a man for forty years,' Elizabeth went on. 'To have done everything together during all that time and then to suddenly find that you're all alone, that you're facing into old age with nobody, with nothing to look forward to. Isn't that right, Penny? Isn't it, Ellen?' Both of them stared back at her blankly. 'What on earth am I asking the pair of you for?' she asked in disgust. 'God only knows where your husband is,' she said, addressing Penny. Then she threw Ellen a look. 'And, as for you, well...' she paused, momentarily at a loss as to how to finish, 'I don't think that you'd even know what to do with one.'

'Ah now Elizabeth, there's no need for that,' said Ana. 'And I–'

'And then I came here and met Colonel Jackson and he was so kind to me from the very first day that I began to think that maybe, just maybe, I wouldn't have to face into old age on my own. You know, it isn't exactly easy to find men at this time of our lives, sure old fellows die like flies – they don't have the sticking power of us women at all. And then you came along, Ana Dunne, and ruined it all. Now he has no time for me. I see him, the way he follows you around like a great big stupid Labrador, practically panting whenever he sees you.'

'Elizabeth, that's nonsense. He's just a harmless flirt, he goes on that way with everyone.'

'You see, you know nothing at all about him. He's besotted with you and the more fool he is for being so.' She turned on her heel. 'Out of my way,' she snapped at Ellen, then pushed her aside and went storming off.

Ana turned to Penny and Ellen.

'God, what did I do to start that off?' she asked, though she had a fair idea.

'At a guess,' said Penny, 'I'd say she heard that the Colonel came over to your house last night for a bit of company – to use your own expression.'

'And who on earth would have told her that?' Ana asked, her eyes settling on Ellen as she remembered the Colonel's greeting to her earlier that morning. 'You wouldn't happen to have any ideas, would you, Ellen?'

'What? God, no,' said Ellen beginning to edge away. 'Is that the time? I should be...'

'It wasn't you by any chance, Ellen?'

'Me?' asked Ellen blushing. 'You think it was me?'

'Yes, I do, actually.'

'Ah Ana, how could you think such a thing? You should know now that I'm not one to gossip, sure I'm not, Penny?'

'God,' said her friend, 'why is everyone so anxious for my opinion this morning?'

'No, indeed I am not,' Ellen carried on. 'If there is something going on between yourself and the Colonel, though I'm not saying there is, well that's your own business, Ana.'

But Ana continued to stare at her accusingly.

'Look Ana, I'd be the last person in the world to go around spreading rumours,' Ellen went on in protest, ignoring Penny's derisive snort. 'You see, I know the harm they can do. Not through personal experience of course,' she hurriedly added, 'but I've seen the damage people can cause by not minding their own business. And I'll give you an example. There's this woman who ... who lives near us at home and, for years and years, she was fierce friendly with one of two brothers who had the farm next door. And of course, you know how it is, in a small place like that people were forever speculating about them, wondering if they'd ever get married. But the fellow was a slow, cautious chap and, although he was always talking about them getting married, he'd never name the day, he just kept on putting it off. And you see, it ruined things for the woman. Because everyone was forever gossiping about the pair of them, nobody else was interested in her. And in the end wasn't she left high and dry?'

Ana stared at her bemused.

'Ellen, what on earth has that got to do with anything?'

Ellen looked back at her, a little puzzled herself as to how she had got on to the subject or what point she was actually trying to make.

'Well, you know, I suppose I'm just saying

that you have to watch yourself when it comes to men. Nobody thinks any the worse of them if they play the field but a woman gets a bad name for herself very quickly if she's not careful.'

'That's great advice, Ellen,' said Ana sarcastically. 'I wouldn't want to get a bad name for myself and ruin my marriage chances, especially at my age.' She began to walk away. 'God, please,' she muttered to herself, 'let Catherine be leaving for Bray soon.'

It was one of those mornings when everyone seemed to be out and about. No sooner had she left Penny and Ellen but she bumped into the Colonel.

'What's wrong with Elizabeth?' he asked as he drew near. 'I saw her a few moments ago and God, she'd a face on her that would give children nightmares. Did she forget to take her happy pill or what?'

'Just don't ask,' groaned Ana.

'I was just on my way over to you,' the Colonel told her.

'Didn't you see enough of me last night?' she demanded crossly feeling annoyed with him. After all, he was the cause of all this morning's fuss.

'What?' He looked at her puzzled.

'Last night, Colonel. You slept with me last night.'

'Well,' he said puffing himself up like a

peacock, 'I'm glad to know I'm still up to it. Everything else seems to be going.'

'Oh, for goodness sake! You know what I mean. You slept in my house. On the couch. And I don't want to hear that you've been going around saying otherwise.'

'Oh.' He looked disappointed for a moment, but quickly recovered. 'So Anastasia, tell me, where are you off to this morning looking so delightfully fresh and lovely?'

'To Bray,' she answered. 'If I can find a way in.'

'Why don't I come with you? We could make a day of it.'

'No thank you, Colonel. I have business to attend to.'

'I see. Well, jolly good,' he said and began walking away but then, seconds later, he called after her. 'Ana, shouldn't you wear a jacket? It's dammed cold.'

'No, no, I'm fine, Colonel.'

Immediately up ahead of her, Ana saw Old Mary, the oldest resident at Rathdowne slowly making her way along the avenue, coaxing the walking-frame she called Horsy to 'gee-up' as she went. Realising that even Mary had probably got wind of her 'carry-on' Ana decided to take a more circuitous but quieter route up to the main house in order to avoid any further encounters and, leaving the path, she pushed her way in through Laurence's shrub border and then headed off across the grass. As she hurried along, it occurred to her that, although she'd only herself to blame for starting off these rumours about herself and the Colonel by letting him stay last night, there was no way she could have anticipated that their 'affair' would be considered quite so big a deal – it just showed how little happened in this place.

But as she slowed down a little, taking time to look around, her mood began to lift. It was so very peaceful here in the gardens. This really was her favourite time of the year, she thought, when everything was on the verge of blooming; everything was so fresh and new. She glanced up at the clear blue sky and saw a single bird flying noiselessly by and she sighed, suddenly feeling calm again and perfectly happy. It was good to be alive.

But then she paused and listened carefully. There was only silence at first and she thought she must have only imagined hearing someone sing. But then she heard it again – somewhere, down towards the far end of the garden, there was definitely a man singing. Her view was obstructed by trees, hedges and the slope of the lawn and she couldn't see anyone but, as she listened, the sound became more distinctive and she recognised the song as Figaro's arietta

'Largo al factotum' from *The Barber of Seville*. Whoever the owner of this mysterious voice was, he was an exceptionally fine opera singer with a powerful baritone voice and was well able to handle the pace of the piece and, only that he was unaccompanied, Ana would have assumed it to be a recording. Nosiness having got the better of her now, she began walking quickly in the direction of the singing and, as she drew near, the voice became gentle and soft, so soft as to be almost inaudible, but just for a few seconds and then it abruptly changed once more becoming fantastically exuberant until it culminated in a mighty *'Traa la-la, la-la la-la la-llaaaa'*. And then, a brief silence, before it started up again. This mysterious singer was thoroughly enjoying himself in the barber's role and, bursting with curiosity now, she crept around the last hedge.

She wasn't sure who she was expecting it to be but not for a moment had she imagined it would be Laurence. But there he stood, putting as much effort into his performance as if he were singing before an audience of thousands. He had his eyes shut tight, his arms were outstretched and his face was red with exertion as he sang with all his might. Ana crept over to a nearby bench and sat down. Oblivious to her presence Laurence carried on, lost in his role until, with a powerful rendition of the closing line *'Sono il factotum della città'*, then a string of *'Fig-a-ro-fig-a-ro-fig-a-ro-fig-a-ro-fig-a-ro, fig-a-rOOOOs'*, he came to the end. He sighed heavily and wiped the sweat from his forehead.

'Bravo!' shouted Ana. She got to her feet and began to applaud. 'More! More!' she called.

Laurence turned around and saw Ana for the first time.

'I didn't realise you were there, Mrs Dunne,' he said, looking a little embarrassed. 'I didn't realise I had an audience.'

'I'm glad that you had. It would've been a pity for such a splendid performance to have gone unheard. So,' she said, looking at him with frank admiration, 'an opera singer disguised as a gardener.' He laughed and looked as if he was about to protest but she went on. 'No, really Laurence, you could be a professional.'

'Well, I used to sing with an operatic company.'

'So used I! With the Ranelagh and Rathmines,' she said referring to a well-known amateur company in Dublin. 'But that was years and years ago. Which one were you in, Laurence?'

'Mainly the Metropolitan Opera – you know, in New York. But I sang with others too.'

Ana wished the ground would swallow her

up. God, with that voice she should have known he meant a professional company.

'The Metropolitan Opera, well, that's pretty impressive.'

He shrugged.

'But tell me, Laurence, why did you give up singing?'

'I didn't give it up. I still sing every day.'

'No, but professionally I mean?'

'Well, nobody objects to me singing while I garden but it doesn't work too well the other way around. Operatic companies are odd that way.'

'So you gave it all up and became a gardener instead?'

'Yes and no. By working as a gardener I get to do the two things I like doing best and at the same time.'

She thought about his answer for a moment, then nodded.

'Yes,' she said. 'I can see the sense in that. But tell me, Laurence, don't you miss all the glamour?'

'I can't say that I was ever one for glamour, Mrs Dunne. To be honest, the whole opera scene was never my thing. You see, I never really decided to become an opera singer as such but, years ago, when my parents and my teacher realised that I'd a bit of a voice nothing would do them but that I should become a professional and, without ever actually deciding that it was what I wanted,

I found myself living in New York and singing with the Metropolitan. Now that sounds more glamorous than it really was, I wasn't exactly the star of the show. In fact, I was usually stuck in the crowd playing a peasant, or servant, or soldier, or whatever. Mind you, now that I think about it, so much of my time was spent lurking in the crowd, waiting to sing, that nobody would have noticed if I had taken a few plants on stage with me and passed the time with a little re-potting.'

Ana laughed. 'Might have even added an air of authenticity to certain roles.'

'True. Better than having us all standing around pretending to be engaged in amazingly interesting conversation with one another.'

'So you don't miss being a professional opera singer at all?'

'Nope. I'm afraid it was never really the right career for me. Unfortunately I'm far too unimaginative and down-to-earth for a lot of it. There were times when I'd be on the stage, milling around in the crowd with all the action going on, and it would bother me that so much of it just didn't make any sense. I suppose you've got to be willing to accept that anything can happen in opera; that two men can go off to a pretend war and come back the very next day in disguise and not be recognised by their girlfriends or that ladies die for no apparent medical reason but just simply collapse from sorrow. And I know little details like that shouldn't be important but, for some reason, they used to bug the hell out of me. I like things to be more realistic, you see. But, as someone once said, opera is where a guy gets stabbed in the back and instead of bleeding, he sings.'

'I know what you're saying but…'

'And it was even worse when I was in operas that were being performed in English,' Laurence continued, for now that he'd started there seemed to be no stopping him. 'Once I was in a production of Schubert's *Alfonso and Estrella* sung in English and God, it was dreadful, so much of what is sung is such nonsense.' And suddenly, without warning, he began to sing the parts of both the King and the Chorus.

'The princess has appeared.

– The Princess?

– The Princess.

– Has she appeared? Has she appeared?

– Yes, she has appeared. She is approaching the palace.

– She is coming here.

– She is approaching the palace, she is coming here.'

'Alright, alright, I get your point,' Ana laughingly interrupted, for Laurence was getting carried away. 'Though I think that's probably your own pretty liberal translation.'

'No, no, it's fairly accurate. Anyway, as I was saying, I eventually realised that I had to get out. What I really prefer is the open air and my own company rather than that of prima donnas and the inside of an opera house. But don't get me wrong, I still love opera.'

He paused for a moment and Ana couldn't help staring at him as she took in all this new information.

'You're quite fond of it yourself, I've noticed,' he went on now. 'I've often heard opera coming from your bungalow when I'm working over that way and I think I'd be right in saying that I've heard you singing along on more than one occasion.'

'Well, you know how it is,' laughed Ana. 'Don't we all fancy ourselves as great singers in the bathtub?'

'What was it I heard you singing the other day?'

He thought for a minute then, very gently, he began singing Giovanni's part in *'Là ci darem'* from the opera *Don Giovanni*. And he sang it beautifully. His voice was every bit as seductive as the role merited and Ana closed her eyes and listened to the sound, so sweet and so simple. When it came to the female part he paused and she opened her eyes and saw him looking at her encouragingly, urging her to join in, but she shook her head, feeling too much in awe of his voice to dare and so he sang the first part again. The second time it came around for her to sing, he prompted her once again and this time, tentatively, she began singing the part of Zerlina, the young peasant girl. She sang nervously at first for, although she knew that she had a passable soprano voice, she felt embarrassed to be singing with someone as talented as Laurence. But gradually, realising that his voice was sure enough to carry hers and that in his company she sounded better than she really was, she gained confidence and began to enjoy herself.

And together they sang out the song. He, in his grubby gardening clothes, leaning against the side of the bench. She, in her green shimmery outfit, sitting there, hat on her head, her handbag resting on her lap. And together they filled the air with the wonderful sound of their voices.

1978

CHAPTER 5

For everything that lives is holy, life delights in life

from *America, 71* by William Blake

Ana had spent all that day peeling, shelling, stoning, dicing, slicing, boiling and baking. She'd laid out plates upon plates of food, made up bowls of punch, counted and recounted plates and glasses, shifted furniture from room to room, rolled back carpets and festooned the entire downstairs of the house in streamers and balloons – all in preparation for the eighty people she was expecting to show for Pierce's 21st birthday party that evening.

'Mom, don't you think that you might be getting just a little bit carried away?' Pierce had asked late in the afternoon when she'd finally managed to coerce him into lending a hand. 'The amount of food you're preparing is crazy. I mean, all that coleslaw, for instance, do you really think people are going to eat all that? There's mountains of the stuff.'

'Out of my way,' she'd snapped, squeezing past him for he was still hanging about in the doorway between kitchen and dining-room, and still holding the bundle of plates she'd handed him ten minutes ago with very clear and very simple instructions as to what he was to do with them.

'I mean, who eats coleslaw anyway?' she'd heard him mutter. 'And what *did* you say I was to do with these plates?'

'Put them on the dining-room table, Pierce, over by the bread rolls,' she'd answered extra-patiently though it was her third time to do so. But, unfortunately for Pierce, she'd worked out that he'd obviously resolved to prove himself completely useless in the hope that she'd eventually decide she no longer required his 'help'. Which of course had just made her all the more determined to keep him there and, not until the first guest, Mr Fowler, Daniel's father, arrived (an hour earlier than the appointed time as it happened) did she allow Pierce to go and get changed.

Now, looking around at the crowd, Ana realised that she might as well have been talking to the wall for all the notice Pierce had taken when, again and again, she'd reminded him that he could invite eighty people and no more. There were at least double that number present already and it was still early on in the evening and, as for the 'crazy' amount of food, it was disappearing at an alarming rate she noticed, even the maligned coleslaw. What had Pierce been thinking of when he'd invited so many? It was hard to believe that he could even know all these people and she was beginning to suspect that he probably didn't, that he'd just indiscriminately invited everyone he happened to bump into over the last week to come along.

At most she knew about a third of the people present. The group horsing around over by the record player she recognised as old school friends of Pierce's who, apart from Daniel, she'd hardly seen since the days when they used to come mooching into the house with Pierce and trail up the stairs after him and then, for hours on end, stay holed up in his bedroom doing mysterious adolescent boy things which consisted of, 'Nothing really,' or so she was told whenever she asked Pierce what it was they did up there.

There was another bunch of lads over by the door, several of whom she knew worked with Pierce at the furniture factory. They were all talking loudly now, all of them cutting across one another.

'Mud,' she heard one of them shout out. 'They'd have to be at number one.'

'Nah. Bay City Rollers are definitely at the top of the list.'

'No, I'd put Pink Floyd at number one

and ah…'

'Ziggy Stardust at number one. Gary Glitter at number two. Bay City Rollers at number three. Pink Floyd at number four and–'

'What about the Carpenters? Nobody's thought of them.'

There was a stunned silence amongst the group. And then loud laughter.

'The Carpenters?' repeated one of the others in disbelief.

'Yeah, why not? They had some fine songs throughout the seventies.'

'The Carpenters? The Carpenters? Jesus, Jimmy!'

'What planet are you on, Jimmy?'

Well, they seemed to be having a good time, thought Ana. Which was more than she could say for their boss – Mr Morgan, the factory owner. He was standing all on his own, she saw now, glass in hand. Apart from herself and that nice Mr Singh from the corner shop, she didn't think anyone else had spent more than five minutes talking to him all evening. It had been thoughtful of Pierce to invite him, surprisingly thoughtful in fact, but it was a pity he wasn't enjoying himself especially since, as he'd told her earlier, he didn't go out much nowadays, not since his wife's death last year. The boys from the factory were staying well clear of him, she noticed, not that she could really blame them. After all, they had to put up with him all day at work and trying to converse with him was quite hard going. He was half-deaf and seemed to think it necessary to shout at the top of his voice and, to make absolutely sure he was heard, he came in really close to his listener so that there was no escaping the spray of spit which accompanied his words, nor his bad breath, nor the permanent smell of stale sweat.

Ana's eyes moved on from him. Amongst the female guests she noticed that there was a preponderance of tall, thin, good-looking girls several of whom she recognised as former girlfriends of Pierce's. Nearby, she noticed Daniel who, having left his buddies, was now desperately trying to chat up one such girl, a head taller than himself, but she was staring down at him with such a bored expression that it was obvious (though apparently not to him) that he was never going to get anywhere with her and it seemed to Ana that, at twenty-one, Daniel was having no more success with girls than she remembered him having at sixteen or seventeen. Watching him, she smiled to herself as she recalled those evenings back then, when he'd often called over to their house only to find that Pierce had already gone out with his girlfriend of the day and, more than once, Daniel had ended up sitting at their kitchen table for the night, drinking coffee with her whilst bemoaning his lack of 'pulling power' as he'd called it. His logic at that time had been strange, she remembered. He seemed to think that if Pierce didn't go out with so many girls then he'd stand a better chance of getting one himself. But now, even though Pierce had a steady girlfriend, Daniel's luck clearly hadn't improved much.

She noticed that the scumbags had shown up – her name for the gang of sad, sorry drop-outs Pierce had started hanging around with that year he'd left school and before he'd started at the furniture factory. God, she hated them. Even now, just the sight of them was enough to make her blood boil. The intervening years hadn't wrought any improvements, quite the opposite in fact and they looked even more lethargic and more stupid than they had in the old days and even less likely to ever do anything with their lives. Pierce had been just awful back then and she'd been so relieved when he'd finally outgrown them and began working at the factory. He'd really taken to that – right from the very first day but then, he'd always been good with his hands. Mr Morgan certainly thought so; even earlier this evening he'd told her that Pierce was one of the best craftsmen he'd ever had working for him and that he'd be sorry to see him go. She noticed one of the scumbags knock against Mr Singh now, spilling his drink, and she smiled to herself as she watched the older man turn and furiously berate the scumbag; clearly all these years spent behind the shop counter had taught him a thing or two about standing up for himself. Suddenly it struck her as somewhat odd that Pierce had invited Mr Singh along to his party.

'Alright, Mrs Harrison?' asked Daniel, coming over now, no doubt having failed in his attempts with the tall, bored-looking girl.

'Fine, Daniel,' she answered, though she was finding it hard to keep a straight face. During the course of the evening, each time she happened to catch a glimpse of him, she couldn't help but smirk at his outfit. He was wearing a shiny purple suit; a black satin shirt with absolutely huge lapels displayed to advantage by the fact that his top three shirt buttons were left open; and black shoes that appeared extraordinarily pointy and uncomfortable to her. His normally bushy hair had been combed back and the top section had been gelled into a quiff.

'So, do you like my gear?' he asked, standing back a little from her and opening up the jacket to give her a better look. 'I've noticed you've been admiring it.'

'Well, it certainly is striking,' she remarked ambiguously.

'You might not know this, Mrs Harrison, but what you're looking at is the height of fashion.'

'Is that right?'

'Oh yeah.' Then he changed the subject. 'You were talking to my dad earlier.'

'Yes, I was.'

As Ana had rushed around, putting the last few finishing touches here and there before the rest of the guests had begun to arrive, Mr Fowler had silently followed her from room to room but, no matter how hard she'd tried to engage him in conversation, all the answer she'd got was a mute nod or shake of the head.

'He told me that the pair of you had a great chat,' Daniel went on.

'Really?'

Both Ana and Daniel glanced over to where Mr Fowler was sitting now. As soon as other people had started arriving, he'd sat himself down in the dead centre of a couch and hadn't budged since. All night he'd sat there, the couch's sole occupant in an otherwise jam-packed room. At some point during the evening somebody, most likely Mr Fowler himself, had turned on the nearby television and, ever since, his eyes hadn't wavered from the screen, though it was certain he couldn't hear a thing over the room's ambient noise level. Now, his eyes were glued to it as Benny Hill silently chased two bikini-clad girls across a park.

'Yeah,' Daniel continued. 'Said that you were able to catch up with all the news. He's looking well, isn't he? You know, I think he's finally beginning to get over Mom's death.'

'I hope so.'

'Of course he gets lonesome at times.'

'I'm sure he does. Mr Morgan was saying the same thing earlier. He lost his wife last year too.'

'I've been telling Dad that he should get out more, that he should join that new bridge club. Do you play bridge, Mrs Harrison?'

'No, I don't.'

'Well, maybe you and he could take it up together. They have a beginners' night every Friday. I think you'd be very good at it, Mrs Harrison.'

Suddenly, it all became very clear to Ana. Mr Fowler was a widower. Mr Morgan was a widower. Mr Singh was a widower. That was the sole reason why they'd all been invited by Pierce to this evening's party. Concerned that she'd be on her own when he left in a few days time to go travelling for the year, Pierce had obviously rounded up all the widowers he knew so as to give her – the widow – a selection of widowers to choose from to keep her company in his absence.

'I'll think about it, Daniel.'

'Will I call him over?' Obviously Daniel

was championing his own father.

'No, no, don't disturb him. I'll go and talk to him later.'

'Alright. Well, Mrs Harrison, I'm afraid I can't let you monopolise me for the night, not when there are so many lovely ladies present.'

'You'd better go so,' she laughed.

She watched as he strutted across the room, hitching up his pants a little and revealing two-inch heels.

'Hello, you must be Pierce's mother?'

Ana turned to see a young girl standing beside her, smiling. She was a twig of a thing, in knee-high boots, wearing a tiny little mini-skirt and top.

'I'm Claudia,' the girl introduced herself. 'I work in the office at the furniture factory. You've probably heard Pierce talking about me.'

'Oh yes, of course,' said Ana. She'd never heard Pierce mention her but she didn't see any reason to say so. 'Nice to meet you, Claudia. I hope that you're enjoying the party.'

'Oh yes.'

'Good. Have you helped yourself to some food?'

'Yes, thank you. It's delicious. I suppose you're going to miss Pierce when he goes. I know we all will at work. Honestly he was the life and soul of the place.' Then, spotting him across the room, she went on. 'Don't you think he's a dead-ringer for Robert Redford?'

'God, don't let him hear you saying that – he has a big enough head as it is.'

Ana turned to where Claudia was looking and saw Pierce talking intently to Mr Singh. Probably listing out all her good qualities she decided, noticing Mr Singh listening carefully to whatever Pierce was saying to him and nodding every now and then. What would those qualities be? Good health, full set of teeth, own home, financially secure. Before she turned away the old man looked over at her as if to confirm some particular point of Pierce's for himself but then, when he saw that she was watching them, he smiled shyly at her and gave a little wave. With little choice, Ana returned his wave but then quickly turned back to Claudia.

'Yes, just like Robert Redford. Only blonder and better-looking. And younger of course,' Claudia went on, still gazing over dreamily. She seemed to have totally forgotten Ana's presence. 'But with Paul Newman's eyes,' she added wistfully.

The girl was being a little bit fanciful, Ana decided, but then, young girls always were she supposed, when they believed themselves to be in love – as this Claudia clearly did.

'The way he smiles, oh it gives me goosebumps. And he's such fun. All the girls in the office just adore him.'

Ana had had enough. It was, she decided, time that she set this Claudia straight.

'Deborah,' she called out to a girl standing nearby. 'Deborah, can you come here a second?'

A pale, serious-looking girl looked over, smiled, then left the group she was with and made her way across to Ana and Claudia.

'Enjoying yourself, Mrs Harrison?' she asked when she'd reached them.

Ana nodded, then asked, 'Deborah, have you met Claudia? Claudia, this is Deborah, Pierce's girlfriend.'

'Hello, Claudia,' said Deborah.

'Hello,' said Claudia, staring at Deborah with undisguised surprise. She was obviously finding it hard to believe that Pierce could be going out with anyone who looked as ordinary as this Deborah.

'And Claudia works in the office down at the furniture factory,' said Ana completing the introductions.

'Mrs Harrison and ... and Deborah,' said Claudia hurriedly, 'nice talking to you both but I think I should be getting back to my friends now. They'll be wondering where I've got to.'

As soon as she'd left, Deborah turned to Ana.

'That was very mean of you. The way she's

been flirting with Pierce all night I'd say I'm the last person in the world she was interested in meeting.'

'Yes, I suppose it was a bit mean. But she was very annoying, gushing on about how wonderful Pierce was. How do you stand it when girls go on like that?'

'Well, they rarely say much to me. They just stare for a few moments, no doubt wondering what Pierce is doing with someone like me and then they carry on flirting with him. Not that he ever notices, he's not exactly the most astute when it comes to women.'

'I'm not so sure about that. He has enough sense to be going out with you.'

'Only after he went through almost every other girl in London.'

'Well yes, but, he didn't stay with any of those others for very long.'

'True,' Deborah agreed and then she laughed. 'He probably only stays with me because he's afraid I'd kill him if he left. Besides, he needs someone like me with him if he's going to spend the year travelling. A lot of good any of his ex-girlfriends would be. And he's not exactly the most practical of people himself.'

'No,' Ana had to agree. 'Although, somehow I don't think that's the only reason he stays with you.'

'Maybe not,' conceded Deborah. 'Imagine,

Mrs Harrison, only four more days to go. I can hardly believe we're actually heading off. I mean, Pierce has been talking about it ever since ... since...' she faltered.

'Ever since Mark died,' Ana finished. 'Well, I'm glad to see that you're both getting the chance. You know, it's such a pity, Deborah, that you never knew Mark.'

'At least I did get to meet him that once.'

Ana smiled, remembering the first time she'd heard of Deborah and the slagging she and Mark had given Pierce over her.

'Pierce was lucky to have you and Daniel around that year,' she said, taking Deborah's hand and patting it fondly. 'You know, I was so glad when you and Pierce finally got together. I always hoped you would. And this trip is such a great opportunity for the pair of you.'

'Did I tell you that Daniel is talking about coming out and meeting us somewhere along the way during his holidays from college?'

'Daniel?' Ana burst out laughing at the thought. 'But how would he fit all his clothes into a rucksack? Wouldn't they get all wrinkled? And what would he do if he couldn't find somewhere to plug in his hairdryer? God, I can't imagine Daniel roughing it.'

'Me neither. But he'll probably undergo yet another complete change of image and become the ultimate traveller. There's nothing he loves better that getting a new look for himself.'

Ana laughed and, still holding Deborah's hand, she went on.

'You're going to have such a wonderful time. And it's good that you've finished your nursing training before setting off and that Mr Morgan is happy to take Pierce on when he comes back again.'

'Speaking of Mr Morgan,' said Deborah with a forced casualness, 'have you been talking to him at all this evening?'

'Briefly,' answered Ana, wondering where this was going.

'He's a really nice man, isn't he?'

So, thought Ana, Deborah was promoting Mr Morgan. Well, she'd really drawn the short straw and Ana certainly wasn't going to make it any easier for her.

'Yes,' she answered, 'if you can get over the smell of stale sweat.'

'Well, yes ... I suppose. But besides that.'

'And if you don't mind someone picking at their ears when they're talking to you.'

'Yes but…'

'And to be honest, though I know it's not a nice thing to say about someone, I'm sure I heard him break wind several times while I was talking to him. I just can't imagine how his poor wife used to put up with him.'

'Yes, but,' Deborah tried again, 'he has

been very good to Pierce and it is nice that they get on so well.'

'In case they should ever become step-father and son, is that what you mean, Deborah?'

'What?' Deborah blushed.

'Deborah, you can drop this matchmaking business. I'm afraid that you, Daniel and Pierce have all been about as subtle as a ton of bricks.'

'What? What do you mean?'

'Deborah, I know what you're all up to. And it's nice that you're concerned about me being on my own when the two of you are away but really, I'd prefer to spend the evenings by myself than to have to listen to Mr Morgan farting on the couch beside me. I mean really – Mr Morgan of all people! Whatever about Daniel's dad or Mr Singh, how could you think I'd be even remotely interested in Mr Morgan? So you might as well go and tell the other two to drop their efforts at playing Cupid so that I can enjoy the rest of the party in peace.'

'Mom,' said Pierce coming over to her with Mr Singh in tow, 'Mr Singh was thinking of joining the new bridge club and he's looking for a partner.'

'Is that right?'

'Yes.' Pierce nodded, not noticing Deborah's warning looks.

'Well then, I've just the solution,' said Ana.

'Mr Singh, would you mind coming with me?'

And, not waiting for an answer, she took Mr Singh by the hand and dragged him across the room, then sat him down on the couch beside Mr Fowler. The two men looked at one another.

'Mr Fowler, meet your new bridge partner Mr Singh. Mr Singh meet Mr Fowler. And, if you need a substitute I'm sure you can call on Mr Morgan. No doubt he's interested in playing bridge too.'

She went back to where Deborah and Pierce were standing, staring at her in astonishment.

'Were you hoping for the wedding before you left, Pierce?' demanded Ana.

'Mom, we were only–'

'Honestly, Pierce, sometimes you are so stupid. I know your heart is in the right place but what were you thinking? That if I hitched up with one of those three I wouldn't be lonesome for you and Deborah? So, no more matchmaking, alright? Just let me enjoy the rest of the party.'

Easter Monday, noonish…

Resuming her search for a spin, Ana left Laurence and carried on through the gardens towards the main house and, as she came in sight of the carpark, she noticed Catherine reversing out. 'Well, thanks be to

God for that,' she muttered to herself, pleased at the prospect of getting away from Rathdowne immediately and, as quickly as she could, she hurried across the lawn, climbed through the border and out onto the driveway and then stood in the middle of it and waited. Moments later, when Catherine's car came around the bend, she flagged it down with her walking-stick.

'Well, if it isn't the Colonel's paramour,' said Catherine having pulled up and wound down her window. 'I'm surprised you haven't had your eyes scratched out.'

'You mean by Elizabeth?'

'Amongst others. You've put quite a few noses out of joint by landing Rathdowne's most eligible bachelor.'

'He's still very much eligible, I can assure you. Anyway, enough about that. Listen, Catherine, if you're on your way home to Bray can I get a lift in with you?'

'Sure, no problem,' answered Catherine. 'Hop in.'

On the twenty-mile trip, Catherine's attempts to draw Ana out proved futile. Ana was having none of it. She blatantly ignored all of Catherine's questions regarding her and the Colonel's 'relationship' as Catherine insisted on calling it and, rather than respond, she took to repeating again and again, 'Yes, it is a fine day, isn't it?' regardless of the question so that in the end, after berating her for being so evasive, Catherine finally gave up.

A half an hour later, just as Ana was getting out of the car on the main street in Bray, it struck her that she'd given no thought as to how she was going to get home again.

'You're not going back to Rathdowne later by any chance, Catherine?' she asked.

'No, but Niamh will be starting work at five,' Catherine told her, referring to her daughter who also worked at Rathdowne. 'I can let her know if you want a lift back.'

That suited Ana and they agreed that she'd wait for Niamh outside the shopping centre at four thirty.

Once they'd said their goodbyes, Ana watched as Catherine pulled away. Then, as soon as the car was out of sight, she went into the nearest restaurant for a bite to eat and, when she came back out again, she crossed the street directly, walked quickly along the other side until she reached the betting shop, came to a halt outside it and, after taking a furtive look up and down the street, she turned quickly and hurried inside.

Ana's entrance did not go unnoticed. A woman in her sixties, dressed up to the nines and all on her own didn't exactly conform to the profile of punters usually seen in Mackey's Bookmakers but, ignoring the stir she was causing amongst the all-male patrons and without so much as a glance left or right, she walked directly to the counter. There, she picked up a betting slip, took a pen from her handbag and was about to start filling out the slip when she was suddenly distracted by someone calling out to her,

'Hey Missus, are you sure you're in the right place?'

Ana looked up. At the far side of the shop stood the speaker, a scruffy-looking fellow in his late teens who was leaning against the wall, staring across at her and grinning saucily. The cheek of him, Ana thought, and was about to give him her most withering look but a quick glance around the shop told her that every single person present shared both his amusement and his interest in her. So instead, conscious of this audience, she slowly began to look around the room, as if she were only now becoming aware of her surroundings. With a puzzled expression on her face, she looked down at the floor – at the discarded betting slips which littered it, then over at the blaring television stuck high up in the corner and then, at each of the customers in turn.

'Oh dear, oh dear,' she tut-tutted in her best old lady voice. 'That will teach me for coming out without my glasses. Why, this isn't the hairdresser's at all. Where, oh where, am I?' she asked, her face full of confusion.

'You're in the bookie's, love,' the young man called over to her, quite openly amused by her foolishness, as was everyone else in the place.

'A bookies? Well, I never!' She looked around again. 'So this is what the inside of a bookmakers looks like. Well, well.' She brought the betting slip she was holding in her hand close up to her face and peered at it. 'This must be a betting slip so and there I was thinking it was an appointment card or the like.' She shook her head in disbelief at her own stupidity, then looked over at the young man again. 'But you know, now that I'm here,' she went on, 'I might as well have a go at filling it in. Might as well have an old flutter on the gee-gees, as they say.'

Taking her time and still conscious that she was the centre of attention, she carefully filled in her choice, then went up to the counter and passed in the slip. Then, she put her handbag up beside her and, in full sight of the watching crowd, she opened it and took out the wad of twenties and handed them over to the astonished assistant.

'Are you sure you know what you're doing, Missus?' asked the young fellow who'd come up behind her and was now looking over her shoulder. 'That's an awful lot of money to be laying on. Wouldn't you be better off lodging it in the post-office?'

'Do you think?'

‘Yes. Course, there’d be no harm in keeping back a fiver, or even a tenner and putting that down and, never fear,’ he said with a wink, ‘I’ll keep an eye on you, make sure you don’t do anything too foolish with it.’

‘Hmm, yes, very kind indeed,’ she muttered sarcastically.

‘Well,’ he went on unwittingly, ‘it’s tough enough for you old folk to get by without stupidly throwing away a month’s pension money on a horse.’

‘Stupidly throwing away a month’s pension money on a horse,’ she repeated. ‘I see.’ She stared at him. ‘So, you think two hundred pounds is too much then?’ And when he nodded in confirmation, she slowly looked him up and down. ‘Yes,’ she said, ‘I can see how it would seem a lot if your sole income is the pocket money you get each week from your mother.’

With that, she turned her back on him and finished placing her bet. Then she took her place in front of the television to await the start of the Irish Grand National at Fairyhouse. There was still some time before the race and she listened as the commentator went through the form and considered the state of the course. She nodded in agreement at much of what he was saying though she was having a little difficulty in hearing as the young man, not being the sort to take offence, had now taken it upon himself to explain things to her. There was a short ad-break and then the commentator came back on and repeated much of his early comments, filling in time as the horses lined up.

And then the race started. Eyes glued to the television, she and everyone else in the place watched as the horses took off.

'Feathered Leader and Manus The Man are taking up the chase. Feathered Leader appears to be travelling best of all.'

The commentator's words came at an impossible speed.

'And Glebe Lad is taking a smooth run up the inner...'

The men around her shouted loudly for their favourites.

'Go for it, Manus the Man!'

'Come on, Feathered Lad!' roared the young fellow, nearly deafening Ana.

'And it looks like it's all over for Papillon...'

'Damn ye to high hell, ye whore ye,' shouted an older man nearby but then, remembering Ana's presence, he looked over at her apologetically. 'Sorry, Missus,' he said.

But Ana hardly heard him, so intent was she on the race.

'And Celtic Giant has been pulled up in the straight...'

'Ah Jaysus,' someone swore.

'And it's all over. Glebe Lad has galloped to glory in Ireland's richest race with a three-length defeat of Feathered Lad and Manus the Man...'

Ana stood there, calmly calculating how much she'd won as most of those around her swore at their own bad luck, ripped up their betting slips and sent them fluttering to the floor.

'Hard luck,' commiserated one man, noticing Ana's calm face and presuming the worst.

'Well yes, maybe I should have put a bit more on.'

Leaving him gobsmacked, she went up to the counter to collect her winnings. At odds of eight to one, her two hundred pound bet had won her fourteen hundred pounds. Not bad for an afternoon's work, she thought, as she bundled the notes into her handbag.

'You were lucky,' said the young fellow begrudgingly having made his way over to her.

'Yes, I suppose I was. Glebe Lad didn't have an ideal preparation and I was worried about that kick he got on the Curragh a week back but then, I didn't think O'Brien would put him in unless he was happy with him. But it was a race that was laid out for him. He'd weight on his side and the ground suited him, so in the end I decided to go with him.'

The young man gaped at her.

'You know a bit about the horses then?' he asked, warily.

'A bit,' said Ana with false modesty.

'And tell me the truth now, you knew what you were at when you came in here, didn't you?'

'Well, I have to say I'd an idea that it wasn't a hairdresser's I was in.'

The young fellow stared at her for a second then, deciding he liked her answer, he broke into loud laughter.

'Well, fair dues to you,' he said and gave her a too-hearty congratulatory wallop on the back. 'You had us fooled alright, hadn't she, lads?'

The men nodded and several of them expressed their congratulations.

'So, tell us, Missus, who'll you be backing at Aintree next Saturday?' one of them asked, curious to see how much of an expert she really was and always anxious to hear an informed tip.

'Well,' began Ana, but then paused, for she was torn between the desire to keep her own counsel and the desire to show off a little. In the end, the latter won out; she was enjoying the attention too much. 'Well, that's always been a hard one to call, only ten or eleven favourites have won it in the last hundred years. Nathan Lad would be an obvious choice but I think if I were betting I'd put my money on Bobbyjo or Merry People. I'd like to see Bobbyjo win, though I know he's an outsider. His trainer Tommy Carberry rode L'escargot in 1975, the last Irish-trained horse to win and his son Paul will be riding Bobbyjo next week. Yes, I think I'd go with Bobbyjo.'

'What about Double Thriller?' shouted out one of the men from the rear of the crowd now gathered around her.

'Maybe, if the ground is dry.'

They threw out another few names and she give what she considered the chances of each. Gradually, the conversation expanded so that everyone was arguing their opinion and as she watched them becoming more and more absorbed in the discussion, she decided that it was time for her to go.

But, just as she was about to leave, the young man tapped her on the shoulder.

'We're going across the road for a pint,' he told her. 'Would you like to join us? To celebrate your winnings?'

She considered his offer.

'Although I don't mean you'd have to have a pint of course,' he clarified. 'You could have a 7-up or a gin and tonic or whatever it is you fancy.'

'Well,' she deliberated. Spending time in a pub in the afternoon with these unlikely companions would be a novel experience for her but then, she'd never been one for turning down anything novel. Besides, wasn't she entitled to celebrate? 'Well, why not?'

In the pub the men went straight into the lounge and sat themselves down around a couple of low-sized tables which they pushed together. They looked unaccustomed to being seated thus and Ana soon realised that, if it wasn't for her presence, then they'd most likely be standing by the counter in the bar. Though she tried to buy the first round, thinking it only fitting given her good luck, the men wouldn't hear of it and, before she knew it, the young fellow had ordered the drinks – a gin and tonic for her and pints for all the others. Since racing was the only thing they had in common, that's what they talked about. After a while another of the men came down with a second round and, as she sipped her drink, she listened to their conversation, contributing whenever she had anything to add. From time to time her mind wandered and she looked around the lounge. She hadn't been in a pub for years. At one table sat a bunch of young people, the boys in monkey suits and the girls in evening dresses, all in good form, all very obviously continuing on the celebrations of the night before. At another table sat the parents of several children who were playing around the lounge, spilling crisps wherever they went, their parents oblivious to the chaos they were creating. Suddenly it struck Ana that she was really enjoying herself; all this was such a change for her, so different to her usual Monday afternoons at Rathdowne. She wondered what Elizabeth would say if she could see her now and she smiled to herself as she imagined her reaction.

'Cheers,' said the young fellow, noticing her smile.

'Cheers,' said Ana.

She came to the end of her drink and, realising that the men would probably be more comfortable if she left, she went up to the bar, paid for their next two rounds, then said her goodbyes and left.

As she walked up the street, Ana thought of the bundle of notes lying snugly in her handbag and felt tempted to spend just a little more of it. After all, the amount she'd won was in excess of what she needed right now. But what to buy was the question for, as she grew older, she found that she'd less and less interest in buying anything for herself; it just seemed she needed so little these days, that she already had everything she wanted. She'd always enjoyed buying gifts for people but so many of those she loved were either dead or far away, so she really hadn't anyone left to spoil on impulse and she found herself envying people like Elizabeth and Penny who had children and grandchildren close at hand.

Elizabeth, she suddenly decided, that's who she'd buy something for – to make up for their quarrel this morning and, noticing a chemist's on the other side of the road, she immediately crossed over and went inside.

She made straight for the perfume counter where there was a baffling array from which to choose but, as she picked up one bottle after another and smelled their contents, she realised that when it came to selecting a perfume for Elizabeth the actual scent itself wasn't nearly as important as the brand and, as long as it was well-known and expensive, Elizabeth was sure to love it and so she picked out the most exclusive brand. Just as she was about to leave the shop it struck her that Elizabeth's reaction to the gift would probably be one of suspicion rather than gratitude; no doubt she'd want to know what exactly was the catch – a notion that tickled Ana's fancy very much and she laughed to herself as she pictured Elizabeth lying in her bed at night, unable to sleep as she tried to figure out precisely what Ana's motives were.

Satisfied with her purchase but still in the mood to spend, she walked up the street until she came to a record shop. That morning, after they'd finished singing, Laurence and she had briefly talked about their musical likes and dislikes and she now recalled Laurence mentioning that he was especially keen on the tenor Francisco Araiza and how annoyed he was with himself for having recently mislaid a favourite CD of his. So, having made up her mind to buy Laurence a replacement copy, she went into the record shop. Once inside however, she immediately saw that she was as out of place in here as she'd been in the bookie's. It was a small shop with two tight aisles packed with customers, all of them young people, males mainly. Every single one of them was industriously fingering through the rows of CDs and she soon found out that they were not at all pleased at being disturbed by a portly old woman such as herself and proved somewhat reluctant to move aside and give her access to the music. Nevertheless, she shoved her way in and wasn't above giving sly and well-placed pokes here and there with her walking-stick followed quickly with apologies which were blatantly insincere but which, because of her age, she got away with. Having eventually managed to find the CD she was looking for, she paid for it and quickly pushed her way out of the claustrophobic shop. Once outside, she glanced down at her watch and saw that it was already twenty to five so she hurried off down the street to meet Niamh, hoping that she hadn't left it too late.

Standing outside the supermarket, Ana looked up and down the busy street but there was no sign of Niamh's car. She glanced down at her watch and saw that it was quarter to five and sighed. Why hadn't she kept better track of the time? 'Not to worry,' she muttered aloud, thinking that at least the price of a taxi wasn't a problem, not now with her nice little stash of cash. She saw an empty cab stuck at the lights and was about to flag it but then, realising that there wasn't any reason for her to go home straight away, she changed her mind. She could take a taxi back at any time and it seemed a pity to waste such a fine evening. A far better use of it, she decided, would be to take a stroll along the waterfront. It was years since she'd been down to the promenade, she couldn't even remember the last time – most likely some Sunday with Celia a long, long time ago, when she was very young.

She made her way along the main street and then turned down one of the smaller streets until she came to the promenade. Then she walked along for a while enjoying the gentle sea-breeze and when she came to a bench by the bandstand she sat down. It was very peaceful sitting there, she thought, looking out onto the water and watching the people strolling by. It struck her now that this part of Bray – with its promenade, bandstand, pier and the terrace of large houses facing out to the water – was a bit of an anomaly really, more like a little bit of England. Yes, that's what it was like, a little bit of England cut off and stuck onto the side of Ireland. It reminded her of Brighton. She tried to recall whether the beer gardens and the arcade at the far end had always been there; she didn't think so but she couldn't be sure. They gave the place a slightly tacky feel which somehow added rather than took from its appeal; seaside towns should have a makeshift, tacky feel to them she felt. Then, as if to confirm her thoughts, she suddenly got the smell of chips in the air and, looking around, she saw that a chip-van had pulled up on the other side of the road – which reminded her that she was hungry again so she got up from the bench, crossed over and took her place at the end of the little queue which had already formed in front of the van. When her turn came she ordered fish and chips and then carried them back to the bench.

Not a very glamorous way of celebrating her winnings, she thought, as she unwrapped the food, but very pleasant nonetheless. Just so long as nobody she knew saw her.

'Mrs Dunne, I thought it was you.'

Ana looked up. Laurence was standing before her, beaming down at her.

'Oh Laurence,' she said, wishing the

ground would swallow her up. 'Ah, hello there.'

'I see you're dining out,' he said facetiously, with a smirk on his face.

'Ahmm yes. Would you ... would you like some chips?' she asked. Her face grew red with mortification for it was obvious that he was finding the sight of her sitting on a bench in all her finery and eating out of a paper bag quite amusing.

'Alright so,' he answered. He leant forward and took a handful.

She wondered if her face was covered in grease. It felt like it was and, not having a hanky on her, she made an attempt to delicately wipe around her mouth with her finger.

'Don't they feed you at that place at all?' he asked, sitting down beside her.

'Oh they do, Laurence, but I have to confess that when it comes to junk food I've a bit of a weakness. So tell me, what brings you into Bray? Do you live here?'

'No, no, I live up past Roundwood. I was just in taking one of the dogs to the vet so I decided to bring them down for a swim – they're stone mad for the water.' Suddenly he gave an ear-splitting whistle. 'Here, boys!' he shouted. 'Tim! Ned! Benjy! Come here!'

Three elkhound pups came bounding up from the shore. When they reached the bench they circled around it a few times in an excited frenzy, shaking water everywhere.

'Good lord, they're not yours?' she laughed. 'Why, they're monsters!'

'And they're not fully grown yet. Only babies, not even a year old.'

'God,' she said staring at them.

They were sniffing around her now having caught the smell of fish and chips so she threw down the remains and watched as they demolished the lot in seconds.

'Savages,' she muttered, still staring.

'Don't listen to her, boys. You're not savages, sure you're not?' He caught a hold of one of them and began scratching him behind the ears. 'Benjy, come back here,' he shouted at another who'd gone tearing off in the direction of a little poodle and its owner both of whom were rooted to the spot, looking as if they might drop dead from fright at any second as the monster drew near. 'Benjy!' shouted Laurence again and, as Benjy turned and came rushing back to Laurence, the poodle and owner visibly relaxed now that the near-certain mauling had been averted. Ever so brave now, the ball of white fluff emitted a defiant 'yap-yap'.

'What are their names again?' asked Ana.

'Tim, Ned and Benjy.'

Ana looked puzzled; she was wondering why these names sounded so familiar.

‘Aren’t they the names of Elizabeth’s grandsons?’ she asked eventually.

‘Are they? Well now, that is a coincidence,’ said Laurence, a smile playing on his lips.

‘You never did, Laurence? You never called them after Elizabeth’s grandsons?’

‘As if I would.’

‘I’m afraid I’m beginning to think that you might. Look at you – you can’t stop grinning.’

‘But why would I do a thing like that?’

‘Pure badness I’d say.’

‘I’m admitting nothing,’ he said with a look on his face that admitted everything. ‘Anyway, Mrs Dunne, tell me, have you gone on the run from Rathdowne or do you intend going back there?’

‘No, no, I’ll head home shortly.’

‘If you like I can drop you back.’

‘Indeed you won’t. I wouldn’t hear of it.’

‘It’s not that far out of my way and how else are you going to get there, tell me?’

‘Well, I was going to get a taxi.’

‘Now wouldn’t that be an awful waste of money? Especially when there’s no need. Look, I’ll drop you back.’

Ana thought for a second.

‘Well, if you’re certain you don’t mind?’

‘Not at all. Will we head now?’

‘Yes, that’s fine.’

They both got up and Ana followed him to where his van was parked – a grimy white

Hiace van with *Wash me please!* scrawled along the side. After first letting the dogs into the back, Laurence then came around and opened the passenger door for Ana and, with a little difficulty but with help from him, she managed to climb up into the front.

'Do you know, Laurence,' she said once he'd got in the other side, 'I don't think I've ever been in one of these vans before.'

'I should think not, Mrs Dunne. A lady like yourself.'

'It's very high off the road, isn't it? Much higher than I'd have thought.' She settled herself down and as Laurence was starting up the engine, she asked, 'Tell me, Laurence, why is that you call me Mrs Dunne but I always call you by your first name? Don't you think we should change that?'

'Alright so. From now on you can call me Mr Hynes,' he joked.

'Very gracious of you indeed,' she laughed.

She remembered the CD in her bag but somehow it didn't feel quite right to give it to him. She'd pictured giving it to him when he was working in the garden and now the confines of the van just seemed the wrong place; it felt far too intimate. Besides, it struck her that he might take it the wrong way.

As they travelled along the road they

chatted about this and that, mainly about the time Laurence had spent in New York and about music in general.

'I hope you're not abducting me, Laurence,' said Ana when he suddenly turned off the main road and began heading in the direction of Roundwood. 'I've heard about you mountainy Wicklow men, how you're all half-cracked from living on your own up in the wilds.'

He looked at her for a second, then laughed loudly.

'You're a right one,' he said. 'Pity a few others in Rathdowne haven't a bit more of your spirit in them. And don't worry, you're perfectly safe from abduction. I've a full house as it is. Haven't I got the dogs? And Patricia? And sorry, I should have told you what I was doing. You see, I decided to drop the dogs off first so that I can head into Ashford for a pint once I've left you at Rathdowne. Is that okay with you? You're not in a hurry back, are you?'

'No, no, that's fine, Laurence.'

They continued on, past occasional groups of bungalows facing out, past tracks of bog, past hectares of conifers and then through stretches of road made dark by overhanging branches. And then through the picturesque little village of Roundwood they went and continued on out the other side and along the narrow road, climbing higher and higher. The sun hadn't set yet and looking around Ana thought how well Wicklow deserved its title as the Garden of Ireland – although garden suggested something tamer than the rugged reality of their immediate surroundings. Everywhere she looked she saw a view worthy of a postcard. On her side, at the road's edge, the land fell away steeply now and she saw a few scraggy trees and bushes hanging on for dear life on the near-vertical slope leading down to a lake at the bottom, slate grey in colour. And over on the far side of the lake, in the distance, her eyes followed the hills, alternate layers in shades of grey and blue.

'Come on, move it,' muttered Laurence crossly and Ana looked to see a trio of sheep dawdling along in the middle of the road just ahead of them. 'Come on,' he repeated and blew the horn at them but they all steadfastly ignored him. He blew it again and the sheep at the rear glanced back with a look which Ana fancied meant it was thinking to itself, 'Look, what's the problem? I mean really, couldn't you just go *around* us? Do you think you own the road, or what?' But then, Laurence gave a longer, more insistent blast of the horn causing their collective nerve to give and they all went scuttling up onto the ditch.

Minutes later, Laurence pulled up outside a little whitewashed cottage with a red tin roof which fronted out onto the road and peered down over the valley on the other side. Attached to one end of the cottage was an old stone outhouse which had caved in on itself. The wild garden was overgrown with native grasses and flowers and was bounded by an old stone wall.

'You're a lucky man to be living in such a marvellous spot, Laurence,' remarked Ana, looking around. Apart from a single house away down in the valley there wasn't another building visible.

'Yes, I am.'

'Were you born here?'

'No, I'm an Arklow man myself but I bought it when I gave up the singing and came back to Ireland and started working at Rathdowne.'

'It must have seemed like heaven after New York.'

'To me anyway, although my wife preferred the bright lights even though she originally came from Wicklow too.' He opened the door of the van but, before climbing down, he turned to her. 'Now, I have to go inside for a second, do you want to come in?' he asked.

'Ah no, I'll wait here.'

'Come on in, I won't be long.'

He got out, came around to Ana's side and helped her down. Then he opened up the doors at the back of the van and the dogs bounded out and went tearing up to the house and he hurried after them. For a few moments Ana stood there, looking around, appreciating the views and the peace of the place. Then she turned and walked up the path to the little cottage.

The front door was open and she called out hello but there was no answer so in she went. Finding herself in a little hall, she called out hello again, but there was no answer and, noticing an open door to the living-room, she went in. The room was stuffed full of old-fashioned furniture and had a crowded, antique feel to it and one of the first things to attract her attention was the number of photographs on display. In particular, a large black and white photograph in an ornate gilt frame hanging over the mantelpiece caught her attention and she went over and studied it. In it, Laurence was seated, looking young and handsome in his wedding suit but serious and solemn as people often did in photos long ago when going to a photographer was a big event. Behind him stood his wife who looked incredibly young and very, very beautiful. In fact, with her impeccably styled hair and that perfectly placed mole right at the corner of her full and ever-so-slightly pouting lips, she looked just like an old-fashioned film star. Turning from the photograph, Ana began to wander around the rest of the room, studying the other photos, and through them was able to trace the history of this family. An early one showed Laurence and his wife – smiling young parents now, holding up a little baby to the camera. Then, in a later one, that little baby boy grown into a toddler and peering into the pram at his newborn sibling. And then, a few years later, two proud little boys dressed in their school uniforms, arms around one another, beaming for the camera. Later still, photos showing the boys – men now, on their own wedding days, posing with their brides. And lastly, a group photo taken on holidays – in Las Vegas or some such place judging by the neon signs in the background and quite recently it seemed from Laurence's appearance. This one showed him and his wife – grandparents now, surrounded by their sons, daughters-in-law and a bunch of giddy grandchildren.

Her curiosity satisfied, Ana went and sat on the couch and waited for Laurence. She could hear the sound of voices coming from somewhere else in the house and, after a few minutes, Laurence popped his head around the door.

'I won't be long,' he said. 'I'm just making Patricia a bite to eat and then we'll be off. She hasn't been too well lately so she's a little bit picky.'

'Oh I'm sorry to hear that. What's the

matter with her?'

'Just a tummy upset but I collected a tonic for her in Bray and I've given her that. It should help. Would you like a cup of tea while you're waiting?'

'No, no, I'm fine. Don't worry about me.'

'Give me five minutes so and I'll be with you,' said Laurence and he disappeared again.

Ana got up from the couch and went to the window and stood there as the minutes ticked by, just gazing out. Everything was so incredibly still. It was so quiet here. Laurence and Patricia were lucky indeed to be living in this beautiful spot, she thought. It was exactly the kind of place she'd once fancied she'd live out the end of her days in. Either somewhere like this or somewhere by the sea.

'Are you right so, Ana?' asked Laurence coming back, now ready to go.

'Yes. All set,' she replied and picked up her handbag, then followed out after him.

'Stay, boys, stay,' shouted Laurence at the dogs as he helped Ana into the van.

By the time Laurence dropped her back at Rathdowne, Ana was feeling very tired. It had been a long and eventful day but very pleasant nonetheless, she thought, as she put her front door key in the lock. Not to mention lucrative. She'd had no idea what she was going to do if she'd lost on the

Grand National. She hadn't even dared let herself think about it. But, thankfully, she hadn't and now she'd enough to cover the service charges at Rathdowne and her money problems were over – well, at least for the next few months. She pushed open the door and picked up the letter lying on the mat and went into the kitchen and, as soon as she'd eased off her shoes, taken off the hat and put on the kettle, she opened it. Seeing that it was from Zanzibar Holdings, the firm in charge of Rathdowne, she sighed in annoyance. They were forever sending letters about some nonsense or other – how it had come to their attention that Regulation 3.1. had been violated in two instances by residents keeping pets in their bungalows or, that they would like to inform residents that Regulation 4.5. would be strictly enforced from here-on-in and that the hanging of washing in the area to the front of the bungalows would no longer be tolerated.

'Blah, blah, blah-de-blah, blah, blah,' she muttered now, her eyes skimming over the first paragraph. But when she came to the second she fell silent and, as she read on, the expression on her face grew increasingly concerned. 'They can't do this,' she muttered to herself. And, wondering if she'd read it correctly, she went over the important bit again, slowly this time, reading it aloud. *'Zanzibar Holdings are giving you due notice that as and from the May 1st, the annual service charge payable to Zanzibar Holdings by each of the residents of Rathdowne Retirement Village will be increased from the current charge of £2,500 to the sum of £5,000 and that henceforth payment will no longer be acceptable by monthly instalment but shall now be payable once yearly, falling due on the 1st of May of each year...'* Ana flung the letter down on the table. 'They can't do this,' she repeated. 'How can it be legal?' How, she asked herself, could they possibly justify doubling the service charge just like that, and then, to add insult to injury, insist that it be paid practically immediately and in full.

At this moment, all the money she had in the world was that which she'd won today, less what she'd spent on Elizabeth and Laurence and on drinks in the pub. Just over £1,700 in all and her only foreseeable income between now and May the 1st was her pension. She couldn't even begin to imagine how she was going to come up with the rest.

1981

CHAPTER 6

Thence we came forth to see the stars again...
from *Divina Commedia 'Inferno'* by Dante

It was seven in the morning when Ana's plane touched down in Nairobi but, even at that early hour, the air inside the airport hung heavy with dust. And had an unfamiliar smell. The smell of Kenya, decided Ana, sniffing the air as she stood there waiting for her baggage to appear on the creaky, slow-moving carousel. There was so much to take in, so many new sights and sounds and she couldn't stop looking around, not for a second. Someone knocked against her and she turned to see a woman with a dark shiny face standing close beside her, studying her carefully. The woman said something in Swahili to Ana and smiled at her, displaying perfectly white, perfectly regular teeth. Ana smiled back but immediately was distracted when, from the other side, she heard someone spit noisily and, when she glanced down, she was disgusted to see a fresh blob of reddish-brown spittle lying just centimetres from her shoe. She might have been a bit more concerned for the state of the spitter's lungs but for the fact that someone had warned her that chewing betel nuts was a common practice in Kenya and one which had the unfortunate effect of turning saliva reddy-brown. She gave the man a long dirty look which he steadfastly ignored and was about to say something to him when, sandwiched between two huge cardboard boxes, she noticed her suitcase making its way around on the carousal so she stepped forward and hauled it off and onto the trolley.

The second she got to the door of the airport she was accosted on all sides by taxi-drivers. Shouts came at her from every direction.

'Lady! Here, here! Come, my taxi this way,' called one presumptuously.

'My taxi this way, lady,' directed another confidently.

'Where you going?' asked a third, falling into step with her, attempting to take her suitcase from the trolley as she wheeled it along.

'Hold on a second,' she laughed, putting a restraining hand on the case, knowing that if she let it into his possession then she'd be as obliged to go with him as if she'd entered into a written contract. 'I've only just got here,' she protested. 'Give me a chance to catch my breath.'

In the days leading up to her departure,

her anxious friends had been full of advice and every one of them had warned the lone, inexperienced female traveller that she'd be a prime target for every chancer under Kenya's sun. But now, as she looked at the eager faces around her, she wondered how on earth she was to decide who was and who wasn't a chancer. And then she saw him, a single taxi-driver, looking on at the commotion, showing not the least inclination to get involved. He was just leaning against the side of his taxi, calmly looking on. Deciding that she liked the look of him, she began pushing her way through the others and over to where he was standing.

'Tell me,' she asked when she reached him. 'Are you a chancer?'

He looked at her puzzled so she went on.

'Never mind. Do you speak English?'

He nodded.

'A little,' he answered.

'Well, can you take me to the Hilton Hotel?'

'Yes, of course.'

Taking the suitcase from her, he put it into the boot as she climbed into the back seat. Then he got in himself and, once he was settled, he turned around, smiled at her, then turned back and attempted to start up the engine but it just gave a little cough and fell silent. He turned to her again, smiled again, a little apologetically this time, and tried the engine a second time but all he got for his efforts was a series of coughs and then nothing. 'Third time lucky,' he said, and this time, he did manage to succeed. As they were pulling away from the kerb, Ana noticed that the other taxi-drivers were now crowding around another traveller – a tall, strikingly handsome, fair-skinned and dark-haired man, one age to herself and who could, she decided, very well be Irish.

Though the seat was covered in red plastic and felt a little clammy, she relaxed back into it and began to look out through the window, anxious not to miss her first sights of Kenya. They turned out of the airport and came out onto the road and almost immediately she noticed a bunch of people, up to twenty in all, sitting on their hunkers on the dry withered verge.

'What are those people doing there?' she asked the driver.

'They wait for *matatu*.'

'For what?'

'For *matatu*. Like that,' he said pointing at a beaten-up van struggling towards them, crawling along at a speed of no more than fifteen miles an hour.

Ana stared in amazement as this crock slowly neared. Squashed into the front alongside the driver she counted five passengers and, as soon as it had passed them by, she turned and, through the rear window, she saw twenty, maybe thirty people piled into the back of it with another seven or eight hanging from the sides.

'Excuse me, you come from England?' asked the driver, glancing at her in his rear-view mirror.

But Ana didn't hear him. She was watching in astonishment as all those people who'd been sitting on the verge got to their feet and began piling into the *matatu* which had pulled up in front of them.

'You come from England?' he repeated.

'I live there but I'm from Ireland,' said Ana, turning around to answer him. She was a little surprised when she noticed a plastic-covered picture of Jesus dangling from the rear-view mirror.

'Excuse me?' he asked, looking at her quizzically in the mirror. 'Where you say?'

'Ireland,' she repeated. 'Have you heard of Ireland?'

'Ah Ireland, yes, I know Ireland. It belonged to England, yes?'

'Well, they might have thought so,' she replied.

Her answer caused him to grin, 'Like our country,' he said. 'But now in Kenya we are independent. You know the name of our Prime Minister?'

'It's Daniel Arap Moi, isn't it?'

'That is right. And what is the name of your Prime Minister, please?'

'Charles Haughey,' she answered.

'Charles Haughey,' he repeated, as if to memorise it for future reference. 'And, Lady, what is your name, please?'

'Anastasia,' she answered.

'Anas ... as...' he tried.

'Ana for short,' she told him.

'Ana,' he repeated after her. 'Ana, my name is Kaninu.'

'Pleased to meet you, Kaninu.'

They lapsed into silence and she rested her head against the back of the seat and gazed out through the window. They passed some girls walking along the dusty roadside in single file, each with a baby sleeping on her back and a basket wedged on her hip or balanced on her head. Together, thought Ana, they'd all the colours of a rainbow for each of them was dressed in a length of brightly-coloured cloth wrapped around her body – known as a *kanga*, Kaninu told her, noticing her looking at them. A little further on, she saw two men in dark, western-style suits made dusty from the road as they cycled to work. And further still, a tall man, slim and erect, dressed in long white robes and walking along slowly, gracefully.

'Is this first time you come to our country, Mama?' asked Kaninu after a while.

'Yes, it is,' she replied.

'I hope you like.'

All these snippets of ordinary life seen

through the car window fascinated her. It was strange to see all these people setting off for wherever and thinking that if she wasn't here they'd still be doing exactly what they were doing now without her ever knowing. She couldn't see any houses but the columns of smoke rising in the distance told her where they'd all come from that morning.

'Are you are married lady, Ana?' Kaninu asked.

She nodded, seeing no reason to explain her exact circumstances to him but, realising he hadn't seen her nod, she answered, 'Yes, I'm married.'

And then her heart sank for it was obvious what his next question was going to be.

'You have children?' he asked, exactly as she'd anticipated.

But if her life depended upon it, she found she couldn't answer.

'You have children?' he repeated.

'I ... I don't understand your question,' she mumbled. 'I'm sorry.'

'You know, little bo-' but then, seeing the anguished look on her face reflected in the mirror he stopped, smiled, then shrugged. 'Excuse me,' he apologised. 'Sometimes my English is not so good.'

They fell silent again.

Gradually the countryside gave way to city and still she stared and stared and, from time to time, was stared back at with matching curiosity.

'This is Hilton Hotel. Very good hotel,' said Kaninu, pulling up. 'I highly recommend.' He got out of the car, went around to the boot, took out her luggage and carried it into the hotel lobby.

Once he'd deposited the suitcase and had come back out again, she paid him the amount he'd asked her for knowing that it was probably over the odds but hoping it wasn't ridiculously so and they said goodbye. But then, just as she was about to go into the hotel, she suddenly turned around again and on impulse hurried back to him.

'This is Lake Nakuru,' she said, showing him a postcard she'd taken from her handbag. 'Do you think you could take me there tomorrow?'

'That is very far away, Mama. Maybe sixty miles. But yes, I take you if it is what you like,' he replied.

'You'll give me a good price?' she asked looking him straight in the face. 'You look like an honest man.'

He nodded but cursed to himself. Now he couldn't overcharge this foreigner staying at a top hotel as he would otherwise have done, not near as much as other taxi-drivers would have but just slightly over the odds, enough to make him feel better about the world's inequalities but not so much that he'd feel guilty about ripping her off. Still, he consoled himself, it was guaranteed work for a whole day and, if things went well, there might even be a few days work in it for him.

After they agreed that he'd collect her the following morning at seven, she checked in and, when she'd unpacked a few things and freshened up, she sat down on the bed and wondered what she'd do with the rest of the day. She wished she didn't feel so washed-out but then, it was only to be expected really given the long flight. Deciding that it would be better if she had a nap before setting out to explore, she slipped off her shoes and lay down on the bed but then, noticing her handbag lying open beside her, she pulled it over, reached into it and took out the postcard of Lake Nakuru again and studied the already very familiar picture. It looked so beautiful, a lake coloured pink by the thousands of flamingos flying over it or just sitting on it, looking around, resting, waiting.

She turned it over now and read it though she knew its contents off by heart.

It was dated September 1980, over a year ago.

Hi Mom,

Having a great holiday in Kenya. Given the short time we have here we decided to hire a car which means we're getting a chance to see lots, a lot more than we did when we were here the last time. Lake Nakuru has to be one of our favourite places – it is just incredibly beautiful. There were millions of flamingos when we visited. Apparently we were lucky as over the last couple of years they've tended to come and go. We'll probably bring Daniel-the-intrepid-explorer (!) up here when he arrives out next week – if he does actually succeed in coming this time though we're not holding our breath given his history of no-shows. In the meantime we're continuing on north. Take care.

Love you,

Pierce and Deborah.

She flipped the card over and stared at the picture again, then leant across the bed and propped it up against the bedside lamp. She lay back down and tried to go to sleep but, exhausted though she was, she remained wide awake for ages, for her mind was racing, buzzing with memories.

But at some point she did eventually fall asleep and by the time she woke again it was dark. So much for doing any exploring, she thought, annoyed with herself for having wasted her first day. Her stomach rumbled, reminding her that she hadn't eaten since the breakfast on the plane and she decided that the simplest option right now was to just get something in the hotel dining-room – there would be time enough to explore

Nairobi when she got back from Lake Nakuru.

Having managed to secure the last empty table, she was studying the menu when a man approached.

'Would you mind if I joined you?' he asked. 'I'm afraid there aren't any tables free.'

Immediately she recognised him as the man from the airport, the other traveller she'd noticed this morning. Going by his accent she realised that she'd been right in guessing he was Irish. Ordinarily she'd have told him that she preferred to eat alone but, feeling depressed and lonesome, she welcomed the distraction.

'Well,' she said, 'I could hardly refuse one of our own although, I have to say, I feel a little hard done by the fact that practically the first person I meet in Kenya happens to be Irish.'

'You're Irish as well?' he asked, looking at her in surprise.

She nodded.

'Yes,' she said. 'And go ahead, please, sit down.' And, as he pulled out the seat, she carried on, 'You didn't have too much trouble getting a taxi from the airport, I take it?' He looked at her puzzled so she explained, 'I saw you there this morning, just after I flew in. Let me introduce myself,

I'm Ana Harrison.'

'Pleased to meet you Ana. I'm Eamon Dunne.'

When the waiter came to take their order, Ana decided to follow Eamon's suggestion and forgo wine in favour of the local beer and, as they waited for the food to arrive, they sipped their beers and chatted. Their conversation was similar to that of many Irish who meet abroad. They began by establishing where in Ireland each of them was from and then, if there was anybody they both knew. Having lived in London for so long, Ana had lost contact with most people but it seemed that Eamon happened to know everyone that she did know. He knew her friend Julie and her husband Tony having bumped into them a few times at a mutual friend's house and also at race meetings at which he was a regular attendee. He was familiar too with Mornington Close where Ana had grown up – a friend of his had lived there for a time and he even thought he'd met Ana's father once or twice, but he couldn't be sure.

'Am I right,' he asked now, 'in thinking that Adrian Lloyd lives in Mornington Close?'

'God, it is a small world,' said Ana, sitting back and shaking her head in wonder. 'Yes, he does. Adrian was a great friend of mine when we were little, like the younger brother

I never had. We used to spend every single day of the summer holidays together. Who knows what we used to be doing but he'd arrive at the house first thing each morning and we'd head off for the day. Tell me, how do you know Adrian?'

'Well, I don't know him as such. But you know, like everyone else, I've heard of him of course.'

'Gosh,' said Ana. 'He used to be so quiet when he was young. He must have really come out of himself, not that I've noticed I have to say. He still seems very quiet to me but then, I don't really see him that much nowadays.'

Just then their meal arrived and they continued on chatting as they ate, Eamon doing most of the talking. He told her that he ran a stud with his brother in County Dublin but that he'd left his brother in charge while he was in Kenya on this combined holiday/work trip. She listened as he explained that he and this brother were part of a business consortium in Dublin which was now considering investing in Kenya, a country he informed her was really taking off tourist-wise. She learned that once his business in Nairobi was finished, he was going to travel down to the coast to look at suitable sites for a five star hotel which their consortium was hoping to build.

As the waiter cleared away their dinner

plates there was a lull in their conversation and it struck Ana that he didn't say much about his domestic life and that he never mentioned a wife or children – just this brother, which was fine with her as she'd no desire to talk about her own circumstances.

'Thanks for the company,' she said finally, finishing the last of her coffee and getting ready to leave. 'It's been a very pleasant evening.'

'I've enjoyed myself too. It's a pity that you're heading up to Lake Nakuru tomorrow and that I'll be gone to Mombasa by the time you get back. Maybe we could meet up again in London. Between one thing and another, I'm over and back all the time. Maybe we could do dinner again?'

Ana thought for a second before answering. Three things struck her about Eamon Dunne. One, that this handsome man had something of the playboy about him which probably meant he was trouble. Two, that she had to admit she was just a little interested in finding out what kind of trouble. Three, and most importantly that, although she liked him, there was no danger that she'd fall in love with him.

'Are you married, Eamon?' she asked.

'No, of course I'm not,' he answered, rather taken aback. 'I'd hardly be asking you to dinner if I was.'

'I know. I just wanted to be sure. Then yes,

dinner would be fine.'

Her sleep pattern was in disarray and she woke several times during the night until eventually, at five in the morning when it was obvious that she wasn't going to get any more sleep, she got up. She stretched, then went over to the window and opened the curtains. It was still dark outside but the front of the hotel was floodlit and she was surprised to see a familiar car, Kaninu's car, parked on the road outside and even more surprised to see him stretched out on the back seat asleep. What had him here at this hour of the morning she wondered. He was over two hours early. Well, at least she didn't have to worry about him not showing up. She looked up at the night-sky; it was clear, not a single cloud obscured the stars, which augured well for a fine day.

She turned from the window and went into the bathroom to run the bath. Then, she came back out and went through her clothes, trying to decide what to wear. Splurging out on a complete new wardrobe for her holiday, like staying in the Hilton, had been part of her resolution to start spending her money instead of letting it sit there in the bank for fear that a rainy day might come along. And anyway, hadn't she just about as many rainy days as anyone was ever likely to have? And even though buying lots of expensive clothes and staying in classy hotels didn't really make things any better, she found that they had some value as short-term relief. Now, she spread the outfit she'd decided upon out on a chair, went back into the bathroom and climbed into the tub. Then, after wallowing in a long, luxurious bath, she dressed, breakfasted and, just before seven, headed down to where Kaninu's car was parked.

He was sitting on the bonnet, waiting for her, and smiled when he saw her coming, then jumped down and hurried to open the rear door for her.

'You were here early, Kaninu,' she commented as she was getting in.

'What?' he asked.

'You arrived here very early this morning. I saw you snoozing in the car when I got up.'

'Yes,' he answered. 'And you sleep well?'

'Not so well. But you certainly were right yesterday when you said that the hotel was very good.'

Once she'd got herself settled, she was surprised to notice a damp towel hanging from the back of the driver's seat which Kaninu immediately took down and quickly shoved into the glove compartment. She noticed that he was wearing the exact same clothes as he'd had on yesterday and it suddenly struck her that maybe he hadn't arrived earlier in the morning at all but had in fact spent the night here in his car. Well, if that was the case, it was his own business – she certainly wasn't going to pry but it did cause her to momentarily reflect on the kind of life a Nairobi taxi-driver might have.

Heading north from Nairobi, they set off, passing through forests first, then along a desolate, broad plateau and down a steep drop, before following along the slopes above Naivasha and then on down an almost vertical precipice into the Rift. Everywhere Ana looked the views were stunning and, for much of the time, she stared out through the window in awe. At one point, she took out the postcard of Lake Nakuru and, looking at it, she wondered for the umpteenth time if it would really be so beautiful in reality.

Now and then, especially as the road descended steeply into the Rift Valley, they'd go around a particularly treacherous bend and find themselves face to face with an overloaded truck trundling along in the middle of the road at speed and, as Kaninu managed to skilfully swerve and save their lives, she'd find her heart in her mouth and tried not to think of just how easy it was to die on these roads.

But Kaninu was a good driver. And he was a good guide. From time to time he'd stop the car at an especially scenic lookout and they'd get out to appreciate the view at their leisure. The binoculars Julie and Tony had given her as a parting present proved very popular with Kaninu and, having spotted something that he felt would be of interest to a foreigner, he'd urge her to, 'Look, look,' and, through the binoculars she'd search out the dusty plains below for whatever he was pointing at. A herd of gazelles crossing the plain. Or a group of tall, lean Maasai in traditional dress herding equally lean cattle along in front of them.

It was still early in the morning when they reached Lake Nakuru and, apart from one young couple, there was no one else about. The lake, Ana saw immediately, lived up to her expectations. It was absolutely stunning. Thousands upon thousands of flamingos were amassed on it giving the scene a surreal pink appearance and she sat at its edge for ages and ages just watching them. She felt so peaceful here, looking out on one of the last sights that her son had seen. She was glad that Pierce had got to see something so beautiful in his life. There was no point in thinking that if he hadn't gone to Kenya, or hadn't come to Lake Nakuru, then he'd be still alive. He wouldn't have been Pierce if he hadn't wanted to travel. Since the trip he'd taken after his twenty-first birthday he hadn't been at home for any longer than a couple of weeks at a time. And, if he'd lived, it would be the same story always, he'd be forever off seeing new places.

Like he was now, in a way. Off on another exploration. She smiled as she imagined the postcard he'd send her.

'Heaven,' he'd write, *'is definitely the best place we've been to yet. The people are really cool here, really friendly. We've met up with this crowd who are heading down to hell for a week or two so we're thinking of going with them – if we can get visas. They say that it gets very crowded and that finding decent accommodation can be a problem sometimes so the going will be tough but we'll go well prepared and bring lots of water, suntan lotion and devil repellent with us.'*

'Ana.'

Ana turned and looked up to see Kaninu standing behind her.

'God, you gave me such a fright,' she said crossly. Aware that her face was wet with tears, she furtively wiped them away. 'I thought you'd gone off somewhere. How long have you being standing there?'

'Not so long. Ana, I want to tell you that the man in charge say there are many hippopotamuses in the lake at other side, would you like to see?'

'Yes,' she answered, getting to her feet. 'I would.'

Together they followed a path around the edge of the lake bounded by acacia forests alive with the sounds of birds and insects. The park was full of all kinds of animals – ostriches, jackals, elands, gazelles, baboons, buffaloes, warthogs and now she was going to see hippopotami.

'Ana,' said Kaninu suddenly, interrupting her thoughts, 'the man who is in charge of this park also tell me there was an accident with motorcars near here and three *watalii* – you know, three tourists – was killed.' He paused, then went on slowly. 'I think one of them was your child.'

There was a long silence. Ana was too stunned to say anything and for a second she even wondered if he possessed some strange African magic. How else could he possibly know?

'Yesterday, when I ask have you children, you have big sadness,' he went on, as if guessing her thoughts. 'And you have in your bag a postcard of this place and it mean much to you. And when we are in motorcar all time you are very, very nervous of all other motorcars. And then I see you sit by the lake with water in your eyes and I put all things I see about you together and I think that one of the people the man talk about is your child.'

'You're right,' said Ana quietly. 'My son.'

They continued walking along side by side. At first Ana didn't say anything. But gradually, she began to talk. Everything she'd kept bottled up until now came pouring out and she talked and talked as if she might never stop. Walking beside this stranger, not having to look at his kind face, gave her privacy, gave her freedom to confide in him in a way she'd never done before with anyone else.

She started with the postcard.

On the morning it had arrived, just after she'd picked it up from inside the doorway where it lay with the rest of the post, the phone had rung and she'd gone to answer it with the card still in her hand and still unread. Since her mother never, ever rang her it took her a few moments to recognise Mrs Moore's voice but, as soon as she did, Ana knew for certain that it wasn't a simple desire to chat about the weather or about her and Ana's health which had her calling and that something serious had to be the matter. At first Ana thought the obvious – that something had happened to her father but her mother had quickly reassured her that he was fine. Then she'd paused and, in an odd sort of a voice, she'd gone on to ask Ana how herself and Pierce were keeping. Fine, Ana had answered and explained that Pierce had just finished a six-month stint with an aid agency in Tanzania where he'd worked as a carpenter and his girlfriend had worked as a nurse and that they were now in Kenya for a few weeks' holiday before returning home.

And then came a strange, strangled sound on the other end of the line – like a whimper that went on and on though Ana asked again and again what the matter was. Eventually, her mother calmed down enough to explain why she'd rung. Moments before, on a radio news bulletin she'd heard that three tourists had been killed in Kenya in a road traffic accident in the Rift Valley. The announcer, she told Ana, had given the names of these tourists as Pierce Harrison, Deborah Thomas and Daniel Something-or-other. Mrs Moore hadn't got his last name.

Ana glanced over at Kaninu as she paused for breath and wondered if he understood everything she'd said. In a way it didn't really matter if he did or didn't, it was just good for her to talk about it. He looked back at her and smiled sadly.

And then she continued, going on to explain the circumstances of the accident as she understood them. That, not far from Lake Nakuru, a man at the wheel of an oncoming car which was being towed by another had fallen asleep so that he'd drifted to the wrong side of the road and into the path of Pierce's car and they'd collided, head-on.

And she told him that Pierce and Deborah had been going to get married when they came home and that Pierce and Daniel had been best friends since the day they'd started school and that, though Daniel had been forever talking about coming out to meet Pierce and Deborah on their travels, this had been the one and only time he actually had.

And she told him how, for weeks after, she'd lain in bed, staring up at the ceiling, not knowing the time of the day, the day of the week, or even what week it was. And not caring. She'd just lain there wondering if every day was going to be the same; if she was going to wake up each morning deadened by the knowledge that her husband Mark and now her son Pierce were gone from her forever. She told him how, for ages after, every single time she'd passed the bathroom she'd missed the sound of Pierce whistling as he showered. And how she couldn't sit in the living-room without imaging him sprawled on the armchair opposite, his legs flung over the armrest, laughing over at her or just reading quietly to himself or watching telly. And how every time the phone rang she wondered, just for a split second, if Pierce was calling to say that he'd 'be home soon, Mom' – as soon as his tennis match was finished. Or, as soon as this crazy mix-up about him being dead was cleared up.

And she talked to him about Mark. How it had been the same when he'd died. How his presence had been everywhere in that little terraced house so that in the end she'd sold it, believing that she'd never recover in a house so cluttered with memories – where, no matter which way she looked, she saw a reason to cry. And how she'd bought a bigger house – Celia's house – as she thought of it, since that's where the money to buy it had come from. But only later, when she was stronger, did she regret letting that other house go and, along with it, its associations with Mark. But she wasn't that strong yet with regard to Pierce. The memories of him were far too vivid in every corner of the house and she knew that she had to get away.

And so, puffy-eyed, carelessly dressed and carrying nothing but a single suitcase she'd left the house and returned to Ireland. Not to Dublin, but to Clifton, where she'd rented an old cottage. There she'd stayed for several months. Hibernating, she'd thought of it. Time for recovery. She'd swum each day in the sea, regardless of the weather; had walked for miles and miles through fields and up mountains; and had spent hours cycling along country lanes, going nowhere. All to make sure that she was thoroughly exhausted by night-time; in the vain hope that she'd sleep dreamlessly.

Winter came and the weather turned cold and blustery and still she hibernated. She didn't want to stay there forever, but her problem was that she didn't know where she wanted to stay, or where she wanted to go. But finally, it was spring and she knew that it was time to find out if she could live with her memories. That it was time to go home.

It had been midday on a bright, sunny morning when she arrived back but the inside of the house was as dark and as still as the inside of a mausoleum. She shivered, put down her case and went directly to the French doors at the end of the hall and pulled back the curtains. And then she saw it – a sea of yellow – the two sloping acres of her back garden were covered in hundreds and hundreds of daffodils, stretching down to the river.

Nobody knew who'd transformed this unkempt grassy area into such a magnificent spectacle in her absence. 'Just think of them as a birthday present,' Julie had told her for Ana, in her sad oblivion, had chosen her birthday to come home. 'Who cares where they came from?' asked Julie. 'Just enjoy them.' And, after a while, she'd stopped trying to figure out the mystery and began to think of them, however foolishly, as a birthday gift from Pierce and Mark for, ever since she'd met Mark she'd received a giant bunch of daffodils every year on her birthday, first from Mark and then, later, from Pierce as he'd carried on his father's tradition. And now an entire garden.

And she began to sleep easy again.

She stayed in the house until the last of the daffodils had withered and then she set off once more. Not running away this time. But going somewhere. Going to see the world, or one part of it at any rate.

Her outpourings had a cathartic effect and as soon as she got back into the car she slept like a baby only waking when Kaninu stopped off in a fragile, dusty-looking town outside an equally fragile and dusty-looking *hoteli*. They went inside and, as soon as he'd helped her order a meal, *ugali* with beef, he disappeared again.

By the time he arrived back she'd almost finished eating and, sitting down opposite her, he made a space on the table.

'I have brought you these,' he said laying four things out in front of her – a camera bag, a notebook, a gold medallion and a copy of Jack Kerouac's novel *On the Road*. She stared for a few moments before she realised what she was looking at. The medallion she recognised as Daniel's – who but he would wear such a monstrosity? The camera bag and its contents had originally belonged to Mark but Pierce had taken it with him to Kenya. The book she remembered was a favourite of Pierce's, one of the few he'd read and reread. The notebook she didn't recognise but when she opened it she saw Deborah's name inscribed on the inside of the front cover and flicking through the pages she saw that they were filled with her neat writing – a diary of their travels, right up to the day they'd died.

'Where did you get all this?' she asked, the tears streaming down her face.

'The man at Lake Nakuru tell me that a person from this town find these things after the motorcar accident. So here I ask people and they tell me where he live and I go to him and say to him that they are not his, that the mother is here and he must give them to her. Now,' he said, leaning forward, 'I take you back to the Hilton Hotel where you sleep away some more of this sadness, yes?'

Tuesday morning...

The first thing that came into Ana's head on waking the next morning was that ominous figure of £5,000.

Yet, this morning, things didn't seem quite as black as they had last night and as she lay there in bed she began to see that there were ways and means. First off, there was Aintree next Saturday. Hadn't she just managed to turn £200 into £1,800 on the Irish Grand National? Who's to say she couldn't do even better the next time? There was every chance. Every *chance* – that was the problem – she wasn't so stupid or so desperate yet as not to see that relying on chance wasn't exactly the smartest thing in the world. But, for the moment, it was her best choice. And, if Aintree didn't work out, well then, she'd just have to sit down and do some serious thinking.

It seemed that the letter from Zanzibar Holdings was preying on everyone's mind and when Ana arrived into the sunroom later in the morning she found several of the residents gathered there, discussing it.

'We should tell Mrs Reynolds about this,' Elizabeth was saying as she waved the letter about, 'and see what she has to say. Maybe she could arrange a meeting between ourselves and Zanzibar. You never know, we might even be able to negotiate a compromise of some sort.'

'I imagine she knows all about the letter already, Elizabeth,' Ana pointed out to her. 'And I don't think you'll find her anywhere near Rathdowne this morning. I went looking for her earlier and she was nowhere to be found. She'll have made herself scarce, no doubt waiting until the fuss dies down.'

'Everyone,' said Penny, bustling into the room with Ellen following after her. 'I've just been on the phone to my solicitor and it seems that Zanzibar Holdings are within their rights to raise the charges in this way. Apparently the lease we've all been stupid enough to sign states that the service charges, including their terms of payment, are open to review subject to Zanzibar's discretion.'

'They can't be,' protested Elizabeth. 'Harry would never have let me sign something like that. He's an accountant, you know. He'd have read through it very carefully. Of course, I'm not saying that coming up with the money is going to be a problem for me, no, not at all, but it's just the principle of the thing really.' Then she noticed Ellen was smirking. 'What, may I ask, is so funny?' she demanded crossly.

'She's pleased that her brother will have to fork out so much money, aren't you, Ellen?' Penny answered before Ellen had a chance.

Still grinning, Ellen nodded. 'I'm just thinking of his wife's face when she finds out, she'll go berserk,' she told them.

'But Penny,' interrupted Ana, 'from what you're saying, even if we do pay up they can still turn around and raise the charges again, anytime they want to.'

'Exactly,' agreed Penny. 'That's the problem.'

'This is just terrible,' cried Elizabeth.

'It seems to me,' Penny went on now, 'that the only reason Zanzibar Holdings are asking for the £5,000 to be paid in full is because they're experiencing financial problems themselves. My guess is that they're having some sort of cash-flow problem.'

'That's exactly what I was thinking,' said Ana.

'Which,' added Penny, 'isn't exactly very reassuring for us.'

'No,' agreed Ana.

Except for the occasional heavy sigh they all sat in silence, each considering their own predicament. Not all of them were going to find it as easy to come up with the money as Ellen and Elizabeth and it didn't seem fair somehow, not at this stage of their lives.

But at least Ana had the comfort of having some semblance of a plan and, remembering that there'd been a piece on Aintree in last Sunday's paper, she resolved to have a read of it later. She hoped she hadn't thrown it out.

But first things first. Leaving the sunroom, she went in search of Laurence. From the outset it had also been part her plan to use some of her Grand National winnings on actualising an idea she'd had in her mind for ages but the letter from Zanzibar had made her reconsider the wisdom of that. But now she saw that it didn't really matter, she was so far off £5,000 that a couple of hundred pounds or so wasn't going to make much difference either way and, once again, she'd made up her mind to go ahead with this idea of hers. But first she needed Laurence's help.

'Ana! Ana!' she suddenly heard someone call and looking over she saw the Colonel peering around the side of his bungalow. 'Over here. Come over here,' he whispered loudly, looking about furtively and affecting a great show of secrecy. 'I've something to show you.'

'What is it?' asked Ana. 'And where have you been? Everyone else is up in the sunroom discussing the letter.'

'What letter?'

'The one from Zanzibar Holdings.'

'Holdings-smoldings. I've more important things to be doing than to be worrying about that shower. Now, come around the back,' he said and, taking her by the arm, he led her down the footpath at the side of the house. 'There,' he said proudly, coming to a stop and nodding at an old Honda 50, a crock of a thing, which was propped up against the wall of his house.

'What's that?' asked Ana, staring at it.

'It's a motorbike of course.'

'Well, I can see that, Colonel. Though maybe that's too grand a title for it, bits of a motorbike more like. But what's it doing here?'

'I got it from Catherine's son Dermot, her eldest fellow. He's into second-hand motorbikes – you know, buying and selling them. So Ana, tell me, what do you think?'

'What do you mean, what do I think?'

'Well, do you like it?'

'As banged up old Hondas go, it's fine.'

'I'm going to fix it up of course.'

'Of course. So how much did Dermot pay you to take it off his hands?'

'Well, I ... well…'

'Ah Colonel, don't tell me you actually paid him money for it?'

'And what if I did?' asked the Colonel indignantly.

'So tell me then, how much?'

'It's none of your business.'

'Twenty pounds?' she guessed, causing the Colonel to snort derisively. 'Forty?' she went on. 'Sixty? Eighty? Ah Colonel, don't tell me you paid him over a hundred?' But the Colonel was staring at her stony-faced. 'Please tell me that you didn't give him more than a hundred and twenty?' But the defiant look on his face told her that he had. 'More than two hundred?' she asked.

'More than two hundred! What do you take me for, Ana? A fool? I paid him one hundred and fifty pounds and considered it a bargain at that price. I had to do a hell of a lot of haggling to get him down to that – a tough lad is that Dermot.'

'Far too tough if you ask me.'

'No, it was a fair price,' said the Colonel, determined not to think otherwise. 'Which you'd realise if you knew anything at all about bikes. Though I'm not saying that there won't be a lot of work involved. Of course there will. But then I've always liked a challenge.'

'Yes, yes. But tell me Colonel, do you know anything at all about fixing up old motorbikes?'

'What I don't know I can learn.'

'At your age?'

'What do you mean – at my age? You think I'm too old, is that it? It's just as well that the American astronaut who flew to the moon at seventy-seven or whatever didn't think that way. Or that man in his seventies who finished the Dublin City Marathon. If I'd known you were going to be so negative, Ana, I wouldn't have bothered showing it to you.'

'I'm sorry, Colonel. I was only taking a rise out of you.'

'And anyway, Laurence promised he'd give me a hand. He knows all about machines. That fellow knows about everything.'

'I'm sure he does. But assuming you'll succeed in getting it running, what are you going to do with it then?'

'Ah for God's sake Ana, you're being very stupid! What do you think I'm going to do – make tea with it? I'm going to go for spins on it of course. Isn't it just the thing to explore the Wicklow mountains? And, despite your bad attitude, you can come too. See here,' he said, patting the seat. 'That's where you'll sit.'

She laughed aloud. 'Do you know, Colonel, you're completely crazy?'

'Laurence even gave me the loan of a pair of overalls. Here, I'll put them on for you, give you a chance to admire the working man.' He climbed into them, fastened the row of buttons up the front, over his fat belly, straightened up, then turned from side to side to give Ana an opportunity to appreciate his figure all the better. 'Well, what do you think?' he asked. 'Don't I look the part?'

'You do,' she lied and managed not to laugh.

'Of course you're not to say a word to Mrs Reynolds about it. I've checked our contract and motorbikes are about the one thing that isn't specifically banned – only because they didn't think to put them in, no doubt. But I'm sure if she finds out she'll try to think up some excuse to make me get rid of it. Nothing would suit her better than to have us spending our days sitting, gaping at the telly – we're easier to manage that way you see. So, not a word to Mrs Reynolds, alrighty?' He knelt down beside the bike, picked up a spanner and was about to set to work but then paused for a moment and looked up at her. 'You and me, Ana, eh?' he said. 'Off up in the mountains with the wind in our hair and a picnic basket strapped on the back. Won't that be something?'

'Sorry to be the one to break the news, Colonel, but you don't have any hair to speak of.'

'I'm well aware of that, Ana. I was speaking metaphorically.'

'I know, Colonel, and you're right, it would be something. Anyway, I'll leave you to it.' She was about to walk away but then paused. 'By the way, Colonel, you didn't see Laurence around?'

'No, but if you find him, will you remind him that he promised to give me a hand with the bike this evening?'

'I will. See you, Colonel.'

And she left him at it.

'Ana, have you seen Ellen about?' called Catherine's daughter Niamh coming in the opposite direction, carrying a great big bunch of flowers.

'Have you tried the sunroom?'

'Yes, but she's gone from there.'

'Well, if she's not in her own bungalow then she might be over at Penny's.' And, looking at the flowers, she asked, 'Are they for Ellen?'

'Yes! Can you believe it? A really nice old man just dropped them in. I can't wait to give them to her, to see her face. Imagine – quiet little Ellen having a boyfriend!'

And off Niamh headed, all excited.

Ana eventually found Laurence sitting on a bench by the lake eating his lunch and reading the paper.

'Hello, Laurence,' she said, sitting down beside him.

'Hello there, Ana.'

'I was just talking to the Colonel and he asked me to remind you about your promise to give him a hand with the new bike this evening. Isn't it great the way he's all fired up about it? When I left him he was busily working away on it.'

'How could you tell?'

'What?'

'How could you tell he was working on it?'

'Well, he'd his overalls on and, you know, he'd a spanner in his hand and he was kneeling down, just about to get started.'

'But you didn't actually see him doing anything, did you?'

'No but…'

Laurence laughed. 'I think it's the notion more than the reality of fixing the bike up that appeals to the Colonel. He hasn't actually done anything yet. I'm not sure he'd know how.'

'It's good that he's got you to give him a hand so.'

'He'll certainly need it. That bike is an awful crock. Catherine's young fellow should be shot for selling it to him.'

'Well, at least it's put him in better form. He

seems a bit strange lately, have you noticed?'

'How do you mean, Ana?'

'He just seems a bit bothered sometimes. Like he forgets what he's talking about or even what he's doing. The other night for example, he was telling me about this golf course he was thinking of starting up but halfway through he lost his train of thought completely and seemed to have absolutely no idea of what he'd just been telling me. At the time I presumed he had too much to drink but later, when I was thinking about it, I realised that the same kind of thing often happens to him. And there's lots of other things as well. Just small things really.' But then she shrugged. 'I don't know. Maybe I'm just imagining things. In fact, he seemed fine when I met him just now.'

'Well, now that you mention it, there was one incident which struck me as very odd at the time. The other day when I was coming out of the shop in Kilmurray, I happened to glance over towards the church carpark and I spotted him there. Now, this might sound very strange, Ana, but it is true, he was actually going around trying the doors of all the cars and then writing things into a little notebook he had with him and, when I went over and asked what he was up to, he wouldn't say but just quietly closed the notebook and shoved it into his pocket. It was odd, you know, especially as we're good friends, but I got the impression that he'd no idea who I was and that he was just letting on that he had. Anyway, I offered him a lift back to Rathdowne and he got in but all the time as we were driving along he kept repeating that I was 'most kind, most kind', as if I were a complete stranger who just happened to do him a good turn.'

'You know,' said Ana, 'I think I'll talk to some of the others, see if they've noticed anything.' Then she changed the subject. 'Anyway, I've come to ask you a favour.'

'Well, if it's to take the bread out of your oven when it's finished baking, I'll have to say no.'

'What?'

'Or to keep an ear out in case your phone rings. Or to post a letter on my way home. Or to…'

'What are you talking about?'

'Lizzy. She can't pass me by without asking me to do something for her.'

'Lizzy? You mean Elizabeth? Don't tell me you call her that?'

'But isn't it her name?'

'No, it's just what the Colonel calls her. You must have picked it up from him. God, she hates it, it drives her mad.'

'That explains the strange looks she's forever giving me. I just thought she was permanently suffering from indigestion or something.'

'But tell me, Laurence, what do you say to her when she asks you to do all these things?'

'"Yes" mostly. Though I'm learning. I'm beginning to realise that the more you do for her, the more she expects from you – she's that kind. Anyway, Ana, tell me what's this favour you're after?'

'I'm not sure I should ask now, you might start thinking I'm just like Elizabeth.'

'Nah, you're a different kind altogether. So tell me, what can I do for you?'

'Well, I was wondering if you could plant some bulbs for me.'

'No problem. What kind?'

'Daffodils.'

'Okay.'

'About five thousand or so but it'll depend on how much they'll cost.'

'Five thousand? That's a hell of a lot. Where would you want me to put them all?'

'In the grassy area in front of my bungalow and down as far as here and on towards the lake. Obviously I'd pay for them, Laurence, so I'm sure Mrs Reynolds won't mind. She's not the kind to look a gift horse in the mouth.'

'That's true,' he agreed. 'Not that it's any of my business, Ana, but why do you want to plant them?'

For just a moment she thought of telling him about the time she'd come home that year to find her entire garden full of daffodils and how, from the very first day she'd been to Rathdowne, she'd had this notion to cover this whole area in the same way.

'It was just an idea I had,' she said instead. 'So, would you be willing to do it?'

'Sure I would.'

'Great.'

'But you'll have to wait until late in the autumn of course.'

'What?' asked Ana, her face falling.

'Spring is the wrong time of the year for planting daffodils.'

'Of course,' said Ana despondently. 'I was never much of a gardener.' She sighed. 'I just completely forgot that you'd have to plant them months in advance.'

'What about some other kind of flower? I could plant something else if you'd like.'

'No, that wouldn't be the same thing at all. You see ... oh, never mind. Anyway, thanks Laurence.'

She got up and walked away.

'Ana,' he called after her. 'Do you want to listen to that CD of Araiza?'

After he'd helped her down from the van the night before, Ana had plucked up the courage to give him the CD and though he'd been surprised he'd seemed very pleased with his present.

'Come on,' he urged, 'you look like you

could do with some cheering up.'

'Yes, I suppose I could,' she agreed glumly.

He bent down to the portable CD player sitting on the ground and switched it on.

'You don't mind if I get back to work?' he asked, just before the music started up.

'Not at all,' said Ana.

He picked up a hoe and resumed where he'd left off before his break and Ana sat back down on the bench to listen to the music. Though she'd been nervous about giving him the CD, thinking that he might take it the wrong way, she was glad now that she had. Knowing that he was married meant that she felt a little more comfortable in his company; she felt easier, and happy that she didn't have to worry about anyone accusing her of having 'designs' on him, as they had in regard to the Colonel. Now, as the first song came to an end, she called out,

'So tell me, Laurence, did Patricia like the CD?'

'What?' asked Laurence, looking up from his work.

'Did your wife enjoy the CD? Did you play it for her?'

Suddenly Laurence burst out laughing.

'What?' demanded Ana. 'What did I say that was so funny?'

'Nothing. Nothing at all. Yes, Patricia loved it. She was singing her head off all night. I had to put a bag over her head in the end to shut her up.'

'Laurence!'

'It's the truth. Tell me, Ana, would you like to meet her?'

'Yes, why not?'

'Well, why don't you come up for a cup of tea and a bite to eat after I finish work? It's a pity she wasn't well yesterday otherwise you could have met her then. But she's grand again now – she was in top form when I left her.'

'Ah Laurence, I don't know. I'd hate to put you to the bother.'

'It's no bother. As it is I'm going to be coming down again later to give the Colonel a hand with his bike so I can drop you back then. So do, come on up home with me.'

'Well, alright so.'

'That's great. Look, I'll meet you in the carpark around five.'

'Fine.'

As she was walking away, Ana saw Ellen and Penny in the distance. Ellen was carrying the flowers in her arms, looking highly embarrassed and in an awful hurry to get back to her bungalow with them but Penny was having none of it. Now, noticing Ana, she called out to her.

'Ana, did you see what was delivered for Ellen earlier?'

Ana saw Ellen pulling at Penny's sleeve, urging her to keep going. But there was no way Penny was going to let her off that easily and she began dragging her reluctant friend over to Ana.

'They're beautiful, Ellen. Do you know who they're from?' asked Ana.

'No,' answered Ellen shortly. 'There was no card with them.'

'Oh right,' laughed Penny. 'Like you've so many admirers you just couldn't possibly guess.'

'Maybe I have for all you know. Anyway, I don't know what all the fuss is about,' protested Ellen, anxious to play the whole thing down. 'They're not even shop-bought, they're only a few old weeds he plucked from his garden.'

'His garden? I thought you said you didn't know who they were from,' pointed out Penny.

'I don't. But I hardly think they're from a woman. Now, will you ever let me go so that I can put them in water?'

1982

CHAPTER 7

Yet knowing how way leads on to way,
I doubted if I should ever be back...
from *The Road Not Taken* by Robert Frost

Since Ana and Kaninu had sat into the car early that morning and set off on the long journey for the airport in Nairobi they'd barely spoken a word to one another; both of them had a lot on their minds and, in any case, neither of them really knew what to say. It was Ana's last day in Kenya and this was their final journey together. She'd come for a four-week holiday and only now, twelve months later, was she finally going home.

It struck Ana that the two of them, driving along like this, was just how it had been when she'd first come out to Kenya, when they'd spent whole days travelling the roads together with Kaninu driving her to the various places of interest which she'd read about in her guide book or had heard about from other tourists. Those times seemed incredibly long ago to her now and it was strange to think that if events hadn't taken the turn they did take, then she'd have been back home ages ago – her brief holiday nothing but a memory with just the photographs she'd taken with Mark's camera to remind her of the wonderful places she'd visited. And she had been to some wonderful places. Mombasa for instance; she'd really loved that coastal town with its narrow lanes lined with old houses and inhabited by people who'd seemed so exotic to her – men in hip-slung *kikoi* wraps and Muslim women dressed in black *bui-buis* which covered them from head to toe. And Lamu had been another favourite of hers, an island of quiet Islamic ambience where the pace of life was dictated by the only mode of transport – the donkey, and where she had spent whole days swaying on a hammock just watching the graceful dhow boats with their outsized triangular sails gliding by on the clear turquoise sea.

But events had taken a different turn when, coming into what should have been her last week, Ana had asked Kaninu if he could take her to Mount Kenya. 'No problem,' he'd answered in his usual obliging way and then happened to tell her that he came from a village just twenty miles east of it where his parents, wife and young family lived and he lived too when there wasn't any taxi-driving work to be had in Nairobi. And, half-jokingly, he'd suggested that Ana should visit the village, maybe stay there for a couple of nights and was more than a little surprised when she said that she'd like to very much.

'Do you remember that day I first arrived in the village?' she asked now, breaking the silence, looking over at him.

'Of course I do, Ansty,' he replied, keeping his eyes on the road.

She recalled now how nervous she'd been that day, so anxious that the arrival of a strange *mzungu* in the village mightn't be as warmly received as Kaninu had assured her it would. How, as they'd trundled along the dirt track in the taxi, a track that grew narrower and narrower as they went further away from the main road, he'd told her that he'd already sent word ahead with his brother, telling them to expect him and a foreign lady. And, as he'd predicted, her worries had proved unfounded for, as soon as she'd stepped out of the car, all the children of the village had clamoured around, the little girls fighting to hold her hand and to take her to the thatched mud hut which was to become her home for the next year, though she didn't know that then. The little boys on the other hand seemed more interested in the taxi and she later learnt that it was the first time Kaninu had ever driven it to the village.

She recalled now her first meeting with

Wanja, Kaninu's wife. Watched by the fascinated infant audience crowded into her hut, Ana had washed in the water brought to her by a couple of the little girls and then she'd come back out of the hut to go in search of Kaninu. She found him talking to a woman, as tall and as good-looking as himself, and, when the pair of them looked over and saw her coming towards them, the woman handed the baby in her arms to Kaninu, walked over to Ana, looked her up and down with frank curiosity and then greeted her,

'*Hujambo*,' she'd said, with a warm, welcoming smile.

'*Sijambo*,' Ana had replied, making use of the Swahili Kaninu had taught her on their journeys.

'*Jina langu Wanja*,' the woman had introduced herself. '*Jina lako nani?*'

'*Ana. Jina langu Ana*,' Ana told her.

She remembered how Wanja had then turned to Kaninu, laughed loudly and had spoken rapidly to him and, when she'd finished, all the adults gathered around had erupted into gales of laughter. Wanja had then nudged her husband, urging him to repeat to Ana what she'd just said.

'My wife say that I am liar,' Kaninu had told her reluctantly. 'My brother tell her that I say I am driving for old lady and that make her happy. But she say I tell lie, that you are not old lady.'

Wanja said something else to him and again, everyone around laughed and once more she'd nudged her husband, prompting him to repeat what she'd said and, though Kaninu shook his head and protested, in the face of his wife's persistence he eventually yielded.

'She say to tell you that if she know you were so ... so nice-looking in the face and in the body she would have worried.'

Wanja had grinned at Ana, confirming that this was so. Then she'd taken Ana firmly by the arm and brought her over to her own *banda* – or hut, sat her down outside it and proceeded to ply her with food which Ana ate, watched closely by a circle of enthralled children and almost as enthralled adults.

During those first few days in the village, Ana had been more than content to pass the time just being part of it all for even the most mundane aspects of its life were new and fascinating to her.

They did take one trip on the second or third day, however, up to the lower reaches of Mount Kenya, taking with them Kaninu's wizened old father. To the Kikuyu tribe, to which they belonged, Mount Kenya is believed to be the resting place of God and for this reason alone the old man despite his aversion to, or more accurately his absolute terror of cars, had come on the journey or what was really a pilgrimage for him and his clenched knuckles and the immutable look of fear on his face as Kaninu's taxi bounced along the dirt roads was as good a testimony to his devotion as any god could want. In addition to the old man, they'd managed to squash Kaninu's three youngest children and five other village children into the car. Or rather, they'd squashed themselves in and, despite the obvious lack of space and Kaninu's threats, entreaties and even physical attempts to get them out, none of them would stay behind. Every time Kaninu actually succeeded in hauling one wriggling, yelling, laughing child out, he or she just clambered back in as Kaninu was attempting to grab hold of another.

Very early on in her stay Ana had come to realise that the car was almost as much a novelty as she was herself and she'd learnt that Kaninu didn't own it but paid the owner, a brother-in-law of his, for its use for part of each month during which time he slept in it at night so that he was ready for business at any hour. The money he made in Nairobi supplemented what was made on the farm, tended by his family in his absence.

Neither Kaninu's wife or mother came on the trip to Mount Kenya and it seemed to

Ana that they, like all the women in the village, enjoyed little free time compared to the men, for the bulk of work, both the domestic and the outdoor, fell to them. Though Ana didn't speak their language, apart from a few basic phrases, she still spent many companionable hours with Wanja and the other women – sitting and watching them work, even lending a hand sometimes though she soon realised that she was more of a hindrance, even if they were far too polite to ever indicate as much. It amazed her to see that the tiniest of children were able to carry far heavier loads than she and for longer distances with seemingly little effort. The children didn't go to school. A *Harambee* school, one of many built in the sixties and seventies in the spirit of co-operation which marked the post-independent period and funded through the donations of 'big men' from the nearby town, now lay empty, the money for the teacher's wages having dried up long ago once the benefactors had received the favourable publicity which lay at the root of their generosity.

Quickly Ana became accustomed to waking to the early morning stirrings of the village as its life kicked into action and she came to know its sounds and smells, heard and smelt through the thin walls of the hut. The door of her hut, like all the others in the village, faced Mount Kenya and when she emerged from it each morning her first sight was its snow-covered twin peaks, a truly magnificent sight at that early hour for only at daybreak and at sunset did the sky clear to reveal its majestic white splendour.

And she found time and, more especially, opportunity to indulge in her new hobby of photography. Since Kaninu had found Mark's cameras and equipment in that village near Lake Nakuru Ana had taken lots of photographs of the places they'd visited and, as the days went by and she became more expert, she found she was becoming increasingly ambitious and was no longer content with a mere record but wanted her photos to be as perfect as possible. When Mark was alive she'd never bothered bringing a camera anywhere with her for there seemed little point in her snapping at something when he was bound to take ten or twelve superior shots of the same thing and, though she'd always been very proud of his skill with a camera, the time and effort he'd usually taken in setting everything up had driven her crazy. But now she found she was fast becoming as particular as he had ever been and that photography was becoming as much of a passion with her as it had been with him. Now she rarely saw anything of interest (and in this village everywhere she looked there was something of interest) without considering how it would look through a lens.

Though she'd come for two nights, she'd extended her stay in the village for a week and, on her final night, the night before her flight back to London when the village was buzzing as the people prepared a special *ngoma* – or feast – to celebrate her stay with them, Ana sought out Kaninu. Over the last couple of days, she'd been doing a lot of thinking and she wanted to tell him of the plan she'd come up with. And her plan, she told him, finding him working on the car, was this – that she wouldn't return to Nairobi with him that following morning as they'd arranged but instead, she'd stay on in the village and run the school for a while, paying for her accommodation and giving her services as teacher voluntarily.

'But how can you teach the children?' she remembered him asking. 'You cannot speak the language. And when you go home, then what happen? The school close and it be as it is now.'

She didn't intend running the school on her own, she'd explained, but wanted to enlist and to pay for the help of Kaninu's niece, a clever young girl called Amina who'd attended school in Nairobi when she'd lived there. Her own role, Ana had told him, would be confined to teaching the children English and to teaching Amina all she could as well as helping her improve her own English.

'But...' began Kaninu.

And, she hurriedly went on to explain, because Amina was young and inexperienced, Ana would help her run the school for a while.

'But...'

Again she cut him off to tell him that of course she'd go on paying Amina's wages when she returned home to England.

'But ... but...' interrupted Kaninu again, convinced that such a plan couldn't be so straightforward.

'Kaninu,' she'd said in exasperation. 'My only child is dead. I have more money than I need. Even in the west I would be considered wealthy and this is the best way I can think of to spend some of this money. Besides, Amina's wages will cost me very little.'

'But ... but...' he'd stuttered, reluctant to accept charity.

'Kaninu, when a very good friend of mine died she left me a lot of money. This woman loved children and I think it would make her happy to see her money being put to such good use.' And, seeing that he was readying himself to protest further, she carried on, not giving him a chance. 'Think of your own children, Kaninu,' she'd said. 'How can you think of refusing my help when it could make such a difference to their futures?'

And so it came to be that Ana got to see Mount Kenya's snowy summit for many more mornings.

But this morning had been her last. It was time for her to go home. For too long she'd been using the school to justify her stay even though for months now Amina had shown herself competent to run it on her own.

Coming up to lunchtime they reached Nairobi and since her flight wasn't for another few hours yet they decided to eat at an Indian restaurant. They ordered and, as they waited for the food to be served, Ana cast covert glances across at a downcast-looking Kaninu and decided that Fate could be a nasty, nasty business. A very nasty business. It seemed so unfair that she, who'd come to Kenya to get over the loss of her son, was now accumulating another loss by her leaving. This time it was this beautiful, kind man sitting opposite her. Whom she'd loved since that day at Lake Nakuru, though it wasn't something she admitted readily. On those occasions, during the past year, when one or other of the children had come running to tell her that Kaninu's car had been seen coming along the track on his way back from Nairobi, bringing film and batteries and whatever else she'd asked for, she'd almost convinced herself that the excitement she felt was just the normal excitement one would feel on hearing the news of a friend's arrival. And those times, when she saw Kaninu and Wanja together, she'd tried to pretend that those disturbing feelings of jealousy were really just the reaction of someone all alone witnessing a happy couple's intimacy. And now she was trying to convince herself that the sadness she was feeling was just the sadness one was bound to feel when saying goodbye to a good friend. But, as usual, she wasn't doing much of a job of convincing herself.

'Ansty,' Kaninu said, interrupting her thoughts.

'Yes?' answered Ana, noting and liking the fact that he used the pet name the village had for her. It had been Kaninu's mother who, feeling that the name Ana was too plain and Anastasia too long, had looked for an alternative and when Ana had told her that Ansty was a common diminutive she'd taken to using it and by the end of Ana's stay it was what everyone in the village called her.

'Ansty, when Wanja say goodbye to me this morning,' Kaninu went on, 'she say that she do not know if I will be back.'

There was a long pause. Ana kept her eyes on the white tablecloth in front of her, not sure exactly where this was leading. Then

Kaninu reached out and stroked the back of her hand where it rested on the cloth – just one stroke.

'My wife is clever lady,' he said. 'She see how I feel about you before I see myself.'

Too startled to answer, Ana just stared at her hand and at his, now lying close by on the white tablecloth – almost, but not quite touching. What he was saying wasn't a complete surprise, she realised. From time to time she'd caught something in his look which had prepared her for this disclosure.

'Maybe I am wrong but I think you have feelings for me too,' he said now.

Ana couldn't bring herself to say anything but her look was enough for Kaninu to know that he wasn't mistaken.

And for five whole minutes they stared at one another. Ana knew that what she would say next could determine the rest of her life. But what could she say? Come with me to England. Let me stay here in Nairobi. Let me and you live here together. And if he were to say yes, then what? For the second time in her life she'd be with a man she loved. But at what cost? A very high one – Wanja's happiness. For Ana had no doubt but that Wanja loved Kaninu as much as she'd ever loved Mark. To take him from her, if it was really in her power, would be to cause Wanja to go through the same loss she'd gone through.

'Do you love Wanja?' Ana asked.

'I think ... I think ... it is possible to love two people.'

Then the cost, Ana decided, was too high. She picked up his hand and held it in hers.

'At least this time,' she said to him. 'I got a chance to say goodbye.'

He looked at her quizzically so she explained.

'One minute Mark was there and the next he was gone. You'll never be gone. I can say goodbye to you now and when I'm back in England I can think of you here in Kenya, with Wanja and your children and the rest of your family where you belong. And I can feel happy knowing that you love me.'

The waiter brought down their meal and they both began to pick at their food glumly. But suddenly, Ana laughed out loud causing Kaninu to look up at her crossly.

'Why you laughing when it is not the time?' he demanded.

But on and on she laughed – a little hysterically really.

'If I don't then I think I might cry,' she answered, having finally calmed down enough to speak. 'I was just thinking,' she explained as he, perplexed and angry now, continued to stare at her, 'of my father's reaction if I arrived home with you. You see, Mark was a Protestant and my family are Catholic and they nearly went mad when I married him.'

'Ah but I am Catholic,' he said triumphantly.

'True. But I don't think it would be enough in your case.' How could she even try to explain? 'There are very few black people in Ireland, hardly any, and if I were to bring home a black Kenyan to meet my parents then it would cause a lot of excitement.'

'Maybe then I will come with you, to give them this excitement.'

'Yes, but you couldn't come as you're dressed now. Shirt and pants wouldn't do at all. They'd expect to see you dressed far more exotically. Or, better still, not dressed at all but wearing a bone through your nose and carrying a spear and a shield.'

'This is how they think all Kenyans look?' asked Kaninu indignantly.

'Some do.'

He looked annoyed but then, gradually, he began to smile.

'Then no problem, I will get me a spear and a bone for my nose.'

So Ana said goodbye to the second man she loved. But at least this time she got to say goodbye.

Tuesday teatime...

The more Ana got to know Laurence the more she was beginning to realise how mistaken she'd been in initially thinking that he was a quiet sort of fellow. Very quickly she was learning that once he got started talking there was no shutting him up. Now, as they drove along the road up to his house, he was in great form and chatted non-stop, barely giving himself a chance to draw breath. He talked about everything and anything that came into his head. Future plans he had for the gardens. His father who'd worked as a gardener at Rathdowne back in the days when it was a private house. His two sons who were living in Las Vegas where they jointly owned a club. Their wives – one of whom worked for an airline which meant Laurence was able to fly back and forth for almost nothing. And his five grandchildren who were growing up as Americans. He talked animatedly, glancing over every now and then to see if Ana was still listening to him and, more than once, she'd anxiously had to remind him to keep his eyes on the road.

'I'm beginning to wonder how Patricia ever gets a word in,' she said when he finally paused to take a breath.

'She's worse than me, Ana,' he laughed. 'You'll see when you meet her.'

'God, it must be a desperately noisy household altogether.'

'Desperate.'

When they'd pulled up outside the cottage, Laurence turned to Ana.

'Ana, before you get out I should tell you that aside from Patricia I have a second reason for bringing you up here.'

'Really?' She looked at him puzzled. 'What is it?'

'It's really the main reason I asked you up and ... well ... let's just say it's a surprise for now.'

'A surprise?' Ana looked worried. 'I'm not sure I like the sound of that. I was never very fond of surprises.'

'I think you'll like this one, Ana. In fact, I'm pretty sure you will.'

'Oh Laurence, I don't really think...'

'Don't worry, Ana, I promise you'll like it. But first let's go inside to Patricia.'

He helped her down from the van and they walked up to the house together.

'Laurence, did you phone Patricia to let her know I was coming with you?' asked Ana as he was putting the key in the door.

'Oh, God. I forgot.'

'Ah Laurence, I hate arriving in on top of her like this.'

'Don't worry, Ana, she's very easygoing.' He unlocked the door and ushered her in before him. Immediately Ned, Tim and Benjy came rushing up the hallway and went bounding out the front door nearly knocking her over in their haste but then, just when she'd recovered her balance, they came tearing back in again and began circling around her excitedly.

'Down boys!' Laurence shouted. 'Now out! Out! Out! Out!'

Instantly they all disappeared outside.

'Why don't you give me your coat, Ana, then take a seat on the couch in the living-room,' he suggested, indicating the room to her right, the one she'd waited in during her previous visit. And, as Ana was taking off her coat, he shouted out loudly, 'Patricia, we've got a visitor! Patricia!'

'Hello, Patricia,' called out Ana politely. 'I hope you don't mind Laurence bringing home an unexpected guest with him.'

There wasn't any response.

'Patricia!' shouted Laurence, but again he was met with silence. He turned to Ana and threw his eyes to heaven. 'In one of her moods, I expect. I'd better go and see.' He took Ana by the arm. 'Come on, into the living-room,' he said guiding her in, 'and I'll just go and have a word with Patricia.'

When he'd left, Ana sat down on the couch. From their wedding photograph above the mantelpiece, Laurence and Patricia stared down at her and once again Ana's attention was drawn to Patricia's face – there was something quite magnetic about it – she really was an exceptionally beautiful woman. But as the minutes passed by and she was left sitting there, Ana gradually began to get restless. What was keeping the pair of them, she wondered. At first there had been only silence but after a while she began to make out the sound of voices coming from the kitchen. Laurence was doing most of the talking and his tone sounded soft, a little cajoling even. The other voice which interrupted him every now and then surprised Ana. It was unpleasantly high-pitched, very harsh and grating and seemed completely at odds with that beautiful face in the photograph. Though Ana could catch very little of what either was actually saying she thought she caught the word 'tea' a couple of times and was mortified to think that they were probably talking, or arguing rather, about her arriving in on Patricia unannounced.

She was beginning to wish that she'd never agreed to come. She glanced at her watch and figured that she'd been left sitting here like this for almost ten minutes. Really, what kind of a woman was Laurence's wife anyway she wondered, getting cross now. Surely she knew that there was a visitor in the house who could hear them arguing. As for Laurence, well, what was he playing at? Why on earth had he dragged her up here when his wife was clearly very odd? One minute he was laughing, telling Ana how easygoing Patricia was and the next minute he was going on about her moods and shoving Ana in here so that he could hurry off to have a 'word' with her. Well, she'd had enough. She wasn't going to sit here any longer. No, she was going to go and find out what was going on.

But just when she'd got as far as the door, there was a sudden ear-piercing screech – a dreadful sound altogether, which was followed by Laurence shouting at his wife, yelling at her to come back, and then came the sound of something – a plate or a cup maybe – crashing to the floor. And then another crash. And then another screech – even more dreadful than the previous. Ana stood frozen to the spot, her hand glued to the doorknob. What was going on? What should she do? God, this was a dreadful situation. Just dreadful, dreadful, dreadful. And what was she doing here in the middle of it all? What if Laurence's wife turned out to be like the crazy wife in Jane Eyre? Or maybe it was Laurence who was the crazy one. For all she knew he could be another Duke Bluebeard with a whole bunch of wives stashed away in this isolated – this very, very isolated cottage. Or maybe both he and she were mad – a mad couple in the habit of enticing people up to their home and doing God knows what to them. Why hadn't she told anyone where she was going? And what had he meant when he'd talked about a surprise earlier – was that a veiled threat of some sort? She shuddered.

Why, oh why, hadn't she told anyone where she was going? She could feel her heart pounding.

Suddenly the door was pushed open from the other side.

'Ana,' began Laurence, putting his head around the door but, taken aback to find her standing there immediately behind the door with such an odd expression on her face, he paused for a second in confusion before going on. 'Ana, I was just coming in to tell you that I think it would be best if you come into the kitchen.'

'Listen, Laurence, I'm not sure if I really want that cup of tea and I know I couldn't eat a thing.'

'Nonsense,' said Laurence.

But Ana went on,

'No really, I wouldn't want to disturb Patricia. No, I think it would be better if I headed back now.'

'But Ana, you've gone to the trouble of coming all the way up to see her, of course you'll come into the kitchen.'

'Really, Laurence, I'd prefer to go now,' insisted Ana.

But he was having none of it. He took a firm hold of her arm.

'There's no way I'm letting you go just like that,' he told her, propelling her down the hallway and into the kitchen.

Anxiously she looked around. There was

no one there. What was going on? It was beginning to look like Laurence was the mad one after all. She thought of Norman Bates. Didn't he used to speak to himself in his dead mother's voice?

'Have some tea!' came a screech from behind the door. *'Have some tea! Have some tea! Have some tea!'*

'Jesus!' cried Ana. She turned but there was no one there.

'Have some tea! Have some tea! Have some tea!'

Then, out from behind the door flew a parrot which circled around the room again and again before coming to rest on the fridge.

'Oh my God,' said Ana, collapsing onto a chair.

Laurence was laughing now.

'Ana,' he said, 'meet Patricia. Patricia meet Ana.'

'This is Patricia?' asked Ana, trying to control her temper.

'Yes,' laughed Laurence.

'I have never, ever got such a fright in all my life.' Anger had very quickly replaced shock. 'Are you right in the head at all? Why in God's name did you pretend to me that this stupid parrot was your wife?'

'I didn't. It was you who decided that Patricia was my wife. At first I couldn't understand why you kept on asking me questions about my parrot and then, only this afternoon, I realised what you were on about.'

Ana was staring at him.

'And you think all this is funny?' she demanded.

'You have to admit that it is a bit, Ana.'

'No! I don't! It's one of the stupidest jokes I've ever had played on me in my whole life. You're sick! So now, if you're finished having fun at my expense, I'll ask you to drop me back down to Rathdowne.'

'Ah Ana, come on. I only meant it as a joke. And you can't go yet, you haven't had your surprise.'

'My surprise! My surprise!' stuttered Ana. 'Listen Laurence, I've had as many surprises as I need right now, thank you very much.' And with that, she turned and stormed out. 'I'll be in the van,' she shouted back.

Once outside she climbed into the van, banged shut the door, sighed, and leant back in her seat. She was trembling with anger. Then seeing Laurence following out after her, she quickly locked her door.

'Ana,' he pleaded through the open passenger's window. 'I'm sorry. Look, I didn't meant to upset you. Please, just let me show you your surprise.'

Ignoring him, she searched for the handle and wound up the window. He tried to open her door but, finding it locked, he began making his way around to the other side but she was too quick and before he'd a chance to open his door, she'd leant over and locked that too.

'Come on, Ana, open the door,' he called to her. 'This is just plain silly.'

'Only if you promise to take me to Rathdowne immediately and without uttering a single word to me.'

'Okay,' he agreed, surprisingly quickly, so she released the lock and he got in.

'Look, Ana,' he began, immediately going back on his word. 'You'll really like this surprise, I promise you. It's the real reason I brought you up here. Please, just let me show it to you.'

'If you don't start this van up straight away I'll start walking.'

'Ana, calm down. Please.'

She put her hand on the door-handle.

'I'm getting out and I'm about to start walking.'

'Listen, if you don't like it then for the next month I'll ... I'll call into Lizzy every morning and see if she has any jobs for me to do.'

'Don't be so childish.' But then she thought for a second. 'Every morning?'

'Yes.'

'For six months?'

'No, for one...' He saw Ana reach again for the door-handle. 'Alright, alright, for six months then.'

'And you'll do everything she asks you?'

'Yes.'

'Alright then, show me the great surprise.'

'Okay. But you must close your eyes.'

'What?'

'Just close them.'

'But Laurence…'

'Close them,' he insisted.

'But…'

'Ana,' he said sternly.

'Alright, alright. I'm closing them. But this had better be good, I'm warning you.'

Laurence started up the van, drove a hundred metres down the road, then pulled up.

'You can open your eyes now, Ana,' he told her.

And when she did she saw a field sloping away from the road and down to a river, a field completely blanketed with daffodils.

'Oh my goodness,' she said looking over this field of yellow, illuminated by the early evening sun. 'They're beautiful.'

'I was going to bring a bunch down to Rathdowne for you, to make up for the fact that you can't plant your own but then I thought that they'd be poor compensation, especially when there's a whole field of them to be had up here.'

'Just beautiful,' said Ana quietly to herself.

She opened the door of the van, stepped

down and walked over to the low stone wall bounding the field. Then she sat down on it and stayed there for ages, just staring. After a while Laurence came up behind her and, noticing a single tear making it's way down her face, he gently wiped it away.

'I don't understand,' she said, turning to him when he'd sat down beside her. 'How come you have all these daffodils?'

'Well, every year I plant them in order to sell them in Bray but when the time comes to cut them I never have the heart, it just doesn't seem worth it for the few bob I'd make on them. I just like being able to look out on them. I can see them from my bedroom window. And you looked so sad when you found out that you couldn't plant the daffodils you wanted in Rathdowne so I decided to bring you up here. That whole Patricia thing was just an excuse really.'

'Thank you so much, Laurence, for thinking to do this. They really are beautiful.'

For a while they stayed there, silently looking out over the field.

'What was it Wordsworth wrote about them again?' asked Laurence.

And Ana recited the first four lines,

'When all at once I saw a crowd,
A host of golden daffodils;
Beside the lake, beneath the trees,
Fluttering and dancing in the breeze.'

And then silence again.

'I've always loved daffodils,' she told him after a long time had passed.

And she knew that sometime she'd tell him why; and that she'd tell him about the bunches Mark and Pierce used to give her each birthday and about the garden of daffodils she'd come home to the year after Pierce had died. Sometime she'd tell him, but not now. Now, she just wanted to keep on looking at them, savouring them.

'Wordsworth's sister wrote about them too, you know,' she said, after a while, her eyes remaining fixed on the scene before her. '*Some rested their heads upon these stones as on a pillow for weariness; and the rest tossed and reeled and danced, and seemed as if they verily laughed with the wind that blew upon them over the lake.*'

Then she looked over at him and smiled.

'Couldn't have put it better myself,' said Laurence, smiling back at her. 'But I'm afraid, Ana, the Colonel will be waiting. We'd better get going. I think if it were up to you, you'd have us here for the night.'

Reluctantly she stood up.

'But first,' said Laurence. 'You must take some with you. Now, I'd be quite happy to drive you up and down everyday so that you could sit here enjoying them but I'm not sure that that would be practical. So come on, let's gather some up.'

'Would you mind?'

'Of course not. Did I not tell you that they're all yours now?'

Both of them collected up as many as they could carry and laden down they returned to the van.

As they were driving back to Rathdowne, Ana thought how very happy she felt at this moment. Things didn't get much better than a van filled with the smell of flowers and the sound of a Verdi opera. She looked over at Laurence and, catching her look, he smiled at her and she smiled back and sighed contentedly.

Or maybe, she reflected, glancing covertly over at him some minutes later, just maybe, things were set to get even better. Maybe it wasn't such a bad thing after all that Patricia had turned out to be a parrot.

As they were nearing the entrance to Rathdowne, they saw Elizabeth's niece Sophie running along the road, coming from the opposite direction. She appeared very distressed and, as Laurence pulled up alongside her, Ana wound down the window to find out what was up.

'Colonel Jackson...' began Sophie, panting loudly. 'Come ... come quickly, I need help,' She paused to catch her breath. 'It's the Colonel,' she continued, 'there's something the matter with him.'

'What?' asked Ana and Laurence together.

'Please, he's acting very strangely. He won't come in off the road for me. I was just on my way into Rathdowne to get someone to help.'

Laurence pulled the van up onto the verge and both he and Ana got out and together all three of them hurried back up the road.

'What exactly happened, Sophie?' asked Laurence.

'I came down on the bus from Dublin, Mr Hynes, and when it pulled up at my stop for Rathdowne the Colonel got on and demanded that the bus-driver show him his licence,' Sophie explained, between breaths. 'When the driver refused the Colonel began trying to arrest him. He was really aggressive. I've never seen him behaving like that before. In the end the driver got so annoyed that he pushed the Colonel off the bus. I think he might be hurt. He landed on his shoulder but I couldn't get him to sit down for me or to come back to Rathdowne. Now he's out in the middle of the road, walking towards Kilmurray. He's not like himself at all.' She was close to tears now. 'Oh Mr Hynes, he doesn't even seem to recognise me.'

Three hundred metres on, they found the Colonel, now sitting on the grass verge, nursing his shoulder but looking remarkably peaceful.

'Lovely, lovely Ana,' said the Colonel smiling up at her. 'Come on, sit down beside me.' He patted the grass. 'Isn't it a perfect evening?'

'Are you alright, Colonel?' asked Ana.

'Fine, fine. What would be the matter with me?'

'Are you sure, Colonel?' asked Laurence.

The Colonel looked at each of the three concerned faces peering down at him.

'And what the hell do you think is the matter with me?' he demanded crossly.

'Come on up, Colonel. I think we should go back to Rathdowne,' said Ana.

Laurence began helping him to his feet.

'Maybe the weather is a bit cold for sitting out,' said the Colonel, getting up docilely. 'Ah Sophie, there you are. Is it your day for the piano, my pet?' Then, realising that Laurence was standing uncomfortably near him, still holding onto his arm, he looked at him distastefully. 'If you don't mind, old chap,' he said, extracting his arm from Laurence's grasp. 'Come along then, Sophie,' he said, linking hers instead. 'Ana, I'm afraid I shall have to postpone the pleasure of your company. It's time for Sophie's piano lesson.'

'Sophie, will I go and tell your grandmother that you've come to see her?' asked Ana.

The girl blushed.

'Well, I'd ... ahmm ... I'd prefer...'

'Ana,' interrupted the Colonel. 'Not a word to Lizzy.' He brought his finger up to his lips.

'Colonel, that's hardly fair…' began Ana.
'No, Ana, not a word. You see, Sophie is here on subterfuge and news of her visit mustn't reach the old battle-axe's ears.'
'Colonel, that's Sophie's grandmother you're talking about.'
'Well, I'm sure she knows what I mean then. If you had that crotchety old woman for a grandmother, would you want her knowing that you were here? Now, Ana my dear, don't be jealous, but I'm afraid it's me that Sophie has come to see. Or rather my piano, for there's little I can teach her. Isn't that right, pet?'
Sophie smiled at him.
'I only have an hour before the bus back, Colonel,' she reminded him.
'Of course, of course. Come along then. Ana, Laurence, you should drop by sometime and listen to this girl, she's an absolute marvel. And her parents want her to study accountancy! But never mind, we'll figure a way around that, won't we, Sophie?' Sophie smiled at him and then reached down and kissed him on the cheek. 'Oh yes we will,' he said patting her arm still linked through his own. 'We'll find a way around it.'
And together they walked back to Rathdowne, in through the main gates and on up the avenue leaving a bemused Ana and Laurence to follow after them.
'Quick, my darling girl,' they heard the

Colonel say to Sophie when he spotted Elizabeth in the distance. 'Quick, before the wicked witch catches you.'

And the pair of them picked up speed.

'Who was that with the Colonel?' Elizabeth demanded of Ana and Laurence as she drew near.

'I have no idea, Elizabeth,' answered Ana.

Elizabeth began to root frantically in her handbag for her glasses but, by the time she found them, it was too late; the Colonel and Sophie had disappeared into his bungalow.

'You don't think Sophie just misread the whole situation,' Ana asked Laurence once Elizabeth had gone.

'I don't think so. She seems a sensible sort of a girl.'

'Yes, that's what I was thinking too. You know, I think I'll go talk to Mrs Reynolds about him.'

'I doubt if she's there now, Ana. She told me early this morning that she was heading into Dublin and wouldn't be back until late.'

'Of course, still keeping a low profile. Well, I'll try and catch her tomorrow.'

'I'd better be off,' said Laurence. 'It doesn't look like the Colonel is going to be interested in doing any work on the bike this evening so I'll just drive the van in and drop off your flowers and then head away.'

1987

CHAPTER 8

There's nothing worth the wear of winning,
But laughter and the love of friends...
from *The Dedicatory Ode*
by Hilaire Belloc

'MOTHER DIED TUESDAY. PEACEFULLY – FATHER.' Short and sweet, thought Ana, reading the telegram one last time before folding it and putting it back in her handbag as the taxi turned into Mornington Close. Not that she imagined he'd have said much more even if he had used the Lloyds' or one of the other neighbours' telephones to contact her, as might have been expected under the circumstances, for there were few people in the world quieter than her father; he'd always had Mother to speak for him. What would he do without her now?

The taxi pulled up and she climbed out, then looked around. The place was far more neglected than she remembered it being a year ago, when she'd last visited. There was almost as much vegetation sprouting from the chimneys and drains of the house as there was in the patchy front garden. As she walked up the cracked path, she searched her bag for the front-door key, found it and was about to insert it into the lock, but then she paused; somehow it didn't feel right to just let herself in and she decided to knock instead. There was no answer and she knocked again. And again. But still no answer. Eventually she unlocked the door and, feeling like an intruder, she went in, calling out to her father as she did.

She found him sitting at the kitchen table, in his usual spot.

'Father,' she called softly, coming up behind him. He remained motionless so she came around to the front of him. She saw that his eyes were closed and was surprised to notice the empty bottle of whiskey on the table beside him – he'd never been a drinker, in fact he'd always been vehemently anti-drinking but, still, it was understandable that he'd take some comfort from it today.

'Father,' she called again gently, but he didn't stir.

She sat down opposite him and wondered should she just leave him be. Probably, she decided, no doubt he could use the sleep. His glasses lay on top of the newspaper spread out on the table beside him and she studied his face now and thought how different he looked without them – like a stranger almost. She didn't think that she'd ever seen him like this before – he seemed very vulnerable, defenceless somehow, and so old. She tried to remember his age – eighty-four, eighty-five maybe. How was he going to survive without his wife? Well, at least he was calm for now.

Too calm, she suddenly realised.

'Oh my God,' she muttered. 'Father,' she called. 'Father! Father, answer me!'

Catching him by the arms she began shaking him but he just flopped back and forth as biddable as a rag-doll. The sudden movements dislodged a pill bottle resting between his legs and it rolled off and hit the floor, vibrating hollowly.

'Oh my God!' she began to cry. 'Oh God! Oh God! Oh God!' She propped him back up on the seat and then, kneeling down in front of him, she rolled up his sleeve, picked up his skinny arm, turned it over and felt for a pulse.

'Hel-llo-oo! Anybody ho-ome?' a voice called, followed by a sharp knock-knock on the front door which Ana had left on the latch.

'In the kitchen, Mrs Lloyd,' shouted Ana, struggling to keep her father upright on the seat.

'So Adrian was right,' Mrs Lloyd said coming down the hallway. 'He said he thought he saw you arriving in a taxi.' She bustled into the kitchen, then stopped in her tracks and stared at Mr Moore whose head was flung right back now, his mouth gaping open. 'Oh sweetest Jesus,' she said. 'What's the matter with Mr Moore?'

'I think he's taken pills. He might have overdosed. There's a faint pulse, I think. Can you call an ambulance?'

'Yes, yes of course,' said Mrs Lloyd and hurried away to the phone in her house.

As soon as she was gone, Ana bent her father right over and stuck her fingers down his throat. She had no idea if what she was doing was the right thing but to her it made sense to try and bring up whatever had gone down.

'What has he taken?' came a voice from directly behind her.

'Oh God, Adrian, you gave me such a fright!' said Ana, 'I'd no idea you were there.' Then, answering his question, she went on, 'I'm not sure but the bottle's there. On the table.'

Adrian picked it up and read the label. 'We'll need to get him in hospital as soon as possible. He'll have to have his stomach pumped.'

By the time Mr Moore was admitted to hospital it was too late. He died some hours later, without ever recovering consciousness.

'Poor Ana, it's been a terrible, terrible day for you,' said Mrs Lloyd, clearing away Ana's plate.

When they'd finally returned from the hospital, Mrs Lloyd had insisted on bringing Ana back to her house where she'd cooked her up some steak and chips. But Ana hadn't made much of a hand of the food and thought that she'd choke on every bite. Instead, she'd just shoved the food around until Mrs Lloyd finally took the plate away.

Now Mrs Lloyd put the teapot and some cups down on the table, then patted Ana on the shoulder.

'Poor, poor Ana,' she said and gently stroked her hair as if she were still the child she'd been a long time ago and not the middle-aged woman she was now. 'You must be feeling dreadful.'

Ana wasn't sure how she felt. She wished she could feel sadder. She wished she could just let go and have a good cry like Mrs Lloyd repeatedly urged her to. But she felt numb, more than anything. And a little shocked – more at having found her father the way she had, than at the fact that he and her mother had both died in the last forty-eight hours.

'I don't know what I'd have done without you,' she said now.

'We were only too happy to help, weren't we, Adrian?' Mrs Lloyd asked her son as he came back into the kitchen. 'Will you have some tea, Adrian? There's plenty in the pot.'

'Yes, I think I might.'

Ana considered him as he went to the cupboard and took out another cup and saucer. Though he looked far older than his age, he hadn't really changed all that much since his childhood. He'd never been healthy and had always looked a little delicate, as Mrs Lloyd used to say when he was young. He'd been a jittery, nervy child and very particular – and still was she could see as she watched him carefully wipe away some crumbs at his place, smooth out the tablecloth and set the cup and saucer down – just so. He poured out his tea, then carefully measured out a level spoon of sugar, added it and stirred it around slowly. Around and around and around and around for what seemed like ages, and with extraordinary care. She wondered if he had ever moved away or if he had lived with his mother all these years. She presumed he had. If he had moved then her own mother would have mentioned as much and on Ana's rare visits home he'd always seemed to be about. She knew that he was a nurse but couldn't remember which hospital he worked in. Either the Rotunda or the Meath. She was almost certain that it was the Meath.

'So are you still nursing at the Meath, Adrian?' she asked after he'd taken a few sips from his tea.

He carefully set the cup back down on the saucer before answering. It suddenly struck her that there was something almost priest-like about him; he was so otherworldly, so gentle.

'No, Ana, I've finished working there now.'

And so precise in his speech, as he was in his actions.

'Oh really? And where are you now?'

'Well ... I'm involved in research at the moment, Ana,' he replied.

'That's right,' said Mrs Lloyd. 'Research. He's doing research. Now, Ana, would you like another drop of tea?'

'Yes, please,' answered Ana, a little puzzled by the abrupt response. She looked from Adrian to Mrs Lloyd and back to Adrian again. They both looked decidedly uncomfortable. She wondered if she had said something wrong.

As Mrs Lloyd poured the tea, Ana suddenly remembered Eamon saying, that first time they'd met in the hotel in Nairobi, that he knew Adrian.

'Adrian,' she asked now, 'do you know an Eamon Dunne? He runs a stud with his brother out near Shankill.'

'You mean Eamon and Brendan Dunne?' asked Mrs Lloyd, before he could answer. 'Brendan Dunne who's married to that politician's daughter, what's-his-name, you know the fellow with the gammy leg? You often see their picture in the papers, at race meetings and the like.' Ana nodded and Mrs Lloyd went on. 'Aren't they worth a fortune, those Dunne brothers?'

'No, I don't know him, Ana,' said Adrian. 'I've heard of him of course. And I've read about him in the newspapers although, to be honest, I can't say that I like the look of him. He strikes me as being a disreputable kind of a character.'

'Adrian, stop now,' cautioned Mrs Lloyd. 'As you say, you don't even know him. Tell me, Ana, are they friends of yours?'

'Yes. Well, Eamon is. I met him in Kenya several years ago but I didn't see him again until this year when I bumped into him in London and we've stayed friends ever since. I just thought I remembered him saying once that he knew Adrian.'

'Really?' said Mrs Lloyd. 'No, no, I doubt it. He must have been thinking about someone else. Adrian doesn't really socialise all that much, sure you don't, Adrian? Although it's not for the want of me encouraging him. I'm forever at him to get out more. His father was the exact opposite, you couldn't keep him inside. But tell me…'

'How do you mean friends?' interrupted Adrian.

'Pardon, Adrian?'

'What do you mean when you say you've remained friends?'

'Well, just that when he comes over to London we meet up, go out to dinner or to the races or whatever.'

'Now, now Adrian,' remonstrated his mother. 'That's Ana's own business. You shouldn't be quizzing her like that. Do I sense a touch of the green-eyed monster? Maybe you still have a soft spot for your childhood sweetheart?'

'Don't be ridiculous, I'm just making conversation,' he snapped.

'Well, aren't we very touchy all of a sudden?' said Mrs Lloyd.

Adrian sighed in exasperation.

'So, Ana,' Mrs Lloyd went on, changing the subject now, 'what do you think you'll do with the house, now that both your parents have passed away?'

'God, I don't know,' Ana answered, remembering that Mrs Lloyd had never been exactly subtle. 'I hadn't thought about it.'

'You could come back from London, Ana, and move in again,' suggested Adrian.

'Maybe, although I don't think so.'

'You poor thing,' said Mrs Lloyd, noticing Ana yawn. 'You must be exhausted with all that's happened today. Coming home to bury one parent only to find that the other has passed away as well. God, it's as much as most people have to put up with in a lifetime. And it's not like you haven't been through the wars already.'

'I am tired. I think I'll go to bed.'

'Are you sure you'll be alright sleeping on your own next door?'

'I'll be fine, Mrs Lloyd.'

'You know you can stay here.'

'No, I'll be fine, really.'

Ana thanked them for all their help and left them.

She did feel completely washed-out she realised and, once she'd locked up, she went straight upstairs to her old room and unpacked her bag, then made up the bed.

But she soon found that she was far too wound up to sleep and a little nervous of sleeping in the house on her own. It was ironic that Eamon had to be in London during the one week she was back here in Ireland. She would have liked his company tonight. She got back out of bed again and was about to go downstairs to make herself a cup of tea but then she changed her mind; she didn't feel like going into the kitchen, it unsettled her to think that her father had died there earlier.

Instead, she wandered through the upstairs of the house thinking, as she did, how much she hated it. There was nothing in the least bit homely about it. Over the last few years, as the assorted lodgers had moved away or died, her parents had stopped replacing them and now most of the bedrooms lay bare, save for some rudimentary furniture – like rooms in some old institution, waiting to be checked into. As she went from room to room, she thought about the people who'd passed through them over the years. It was odd how her parents had always managed to find dour, quiet people like themselves, people she could never imagine having any fun. As a teenager, she'd always pictured them behind their closed doors, sitting on their beds and staring into space, their heads full of sad thoughts. Celia was the exception – the only one who'd lived in the house over the years who Ana remembered with affection. Often, when Ana thought of Celia, she wondered why she'd gone on living in Mornington Close. She remembered asking her as much once and vaguely recalled Celia laughing and saying that she'd be mad to move; for where else would she find such a lovely girl to keep her company?

Ana came to the last room on the third floor. When she turned on the light she was surprised to see that, in contrast to the other rooms, this one was chock-a-block with all sorts of things, that it was full of old furniture, boxes of clothes, books, paintings, broken kitchen appliances – even an old fridge, things that most people would have thrown out long ago. In the corner nearest, resting on a busted old armchair, she noticed a bundle of presents all still in their wrapping paper. There was something oddly familiar about the bundle and she went over, picked up one of the parcels and examined it. The wrapping had been torn away just enough to establish what was inside and she was surprised to see that it was the electric blanket she'd sent her parents for Christmas last year. She began to look through the rest of the parcels. Like the first, the wrapping on each had been partially torn away and she recognised every single item as being either a Christmas or a birthday present that she'd given them over the years. Obviously they'd had no use for anything she'd sent them. She thought of all the time she'd spend each year choosing something she imagined they'd like – ignoring the fact that it had been a long time since she'd received anything in return. Why had she bothered, she wondered now. Probably the only joy her mother had got from these presents was that which she'd felt when ridiculing them. She could almost hear her scornfully remarking to her father, 'An electric blanket? God, some people don't know what end of them is up.'

Idly, she opened the wardrobe she was standing beside and, as she registered its contents, she became increasingly bewildered. It was packed full of women's clothes – beautiful clothes, all brand new and very, very expensive, the price tags still hanging from the sleeves of some. There was a short fur jacket, a full-length fur jacket, suits in linen and wool, evening dresses in silk and velvet, and scores of high-heeled shoes. Down low, amidst the elegant footwear, Ana spotted a vanity case and she bent down and opened it and found dozens of tubes and bottles of expensive perfumes, make-up and creams – all unused. Did these and all the clothes and shoes belong to her mother? And, if so, where had she got the money for them? She'd always given Ana the impression that, if it wasn't for pride, they'd have been regulars at the St Vincent De Paul – though she'd scathingly rejected any offers of help from Ana. Whatever could her mother have wanted with these things? As far as Ana knew, she never wore anything other than dark slacks, jumpers and flat lace-up shoes, and the only aid to beauty care that Ana had ever seen on her dressing-table was a comb with more blank spaces than teeth in it. Why had her mother bought all this stuff? When had she bought it? Why didn't she ever use or wear any of it? It was all very puzzling.

Underneath the vanity case sat a box covered in red fabric. Ana lifted it out, opened it and found dozens of letters inside. She recognised her father's neat, tiny handwriting and, flicking through the envelopes, she saw that each of them was addressed to her mother. The date stamps on each showed that they'd all been sent many years prior to her parents' marriage.

She closed the wardrobe, cleared the presents off the busted armchair, sat down and put the box on her lap. These letters had her intrigued. She'd no idea how her parents had met, or when, it wasn't the kind of information they'd cared to impart or that she'd have dared to seek. She stared down at the letters now, deliberating. If her father hadn't wanted her to find them, she told herself, then he could have burned them before sitting down with his bottle of pills. So, should she read them? Yes or no?

As if her mind hadn't been made up from the moment she'd set eyes on them.

Taking them out of the box, she saw that they'd been carefully filed away in chronological order. She started at the earliest one; it was dated the 4th of July 1924.

My Darling Marguerite,

Weren't you well named when they called you that? A beautiful name for a beautiful girl. Can it really be only two weeks since I last saw your lovely face? It can't be. It has to be months. Years even. At least that's the way it feels to me.

Well, Marguerite, London is all that they say it is but I'm afraid without you here I'm finding it a drab place indeed. Forget Big Ben and London Bridge – the most wonderful sight in the whole of this city is your photograph standing before me now. But a photograph is a poor substitute for the real thing. You can't feel or smell or kiss a photo. Well, you can but the two lads I'm sharing with will have the men in white coats around pretty quick if they catch me at it one more time. Ha! Ha!

So Marguerite, you'll be glad to know that I've started work – general labouring, which pays good money. Not as good as if I had a trade but I'll keep going at it for the moment until I figure out what's the best step from here. And it's true what they say, Marguerite – this is a city full of opportunity, especially for a young fellow with a head full of notions – as you would have it. And you're right – my head is fit to burst but then, who got anywhere without a dream or two. And with a little bit of determination, they'll be more than that. When you're sitting in the big house I'll build for you one day, you'll see how right I was. And all you'll have to do is fill it up with little Marguerites and little Jimmys – lots of them – with a little help from me of course! Ha! Ha!

Marguerite, I know that you're anxious to come over straightaway but I think you're better off where you are for the moment even though I know that you're not happy there, how could you be? But the way I see it, at least you'll get an education out of the nuns. So please be patient and stay put until I've enough money saved for us to do things properly and until you have your Leaving Cert completed.

I think about you all the time, Marguerite. And miss you, like you wouldn't believe. And worry about you of course. But, if you keep your head down, you won't come to any harm – the girls' side is nowhere near as bad as the boys' – how could it be? It's good that I got away when I did. Another day there and God knows I'd have exploded and, as we know from experience, that never gets anyone anywhere in Kilmore – it just gives them another reason to beat the living daylights out of a chap. I'll say goodbye now, Marguerite, but I'll write again soon,

All my love,

Jimmy.

P.S.-Keep at the books.

P.P.S. – Don't be annoyed that I've spent some of my wages on you. Not a lot, but please wear it and think of me. And I can think of you, looking even more beautiful. Blue was always my girl's colour.

Ana put the letter down. She felt dazed. Everything about it came as a surprise to her. The whole loving tone of it was so at odds with what she knew of her father. Ana had almost forgotten that her mother had such a pretty name; she didn't think she'd ever heard her father calling her that but then, she didn't remember him calling her anything. And 'My darling' – that certainly didn't sound like him. And could he really be referring to her mother when he'd written, 'Blue was always my girl's colour'?

Ana had never seen her dressed in blue, or in any pretty colour. And her father had even cracked a joke. Two jokes, in fact. Which was two more that she'd heard from him in all of her life.

But the actual content of the letter was even more of a mystery. Living in London? Getting an education out of the nuns? Boys' side? Girls' side? Having the living daylights beaten out of him? And Kilmore? Did he mean Kilmore, the orphanage in Co. Kildare? True, she'd always thought it odd, and Mark had thought it completely bizarre, that she knew nothing of her grandparents or any other relatives. But never in a million years would she have guessed the reason why.

She began to read through the other letters. A good part of each was devoted to expressing his love for Marguerite and the remainder related his progress in London. And it was a rapid progress. She read that within a couple of months he'd got an apprenticeship as a bricklayer. Then, not long after that, he'd switched and became a scaffolder on high-rise developments because the money was so good due to the risks involved but, being as sure-footed as he was, he was in no danger; the other men, he told Marguerite, didn't call him Monkeyman Moran for nothing. And then, in a letter written two years later than the first, he told her that he was going into business with another Irish fellow and that this other fellow would supply the money and the contacts whilst he'd supply the know-how. And it seemed this partnership quickly went from strength to strength. Letter after letter was full of the new building contracts they'd won, the sums of money he was putting aside and how that soon, when he felt really financially secure, he'd start building their own house, or mansion rather, judging from the detailed descriptions he gave – and that finally, Marguerite would come over to England to be with him.

Up to that point the letters had been written on a weekly basis but then they became less regular and the tone of them started to change. The determination and exuberance which had marked his earlier correspondence began to disappear. And with good reason, as she found out.

For the bubble had burst. Jimmy Moran and partner had been overly ambitious. First he mentioned that their business had hit a bad patch. Then, that their debts were beginning to mount up. Later he wrote that his partner had absconded with what little money they'd left, leaving him to face the music. And things just got steadily worse. She read that her father discovered that his partner was heavily involved with the republican movement and had been funding them through their business. And when the police finally swooped his partner was long gone and it was Jimmy they arrested. The perfect scapegoat didn't stand a chance. Poor orphan Jimmy was sent down for seven years.

He wrote regularly from prison, though not very frequently. Short, simple letters with few traces of the romance of his earlier ones though his concern for his Marguerite was still very much evident. Reading between the lines of these accounts of his daily routine it was fairly obvious to Ana that an English jail was not exactly a pleasant place, particularly for someone like him.

But he managed to survive it and finally he wrote to tell her that he was getting out in a couple of weeks and that when he did he was going to start up his business all over again. If he could do it once, he told her, then he could do it again. And then he'd send for her.

But things didn't work out as well as he'd planned. Ana opened the last letter.

My darling Marguerite,

I'm afraid I'm knocking my head against a brick wall here. It's a million times harder setting up this second time around. My 'reputation' precedes me.

I'm coming home, my love. The feeling that

I've let you down is the hardest part to take.
Love as always,
Jimmy.

Ana sat there, stunned. She didn't know what to think. Or feel. She felt too many things. Bewildered, for one. It just seemed impossible to reconcile her memory of her father – a man who'd sat day after day at the kitchen table, reading the newspaper, or staring at it in any case, who'd almost never left the house – with this scaffolder-turned-entrepreneur, this Monkeyman Moran. She felt sad too – to think that life had changed him so much, had caused him to give up on it so completely. And she felt just a little happy – she'd always imagined that her parents had stayed together out of habit and doubted that they'd ever even been in love and now she found it comforting to think that they'd meant so much to one other. But then, she reflected, she should have known. Though they'd never talked much, neither had they ever fought. In fact, she couldn't remember a single instance of either of them ever criticising the other, or of disagreeing on anything.

But most of all, she realised, she felt angry. Really, really angry. Why had they excluded her so much? What hadn't they told her about their past, explained it to her? It was as if they'd decided to trust no one, to let no one else into their own private world, not even their daughter. Maybe she was a disappointment to them – a single Marguerite when they'd once envisioned lots of little Jimmys and Marguerites.

What good was there in finding out all these things now, she asked herself bitterly. What good was there in being able to understand them a little better? They were dead. It was too late now.

She returned the letters to the box and put it back down in the wardrobe where she'd found it. Noticing a heap of old papers in the other corner she realised with a sinking feeling that she'd have to face sorting out all their effects at some point. The papers looked like legal documents and she pulled them out to have a quick look. But they were confusing. At first, as she flicked through them, she thought that she was looking at duplicates of the deeds for this house but then realised that they were in fact the deeds for several houses scattered all around Dublin. There was one in Balbriggan. A second in Balbriggan. One in Ranelagh. One in Rathmines. Another in Rathmines. One in Terenure. And a third in Balbriggan. All in her parents' name. All bought at different times over the last forty years. So it seemed that all the time her mother had been complaining about having to take in lodgers to make ends meet they had all this property dotted around the city and that all the time they'd been penny-pinching they could have afforded to do anything they wanted to do. She'd grown up listening to her mother say that going on holidays, or buying nice clothes, or eating out in restaurants wasn't for likes of them. Now, Ana saw that there had been no need for any of it. And though, as evidenced by the expensive clothes hanging in the wardrobe, her mother had finally felt secure enough to spend some of their money, it was too late; she'd become far too entrenched in her penny-pinching, putting-aside-for-a-rainy-day ways to enjoy it.

But at least, thought Ana, getting to her feet and closing the wardrobe, some of their spirit had managed to survive. It was a pity it had only been their entrepreneurial spirit.

Thursday morning...

Ana sat on the bench with her eyes closed, basking in the warmth of the early-morning sun. It was a beautiful spring day and she was feeling happy. Part of that happy feeling was due to the fine weather and part, she admitted somewhat reluctantly, was due to Laurence's presence nearby – he was busily working away just metres from her, singing heartily, for both his own and for her pleasure. But her good feeling went deeper than that. At this precise moment she just felt completely contented – strangely so for someone whose continued stay in Rathdowne was so tenuous. It occurred to her that it was just as well that nobody else had any idea of how foolish she actually was; that they had no idea that she bet on horses to raise money to pay her service charges.

But there was no doubt about it that, when it came to money she had been, and still was, incredibly foolish. Not that she regretted that this was the case. On the contrary – her only regret was that she and Mark had been too sensible and that he'd wasted precious years in the classroom whilst Celia's money had lain idle in the bank. And as for her parents, hadn't they been the epitome of sensible thrift – and what happiness had it brought them? None, in a word. After their deaths she'd resolved to spend like there was no tomorrow and proceeded to carry out this resolution with remarkable dedication. Well-off even before they'd died, afterwards she was positively 'rolling in it' to put it crudely, and able to bankroll any foolish whim of hers. Which she did. Alarmed at her friend's increasingly extravagant lifestyle, Julie had disparagingly described it as a pathetic, delayed, middle-aged rebellion against her parents. Delayed – yes, middle-aged – yes, Ana had agreed, but pathetic – no. For, as she'd tried to explain to Julie, she was intent on building up a bank of happy memories – with her current surplus of unhappy ones, she needed a few good ones to balance the books. And as she'd told Julie when her friend had cautioned her when she was going through a particularly extravagant period, if the worst came to the worst, then she'd manage to get by on a state pension – for memories, not money were going to be her old-age security. Even if she did have to spend the last of her days wearing badly-knitted cardigans kindly donated to her by charitable souls, well then, she'd gladly wear them happy in the knowledge that she knew what a Christian Dior outfit felt like to wear. And so what if she squandered money on expensive meals, she'd told Julie, it was just an investment for the day she might find herself old and broke and living in a crappy old room somewhere, subsisting on tinned beans.

If, in the unlikely event, Ana did end up in a crappy room then it would be her own fault, an annoyed Julie had pointed out and anyway, wasn't it all hypothetical for no matter how extravagant Ana was there was no way she was going to get through all of her money. But Ana had disagreed. Chance, she'd tried to explain to Julie, could take everything away in a flash, so what was the point in hoarding?

And, in the end, it had turned out that she and not Julie had been right. Now the only money Ana possessed was that which she'd won the Monday before on the Irish Grand National. Yet still she felt optimistic on this bright and sunny morning. She wasn't going to lose on Aintree – she could feel it in her bones. Things would work out okay for her.

She wished she could say the same for the Colonel and she frowned now as she thought about him and the strange way he'd been behaving. It was time to go and have another look for Mrs Reynolds she decided, getting up from the bench.

'See you later, Laurence,' she called as he came to the end of the song. 'I'm just going to see if I can find Mrs Reynolds – to talk to her about the Colonel.'

'Will you let me know how you get on if you manage to find her?'

'I will.'

Though Mrs Reynolds' car was parked at the front of the main house, Ana couldn't find her anywhere. Several people had seen her earlier in the morning but nobody knew where she was now. As she was walking past the sunroom, Ana glanced in and saw that she wasn't there either. But Penny, Ellen and Elizabeth were – maybe they'd seen her. She climbed up the steps and went in through one of the French windows.

'Did any of you see Mrs Reynolds?' she asked the trio who were huddled together in a circle, deep in conversation. 'She's nowhere to be found.'

All three women glanced up, shook their heads and answered no.

'I'm telling you,' Penny then continued, 'the Colonel definitely has a drink problem. You only have to look at his complexion to know that.' Catching her words, Ana stopped to listen. 'Believe me, he didn't get that colour from drinking tea,' Penny went on. 'No sir. The big red face on him, you wouldn't see the like of it on Santa Claus.'

'Isn't it terrible what drink does to a man all the same?' remarked Ellen. 'And do you know something, I think the older they are when they take to it, the worse eejets it makes of them. There are these two brothers,' she said, settling back into her seat, 'living not far from my home place. Jack and Francis we'll call them. Now, their father died when they were just young fellows and so the burden of farming the fifty-four acres fell to the pair of them. Well, you know, they worked away at it over the years and made a good fist of it. And looked after the mother – an invalid *supposedly* – who, let me tell you, was a demon of a woman. By Christ, but did she rule the roost in that house. There was nothing whatsoever the two boys could do without her say. They couldn't go to the pub nor to dances and any girl Jack – and I'm sure Francis too – brought home, well, she soon sent them packing. So anyway, the three of them carried on living the quiet life, each of them getting older and older until finally, about a year ago, the mother – God, she must have been nearly a hundred at this stage – dropped down dead. Well, the two boys were fierce cut up about it; there was no consoling them. I suppose no matter how bad a mother is, it's hard not to get attached. 'A drink is what those fellows need,' said one of the neighbours seeing the two boys standing there with their long auld faces in the pub after the funeral and off he goes to the bar and brings them down their very first pints of Guinness. Well, the boys swallowed it down like it was mother's milk and back up they went directly and ordered more pints for themselves. And I'll tell you now, that night was the ruination of them – it was the first of many that they didn't manage to make it home but found a bed for themselves on the side of a boreen.' She paused. 'And that,' she said emphatically, 'is what drink can do to a man. Even to good men like Jack and Francis.'

She sighed heavily from the exertion of her storytelling then looked around to see the impact her tale had. The others were staring at her bemused.

'Well,' said Elizabeth eventually. 'That place you come from gets more interesting by the day.'

'Maybe we should hire a mini-bus and take a trip out to see it one of these days,' added Penny.

'Do you think we'd get the numbers?' asked Ellen. 'Would there be that many interested in going?'

Penny sighed. She was about to explain that she was being sarcastic and that wild horses wouldn't drag her up to such a godforsaken-sounding place. But then she decided that there wasn't much point; sarcasm was not something Ellen's literal way of thinking grasped easily.

'By the way, Ellen,' asked Penny, a thought having suddenly struck her, 'would either of these brothers know anything about those flowers you got the other day?'

'What?' asked Ellen, blushing furiously. 'Penny, don't be talking foolishly.'

For a full minute Penny stared at her with a disbelieving expression on her face.

'Ah no, Penny, you've got it all wrong,' stammered Ellen, continuing to redden under her stare. 'Sure Jack is just a neighbour – that's all.'

'So it's Jack then, is it?'

'Ah now, Penny, stop it. Wasn't I just saying he had a bit of a drink problem? Now why would I be interested in someone like that?'

'Alright then, have it your way – keep it to yourself,' said Penny, annoyed. 'Anyway, where were we before Ellen distracted us? Oh yes, the Colonel. Well, if he really is an alcoholic and he certainly has been acting strangely lately then I don't see how he can be let stay here. It's a retirement village, not a nursing home. We're meant to be able to look after ourselves. He could become a danger to himself, not to mind to the rest of us. What if he left his cooker on one night? Why, with the bungalows being packed so close together we'd all go up in smoke.'

'Couldn't they move him into the main house?' asked Ellen.

'No,' answered Penny. 'The nursing facilities are only there for temporary care – say, if you were convalescing after coming out of hospital or if you had the flu. You can't stay there indefinitely.'

'But where would he go if he had to leave here?' asked Ellen.

'I'm sure one of those rich relatives he's forever talking about could spare a room in one of their mansions,' observed Elizabeth.

'Well, I think we should talk to a doctor,' suggested Ellen. 'He'd know what to do for the best. Maybe he could get the Colonel into one of those detox programmes, or whatever they call them.'

Things were moving just a little too quickly, thought Ana. From a drink problem to full-blown alcoholism requiring immediate detoxification – all within minutes. At this rate, the Colonel would be lucky if he didn't wake up strapped to a strange bed by morning.

'I think Elizabeth is right and we should seek professional advice,' she interrupted. 'There's definitely something the matter with him but I don't think it's drink.'

'No?' asked Penny raising an eyebrow sceptically. 'Well, take a look at the state of him now.'

The other three women followed Penny's look and saw the Colonel standing at the far side of the French doors fumbling with the handles and cursing under his breath. His face was flushed red and the few strands of hair that he usually so carefully combed over his crown were flapping down over one ear. Just as Ana was about to go and help him he succeeded in opening the doors and then stepped into the sunroom looking very agitated.

'Ana,' he asked. 'Have you seen the woman who runs this place? She's never around when you need her.'

'No, I haven't, Colonel. I'm looking for her myself. Is there something up?'

'Yes, there bloody well is. Someone has damn well broken into my bungalow.'

'Really?' asked Ellen, her eyes opened to twice their normal size.

'When?' asked Elizabeth, all agog.

'I don't know. Sometime during the night,

I presume. I could have been killed in my bed. Some hooligan out from Bray, or down from Dublin, no doubt.'

'What did he steal, Colonel?' asked Ana.

'Probably a whole bunch of hooligans. They never travel alone. Ladies, you should check your own bungalows.'

'Colonel, what they steal?' repeated Ana.

'Lots of things. He – or they – took my keys and my wallet and a pair of ... of ... of ... those,' he said staring down at his shoes.

'They stole a pair of your shoes?' asked Elizabeth.

'Yes. They were the first thing that I noticed missing. And they rifled through all my drawers and my wardrobe. I'll have to do a thorough check before I can ascertain the extent of their thieving. It's an abomination. An absolute abomination.'

'Colonel,' asked Penny, 'what would they want with your keys when they must have already been inside your bungalow?'

'How would I know? Who knows what goes on in the criminal mind?'

'And what on earth would they want with your shoes?' asked Elizabeth, giving Penny an incredulous smirk.

'You watch out,' said the Colonel, catching her look and angry that the situation wasn't being taken as seriously as he felt it warranted. 'They might have set their sights on your witch's den next. And mind what you say, for I know a lot more about you than you think.'

'I beg your pardon?'

'Beg away.'

'Colonel,' said Elizabeth, stung by his insults, 'to be honest I don't think anything was stolen. I think the drink has you confused. Either that, or you're going senile.'

A look of uncertainty passed over the Colonel's face. 'I ... I...' he stuttered, looking from one of them to the other.

'Colonel, come on,' said Ana, taking him by the arm. 'Let's go and find Mrs Reynolds.'

Mrs Reynolds was feeling more than a little confused by the Colonel's recounting of events.

'Yes, yes, I think they probably got in through that window,' he was saying to her now, pointing at the one alongside his bed. 'You see, it's the only one I leave open at night.'

'But I thought that you said you were asleep when they broke in.'

'And I was.'

'But, Mr Jackson, if you were in bed when they came in through that window then they'd have had to climb in over you. Surely you would have heard, if not felt them. And to be honest, I don't think they could have even fitted through it – not unless they were a band of midgets.'

'For all we know they could have been children,' said Ana. She didn't much like Mrs Reynolds at the best of times and she certainly didn't like the way she was treating the Colonel. 'And maybe *Colonel* Jackson,' she said, pointedly correcting her now, 'was using the bathroom at the time or getting himself a glass of water.'

'Yes, maybe that was it,' said the Colonel, nodding his head vigorously, glad to have a plausible explanation put forward.

'But then you'd have been awake,' Mrs Reynolds sighed in exasperation. 'And presumably you would have heard them.'

'Then I can't have been in the bathroom. I must have been in bed so.'

'And did you hear or feel them getting in?' Mrs Reynolds asked.

'I don't think so. I can't be sure.'

'But,' said Mrs Reynolds getting more and more annoyed, 'they couldn't have got in over you without doing you an injury.' She was beginning to wonder, not for the first time, what on earth had possessed her to get involved in the running of this place.

'Look here,' said the Colonel, suddenly getting very annoyed, 'I don't know when, or how, they got in but they did and my things are missing. I demand that the police be brought in to investigate this matter immediately.' Then he looked at her and nodded knowingly. 'Ah, now I see your game. You want to hush this whole matter up – it wouldn't do this place much good if it got out.'

'Mrs Reynolds,' interrupted Ana before the Colonel went any further, 'why don't I go through the place with the Colonel? We can make out a list of all the items taken.'

'I don't know if there's much point. I'm beginning to think that this whole break-in is in his mind.'

'How dare you?' shouted the Colonel. 'How dare you ... you – you four-eyed – bitch.'

Ana looked at him shocked whilst Mrs Reynolds stared at him sourly.

'Oh you'd want to tread very carefully, Mr Jackson,' she warned him. 'I've better things to be doing with my time than to be wasting it in humouring an old fool like you.'

And with that she left, leaving Ana and the Colonel standing there, looking at one another.

'Whatever happened to the courteous Colonel that used to be?' asked Ana gently. 'Why did you have to call her that?'

The Colonel threw his hands in the air.

'I don't know Ana. I just don't know. Sometimes I think my mi–' he stopped, then stared at her sadly. 'Oh Ana, I don't know. I'm just tired.'

'Colonel, why don't you take a rest? Come on, leave it to me to find out what's missing.

I think this break-in has been a strain on you.'

'Maybe you're right, Ana.'

Ana led him over to the bed. He sat down and she helped him take off his shoes.

'Maybe you're not feeling the best,' she suggested. 'Do you think we should get someone to take a look at you?'

'I'm just tired, Ana.'

'Maybe tomorrow?'

'Maybe,' he agreed, resting his head down on the pillow. 'But not that Nurse Boo,' he warned. 'I don't want him anywhere near me.'

'Ah Colonel, you know he's a friend of mine. Will you stop talking about him like that? Why can't you call him Adrian?'

But all the response she got to that suggestion was a dismissive snort.

'Ana,' he called, after she'd drawn the curtains and was just about to leave.

'Yes?'

'Why wait until we're married? Why don't you take off your things and slip in beside me now?'

'You never give up trying, do you, Colonel?' she laughed.

'No harm in trying, is there now?' he said, settling himself down.

'No, Colonel, I suppose there isn't.'

'Spring,' he called out as she was shutting the door. 'The spring's a nice time of the year to get married.'

Ana went into the sitting-room. Looking about, she realised that it was the first time she'd ever been there. The Colonel wasn't much of one for enjoying his own company and rarely stopped in on his own and, since Ana could hardly step outside her own front door without bumping into him, there was very little reason ever to call on him. Looking around now, she saw that there wasn't any obvious sign of a break-in and noticed that the room was meticulous, as might be expected from a military man. She remembered Elizabeth, who'd made it her business to extract as much information as she could from the Colonel, telling her that his wife had died over twenty years ago and that they'd had no children. Noticing two photographs standing on the piano she automatically went towards them. The first was a black and white portrait shot of a woman the Colonel's wife in her youth, Ana presumed. She picked it up to have a closer look and saw a plain, bossy-looking woman scowling back at her; then, putting it back down again, she examined the other photograph. It took her a few seconds to recognise that it was Sophie she was looking at, partly because she just didn't expect to see Elizabeth's granddaughter smiling out at her from a photo on the Colonel's piano but also because she looked so different, so very grown up. She was wearing a long evening dress and was standing on a platform beside a piano and smiling at a man dressed in a tuxedo who was presenting her with a trophy. The photo surprised Ana, she'd no idea that Sophie and the Colonel were that close – close enough for her photo to merit a place on his piano.

She left the little sitting-room, came into the kitchen and went directly to the phone on the wall and dialled Adrian Lloyd's number. Then, when the answering machine came on she left a message asking Adrian to ring her back – that it was in connection with her friend Colonel Jackson and that it was urgent. Having hung up, she looked around and saw that here too everything was perfectly neat. And again – no sign of a break-in. A single open drawer was the only disruption to the room's order and she went to close it. A silver pen caught her attention and she reached in, took it out and stared at it somewhat puzzled. It was a Cross-pen identical to one she'd recently lost and when she examined it further she saw that it had her initials engraved on it. She opened the drawer wide and stood there for a few moments trying to make sense of its contents for it was chock-full of pens, lighters, magazines, sets of keys – all sorts of things which she recognised as belonging to other residents. She picked out a *Statue of Liberty* lighter, the very one Penny's daughter had brought her back from New York lately. Only yesterday, Penny had complained that it had gone missing. The copies of *Hello* magazine probably belonged to Elizabeth. Whenever she mislaid them, which seemed to be very often, she always accused Ellen of 'whipping' them, a charge Ellen vehemently denied – quite rightly it seemed now. But what on earth did the Colonel want with all these things? Most of the stuff was of absolutely no use to him. She couldn't imagine him being so interested in reading *Hello* that he'd resort to stealing it.

Ana rooted through the drawer to see if the Colonel had taken anything of real value but, apart from her pen, she found that it was all junk. Except for the sets of keys; somehow she'd have to return those to their rightful owners. Then she noticed a bundle of letters buried deep in the bottom – they'd definitely have to go back as well she decided but, as she took them out, a scrap of newspaper became dislodged from the bundle and fluttered to the floor. She picked it up and without thinking began to read an ad at the top which was ringed heavily with thick red marker. *'RETIRED GENT seeks lady,'* it read. *'Financially secure, trim, ex-army man in his late 50s and considered good-looking seeks elegant, mature lady to woo, wine, dine and charm.'* Ana burst out laughing. The liar, she thought. Why, he hadn't seen his fifties for years. And trim? Hardly. And exactly who considered him good-looking? Her eyes scanned the rest of the ads and she saw that his was far from the worst. Who in God's name, she wondered, would reply to someone who described himself as a *'7-year-itch sufferer / mid-life crisisee'* who sought *'ladies for discreet fun and excitement.'* And who, she wondered, flicking through the envelopes in various pastel shades, were all these ladies who'd written to the Colonel at P.O. Box 7385, in the hopes of being wooed, wined, dined and charmed by him. She stood for a while, wondering if she dared to peek – just at one. After all, it wasn't like she knew these people. Just one, she thought. Like that one without an envelope, for instance.

She dithered for all of one second and then she dared. It was dated January 4th she noted, a week before she'd arrived at Rathdowne.

Dear Retired Gent

This is the very first time I have replied to a personal ad and I only do so because your ad seemed written for me. I felt that it was calling out to me.

How would I describe myself? An old-fashioned romantic I suppose, someone who believes in love. Though life has really given me no reason to, but I do, I still believe. All my life I have been waiting to be wooed and charmed and sadly, am still waiting. But perhaps, not for much longer!!

I married young, you see, though not to a gent – I say no more – he is no longer with us. Enough to say it was not a happy marriage. An unfortunate mismatch. Just think – Jackie Kennedy and Aristotle Onassis. Think – Princess Diana and Prince Charles.

So my dear retired gent, reply to my letter. And woo me. Wine me. Dine me. Charm me. Yes, please, please charm me. And perhaps even grow to love me...

Good lord, thought Ana,

Yours in anticipation (and in confidence I presume) – Elizabeth Daly.

'Good, good lord,' said Ana aloud.

'Colonel!' called Elizabeth from the front door. 'Ana!'

'Ah, in here, Elizabeth, in the kitchen,' called out Ana, shoving everything back into the drawer and hurriedly closing it.

Elizabeth came in and looked around, 'Where's the Colonel?' she asked.

'He's sleeping.'

'Good, he needs a rest. And tell me, was he burgled?'

'To be honest I don't think so,' Ana told her.

'Ana, why are you staring at me like that?'

'Oh I'm sorry, Elizabeth, I didn't mean to.

I was a million miles away.'

But she found it hard not to stare. God, the world was full of surprises. Who'd have thought that underneath that brown cardigan such a passionate heart was beating. And that Elizabeth's no-nonsense hair-do covered an old head full of romantic notions. But, wondered Ana, why was Elizabeth always so anxious to pretend that she'd had the perfect marriage when it seemed the opposite was the case? All part of keeping up appearances, no doubt. Wasn't she guilty of the same thing? As no doubt were others in Rathdowne. Well, at least the Colonel had kept Elizabeth's secret. But then, he could hardly divulge it, not unless he was prepared to let people know that he'd written the ad in the first place. She smirked, thinking of what torture it must have been for him not to be able to tease her about it.

'I know that we've had our differences concerning the Colonel,' Elizabeth was saying. 'But Ana, I'm as worried about him as you are. He's been a bit odd lately, but he has a good heart. I'm very anxious about him.'

'So am I, Elizabeth. That's why I've left a message on Adrian Lloyd's home phone asking him to ring back.'

'Who?'

'Adrian Lloyd. You know, the nurse who

runs the surgery up at the main house.'

'Oh, you mean Nurse Boo? Oh Ana, I don't know about him,' said Elizabeth, looking doubtful. 'Are you sure he's the right person? I mean…'

'Well, I've known him for a long time, Elizabeth, and I thought I'd just talk to him, as a first step.'

'Yes, I suppose that's something.'

'Come on, let's have a cup of tea,' said Ana. And she went and put on the kettle.

1990

CHAPTER 9

There is no duty we so understand as the duty of being happy

from *Virginibus Puerisque 'El Dorado'* by
Robert Louis Stevenson

'Now wasn't I right to persuade you to buy that outfit?' asked Eamon, looking at Ana admiringly.

'You didn't persuade me, Eamon. I was going to buy it anyway.'

'Then why were you dithering about it so much in the shop yesterday?' he asked.

'Well, you know–' she began.

'Hello there, Maurice. Hello, Jeanie,' Eamon interrupted her, calling to a couple who were passing by at a distance. As they shouted back their hellos, he beamed over at them. 'Jeanie, you're looking absolutely wonderful,' he called to the woman.

All morning he'd been the same, recognising and greeting practically every second person he saw but then, it was only to be expected, allowed Ana. After all, the annual horseshow at the RDS was the absolute ultimate for him, being a highlight in both the Dublin Society calendar and in horsey circles – the two worlds he loved the most.

'Well, you know,' she began again when he'd turned back to her, 'it was just so expensive I felt I had to be sure.'

'Ana, will you just listen to yourself? Don't you know that you alone have more money than the pair of us will ever be able to get through? Just on your parents' money we could manage very nicely, not to mention what's left of Celia's or what you're making on your book. Which is just as well since you insist on tying all that up in your little Kenyan project.'

'Why do you have to be so condescending, Eamon? My little Kenyan project! God – listen to yourself. Just because my budget isn't in the millions it doesn't mean that it's any less important than your big-time, megabucks business projects. At least my little Kenyan project does some good.'

'Even that's debatable. Some might say that you should leave well enough alone. Tell me, when the children you're financing through college finally graduate, what do you think they're going to do then?'

'Oh God,' groaned Ana. 'How many times do we have to have this discussion? You already know what I think, Eamon.'

'I do. And I can't believe that you assume that once they finish college they'll go back to the village.'

'I never said that. I happen to think that some will go back and some won't. But even those that don't are likely to send money home and that will help raise the standard of living. Overall, an education has to be a good thing even if it will bring about social changes – they're going to happen anyway. Young people do go away, that's the nature of things, so they might as well be in a position to get a decent job when they do. Anyway, what's the point in having this discussion? You're not going to change my views and I'm not going to change yours. But in his last letter Kaninu told me that...'

'Ah Kaninu – the taxi-driving oracle. Pray tell, what does the Great One say?'

'Oh shut up, Eamon, now you're being nasty. Anyway, that's not what we were talking about. We were talking about trying to justify how much we spend on ourselves.'

'No, no. You were. I've no problem with how much we spend.'

'Well I do, or at least I'd never try to justify it. How could I? The other day Julie asked me how much the carpets in the new house were costing and I was too embarrassed to tell her the real price so I pretended that they cost half that. And do you know what? She was still shocked.'

'Ana, do you remember what you said when your parents died and you found out how much money they had?'

'Yes. Of course I do.'

'You said that you were going to be the exact opposite to them. That you were going to enjoy it all while you were alive.'

'And you can hardly fault me on that score. This year alone we've been to New York twice, over and back to London I don't know how many times, and to Italy once. The amount that we've spent on buying the new house here and on doing up my house in London doesn't bear thinking about and, in the last year, I've acquired so many clothes that I'd need to change twice a day if I'm ever to get around to wearing them all. And to top it all, I, at the age of fifty-six, am presently being talked into buying a convertible by you, my even more foolish soon-to-be husband. And if that's not ridiculous, then I don't know what is. At a time of my life when I should be getting sense, I've suddenly and completely lost the run of myself. And I blame it all on you, Eamon Dunne. You are a very, very bad influence.'

'So you're not enjoying yourself?'

Ana appeared to consider his question for a second, then she laughed.

'Of course I am.'

'Anyway, where are Julie and Tony?' asked Eamon, looking around. 'If they don't come soon we'll have to go into lunch without them. By the way, Ana, what I'd begun to say before we got side-tracked is that you're looking lovely. That dress suits you. If I hadn't done so already, I'd be sorely tempted to ask you to marry me.'

'Is that right?' she laughed, then leant forward and kissed him. 'And how do you know that I'd say yes a second time?' she teased.

'Ahh, would you look at the pair of love-birds,' said Julie coming up behind them. 'Tony, were we as bad as them before we got married?'

'That was years ago,' grumbled Tony, who was following along after her. 'How can I be expected to remember?'

'Much worse, as I recall,' answered Ana. 'And less of the lovebirds if you don't mind. After all, I am a mature woman in my fifties.'

'Sssh, Ana, not so loud. How will people believe me when I say I'm in my forties if you go around saying that? Anyway, tell me, how are the plans for the big day coming along? You know, I really wish you'd let me wear something other than a suit. A brides-maid in a suit – honestly! It's just not the thing.'

'Nor is a bridesmaid in her fifties – sorry, forties – but you're insisting.'

'And who else would you have? Aren't I the best qualified for the job? After all, I'm the only one who's done it for you before.'

Then she paused and looked around. 'Do you know, I think there's a bigger crowd here this year than any other!'

'You said the same thing last year,' Ana pointed out.

'She says it every year,' said Tony. Then he turned to Eamon. 'So, tell me Eamon, are you feeling lucky today?'

'Luck has little to do with it, Tony,' answered Eamon. 'But I have to admit that I've a feeling today will turn out to be pretty lucrative alright.'

'You'll be able to give a few good tips so,' said Tony.

'Oh God, Ana,' Julie interrupted her husband, suddenly remembering her news. 'I knew I had something to tell you! Guess who I saw earlier?' And without giving Ana any opportunity to guess, she went on. 'Just after we arrived in we met some friends of ours so we stopped to talk to them but, after a while, as we were standing there chatting I got the strangest feeling – like when you know someone is staring at you – so, I turned around and there was this peculiar-looking man just standing there, staring over at me – with a real intense look on his face but when he saw me looking at him, he turned away immediately and scurried off into the crowd. Anyway, it was only after he'd gone and we'd moved on that I suddenly remembered who he was. Remember that neighbour of yours who used to trail home after us from secondary school every day? You know, the little skinny fellow with the eye-patch and with his socks forever hanging down around his ankles? Do you know who I'm talking about? Remember he was in the–'

'Adrian Lloyd?'

'Yes, yes – him. I couldn't think of his name but I was telling Tony all about him, you know how–' Suddenly she broke off and grabbed Ana by the arm. 'Oh God, he's there again. Don't look around now, he's behind your back. We don't want to draw him on us. Keep talking.'

'Julie, for God's sake, let go of my arm! If it is Adrian Lloyd then of course I want to meet him.'

'Ah, Ana, no. You can't possibly, not after...'

'Julie, I know you never liked him. But I grew up with Adrian. He was practically like a brother and his mother was always very good to me. Of course I want to talk to him if he's here.'

Ana turned and saw Adrian staring over at her but, before she could call out to him, he'd turned on his heel and disappeared back into the crowd. Knowing how shy he'd always been, Ana hurried after him watched by the others and, much to their dismay, she arrived back with him in tow a minute later.

'Adrian, let me introduce you to everyone. You might remember Julie – she was in my class in school and this is her husband Tony. Julie, Tony, this is Adrian. And Adrian, this is Eamon Dunne. Eamon and I are getting married next month.'

Eamon, Tony and Julie nodded at Adrian.

'So,' said Eamon, turning back to Julie and Tony, 'Friday suits you then?'

'Yes, I think so,' answered Julie. 'We don't have anything else on, sure we don't, Tony?'

'No, not that I can think of.'

Ana was mortified. She couldn't believe they were being so rude. Certainly Adrian was a little odd and she could see how he must appear to others. Like now, the way he alternated between pushing the glasses back up along his nose and nervously rubbing his hands together. But that certainly didn't excuse Eamon and the other two.

'So Adrian,' said Ana, determined to make the best of this awkward situation, 'how have you been keeping?'

'Not too bad, Ana.'

Suddenly he dropped the programme he'd been holding and bent to pick it up but, as he did, his glasses fell from his face so he reached down for them only to drop the programme again. Ana noticed Julie and Eamon glance at one another, then scornfully raise their eyes to heaven. He was so jittery that he was beginning to make Ana feel the same way and she wished now that she hadn't embarrassed him by dragging him over like this. She should have just talked to him on his own.

'Of course, since my mother died it's been strange,' Adrian continued, when he'd eventually composed himself. 'But well, her time had come, I suppose. She was eighty-two, you know. Your mass card was very much appreciated, Ana.'

'I'd have come for the funeral but by the time I'd heard it was too late.'

'I thought as much.'

There was an awkward silence as Ana tried to think of something else to say.

'So are you still living in Mornington Close?'

'Sure where else would I live? And I won't be moving out now. I've been there too long.'

'And tell me, how's the research going?'

'Hmm?'

'Your research? Hadn't you given up practical nursing and gone into some sort of research?'

'Yes.' Adrian hesitated for a second. 'Yes, that's right. I had. But I've gone back to nursing again. Just part-time. In a retirement village down in County Wicklow. You might have heard of it? Rathdowne Retirement Village? I run a clinic there twice a week.'

'I see. And do you like it?'

'Yes, I do. It's a great opportunity for me. You know, after everything.'

'Pardon?'

But Adrian had moved on. 'And are you still living in Burnhill?'

'Partly. Eamon and I have just bought a house here in Dublin, so we intend dividing our time between the two.'

'Burnhill is one of the nicest parts of London, I've always thought so. And you were wise to hang onto your house there, just in case.'

'Pardon?'

'You know – for security.' Then he changed the subject. 'Ana, I really liked your book *A Year in a Kenyan Village*.'

'Oh you've seen it then? I'm glad you liked it.'

'I never realised that you were such a gifted photographer, though it doesn't surprise me. I thought the photographs of the children were particularly good. I hate to ask, but do you think you could sign some copies for me, if I send them to you?'

'Well, if you'd really like me to, then yes, of course. Let me give you my address.'

'No, no, that's fine. I'm sure it's in the address book at home.'

'Ana,' interrupted Eamon. 'We're about to go for lunch, are you coming?'

'Yes, yes. Just a moment.'

It suddenly struck Ana that apart from

racing fanatics only the completely alone would come on their own to such a social event as this and a wave of pity for Adrian passed over her. He exuded such utter lonesomeness. She imagined him back in Mornington Close that morning, getting all dressed up to head off to the races on his own.

'Adrian, would you like to join us?' she asked, thinking, to hell with the others. If they didn't like it – well, stuff them.

'Actually, Ana,' Eamon interrupted, 'we've only booked a table for four.'

'Squeezing in one more person is hardly going to be a problem. I'm sure Adrian won't mind the tight fit and no doubt you can charm one of the waitresses into obliging us by setting an extra place.'

Eamon stared at her coldly.

'I don't think so,' he replied.

Ana stared angrily back at him. He was making it so obvious that he didn't want Adrian along and she realised that if she insisted any further then the situation was only going to get even more embarrassing.

'Ana,' said Adrian, 'if you don't mind I think I'll skip the invitation. Thanks all the same. But, if it's okay with you, I'll forward those books for you to sign.'

'Yes, of course. And it was very nice meeting you again, Adrian.'

'You too, Ana.'

They all watched as he walked away.

'Well, thanks be to God he's gone,' said Julie.

Ana turned on all three.

'I have never been so embarrassed in all my life,' she said furiously. 'I can't believe that all of you could be so rude.'

'Ah come on, Ana,' said Eamon. 'You could hardly expect us to invite him along to lunch.'

'And why not? He's a friend of mine.'

'Ana, how can you say–'

'I would never be that rude to any of your friends,' she interrupted. 'And I can tell you that there are quite a few of them who deserve it.'

'I think we should drop the subject,' Tony intervened, 'or the whole day will be ruined. Come on, let's go in for lunch.'

'Yes. And come on, Ana, lighten up,' said Eamon, putting his arm around her shoulders. 'We're sorry.'

She shrugged off his arm.

'It's a bit too late for that now. And anyway, as far as I'm concerned the whole day is already ruined.'

Friday afternoon...

'And you went up to Laurence's house on your own?' Elizabeth asked Ana incredulously.

The two of them, together with Penny and

Ellen, were sitting in the sunroom once again.

'Yes, but that's not the–' Ana tried to explain.

'God, Ana, were you wise to do that?' Ellen cut in. 'I remember a neighbour of mine telling me once that–'

'Ah not now, Ellen,' snapped Elizabeth. 'Can we not have a single conversation without having your neighbours dragged into it. But tell me, Ana, did you really go up there on your own?'

'Yes, yes, yes, but that's neither here nor there, you're getting me side-tracked. All I was trying to do was amuse you by telling you a silly story about going up there with the completely wrong impression that Patricia was Laurence's wife when in fact she was his parrot. I was just telling you because I thought that you might find it funny. But,' she said, looking in turn at each of the three stony faces, 'obviously not.'

'No,' said Elizabeth. 'It all sounds a bit stupid to me.'

'And me,' agreed Penny. 'Especially when Laurence's wife lives in Las Vegas.'

'What?' asked Ana.

'Are you sure it's Las Vegas?' asked Elizabeth. 'I think it's Los Angeles.'

'No, no. It's Las Vegas definitely,' said Penny. 'I should know. Didn't I go to see her show when I was there a few years ago with

Olive, my eldest. And I'm telling you now – it was something else! Absolutely spectacular! She even had Sammy Davis Junior on with her for a couple of songs.'

'Oh God,' said Elizabeth in disgust. 'I can't stand that fellow.'

'Hold on a minute,' interrupted Ana, 'I thought Laurence was a widower. Are you saying now that his wife is alive and that she's a singer in Las Vegas?'

'Yes,' said Penny. 'Dawn DuBois. You must have heard of her. She was huge in the States back in the sixties.'

'Didn't she start out as an opera singer?' asked Elizabeth.

'Did she? I never knew that,' said Penny.

'Yes, I'm sure she did. But she wasn't known as Dawn DuBois then of course,' Elizabeth told them. 'Sinéad O'Shea I think she was called, or maybe Siobhan O'Shea, one or the other. Oh, she was a beautiful-looking woman in her day. Beautiful. I'd say Laurence must have been gutted when they split up, absolutely gutted.'

'No doubt,' agreed Penny. 'I don't think he's over her yet. Isn't he back and forth all the time to Las Vegas? Maybe he's still hoping that they'll get back together again. I can't say I blame him, she's still a very good-looking woman.' Then she looked at Ana. 'So you thought he was a widower then?'

Ana shrugged.

'I hope you weren't developing a little crush on him,' said Elizabeth, raising an eyebrow.

'Don't be stupid, Elizabeth,' snapped Ana. 'A crush is what teenagers develop.'

Just then, Ellen got up.

'There's something on the telly I want to watch,' she said. 'I'm going to go back down to my bungalow.'

'But why don't you watch it here?' asked Elizabeth.

'No, I think I'll watch it down below.'

'Ah stay here. What is it you want to see? We can all watch it with you,' insisted Elizabeth.

'Elizabeth,' warned Penny, 'will you just leave her go? The reason she doesn't want to watch it here is because there is nothing worse than trying to look at something with you in the room. You give a non-stop commentary on what you think is going to happen, and on what happened last week, so that nobody has any idea of what is actually happening.'

'I see,' said Elizabeth, clearly upset.

'Ah Elizabeth,' began Ellen, 'that's not exactly–'

'No, no, it's all right,' said Elizabeth huffily. 'Don't mind my feelings.'

'Ah Elizabeth please don't think–'

'Ellen,' interrupted Ana. 'I'm heading back down now, if you're coming.'

Together Ellen and Ana walked back to their bungalows; their slow pace set by Ellen.

'I suppose I'll have to get it done sometime,' said Ellen, out of the blue.

'Get what done?' asked Ana.

'The old hip. I don't suppose I can keep putting the operation off forever. But you see, I've an awful fear of needles and being put to sleep; all that sort of thing gives me the willies. And I'm telling you, I've heard stories that would cause the hairs on the back of your neck to rise up. Awful stories altogether. A neighbour from home was in hospital there a while back–'

But then she broke off. 'Oh I forgot,' she said, 'I'm not meant to mention my neighbours.'

'Ellen, don't mind Elizabeth. Go on, what were you going to say?'

'Well, just that some of the things the other patients on the ward told him were absolutely frightful. This neighbour told me that one of them knew a fellow who knew someone who was awake during the entire operation. Can you imagine that? Wouldn't you only die? And because this fellow was paralysed he couldn't alert anyone to his predicament but had to lie there, completely powerless, while they sawed and hacked away at him. Oh Ana, I don't think I could bear it. I couldn't, I really couldn't.'

'Ellen, Ellen, calm down,' Ana said gently for Ellen was working herself into a state. 'There's no chance that you'd wake up during it.'

'Oh God, I don't know if you're right at all.'

'Listen to me, things are very sophisticated now. You won't feel a thing. They'll just put you to sleep and you won't wake up again until you're back in the bed with a new hip in place.'

'Do you think?'

'Definitely.'

'But what if they read the wrong patient's notes and say ... say they gave me a bypass by mistake? Or a transplant?'

'I really don't think that that's going to happen.'

'Or they might give me contaminated blood and I'd end up catching AIDS.'

'Really, Ellen, it's very, very unlikely. I think you're worrying about it too much.'

As they rounded the bend, Ana was the first to notice the elderly man sitting on the doorstep of Ellen's bungalow.

'Looks like you've got a visitor,' she said.

'Well, Holy Mother of God!' cried Ellen. 'Will you look at who it is? Jack Duffy!'

On seeing the two women approach, the man got to his feet and began straightening his tie.

'Well, well, well,' said Ellen. 'Isn't this a turn-up for the books? We were just talking about you, Jack Duffy, and that time you were in hospital and what that fellow in the bed next to you was telling you.'

So this was the neighbour Ellen was forever talking about. Ana took a good look at him. The most striking aspect of his appearance was his hair, both the quantity and quality of it; he'd great bushy white eyebrows, and tufts of white hair sprouted from his nostrils and probably from his ears, Ana imagined, though they weren't visible under his head of incredibly thick, incredibly messy white hair. His rugged red face was made redder than usual by a recent and close shave as evidenced by several fresh little cuts. On his gaunt, stooped frame hung a black, old-fashioned suit, the jacket of which was unbuttoned and revealed a grey-white shirt and, knotted tightly at the base of his scrawny neck, was a skinny black tie. His pants, Ana noticed, stopped an inch short of his shoes. His socks were whitish in colour and the shoes, though well polished, had seen better days. His rough red hands, the size of shovels, were now clasped tightly before him.

'Well, you're a long way from home, Jack Duffy,' said Ellen.

'Hello, Ellen,' said Jack, nervously shifting from foot to foot. 'You're looking well. This place must be suiting you.'

'There's not much I could do if it wasn't. Are you on your way to a funeral or what?' she asked, taking in the clothes and the fresh shave.

'Ellen, I'll see you later,' interrupted Ana.

'Indeed you won't,' Ellen hurriedly told her, catching a restraining hold of her arm. 'Stay where you are. He won't be stopping long. So Jack, what is it that you want?'

'Ellen,' he began nervously, 'tell me first, did you get my flowers?'

'I did.'

'And Ellen, did you like them?' he asked eagerly.

'I suppose I did,' she conceded begrudgingly.

'I knew you would.'

'Did you now?'

'I did. You see, Francis brought home an article from a woman's magazine he came across in the dentist's surgery and showed it to me and it said that the one sure way to win a woman back was with flowers; it said that all women love flowers.'

'And you had to read a magazine to find that out?'

'Ha?'

Ellen didn't answer him.

'So tell me,' she said instead, 'what is it that you want?'

'Well, it's like this, I ... I...' He looked over

at Ana, obviously embarrassed at having to talk in front of her.

'I'll go, Ellen – leave you two to it,' said Ana, understanding his discomfort.

'Indeed you won't,' insisted Ellen, keeping a firm hold of Ana's arm. 'Go on, Jack, say whatever it is you have to say for I'll have to go soon.'

'Well ... well, I was wondering if ... if...' He sighed, then started again. 'Ellen, I was wondering if...' Ana watched his neck getting redder and redder as he hummed and hawed and shuffled from one foot to the other. 'You see, Ellen, the ways things are I thought... You see, I know things never really got going between the two of us but ... but you know yourself how things stood, if it wasn't one thing, it was another. But now everything is sorted. After Mammy died we took it bad as you know, both Francis and myself, but neither of us have touched a drop now in over three months and won't again, I can swear to you. And I've discussed everything with Francis so he knows I'm here and...'

'Have you any idea what he's talking about, Ana? God help us, but he's not making a bit of sense to me.'

'Ellen, I came over to ask you to ... to...' And to the two women's astonishment, Jack suddenly dropped to his knees. 'Would you, Ellen Madden,' he asked in a stilted, formal voice, 'kindly do me the honour of becoming my wife?'

Ellen stared at him. Ana stared at him. And at Ellen. She was aware that she should just walk away but this was compelling stuff indeed and both of them seemed to have forgotten her presence. Ellen kept on staring down at him and, as the seconds dragged by, Ana wanted to prod her and tell her to put the old man out of his misery, to give him an answer – whatever it might be, and to let him get back up off his knees.

'Ellen?' entreated Jack. 'Ellen? Answer me, can't you? Did you hear me?'

'I hear you,' snapped Ellen. 'And now, you hear me, Jack Duffy. I waited for years and years for you to ask me that question and to mean it but you've left it too late, far too late and my answer to you today is no.'

'But things are different now, Ellen. The time is right now.'

'No, Jack, it isn't. The time is forty years too late.'

'Well, I understand that we wouldn't be able to have children it being too late–'

'Jesus, Mary and Joseph! What kind of an amadán is he at all? Wouldn't be able to have children! Did you ever hear the like? Jesus, Jack, who told you that? That's awful news. Are you sure it's true? Maybe we should consult a doctor, just to be certain.'

'I understand you're cross, Ellen. But

listen to me, we could be married within a few months and you could come back and live with Francis and me.'

'Jack Duffy, I'd sooner go live in a tent on the top of the Sugarloaf than go live with you and your brother. What use are you to me now? For years I've waited, all the time listening to your excuses as to why it was never the right time. "Ah Ellen, wait a while – my father's not well. Ah Ellen, not now – not when my father has just died. Ah Ellen, wait until my mother gets used to the idea. Ah Ellen, wait until I get a bit of money together." Ah Ellen, ah Ellen, ah Ellen. Wait, wait, wait – that's all I've heard from you. Well, I've waited too long and that's an end to it.'

'Ah Ellen...'

'Sure what good are you to me now? I'd be only coming to look after you in your old age. I'm happy here and here I'm staying. So goodbye to you.'

She found her key in her handbag, inserted it into the lock and was about to open the door when she suddenly turned around.

'Not that it's any concern of mine but tell me, Jack, how are you getting back home?'

'Your brother is collecting me.'

'Ah-ha! So my brother is involved in all of this. Yes, I can see his and the Blondie Trollop's stamp on it alright – egging you along, thinking of all the money they'd save by having me go live with you. Well, he's in for a nasty shock. When he comes to collect you, Jack Duffy, you can give him this from me.' She paused and rooted around in her handbag until she found what she was looking for. 'Here,' she said, handing him the letter from Zanzibar Holdings, 'give him this with my compliments.'

And she stepped into her bungalow and banged the door behind her.

Jack looked at Ana, then nodded to her,

'Nice meeting you,' he said.

'You too,' she replied, then watched him walk off down the avenue.

Almost as soon as Ana had gone into her own bungalow, a knock came on her door.

'Door's open,' she shouted from the kitchen, assuming it was the Colonel. She'd passed him and Laurence earlier as they were both working on his motorbike (or rather Laurence was working and the Colonel was looking on) and he'd told her then that he might drop over later. He'd seemed fine she'd noted, back to his old form, as if nothing had ever happened yesterday. 'Is that you, Colonel?' she called out now.

'No, Ana. It's me, Laurence.'

Ana's heart skipped a beat.

'Come on in, Laurence,' she called, as

calmly as she could.

That it was Laurence surprised her. He'd never called to her before and she didn't exactly welcome his visit right now. In fact, he was the last person in the world she wanted to see. She needed time to think about things, to sort out how she felt. One minute she'd thought that he was married and was happy just being friends with him. The next, she'd believed he was widowed and had begun feeling like some love-struck teenager. And now, she'd just learnt that he had a wife from whom he was separated but with whom he was still on very good terms, news which had upset her more than she could have imagined. It was all too confusing and unsettling.

'I'm in the kitchen,' she called out to him.

She wondered if she looked flustered. She certainly felt it.

'I hope you don't mind me calling like this?' she heard him say as he came down the hall.

'No, not at all.'

He came into the kitchen, smiling.

'So, how's the work going on the motor-bike?' she asked, trying to act as if nothing had changed. And nothing had – apart from her perception. He was still a lovely man and hadn't they started to become friends before she began getting stupid ideas? She should try to be content with just that.

'Not too bad,' he answered.

'Tell me, is the Colonel any help?'

'Oh yes, he's a great help,' said Laurence, not very convincingly.

'Really?' she asked, looking at him in disbelief.

'Well, all I can say is that I've never met a man better than him for saying what he thought I should do next or where he thought I should put this, that, or the other.' Then suddenly, he started laughing.

'What?' demanded Ana.

'Well ... when ... when...'

But he couldn't continue for whatever he was trying to say was proving too funny. Ana stared at him, bemused but then, gradually, she too began laughing, though she'd no idea at what. But it was impossible not to.

'What?' she finally managed to ask again. 'What are you laughing at? What am I laughing at?'

'Well, after I put my tools back in the box after we'd finished up, I happened to look around and I saw the Colonel wipe a finger along the bike and...'

'And?' demanded Ana, for Laurence was laughing again.

'And then I saw him bend down so that he could see his face in the mirror and I watched as he very carefully smeared two streaks of oil on his face, one across his cheek and one on his chin. When he'd straightened up again, he ran a few more streaks along his overalls which up to that point had been absolutely spotless and then, noticing me looking at him, he says, 'Wouldn't you get filthy from it, Laurence? Look at the state of me!'

Ana laughed at the image.

'So, you thought he was alright then?' she asked.

'Yeah, he was fine.'

'Did he mention anything about yesterday?'

'No? Why, what happened?'

'Well, he got it into his head that someone had tried to break into his bungalow and he was really agitated about it so I went down with Mrs Reynolds to check what had been taken but there was no sign of a break-in or of anything having been stolen. I really think it was all just in his head. I don't want to be scare-mongering, Laurence, but I'm beginning to feel that there's definitely something seriously the matter with him. Anyway, I've left a message for Adrian Lloyd – you know, the nurse – and asked him to call me back. I haven't heard from him yet but then, I haven't been here a lot of time since so I could have easily missed his call. You know, I'd just feel better if I could talk to Adrian about him. Mrs Reynolds doesn't want to hear a thing about it. Do you think I did the right thing?'

'Absolutely.'

'I might be all wrong, of course. I hope I am.' Then, changing the subject, she asked, 'So anyway, Laurence, what can I do for you?'

'Ana, when I was working on the bike, the Colonel and I were talking and you happened to come into the conversation and, you see, up to now, from the way he went on about you I thought that you and him had ... had a thing going. You see, he's confided in me a lot from time to time, told me how he felt about you and how he hoped the pair of you might get married one day. Now, initially I thought it was all on his side, but then, well, you know how small this place is, I heard how he stays over at your place and–'

'I beg your pardon?'

'Not that it's any of my business of course but–'

'No, it isn't, Laurence.'

'Of course it isn't. More power to the pair of you that's what I say. It was good to learn that some people were having fun in this place. Of course now I kn–'

'Laurence, this is the most extraordinary conversation and I'd like to know where you're going with it.'

'Ana, it's difficult for me but I'm actually trying to ask you if you'd like to go out with me sometime. Maybe you could come–'

'Hang on a second, let me get this straight. You heard that the Colonel and I were carrying on but because it wasn't serious you felt you'd like to get in on the action, is that it?'

'No, no, Ana, you're taking me up all wrong. I'm not making myself clear.'

'I think you're making yourself perfectly clear. And tell me, Laurence, how does your wife fit into all this? For you do have a wife, don't you? And I'm not talking about Patricia-the-bloody-parrot either.'

'Yes I do, Ana, but–'

'I don't want to hear another word from you, Laurence. So please, can you just leave? Right now?'

'Ana, please, can I just explain?'

'No, no, no, I'm not listening to another word. I don't think I've ever been so insulted in my life.'

'Ana, let me explain...'

Ana went to the radio and turned it on at full volume and though Laurence attempted to talk to her over the noise, he soon realised that it was hopeless and eventually, admitting defeat, he left.

As soon as Ana saw that he'd gone, she turned the radio off again. She was shaking with rage. What kind of woman did he think she was? The cheek of him! God, she felt just so mad. Taking deep breaths, she tried to calm herself, but it was no good. Her blood was boiling. She couldn't stop shaking.

A bath, that's what she needed. That

might relax her a bit. She went to the bathroom, turned on the taps, then took some towels from the airing cupboard. But, just as she was about to undress, the phone rang so she turned off the water and went to answer it.

It was Adrian Lloyd.

'Adrian, thanks for ringing back. It's about Colonel Jackson. You see, I'm just a little concerned about him, he's been acting very oddly and I'd hoped that you might come down and have a look at him. Just informally. What? Lots of things really. He's very forgetful sometimes. And he does strange things and gets funny ideas. An example? Well, yesterday morning he thought that his house was broken into but I'm fairly sure he just imagined it. I think he'd mislaid some of his things and was so frustrated that he decided someone else had to be to blame. And another thing, he's been taking silly, useless things from the other residents, things he couldn't possibly have any need for. I've also seen him being quite abusive to Mrs Reynolds and to Elizabeth Daly, one of the other residents, which isn't his usual style at all but, according to some of the others, he's been that way to a lot of people lately.'

Having heard her out, Adrian agreed to pop in to see the Colonel after his morning clinic the following day and, at her request, he promised that he wouldn't let on to the

Colonel that she had asked him to call.

After thanking him, Ana hung up and then headed back down to the bathroom but, before she'd reached it, there was a volley of sharp knocks on the door.

'I thought I made myself perfectly clear,' she shouted out.

'Ana, it's me, Elizabeth. What on earth are you talking about? Let me in, quick.'

'Sorry, Elizabeth, I thought…'

As Ana was opening the door, Elizabeth pushed it in, knocking her aside.

'Come in, why don't you?' said Ana as Elizabeth went hurrying down to the kitchen. Shutting out the door, Ana followed her.

'Oh God, Ana, the worst thing in the world is after happening. But first, let me sit down before I collapse,' said Elizabeth, flopping down on a chair.

Only now did Ana notice how pale Elizabeth looked and that she was trembling.

'What?' she demanded. 'Elizabeth, what's after happening?'

'Oh Ana, it's dreadful.'

'What is?'

'Only dreadful.'

'What Elizabeth? What's dreadful?'

'The Colonel, Ana, the Colonel is dead.' And she burst into tears. 'Ana, the Colonel is dead.'

'What?'

But Elizabeth couldn't answer, she was

crying too much.

'What happened? Tell me, what happened to him?'

'Oh Ana, it's just awful,' she sobbed. 'He was knocked down and killed, stone dead. You should see him lying there on the ground. He's in an awful way. There's blood everywhere. Everywhere. It's terrible. They're not moving him until the ambulance arrives but there's no doubt about it, he's dead alright.'

Too shocked to speak, Ana sat down herself, then reached out and took one of Elizabeth's hands in hers.

'And, Ana, it was Laurence who knocked him down. He came tearing out of the avenue in his van and ran straight into him. Catherine's daughter, what's-her-name, the one who works in the kitchen, saw it all on her way into work. The Colonel was wandering along in the middle of the road when Laurence came out of the avenue and though he tried his best to avoid him he couldn't, he hadn't a hope. Then, after he hit the Colonel, the van just carried on until it smashed into the high wall on the other side of the road. There was no way Laurence could have avoided hitting him. The van's a complete write-off and Laurence is badly injured as well. Oh Ana,' cried Elizabeth, the tears streaming down her face, 'isn't it just awful?'

1992

CHAPTER 10

If you can make one heap of all your winnings
And risk it on one game of pitch-and-toss...
from *If* by Rudyard Kipling

The couple, acquaintances of Eamon's, had arrived into the restaurant moments before and, en route to their own table, had stopped briefly at Ana and Eamon's and invited them to a dinner party in their house on the following Friday.

'Sounds wonderful,' Eamon said to them, then looked over at Ana. 'I'm fairly certain that we haven't anything else planned, sure we don't, Ana?'

'Pardon?' said Ana, staring at him frostily.

'We're free on Friday, aren't we?' he asked.

Ana nodded.

'There'll be a dozen or so guests altogether,' the woman told them.

'And you'll probably know several of them,' added the man. 'You know Maurice and Jeanie O'Donnell, don't you? And Jonathan Brennan and his fiancée?'

'Is Jonathan Brennan back in Dublin again?' asked Eamon. 'I thought he'd moved to New York.'

'He had,' said the man, 'but I don't think things worked out for him there as well as he'd hoped. So, we'll take it that you'll come then?'

'Definitely. We'll be looking forward to it, won't we, Ana?'

Again Ana just nodded; she didn't trust herself to speak.

And, as Eamon continued on chatting light-heartedly, Ana couldn't help but stare at him. That he could be capable of appearing so carefree and genial at a time like this truly amazed her. Why didn't he just let the couple move on to their own table? Why was he delaying them by asking questions about this Jonathan Brennan?

As she sat there staring at him, it suddenly struck her how odd it was that, in the last two years, not once had he ever asked her why she'd changed her mind and agreed to marry him. Typically he'd just accepted that she had, just as he accepted all his good fortune. Or expected it even. And why had she agreed to marry him? Certainly not because she'd fallen in love with him. She had loved him of course but, right from the start, she'd known that she'd never feel the same way about him as she had about Mark or Kaninu. She wondered was he, or had he, ever been in love with her and, though he was blue in the face from telling her that he was, she had her doubts. After all, he wouldn't have acted the way he had if he really loved her. And had she been right to marry him without being in love with him? Well, she'd thought so at the time. When the alternative was being on her own it had seemed enough that he was such good company, that he was handsome, that he was kind and that she'd felt certain she'd enjoy life with him. She'd weighed up loneliness against companionship, fun and excitement and the obvious had won out.

'So Jonathan Brennan is back in Ireland again,' remarked Eamon, turning back to Ana now that the couple had finally left. 'He didn't exactly last long in New York, did he?'

Ana didn't respond; she just stared at him, half-amazed, half-disgusted.

'Let me guess,' Eamon said, noticing her look. 'You're not interested in discussing Jonathan Brennan right now because you're anxious to resume telling me why you're leaving me.'

'In the middle of which, quite incredibly really, you decide to call that couple over and accept a dinner invitation on our behalf.'

'I didn't call them over, Ana. Unless we both got down on our knees and hid under the table until they'd passed us by, there was little chance of avoiding them. And what would you have had me say to them? That sorry, we can't come on Friday because we're in the middle of splitting up and you lucky people are the first to hear our news.' He sat back in his seat. 'So, Ana, why don't you pick up where you were before we were interrupted and explain why you're leaving me.'

'It's fairly simple, Eamon. You're a lying cheat.'

'You think I cheated on you with someone else?'

'That's not what I'm saying. There are other ways of cheating.'

'Sorry but you've lost me now.'

'Eamon, is there anything you want to tell me? Anything at all?'

'Like what?'

'Well, let's start with the house in Burnhill and the fact that it's come on the market. Maybe you'd like to tell me how that has come about?'

He laughed.

'Is that what all this is about? Ana, I meant to tell you but it just slipped my mind. Between one thing and another, I just didn't get a chance. You know how hectic things have been lately.'

'So you're admitting that you've put it on the market then?'

'Yes of course but…'

'Behind my back.'

'Behind your back? Ana, you're making me sound very conniving. It's not like that at all. I just didn't get a chance to tell you. I'd no intention of actually selling it. I just wanted to suss out the market, get an idea of how much it might be worth.'

'Sure,' she snorted incredulously.

'Ana, believe me. That's the truth. You can hardly think otherwise.'

'Actually, I can. In fact, I do.'

'But why would I do a thing like that?'

'For the obvious reason.'

'Which is?'

'The little matter of a cash shortage?'

'Ana, Ana, Ana,' he shook his head fondly. 'That's nothing to worry about. That's the nature of business. It's all up and downs, you know that.'

'And right now is a down?'

'Yes.'

'And that's why my personal account is cleared out?'

'Ana…'

'Answer me, Eamon, is that why you've cleared out my personal account?'

'Ana, you know that the way we live doesn't come cheap.'

'Yes, I do. But it certainly didn't cost us half a million pounds within the last six months so don't try telling me that it did.'

'Okay, okay. I did withdraw some money from it for business reasons. But only as a temporary measure. The hotel in Kenya hasn't being doing so well lately, you know that. And we've had that string of bad luck with the horses, between having to put down two of our best and not having had a winner in so long. It's only a temporary situation. I will be putting the money back into the account. And anyway, I didn't know you still considered it *your* account. After all, we are married. You don't hear me going around saying that I've paid for this or that. It all balances out in the end, you know.'

'That's just it. It actually doesn't balance out – which is precisely what I've begun to realise lately. All our personal expenses, absolutely everything, comes out of my account.'

'That's not true at all.'

'Eamon, it is. I don't know how I never noticed before but I practically cover all our private expenses. And, if that's not enough, now you've started using my money for your business purposes. I mean, even if you'd asked me, we could have talked about it. I'd probably have ended up giving you the money anyway.'

'Of course. I knew that, that's why…'

'No, you didn't know that. You know, Eamon, the part that really gets to me is all your sneaking around behind my back. How could you put the house in Burnhill on the market without telling me? Wasn't it enough for you that I'd already sold all the houses in Dublin at your persuasion? And against my better judgement.' She paused, reminding herself to stay calm. 'So, if it is a temporary cash shortage then that presumably means you're expecting to resolve it in the near future. Might I ask when?'

'Well, it's like this. You know I've always said that you need to speculate to accumulate.'

'Yes?'

'Well, I'm going to need some more capital first.'

'Really?'

'Yes, that's the only reason I was scouting – just scouting mind – the market for the house in Burnhill. Obviously if you feel so strongly about not selling it then we won't. But I just thought that since we seem to be spending more and more of our time in Dublin it made sense to consider selling it. Anyway, there's no pressing need. I mean, your book is still making a surprising amount of money.'

'My book money? Are you suggesting that we use the book money to give your business a cash injection?'

'Why not? I know we're not exactly talking about a fortune but it would still help. And you can't go pumping money into that village forever. The idea was to make it autonomous, wasn't it? You're going to have to pull out some time, for the good of the village.'

'It's touching to see your concern.'

'I'm not denying I could use the book money, but I do also happen to think that you need to pull out.'

'I see. And I happen to disagree. But do you know something? I'm actually beginning to agree with you on one thing. I'm beginning to think that putting the house in Burnhill on the market is a good idea after all.'

'Really?'

'Yes.'

'I knew you'd come up trumps. That's my girl.' He leant over to kiss her but she turned away.

'With the money I make on it I should be able to buy a smaller house somewhere else and still have enough to live on,' she told him.

'What are you saying?'

'What I began trying to tell you half an hour ago. I'm leaving you.'

'But...'

'Now listen to me, Eamon, very carefully. Today I went to my solicitor and explained to him how you'd taken every single penny belonging to me and he suggested the obvious, that I take you to court and try to retrieve some or all of that money. Now, I could heed his advice and if I were sensible I probably would but the thought of spending the coming years in and out of court is not a prospect I find particularly appealing. And, even if I did win, I'd rate my chances of actually getting any money out of you as being very slim.

'So, as I see it, I have another option and that's to cut my losses and not waste the next five years of my life fighting you. I've already wasted enough time on you. Obviously the major disadvantage is that you get off scot-free. Now, most people would probably think me crazy but I really don't want to waste any more of my time on you. So Eamon, you've struck lucky but don't you even dare think of trying to get any money out of the sale of Burnhill.'

Saturday morning...

As she was pulling out her front door, Ana noticed Sophie sitting on the bench across from the Colonel's bungalow. She was slumped forward and had her head buried in her lap.

'Sophie,' asked Ana, going over to her, 'are you alright?'

The girl didn't answer and, from the manner in which her body was heaving up and down, together with the strange muffled sounds she was emitting, it was obvious that she couldn't, that she was crying too much and so Ana sat down on the bench beside her and gently began to stroke her hair. Gradually, Sophie grew calmer, then straightened up and wiped her eyes. She looked over at Ana and smiled weakly at her whilst feeling her pockets for a hankie, but in vain, so Ana took one from her handbag and passed it to her.

Sophie loudly blew her nose several times and then she was finally ready to talk but her words came tumbling out so quickly as to be almost incomprehensible.

'Mrs Dunne, I've just found out that the Colonel is dead. I came down on the bus for my piano lesson and I couldn't find him anywhere. He wasn't in his bungalow or in the gardens and then I heard those two women, Penny and Ellen, talking about what had happened to him. Mrs Dunne, nobody told me, I never knew he was dead. I can't believe it.'

She threw her head back down on her lap and started crying again.

'There, there,' said Ana, patting her gently on the back.

Her comforting gesture caused the young girl's strangled, hiccuped sobs to intensify but Ana continued stroking and, gradually, Sophie began to calm down. It occurred to Ana that the Colonel was possibly the first person Sophie was close to who had died. It was terrible that she'd found out this way and Ana was annoyed with herself for not having thought to let her know.

'I just can't believe I'll never see him again, Mrs Dunne,' said Sophie when she was composed enough to talk. 'I can't believe it.' And immediately she started crying again.

'Sophie, Sophie,' murmured Ana consolingly but Sophie continued crying. 'Come on,' said Ana, getting up. 'Come with me.'

Ana brought her over to her bungalow and into the living-room where she put her sitting on the couch. Then she went out to the kitchen and prepared some tea and sandwiches, came back with them and set them down on the table. As she poured Sophie a cup of tea and passed it to her, she saw that the young girl appeared to be a little calmer now.

'Sugar, Sophie?' she asked.

'No thanks, Mrs Dunne.'

'Milk?'

'Yes. Please.' Sophie held out her cup and Ana poured. 'That's plenty, thanks.'

Ana sat down. For a few minutes the only sound was the clink of cups on saucers for though she knew she should try to say some words of comfort, Ana was too much in need of comfort herself to feel quite up to the task.

'Mrs Dunne, is that your son?' Sophie asked politely after a while, looking at a photograph Ana had recently had framed and which now hung on the wall opposite.

'Yes, it is.'

'He's very handsome,' Sophie said after considering him for a few moments. 'He's a bit like Brad Pitt.'

'Who?'

'Brad Pitt, the actor?'

'That's funny. It used to be Robert Redford that people said he looked like.'

'Who?'

Ana smiled.

'Never mind,' she said. 'You've probably never heard of him. He's an actor as well.'

'Does your son live in Dublin, Mrs Dunne?'

'No, he ... well, he died shortly after that photograph was taken. A long time ago.'

'I am sorry.'

There was an awkward silence.

'Drink up your tea,' coaxed Ana.

'Oh Mrs Dunne, isn't life just so sad?' Sophie suddenly burst out. 'I mean, what's the point of it all? One day, the Colonel is here, teasing me and listening to me practise the piano and the next he's gone. And look at you; you lost your lovely son. How can you bear it, Mrs Dunne? It's all so unfair.'

'Ah now, now, Sophie,' said Ana, going over and sitting beside her.

'It's all just so sad. Having someone die must be the saddest thing in the world. One minute they're here and the next minute they're gone. It's just, it's just unbelievable.'

'Sophie, Sophie,' said Ana gently. 'Listen to me. As long as you remember them then they're never really gone.'

'Yes, they are.'

'Sophie, listen. When I was young, I was really close to an old woman, like you were to the Colonel. She's been dead over thirty years but I still think about her. If I'd never known her I'd be a different person than I am now. And the same with my husband Mark, and my son Pierce. Their deaths were the worst things that happened in my life but, if I had a choice, I'd pick having them and losing them over never having had them at all. And they're not gone, not as long as I still remember them.'

Suddenly, she got up and went to the bookcase, took down a book and handed it to Sophie.

'*A Year in a Kenyan Village* by Ana Harrison,' Sophie read, then looked up at Ana quizzically. 'Did you write this?'

'Yes, Harrison was my surname before I married my second husband.'

Sophie opened the book and began looking through the photographs.

'Why, these are beautiful! Did you take them? All of them?'

'Yes.'

'And did you really live in Kenya for a year?' When Ana nodded, she went on, 'What made you go there, Mrs Dunne?'

'That's where Pierce died. In a road traffic accident along with his best friend and his girlfriend. Afterwards, I just wanted to see what the country was like – Pierce really loved it, you see. And then, having nothing to come back to at the time, I ended up staying in this village for almost a year. But Sophie, do you see all those children?' She pointed at the photograph on the page on which the book lay open. In it, Kaninu, his father and a bunch of children were smiling and waving from Kaninu's over-crowded taxi, all set to embark on their trip to Mount Kenya. 'Well, if Pierce hadn't died, I wouldn't have met them, nor would I have had the opportunity to set up a school for them or to fund some of them through college. These children got an education because of me, because of Pierce dying. I guess what I'm trying to say is that everything is connected and that some good even came from Pierce's death.'

'I see what you mean, Mrs Dunne. But ... but ... but how can you bear the fact that he's dead?'

'Well, what I sometimes do,' said Ana, 'is that I pretend he's just on holidays. You don't really miss someone all the time when they're away, just now and then – when you think about them. But, because you believe that they're having a good time and you know they'll be back again, you're not really sad. Knowing that someone is not coming back is the hardest part to take when someone dies, so pretending that they're on holidays makes it easier.'

Sophie looked at Ana sceptically.

'And does it work?' she asked.

'Yes,' answered Ana.

Sophie's look told her that she wasn't convinced.

'Well, only sometimes,' Ana admitted with a smile. 'But look at the two of us sitting here – getting to know one another. If it wasn't for the Colonel then that would never have happened.'

'That's true.'

'Sophie, try to dwell on happy memories. Like, I'll always remember my husband Mark on the day of our wedding. I can still see how he looked, so incredibly young and so excited as I came up the aisle. And I can still remember what it felt like when Pierce was a little boy and he used to climb into our bed and cuddle up to me. So Sophie, don't dwell on the fact the Colonel is dead, just try and remember what he was like when he was alive.'

'I'll try.' But then she sighed heavily. 'Oh Mrs Dunne, you're so brave. The Colonel's death must be far worse for you, seeing as how you and he were going to get married.'

'Ah Sophie, that was all talk,' said Ana. 'The Colonel didn't really mean anything by all that nonsense.'

'Oh but he did, Mrs Dunne, he did. He was always talking about you. He really did want to marry you.'

Ana wasn't sure what to say, there seemed little point in trying to persuade Sophie otherwise and she decided that she might as well leave it go for now.

'But wasn't it funny how he became the Colonel?' Sophie went on.

'What do mean?' asked Ana, puzzled.

'Well, you know, when he wasn't a Colonel at all.'

'What?' asked Ana, but Sophie didn't hear her for she was noisily blowing her nose.

'It suited him though, didn't it?' she went on when she'd put the handkerchief away. 'Once he told me that his English colleagues at the station started calling him the Colonel on the very first day he started working there. And you can see why, can't you? He really did act and look exactly the way you'd imagine a Colonel would. Did you know that it was only when he came home to Ireland after retiring that he started calling himself the Colonel? He told me once how it all started; how he was so sick of being put on hold or being told to ring back tomorrow whenever he tried to sort something out over the phone that he began talking in a posh accent and started introducing himself as Colonel Jackson. He said it really worked too and that it was far more fun being Colonel Jackson than a retired policeman. You know, I think he just liked feeling that people thought he was important.'

'Sophie,' Ana began, wondering how exactly she should put this. 'You know that most of the people here really believe he was a Colonel and, well, you see, I think if they found out now that he wasn't then they'd be upset by the fact that he'd lied to them.'

'Yes, I see what you mean.'

'And,' Ana went on, choosing her words carefully, hoping that Sophie wouldn't be insulted, 'it probably would be better if you didn't say anything to your grandmother about the Colonel not being a Colonel.'

'As if I would? God, Granny would spread it around like wildfire. I'm only saying it to you because you already know, seeing as how you were his fiancée.'

'Well, not exactly.'

'No, but as good as.' Sophie blew her nose again. 'What time is the funeral, Mrs Dunne?' she asked.

'Monday, at twelve.'

'There's a bus back to Dublin soon, so I'd better get going,' said Sophie, getting up. 'Thanks for cheering me up a bit, and for the tea and sandwiches.'

After seeing Sophie out, Ana returned to the living-room, sat back down and poured herself another cup of tea. She tried to drink it calmly but suddenly she slammed the cup down on the saucer. Dead and all as the

Colonel was, or whatever she should call him now, she felt really mad at him. She looked around for something to kick but then thought better of it. There was no point in doing herself an injury. She wasn't the one she was mad with. It shouldn't matter that he'd lied, she told herself, but it did. She hated the idea that she'd been fooled along with everyone else; that he'd made as big an eejet out of her as he had out of everyone. Of course she'd always suspected him of embellishing his stories but there was a difference between that and being a complete pretender. In all the time she'd known him he probably hadn't uttered a word of truth to her. If he'd lied about being a Colonel then it was highly likely that he'd lied about everything else – all that stupid nonsense about his wealthy family, and his plans for the golf-course, and knowing the President – everything. Not that it should matter, but it did. He'd treated her just like he had everyone else, lying to her and probably laughing at her gullibility behind her back. And she'd thought that they were friends.

Suddenly there was a loud knocking on the door and when Ana went to open it she found a furious-looking Elizabeth standing there and, before she'd even a chance to say hello, Elizabeth launched her attack.

'Sophie said you had her here for tea?' she

said accusingly.

'Yes,' answered Ana. 'I did. So?'

'Will you stop at nothing, Ana Dunne?' Elizabeth demanded, her face bright red with anger. 'Is there no limit to how low you'll go?'

'What are you talking about, Elizabeth?'

'Can't you just leave people alone? First you take the Colonel and now you're trying to take my own grandchild away, my only granddaughter. You're a pathetic old woman trying to inveigle your way into other people's affection just because you've no one of your own.'

'Elizabeth, calm down.'

'How ... how ... how dare you tell me to calm down?' Elizabeth stammered in fury.

'And how dare you come barging in here, making these stupid accusations. Elizabeth, I'm not taking anyone from you. You can't take people.'

'Well, you're making a good job of trying! Enticing her over here when she should have been with me! I wouldn't have known a bit about it only that I happened to meet her on her way out.'

'Elizabeth, she was upset about the Colonel, she needed some attention.'

'And naturally you were the one for her to come to and not her own grandmother. You should have sent her over to me. You're nothing but a lonely old woman, Ana

Dunne, and I'll thank you to stay well clear of my granddaughter in the future.'

Ana had enough. She took Elizabeth by the arm and began turning her around.

'I beg your pardon! Ana Dunne! Let go of me! What are you doing? Take your hands off me at once!'

None too gently, Ana propelled Elizabeth down the steps.

'You can't manhandle me like this. I'll ... I'll report you to Mrs Reynolds.'

'You do that.'

Ana banged the door and for five minutes she leaned against it, breathing heavily. Then, realising that she just couldn't stay cooped up inside, that she had to get out, she decided that she'd go and walk off some of her anger. The coast should be clear by now she reckoned.

As soon as she stepped outside she noticed Ellen's friend Jack sitting on Ellen's doorstep. She'd thought she'd seen him around earlier in the morning and had half-noticed him when she'd been removing Elizabeth from the premises, so to speak. She wondered now what he must think of such carry-on.

As she passed him by she nodded to him and, immediately, he got to his feet and hurried over to her.

'Excuse me, excuse me, Ma'am, you might remember me. I met you yesterday when you were with Ellen. I'm Jack Duffy. Ellen's boyfriend.'

'Yes, yes, of course I do,' answered Ana, smirking at this unlikely description. She wondered how Ellen would feel about it.

'I'm sorry to be bothering you and I wouldn't only I don't know what else to do. You see, I want to ask you for a bit of help.'

'Well, I don't kn–'

'You see, I came over early this morning to try and talk to Ellen but she won't let me. She refuses to even come out of the house, she's been stuck inside there the whole day. And all I want to do is to try and explain things to her. I know she has a right to be mad at me but she took me up all wrong yesterday – thinking that I only wanted to marry her so that she'd come and look after Francis and myself. Sure, that's just nonsense. She should know that in our house it was always the men who looked after the women – well, the one woman, the mother – she saw to that. But if Ellen were to come and live with us she wouldn't have to do a tap, she'd have the life of Riley with me and Francis waiting on her hand and foot, especially after the hip operation and she'll need someone then. And the other thing she should know is that I'm not in cahoots with her brother. Doesn't she know I've no time for him? The way he packed her off to live with strangers when she'd every right to go on living at home. That was just terrible. And it doesn't matter how much he's paying or how fancy this place is, she shouldn't have been shipped off like that. But once the brother's wife said she had to go, well then that was it, she had to go. And Ellen should–'

'Jack, Jack,' interrupted Ana. 'Shouldn't you be telling Ellen all this, not me?'

'Sorry, sorry. I just got carried away. Since I left here I've done nothing but think about Ellen and what I should do and it's all been sort of boiling up inside me so it just sort of came gushing out, if you know what I mean. What I really wanted to ask you was would you mind giving Ellen this letter from me? It explains things better than I might say them myself. Things always seem to come out arse-ways when I'm talking to her.'

'Yes, of course I will.'

'Will you make sure that she reads it and doesn't just throw it away?'

'I'll do my best.'

He held it out to her but, as she reached for it, he suddenly changed his mind and withdrew it.

'I'm not much of a hand at writing. Maybe I should read it out to you first so that you can tell me what you think?'

'I don't think so, Jack. Letters of that kind are private affairs really.'

'Sure I'll give it a go.' He coughed, then

coloured slightly. 'I suppose it's more of a poem really,' he confessed. He gave a quick glance up at Ellen's front window and, following his look, Ana saw a silhouette behind the net curtain and suddenly realised that Jack was far cleverer than she had given him credit for. All he was saying was for the benefit of Ellen and she, Ana, was just the excuse.

And then he began:

'Ellen, do you remember the day you started school?
I do.
Your mother says to me, take her along with you now, Jack,
And mind her, for she's only a scrap of a thing.
And I did, I minded you, didn't I?

And then your first dance. Do you remember it, Ellen?
I do.
And your mother says to me, watch out for her now, Jack,
For fear she'd go off with a yolk from the town.
And I did, I watched out for you, didn't I?

But then, Ellen, somewhere along the line I forgot what my job was,
To mind you. To watch out for you.
For you didn't seem to need much minding,
Or watching.
Not when you were there so close, weren't you?

And Ellen, did we ever expect to grow old?
That time would pass this quickly,
How could we have foretold?
And now we're both old crocks, who the passing of time mocks
Too old for love, or are we?

Ellen, when I look at your face,
I can see yours and my
Spring, summer, autumn and maybe winter.
Please, Ellen, I know I've left it late.
But please don't say too late.'

When he'd finished, he looked over a little bashfully at Ana.

'It isn't up to much, I know. It's the first poem I've ever written but Ellen always liked poems and all that sort of stuff so I thought I'd give it a go. And my brother Francis gave me a hand with the rhymes though we couldn't find any for some of the lines. Do you hear that? Lines and rhymes. What do you know? I must be getting better at this lark.'

Suddenly Ellen appeared at her door.

'What do you think you're playing at, Jack Duffy? Making a complete fool of me you are!' she shouted at him crossly.

'Oh Ellen, I'm sorry. I didn't know you were listening.'

'I wasn't listening. I just couldn't avoid

overhearing. The whole place probably heard you. And anyway it's limes, not lines.'

'What?'

'Limes rhymes with rhymes, not lines.'

'But did you like the poem, Ellen?'

'Well, as these things go it wasn't too bad, I suppose. But whatever has you out here, bawling it out like that is beyond me. Trying to mortify me you are.'

'Ah Ellen, I wasn't trying to mortify you. I'm only out here because you wouldn't let me inside to say what I had to say. Haven't we wasted enough time now without wasting any more? We're getting older by the minute and I know we did a fair share of kissing but we've hardly ever even–'

Ellen cut him off.

'Come on, inside,' she ordered, 'before you tell the world the rest of our business though there's precious little left to tell.'

'Answer me first, will you marry me, Ellen?'

'Yes, I'll bloody well marry you. Now come on, inside with you.'

1997

CHAPTER 11

Chaos often breeds life, when order breeds habit...

from *The Education of Henry Adams* by Henry Brooks Adams

The rain lashed against the window then came flowing down in rivulets, distorting the shapes of the world outside. Ana could just make out the motion of the waves bashing against the rocks far, far below at the bottom of the cliff – a sudden burst of white hitting off the greys. Something yellow flew past close to the window, a broken umbrella she guessed, being carried in a great gust of wind.

She took another sip of coffee, then turned to the others.

'I've decided to move back to Ireland,' she announced.

'You've what?' demanded Mavis, setting her cup back down in its saucer and staring at her friend, absolutely astonished.

'What?' chorused Win and Netta.

'I said, I've decided to move back to Ireland,' Ana repeated.

'Ana, are you crazy?' demanded Mavis.

'What are you talking about?'

'What ... what will we do without you?' asked Netta.

'You won't know anyone there, Ana!' cried Win. 'Aren't they all dead by now?'

For the last five years, hardly a week had gone by that the four women hadn't met for morning coffee in this hotel lounge. Every Friday morning, regardless of the weather, they'd cosily ensconced themselves in the large, overstuffed armchairs circled around the open fire and then they'd spend the hours chatting. Ana considered herself fortunate to have met Mavis, Netta and Win when she'd first moved to Brighton and together they'd made up a golfing and bridge foursome. They'd gone for walks, went shopping – they'd done almost everything together. And now, here she was, dropping this bombshell and disrupting their cosy companionship.

'But Ana, your friends are here.' said Win. 'We're your friends. Haven't you lived in England longer than you did in Ireland?'

'Yes. Yes, I have,' snapped Ana crossly, annoyed to know that they were all making sense.

'And didn't you try it for a while when you were married to that horsy fellow?' persisted Win.

'Well, not really, not properly. We were over and back all the time.'

‘If you ask me,’ said Netta, ‘I’ve never heard of anything so ridiculous in my life.’

Ana knew that Netta was right. To go on living in Brighton was the obvious thing, the sensible thing to do. Going back home to Ireland made no sense whatsoever. Even saying that she was going ‘back home to Ireland’ was an absurdity, for really Brighton, England, was her home now. This was where she belonged, here with her good friends, Win, Mavis and Netta. Apart from her rather flamboyant dress sense there was little to distinguish her from her friends, all of them nice, middleclass women on their own, enjoying their latter years in the pleasant seaside town. Her accent had changed over the years and the only time she now sounded unmistakably Irish was when she met someone from home and then her words came out at twice their usual speed and the ‘Dublin’ broke through in every sentence. Though her friends considered her one of them, her Irishness set her apart in her own head, if not in theirs. Only occasionally was that difference jarringly obvious: when they included Ireland in their definition of the United Kingdom and she felt compelled to correct them or when she felt obliged to explain that few Irish condoned the latest bombing atrocity; or sometimes, when she used a colloquial expression – when she told them that she thought so-and-so was an eejet for example, only to see her friends looking at her uncomprehendingly.

But she wasn't English and, however irrational, she was feeling increasingly lonesome for a home she'd left years ago. Against all better judgement, her desire to go back to Ireland was as compelling and instinctive as that which tells a bird it's time to fly south for the winter.

And besides, although life in Brighton was certainly congenial she sometimes found it stifling. It scared her to think that the rest of her future would be spent in exactly the same way, in the same town, with the four of them having variations of their same few conversations and doing the same things day after day after day. A running joke amongst them was that when one of them died the others were going to have to hold interviews to find a suitable replacement. But Ana found the joke unsettlingly close to the bone.

'And, if it doesn't work out?' demanded Netta.

'I can always come back.'

'And who's going to take your place at bridge?' asked Win. 'And at golf?'

'I'm sure you'll find someone.'

'We'll have to hold interviews,' joked Netta.

'Ridiculous,' muttered Mavis. 'Absolutely ridiculous.'

Monday Morning...

As she sat there waiting, she asked herself for the umpteenth time why she hadn't just stuck with Bobbyjo. God, she'd really made a mess of Aintree.

'I'll give you £250 for the lot, Mrs Dunne,' said the jeweller, finally looking up. 'I can't do any better than that.'

Ana stared at him. She was certain she must have misheard him.

'Pardon?' she asked after a couple of moments.

'£250, and that's the best I can do, Mrs Dunne.'

'£250?'

'Yes.'

Ana turned her gaze from him and looked down at Celia's jewellery spread out on the desk between them.

'£250,' she muttered to herself. Reaching out, she picked up the large ruby brooch and fingered it for a few moments as she struggled to compose herself. 'This brooch alone is worth thousands, Mr Carey,' she said eventually, as calmly as she could. 'I've had this jewellery valued before so I know what I'm talking about. I'm telling you, altogether it's worth over £15,000 at least.'

'Mrs Dunne, I'm afraid...'

But she wasn't finished.

'*At least*, Mr Carey,' she repeated. 'I was

surprised to find out that it was worth so much that last time I had it valued because as a child I used to play with it as carelessly as if was just costume jewellery, as if it was all just worthless trinkets. And now you've the cheek to tell me that you'll give me £250. Mr Carey, you must think I'm a complete fool.'

'Mrs Dunne–'

'Offering me £250! I mean, really!'

'Mrs Dunne–'

'You have some nerve!'

'Mrs Dunne, please, let me speak. Look, I'm not sure who valued it for you that time but all I can tell you now is that the jewellery lying on the desk before us is relatively worthless – every single piece. Any jeweller will tell you the same thing.' He picked up one of the rings. 'Look – that's just gold plating. And see here – coloured glass, it's just coloured glass. And it's the same story with every piece.'

'It can't be. I'm telling you that when I got it valued before I was told that it was worth £15,000 and that was by a very reputable jeweller in London.'

Mr Carey sat back in his seat, sighed, then took off his glasses.

'Well, Mrs Dunne, if that really is the case then you need to consider if there is anyone you can think of who was in a position to get copies made of the originals – someone close to you, someone who might have had money problems.'

'What?'

'Mrs Dunne, it wouldn't be the first time a husband found the solution to his financial difficulties in his wife's jewellery box or, equally so, some other member of the family. Or perhaps a close friend might have been tempted. In fact, I came across just such a situation myself before though it was a long time ago. Do you understand what I'm trying to say to you, Mrs Dunne?'

'Yes,' she said quietly.

Eamon – it was him, there wasn't a doubt in her mind. The low-down, filthy, dirty, rotten scumbag. For a few moments she sat there motionless, too shocked to move, the colour completely drained from her face. It struck her that although she'd never anticipated ever actually selling it until this morning, Celia's jewellery had always been her safety-net and, though she'd worried a lot of late about where she was going to find the money for this or that, in particular for the service charges, she'd known that if all else failed there was always the jewellery to fall back on. Knowing that had made it easier for her to take the risks she did, like betting on the Grand National last week and on Aintree the day before and, although she hadn't expected to lose on either occasion, at least she'd known that she'd still have the security of Celia's jewellery if she did. Or so she'd thought. But she'd lost the bet and the last of her money on Aintree and now it seemed that this jewellery, her little nest-egg, was worthless. It was utterly worthless and she was utterly penniless.

'Mrs Dunne, are you alright?'

'Yes, yes, fine, Mr Carey.' She got up from the seat and hurriedly collected up the pieces of jewellery and put them back into her handbag. 'I'm very sorry for wasting your time but thank you very much for seeing me at such short notice.'

'Not at all, Mrs Dunne, and I'm sorry that it's been a disappointment to you.' He helped her on with her coat. 'Let me see you out.'

Although she'd over an hour to wait she went directly to the bus stop. It was the easiest thing to do since she hadn't the composure to do or to go anywhere else. There she sat down on a seat in the shelter but within seconds she was on her feet again and pacing up and down the footpath. The thought of Eamon ripping her off like that, knowing that he'd already taken almost everything else, had her raging and she only wished that he was still alive so that she could go and kill him herself right this minute. What an absolute bastard! She suddenly remembered the last time they'd met – a couple of months before he'd died –

and she recalled now how he'd been full of jokes and compliments – as charming as ever, so much so, that she'd even wondered (just for a split-second) if she'd been too hasty in leaving him. She remembered him asking her how she was getting on and even remembered him saying that he hoped things were going well for her. The two-faced hypocrite!

But what a fix she was in now. Why, oh why hadn't she just stuck with Bobbyjo? What had made her change her choice of horses at the very last minute? And anyway, how could she have been so stupid as to be convinced that she, of all people, would be lucky? It should, she thought, be obvious to her at this stage of her life that luck was not something she was blessed with.

The bus finally came and she made her way on, then down the aisle and sat in the one free window seat available. Immediately the bus started up and as it travelled the twenty-mile journey back to Rathdowne, she stared fixedly out of the window but saw nothing. She'd rarely felt so low. Days didn't come much worse than this – stony-broke and on her way back to the poor old Colonel's funeral.

The funeral was held in Kilmurray church, said by some to be the smallest church in Leinster. Which was just as well, thought Ana, looking around at the very modest crowd about her as they came filing out. Besides the staff and residents of Rathdowne, there were very few others present. Sophie was there, of course. And Jack Duffy – standing proudly alongside Ellen in his new role as supportive fiancé. Laurence wasn't there – he was in the hospital, still unconscious though it seemed the doctors were optimistic that he'd make a full recovery. Throughout the mass, Ana had cringed each time she heard the priest refer to the Colonel as Mister Jackson and wondered what Elizabeth and the others had made of it. But at least the ceremony had been short and it was obvious from the priest's eulogy that he'd barely known the Colonel. He'd stuck to a stock of platitudes and the congregation were safe from having their heartstrings tugged any more than they already were. Although poor Sophie had cried the whole way through the ceremony.

And was still crying, Ana saw now, noticing her up ahead. She was shuffling along with her head bent low – the single young person amidst all the old people soberly making their way to the adjacent graveyard. Thinking that Sophie could do with her grandmother right now, Ana looked around and spotted her at the front of the little crowd, busily gaping about and she tried to catch her attention but Elizabeth was too preoccupied to notice.

Her eyes were scanning the crowd and her lips appeared to be moving and it seemed to Ana that she was counting the number of people present – which wouldn't really surprise her. Knowing that Elizabeth would be annoyed at her for muscling in on her territory but deciding to hell with her – for if Elizabeth wasn't going to give Sophie the comfort she evidently needed, then she would – she stood in beside the young girl as the crowd gathered around the open grave.

'How are you getting on?' she asked Sophie.

Sophie sniffed.

'I'm okay, Mrs Dunne.'

Having spotted Ana talking to her granddaughter and no doubt anxious to prevent any further contact, Elizabeth immediately came hurrying over and pushed her way in between the two of them.

'Have you enough room there, Elizabeth?' Ana asked as she found herself being roughly shoved aside.

Elizabeth didn't deign to answer for she was still put out with Ana.

'The poor, poor fellow,' she muttered after a few moments, shaking her head sadly. 'He'll be sorely missed, won't he, Sophie?'

Glum-faced and staring down at the ground, Sophie barely nodded.

'God, isn't the drink a terrible thing?' Elizabeth went on. 'A terrible, terrible thing.'

Sophie looked at her crossly.

'Granny, don't going around saying that,' she snapped. 'You know it wasn't the drink.'

'Of course, of course. Alzheimer's, that's what we're saying was the cause of the accident, isn't it?'

'Only because it most likely was.'

'Of course,' agreed Elizabeth, though the look on her face made it clear that she was only humouring the child. 'What I'd like to know,' she said, changing the subject, 'is where they got that priest. Wasn't he only dreadful? Why, he could have been talking about anyone. And did you hear him calling him Mister Jackson? I mean, really! If he wasn't a priest, I'd give him a piece of my mind.' She paused and looked about her as people continued to collect around the grave. 'You'd have expected more here,' she remarked. 'Apart from ourselves there's hardly a sinner.'

'Did you count them?' asked Ana.

'Of course I didn't count them,' snapped Elizabeth. 'But seeing as how he was such an important man, I'd have expected the crowd to be bigger. And there's no sign of any of his family.'

'Gran, if you don't have anything nice to say about the Colonel, why say anything at all? Why did you bother coming to his funeral if you're just going to be so horrible about him?'

'I – I beg you pardon,' stuttered Elizabeth.

'Beg away, as the Colonel might have said.'

'For goodness sake, Sophie, all I said was that I thought the crowd would be bigger. The way the Colonel used to go on I'd have expected all sorts of important people to be here.' Then she noticed that neither Ana nor Sophie was paying her any attention but that they were both staring over her shoulder. 'What are you two gawking at?' she asked crossly, turning around herself to have a look.

'Hush,' they both urged her as they stared at the black limousine which was pulling up outside the graveyard wall.

'Oh my goodness,' Elizabeth now whispered in awe, for this limousine was no clapped-out, twenty-year-old affair hired from the local undertakers. No, this was the real McCoy. 'Whoever could that be?'

Every single person in the graveyard stood in silence watching, waiting to see who'd get out. Then, from the front, stepped a youngish man, dressed in a suit.

'Who's that, Sophie?' demanded Elizabeth. 'I can't see. I don't have my glasses with me.'

'Nobody.'

'What do you mean, nobody? Tell me, who is it?'

'Nobody you'd know, Granny,' Sophie answered crossly.

A second man stepped out.
'Who's that then?'
'Nobody.'
A third man stepped out.
'And what about him?'
'Nobody either.'
'A limousine full of nobodies, I'm not missing much, am I?' But then, seeing a woman step out, she remarked, 'And I suppose she's nobody either.'
Sophie let out a gasp.
'Sophie, Sophie, who is it?' demanded Elizabeth. But Sophie didn't answer for she was far too engrossed. 'Who is it, Sophie? I can't see without my glasses. Sophie? Answer me.'
'It's the President, Granny.'
The priest, having managed to overcome his initial shock, was now making his way over to the newcomers.
'What president?' demanded Elizabeth.
'Sssh Granny, I want to hear what they're saying.'
'What president?'
'The President of Ireland of course. Where did you think? America?'
Everyone watched. The President appeared to be apologising for being late but the priest was waving his hands about in protest, obviously dismissing her apology as being unnecessary.
'Not at all,' Ana heard him say. 'If only I'd

known, we would have delayed the proceedings.'

Then, together, they came walking over towards the crowd.

'Would the President like to say a few words?' the priest asked as they came to a stop.

'I really came down here in a private capacity, Father,' said the President. 'But if it would be alright with you, then yes, I'd like to very much.'

'It would be an honour, Madam President.'

The President stepped forward, looked around at the crowd, then nodded at those who caught her eye, cleared her throat and began,

'As many of you will probably know, even before Gilbert retired and came back to live in Ireland hardly a summer went by without him spending some time in Wicklow and it was my good fortune to meet him many years ago when I too was here on holiday and my even better fortune to have remained friends with him ever since. And what can I say about him here today, on this saddest of occasions?' She paused for a second, visibly upset, obviously needing time to compose herself. 'Well, you don't need me to tell you,' she went on eventually though her voice was shaky, 'that he was a kind, caring man, full of life and always fun to be with. But perhaps I might tell you one story to show what he meant to me. When I decided to run for president most people thought I was crazy and told me so, told me that I hadn't a chance – even some of the people closest to me. But, when I told Gilbert, immediately he asked me to keep a seat for him at my inauguration. Not for one second did it cross his mind that I might lose. That's the kind he was, always his friend's number one champion. I just wish now that I'd told him how dear he was to me when he was alive.' She bent her head, closed her eyes for a second, holding back her tears. Then she breathed deeply before going on. 'So goodbye, Gilbert,' she said quietly, almost inaudibly. 'Goodbye, my very dear friend Gilbert.'

The priest thanked her for her kind words and the President stepped back into the body of the small crowd, in beside Sophie.

As the priest began to read the burial rites, Ana tried to concentrate but she was finding Elizabeth's carry-on too much of a distraction. Though she was trying to be discreet, Ana noticed her easing her way behind Sophie's back to get to where she wanted to be – right beside the President.

'Excuse me your – Lady – Madam President,' she said once the priest had finished. 'On behalf of Gilbert, I'd like to thank you for coming. I'm sure it would have made his day, if he were alive to see it, if you know what I mean.'

'Thank you,' said the President.

'He often talked about you, Madam President.'

'That is nice to hear,' the President answered. Then she looked over at Sophie. 'Tell me, are you one of his grandnieces?'

'No, no, Madam President,' answered Elizabeth. 'She's my granddaughter. Sophie's her name. The Colonel was very fond of her on account of how she's my grandchild. You see the Colonel and I were, well, we were...'

Suddenly the President laughed.

'So he was still carrying on with that nonsense? Still calling himself the Colonel?'

'...very close.' Then the President's words hit Elizabeth. 'Pardon?' she asked.

But the President didn't hear her.

'So, none of his family are here then,' she remarked, looking around.

'No, no, I didn't see any of them,' answered Elizabeth.

Ana could see the conflict in Elizabeth's face. She was in a Catch 22 situation. If she asked all the questions she so clearly wanted to then it would be obvious to the President that she wasn't quite so close to the Colonel as she'd let on.

'So you know the Col – er – Gilbert's family well then, Madam President?' she asked, not being able to resist fishing just a little.

'Yes, though I can't say I've ever had much time for them.'

'No, no,' murmured Elizabeth in concurrence. 'Me neither.'

'A pompous shower, every last one of them. Even those half-brothers he admired so much. As for his father, well, he was the worst of the lot of them when he was alive.'

'Oh, by far.' Elizabeth nodded knowingly.

'No, Gilbert was far better off without them, even if he didn't think so himself.'

'Oh, far better.'

'I could never understand why he was so anxious to be considered one of them. I mean, those schemes he was always coming up with – the golf course, the polo pitch, the model village, all of them – I don't know how he ever thought he'd get his father interested in them. I'm not saying that they were bad schemes – on the contrary some of them had real merit – but the old man only thought he was trying to wrangle money out of him. He could never see that Gilbert just wanted the two of them to be involved in something together, that Gilbert wanted to make him proud and to acknowledge him as his son. Fools, the lot of them,' she finished angrily.

'Fools,' agreed Elizabeth.

'For all their money and connections.'

'Yes. Indeed. For all that.'

'But it's the classic situation, isn't it? The

illegitimate son growing up unrecognised in the shadow of his wealthy family.'

'Classic,' agreed Elizabeth. She waited for the President to go on but she seemed to be finished for the moment. 'And, Mrs President,' she finally asked, 'would ... would that be tied in with ... with ... that Colonel nonsense, do you think?'

'Yes, maybe. You know I never thought of it that way before but you may have something there. A lot of the O'Brien-Smiths were quite high up in the British army. Yes, that might explain why he went about ridiculously calling himself the Colonel after he came back here to live.'

Ana saw by the look on Elizabeth's face that she recognised the name, as she did herself – the O'Brien-Smiths owned half of County Wicklow.

'Well, ladies, it was nice meeting you.'

'And you, Madam President. Goodbye now,' said Elizabeth and, just for a second, Ana thought she was going to curtsey but instead she settled for grabbing the President's hand and giving it a very hearty handshake.

Ana, Sophie and Elizabeth, together with the rest of the crowd, watched as the President got back into the car.

'Ana, Sophie,' said Elizabeth, turning around as soon as the limo had departed, 'I really don't think there's any need to repeat what the President has just told us. You know, about the Colonel not being a Colonel. I don't see any reason why the other residents should find out.'

'No, no, of course not,' answered Ana, finding it hard to keep a straight face, such was her surprise at Elizabeth's unexpected discretion.

Although Elizabeth's words convinced Ana that she wouldn't spread the Colonel's secret around, Sophie remained far more sceptical.

'Why do you think she was so anxious to go in Mrs Reynolds' car?' she asked Ana as they walked along the road together. 'I bet it was so that she could tell her everything she's just heard.'

While the older and frailer residents were being driven back to Rathdowne by the staff, Ana and Sophie and the others were walking the half-mile. Well, one not-so-frail-nor-old resident, namely Elizabeth, had managed to wrangle a lift with Mrs Reynolds and, as Ana had watched Elizabeth nearly knock Old Mary to the ground in her haste to get into the passenger seat, it had occurred to her that Elizabeth's curiosity must be great indeed given that she was prepared to temporarily relax her vigilant watch against Ana's attempts to get her claws into her granddaughter.

‘I imagine Mrs Reynolds already has an idea about the Colonel,’ she said to Sophie now. ‘I’d say Elizabeth just wants to ferret around, to see if she can find out any more.’

Sophie shook her head.

‘No, I bet Granny is just blabbing away, telling Mrs Reynolds everything she’s just heard,’ said Sophie. ‘I know what she’s like.’

‘Sophie, don’t you think you’re being a little bit hard on her?’

‘No, Mrs Dunne, you just don’t know her as well as I do.’ Then she sighed. ‘You know, Mrs Dunne, I wish you were my grandmother. I know it’s a terrible thing to say, but I do.’

‘Ah Sophie, you don’t really mean that.’

‘I do. Granny never has any time for me. She can’t stand me. It’s only the boys and my father she’s interested in. She just dotes on them and never sees any wrong in anything they do. And it was the same with my grandfather when he was alive and he was a horrible man. He was awful to everyone, including her, but she always stood up for him.’

Suddenly Ana remembered that letter Elizabeth had written in response to the Colonel’s advertisement and the negative comments about her husband it had contained and, just for a second, she thought of telling Sophie about it but she decided not to. After all, it was Elizabeth’s private affair, Ana shouldn't even know about it herself.

'Sophie,' she said instead. 'I don't think that your grandmother is a very happy person. And sometimes, when someone isn't happy it can make them ... well ... a little unpleasant. Maybe you should take time to try and get to know her a bit better. You know, sometimes it can be lonesome when you're old. Why don't you think about coming down on your own some day, without your mother and father, just to spend some time with her?'

'Oh I don't know.'

'Sophie, there's no point in regretting that you didn't make the effort when it's too late.'

Sophie shrugged.

'Anyway,' said Ana, 'it must be nearly time for your bus.'

'Yes,' said Sophie, looking down at her watch. 'In five minutes. Mrs Dunne, I know you're right but if I did come down to see her, could I call in to you as well?'

'What? Do you want me to get knifed in my bed by Elizabeth?' joked Ana, but then added, 'Sophie, you don't even have to ask.'

'Would you mind?'

'Would I mind? Of course I wouldn't. I'd be delighted.'

'Obviously I'm not the only one who's feeling down and in need of some company then,' said Ana as she came through the French windows and into the sunroom some hours later. Settling down on the couch beside Ellen, she found her place in the book she was reading but then rested it page-down on her lap. 'The place seems so much quieter without him, doesn't it?' she remarked. 'It's going to be so strange not having him around any more. You know, I keep expecting...' But then she broke off, now noticing the hostile stares directed at her from Penny, Elizabeth and Ellen.

'What?' she asked, looking from one to the other. 'Why are you all looking at me like that? What is it?'

Silence reigned as all three stared at her accusingly.

'What?' Ana asked again. 'What did I do?'

Penny left out a derisory snort. 'You tell us,' she demanded.

'Yes,' echoed Ellen. 'You tell us.'

'Tell you what?' asked Ana. None of the three obliged her with an answer but all eyes remained steadfastly upon her; they didn't appear to be even blinking. She sighed. 'This is about my bungalow, isn't it?' she asked finally. 'Obviously Mrs Reynolds has been busy spreading the news. God, she certainly didn't lose much time – it can hardly have been an hour since I told her.'

'Wasn't it just as well she did tell us?' asked Penny.

'Yes,' agreed Elizabeth. 'If it was up to you I don't suppose we'd have known a thing until the removals van pulled up outside your door.'

'That's not fair,' Ana protested. 'I was going to tell you.'

Penny snorted again. 'Sure you were.'

'Of course I was. I only made the decision today and with the Colonel's funeral going on it was hardly the right time and anyway, there just wasn't an opportunity to tell you. Besides, I won't be going for ages yet, who knows how long it will take to sell it.'

'Did you not settle here, Ana, is that it?' asked Ellen. 'Did you not like it?'

'Of course I did. If I had my choice I wouldn't be going at all. But I have to leave.'

'But why do you have to leave?' asked Penny.

'Because I'm a stupid old woman without an iota of sense, one who's been foolish with her money and now finds she can't afford to go on living here. Alright?'

There was an embarrassed silence.

'I see,' said Penny, after a while.

'That's just awful,' said Ellen.

'God, there'll be nobody left here soon,' said Penny. 'First the poor Colonel. Now you, Ana. And it's only a matter of time before Ellen deserts me for her old Romeo. Soon, Elizabeth, it will be just yourself and myself.'

'Well, actually I...'

'What? What? Ah Elizabeth, don't tell me you're thinking of leaving as well?'

'Not exactly. It's just that Harry ... well ... it's just that Harry thinks that maybe I should give it some consideration.'

'But why, Elizabeth?'

'He's worried for me. He's concerned that this place isn't run as well as it should be and even more so since the Colonel's death. He feels that staff negligence may have been a contributory factor, that someone should have picked up on the fact that the Colonel was an alcoholic...'

'Elizabeth,' interrupted Ana, 'you know that wasn't the case.'

'...was an alcoholic or had Alzheimer's disease, whatever, and that something should have been done for him.'

'Elizabeth,' protested Penny, 'none of us realised that there was anything the matter with him until it was too late and we were a lot closer to him.'

'Yes but we're not health professionals. As Harry says, you have to only look at the quality of the nursing staff to be concerned. I mean, take Nurse Boo for example. Given how much we pay out each month it's an insult to have the likes of him looking after us but then, Zanzibar Holdings can probably get away with paying him next to nothing. And if...'

'Excuse me–' interrupted Ana.

'Yes, yes, I know. He's a great friend of yours. You won't hear a word said against him. But, as I was about to say, if Zanzibar Holdings are facing financial difficulties then the standard of services is just going to deteriorate further. And what if they were to pull out altogether? It could happen you know, then where would we be?'

'Elizabeth, it's only natural that Harry should be concerned,' acknowledged Penny. 'but…'

But Elizabeth cut her off.

'And if Zanzibar run into serious financial problems and it becomes public knowledge, then it will be impossible to sell any of the bungalows here, nobody will want them.'

'And what will we care about selling them when we're six foot under?' demanded Penny.

'Yes, but what about the families we all leave behind?' asked Elizabeth. 'They'd lose out.'

'So what, Elizabeth?' asked Ana. 'Doesn't your son Harry already have a house, a mansion from all accounts? It sounds like he's got so much money that it couldn't possibly matter to him what your bungalow is worth. Anyway, surely the important thing is that you're happy with where you're living?'

'Since you've never had children, Ana, you can hardly be expected to understand how a mother feels – that no matter how old your children are, you still want to do the best for them.'

'Actually Elizabeth...' began Ana but then changed her mind.

'But where would you live if you sold your bungalow, Elizabeth?' asked Penny.

'Well, with Harry I expect.'

'You expect? Has he not said so?' demanded Penny.

'Well, not in so many words but then he hardly needs to. He wouldn't be urging me to sell if he didn't want me to move in with him.'

'But Harry can't make you sell, can he?'

'You're making it sound like he's forcing me to.'

'I don't mean to, I'm just asking.'

'As it happens he could stop paying the service charges, I suppose. I own the bungalow but he pays those. But that's not the issue.'

'Well, if you own it–'

'Penny, will you just shut up?' shouted Elizabeth, losing her temper. 'Why are you hassling me like this? What you don't seem to understand is that I actually want to go and live with Harry and Janet and besides, I don't want to upset them by refusing to sell if that's what they want. I don't want to fall out with them. If I do, then who would I have?'

'But–' began Penny.

'And what you really don't understand is that I hate living on my own. I hate it. The silence, the way the hours stretch out in front of you in the evening so that there's nothing to do but to take yourself off to bed early. I ... I ... I just *hate* it. Understand?'

'Ah Elizabeth, it's not like you're short of company here,' said Ellen.

'It's not the same thing at all. It's all right for you, going off marrying Jack, you've no idea how much I envy you. I'm just not cut out for living on my own. You know,' she paused for a second before deciding to go on, 'for a while I really thought that maybe the Colonel and myself might ... might get together. Of course that was before you came along, Ana, and set your cap on him.'

'Elizabeth, I didn't set my cap on him, as you put it.'

'If you say so. Do you know,' she began, but she paused, debating as to whether or not she should continue, 'do you know that once I even replied to a personal ad in the newspaper? Now, it's not the kind of thing I normally do as you can imagine but this ad seemed, well, it seemed written especially for me. And I got a letter back too, a wonderful letter. Oh he sounded just lovely, a real gentleman. He told me that of all the responses he'd received mine was the one which appealed to him the most but that, unfortunately, his circumstances had changed and he'd been called out of retirement and had no choice but to go abroad for a while to work. He'd have liked very much to meet me, he said, but didn't think it fair to start a relationship under such uncertain conditions. I got the impression from his letter that the work he was going to be involved in was quite dangerous, something pretty secretive and at a fairly high level. You know, I often wonder how it would have turned out between us if we'd actually met. Who knows, maybe we'd have even ended up marrying. Maybe he was my soulmate. But I'll never know.'

'Ah poor Elizabeth,' said Ellen, reaching out and patting her hand.

'God,' said Penny, 'the last thing in the world I'd want is another husband. In all the time mine was around he hardly did a day's work. He left the running of the shop to me though he was happy to take the credit and to waste away the profits until I threw him out. To this day I ask myself why I ever married him.'

'I often ask myself the same question with regard to Roddie,' said Elizabeth but then her jaw dropped. She looked as if she could hardly believe what she'd just said. 'Do you know, that's the first time I've ever said that to anyone? I must be feeling a bit emotional after poor Gilbert's death. But I've said it now and it's true. Roddie was an awfully mean man. He expected everything and gave nothing. He'd no spirit in him at all. That's the truth. But you know, I suppose I got used to having him around and I have to admit that I'd prefer to have someone than nobody at all.'

'Rubbish! Better off without him!' Old Mary piped up from the corner. 'Slugs, the lot of them! The happiest day of my life was the day Finbarr kicked the bucket.'

'Mary, you can't really mean that,' protested Elizabeth.

'Slugs, every last one of them.'

'God,' said Ana. 'First Penny, then Elizabeth and now you Mary. This is turning into an episode of the Oprah Winfrey Show. Today's topic – *The Truth About These Widows' Dead Husbands*.'

'Carrying on with that bitch all those years,' Mary ranted. 'My own sister, even when I was inside in the hospital giving birth. Right there in my own house.'

'Mary, Mary calm down,' coaxed Ellen.

'And I'd like to know who the father of her youngest really is.' But then, suddenly, she lost all interest in the topic, settled back down again and continued her snooze.

'You're lucky, Ana,' resumed Elizabeth. 'At least you're used to being on your own.'

'How do you mean, Elizabeth?'

'Well, what with your marriage breaking

up and never having had any children at least you don't have to go through the shock of suddenly finding yourself all alone so late in life.'

'Is that right?'

'I've been thinking, and you know, I suppose I can understand how you're so anxious to make a pet out of my granddaughter and I can't say I blame you.'

'Really?'

'Maybe one never gets completely used to being on one's own. Maybe that's why you were so anxious to nab the Colonel or Laurence. And how were you to know that one was going to die and the other was already married? Still, there's always Nurse Boo left.'

Ellen and Penny were both looking at each other anxiously.

'Ana, I'm sure that Elizabeth doesn't–' began Ellen.

'Elizabeth, I think it's about time I set you straight on a few things,' said Ana, her patience having finally snapped. 'First, you think you're subtle when you go prying into other people's lives – well you're not. You're about the least subtle person I've ever met and that's why I never answer any of your nosy little questions. Second, just because I don't tell you anything that doesn't give you licence to fill in the blanks anyway you fancy. When you say my marriage broke up, can I ask if you are referring to my first or my second marriage? Having my first husband stabbed to death can hardly be what you mean – even you wouldn't be so insensitive or stupid as to call that a break-up. As for my second husband, yes we did split up after I found out that he'd taken everything I owned – maybe that's what you mean. And, as for children, it's not strictly true to say that I never had any. You see Elizabeth, I did have a son but unfortunately he was killed when he was in his early twenties.

'But can I tell you one thing? I *am* jealous of you – so jealous that you have a lovely, lovely granddaughter like Sophie. If she were mine I wouldn't waste her like you do. Do you know anything about her at all? Do you know that all she wants to be is a pianist? Do you know that she used to come down here a couple of times a week to visit the Colonel and to practice on his piano? Do you know that she thinks her own grandmother has absolutely no time for her? And it would appear she's right.'

And with that Ana turned on her heel and left them.

1998

CHAPTER 12

Oh, who could have foretold
That the heart grows old?

from *A Song* by W B Yeats

Ana glanced first at the bunched-up traffic coming towards her and then to the other side of the road and tried to gauge how long it would take her to cross over. Deciding she could make it, just about, she stepped out but the sight of the cars bearing down so quickly caused her nerve to give and she hurriedly retreated back onto the pavement. Seconds later, the traffic went whooshing past. 'Damn,' she muttered. She'd missed her chance; now she'd never get across. A great big articulated lorry trundled by, belching smoke, causing her to cough. Then, almost immediately, a dirty old bus repeated the insult. 'Disgusting,' she muttered, waving away the fumes.

She wanted to cross the road here, at this point, but it was becoming clear to her that she'd have to give in and walk two hundred metres down this side of the road to where the traffic-lights were, only to retrace her footsteps back up again on the other side.

This annoyed her for it seemed such a waste of effort but, having no choice, she set off. On reaching the traffic-lights, she pressed the button and waited for the green man to appear. Beside her stood an old woman, also waiting, and almost immediately this other woman reached across Ana and pressed the button herself. Seconds later, she reached across and pressed it again. And, just as she was about to reach out to press it for a third time, a young girl pushed past her and then ran out onto the road, darting easily between the vehicles, and over to the other side.

'Not a bother to her,' commented the other woman, nodding after the young girl and Ana murmured her agreement. Then, seconds later, and to Ana's surprise, the woman suddenly snarled. 'The fecking dogs. The fecking, fecking dogs,' she said, spitting her words out in anger. Catching Ana's startled glance, she demanded crossly, 'Amn't I right though, amn't I?'

'Pardon?' asked Ana.

'Dublin. It's gone to the fecking dogs. I remember when this was a quiet street and, let me tell you, Missus, that's not so long ago either. It's gone so bad now that I have to have my route all worked out in my head before I ever set foot outside my front door so that I'll have as few roads to cross as possible. That's how bad it's got. And I'll tell you another thing,' she went on, now jabbing Ana in the chest much to her annoyance. 'No one is thinking of us old people when they're planning all them duel carriageways and flyovers and roundabouts and what-have-you. No, nobody is considering how we're going to get about, sure they're not? I've even given up going to Mass each morning, the bother was too much.' The lights changed. 'And it takes me twice as long to do my shopping,' continued the woman as they made their way across. 'Prisoners in our own homes, that's what we've become.' The green light began flashing, then turned red prompting a motorist to beep impatiently at the two women who were delaying him by all of five seconds. 'Gone to the dogs. It's no place for us old people, at all, at all.'

And then, without further ado, she left Ana and continued on her own way.

She was right though, Ana reflected, as she carried on walking. Dublin wasn't a place for old people. Worse still, it was making her feel old. Why, not so long ago she'd have felt positively insulted to have been included in a stranger's definition of 'us old people'. But not any longer. No, now she could identify with exactly how this woman felt. She just felt so weary herself these days, and today more than ever. Everything seemed a battle of late – crossing the road, making her way along pavements full of people shoving their way against her, trying to attract the attention of surly shop assistants who paid her no heed. Before, she wouldn't have been slow to tell a shop assistant to stop gossiping and demand that he or she do their job and serve her straight away, or to give anyone who shoved into her a shove back and a quick lash of her tongue. Now, she just didn't have the spirit any more.

Although she wasn't quite ready to give in just yet, Ana was beginning to feel that her move to Dublin had been a huge mistake and she wished now that she hadn't been so hasty in selling her house in Brighton. After months of house-hunting she'd discovered that the money she'd made on that sale wasn't going to buy her very much in Dublin; certainly nothing decent in any of the seaside areas she'd been so foolishly thinking of when she'd first arrived. It seemed that the only houses within her price range were either stuck at the edge of a forever sprawling suburbia, lacking both shops and public transport, or 'artisan cottages' as estate agents were so fond of calling every little inner-city terraced house over fifty years old, whilst unabashedly presenting their lack of an inside toilet, together with backyards that were rarely bigger than a good-sized tablecloth, as a 'challenge'. If she wanted a challenge at this time of her life, she'd told one of them only last week, she could think of more exciting things to do with her time; like taking up bungee-jumping for instance.

Despite the constant beat of music from the flat across the hall, the incessant screaming from the one overhead, and the steady stream of visitors noisily traipsing in and up the stairs at all times of the day and night, Ana had resigned herself to renting her current flat until such time as she could find somewhere suitable to buy. But, the other night, she'd walked in on two young thugs who'd broken in and, even though this cowardly duo had fled at the sight of her and no real harm had been done, it had really rattled her and afterwards she'd hardly slept a wink. That hers was a ground-floor flat made her feel especially vulnerable. But the last straw had come this morning when she'd asked her gum-chewing, surly, cute-country landlord, barely one third of her age, to install an alarm and he'd just looked at her as incredulously as if she'd just demanded a team of around-the-clock security guards. He had then simply walked off without a single word, leaving her standing there, staring after him.

But there was no doubt about it, she was definitely going to have to get somewhere else to rent in Dublin. Either that or she'd just have to pack up and go back to Brighton.

The rain which had been threatening all morning was now falling in a heavy drizzle and, glancing up at the grey sky, Ana decided that it didn't look like it was going to let up for the day; it looked set to get heavier if anything and briefly she considered going back to the flat but the thought of it depressed her too much. She didn't think she could bear being cooped up on such a damp, dismal day, listening to the sounds of other peoples' lives through thin walls and floors and, just as she was passing the bus stop, a bus pulled up so making up her mind to go into town, into Bewley's, she impulsively climbed on.

The fogged up inside of the bus smelt of damp clothes and everybody looked about as depressed as the weather outside. A young girl stood up and offered Ana her seat and she took it gratefully for, right now, she really did feel like the old person the girl so obviously considered her to be.

Getting off near Westmoreland Street, Ana went directly into Bewley's and, as she was standing at the counter, waiting for the hot chocolate she'd ordered, she noticed that the tightness in her chest had returned. It had been coming and going all morning but now it felt worse than ever and, just as she was reaching out to take the mug of hot chocolate, she suddenly collapsed and fell to the floor.

'Oh my God, oh my God,' screamed the girl behind the counter. 'There's an old lady dying!'

The other customers were already crowding around her.

'Give her some brandy,' someone told the waitress.

'And where am I to get brandy?' she demanded.

From the back of the crowd came a male voice. 'Excuse me, excuse me, can you let me through? I can help. Please, let me have a look at her!'

'Loosen her blouse,' ordered a woman near the front.

'Someone ring for an ambulance,' cried another.

'Please! I'm a nurse. Let me through!' came the voice from the back.

'Don't move her,' someone cautioned.

'Please,' came the voice from the back again, 'I'm a nurse. Please, let me through. I believe I know this woman.'

'Stand back,' shouted a burly man with considerably more presence than Adrian Lloyd. 'There's a gentleman here who says he's a nurse.' He began pushing Adrian forward. 'Will ye for God's sake stand back and let this man attend to the lady.'

Once he'd been propelled to the front of the crowd, Adrian knelt down beside Ana.

'Ana, are you okay? Can you breathe?' He

opened her top few buttons. 'Please, can everyone stand back a little and give this lady some room, you're crowding her. Has someone called for an ambulance?' Seeing Ana's eyelids flutter slightly, he leaned forward. 'Ana,' he called gently, 'do you recognise me? It's me – Adrian.'

'Hello, Adrian,' Ana managed to respond.

'There now, Ana, don't worry about a thing. There's an ambulance on its way.'

Ana nodded weakly.

'Thanks, Adrian,' she managed to say.

'You just lay still, Ana. You'll be fine. Aren't I here to take care of you now?'

The Sunday following Easter…

'It's all right for the three of you,' said Penny, looking around at the others, 'but what about me? When you're gone all I'll be left with is the likes of Old Mary there,' she said, nodding in the direction of the old woman who was dozing at the far side of the sunroom. Mary's head was flung back, her mouth was wide open and she was emitting a steady stream of little grunts, snores, sighs and mumbles. 'And you wouldn't exactly call her good company, now would you?' asked Penny in disgust, frowning at the sight and sound of Mary. 'You know, I'd swear she hasn't budged from that seat all week.' She turned back to the others. 'But really, what will I do when you're all gone? Spend my days napping alongside Mary? You know, when I moved into Rathdowne the last thing I expected was that everyone I'd make friends with would suddenly decide to up and leave to set up new lives elsewhere. After all, it's called a retirement village for a reason – when people come here they're meant to stay put.'

'Well, it's not exactly through choice that I'm leaving, Penny,' Ana pointed out.

'That's true. Tell me, have you sorted out where you're going to go yet?'

'I think so.'

'So, tell us?'

Ana shook her head.

'Wait until I've everything finalised.'

'I'll forgive you so for going but,' Penny paused and looked over at Elizabeth and Ellen, 'as for you two, you're nothing but deserters.'

'So it's been decided then, Elizabeth, that you're going to live with Harry?' asked Ana.

Since their bust-up the week before, Elizabeth had refused to talk to Ana and, although Ana had meant everything she'd said and still didn't regret any of it, she'd no desire to remain on bad terms with Elizabeth. But, if she wanted things to be resolved between them, it was obvious that it was going to be up to her to make all the moves.

'Yes,' Elizabeth answered frostily.

'You're selling the bungalow then?'

'Yes.'

'And will it be coming on the market soon?'

Anxious to show that she was still odd, Elizabeth loudly sighed in annoyance but she condescended to answer.

'Yes.'

'Isn't it grand for all of you?' moaned Penny. 'The highlight of my week will be the family's Sunday visit. By the way, what time is it?'

'Just gone twelve,' Ellen told her.

'It'll be a while so before any of my lot show up,' said Penny.

'Penny, did I tell you Jack's coming over today?' asked Ellen excitedly.

'Jesus, Ellen,' Penny suddenly snapped, 'can't you give it a rest? Jack this, Jack that. If I hear another word about Jack I'll... I'll...' She broke off and glared over at Old Mary who was now snoring extra loudly. 'God, would someone ever throw a cushion at her to shut her up?'

'Ah Penny,' said Ellen, 'I'm sorry. I didn't realise I was going on so much.'

'Well, you are,' answered Penny crossly.

For a few moments there was an awkward silence between the women and Mary's snoring was the only sound to be heard in the room.

'Ana, Elizabeth, why don't we do something to cheer Penny up?' suggested Ellen.

'We could go somewhere maybe. We're forever saying we will, or that we'll do something special, but we never do and soon we'll all have split up and it'll be too late.'

'Like what?' asked Elizabeth.

'I don't know. Maybe we could go up to Dublin some evening for a meal and then on to the pictures or to a show afterwards.'

'The Chippendales are coming to Dublin next week. We could go to see them,' suggested Penny, suddenly perking up at this talk of an outing. 'Two of my daughters went the last time they were on and said that they were only marvellous, that it was well worth going to see them.'

'Penny,' protested Elizabeth, slightly shocked, 'you're having us on. You can't really want to go to see those fellows?'

'Why not?'

'Well, I think it's a great idea,' said Ellen, anxious to back her friend up.

'Ellen, the Chippendales are a – a – a male dance troupe,' Elizabeth explained.

'So? And what's wrong with male dancers? I've nothing against them. Some of them are every bit as good as women. Remember that foxy-haired fellow in *Riverdance*, wasn't he only marvellous?'

'But, Ellen, it's not just dancing,' Elizabeth tried to explain. 'It's more of a show really.'

'Oh I see,' said Ellen. 'And you think that I'm not sophisticated enough to appreciate a show, is that it?'

'No, but–'

'Just because I'm not from the city like yourself?'

'Ellen,' Elizabeth tried again, 'the show isn't exactly what you–'

'Well, my vote is with this Chippendale thing,' Ellen said defiantly.

'For God's sake, Ellen,' said Elizabeth crossly. 'They're male strippers.'

'Oh, right. Well, why didn't you say?'

'What about a pub crawl?' Penny asked.

'Or Daniel O'Donnell?' suggested Elizabeth hastily as an alternative to Penny's which wasn't at all to her taste. 'He's coming to the Point soon, we could go to see him.'

'Yes,' agreed Ellen. 'I wouldn't mind going to see Daniel. What about you, Ana?'

'Well, I don't really…'

'You can stop right there,' interrupted Penny. 'I'd sooner spend the night in bed with Nurse Boo.'

'Elizabeth, do they take all their clothes off?' interrupted Ellen.

'Who?' asked Elizabeth crossly. 'What are you on about?'

'That male dance troupe?'

'Ellen, we've moved on from that. They've been ruled out.'

'I know, I know. I was just curious. So, do they?'

'Yes, they do,' snapped Elizabeth, not

having any idea whether they really did or not. 'Now, enough nonsense. Let's decide on where we're going.'

'Everything?' persisted Ellen.

'Yes.'

'Well, fancy that!'

'So, where are we going to go?' asked Penny.

'You know, I fancy the idea of a day's outing but it shouldn't be to anywhere too far,' said Ellen, 'but to some place where we'd be able to get a bite to eat.'

'And get a couple of drinks,' said Penny.

'Somewhere in the country maybe,' suggested Elizabeth.

'Maybe,' agreed Penny. 'As long as we didn't have to do too much walking. Maybe Glendalough?'

'No.' Ellen shook her head. 'I've been there too many times. What about Avoca?'

'Look, we can agree on what or where later,' said Penny. 'But it's a great idea. We'll definitely have to do something before you all desert me.' Then she noticed a bunch of people crossing the lawn. 'What time did you say it was again?'

'Just coming up for ten past,' answered Ellen.

'Your son and his family are down early then, Elizabeth,' said Penny and, almost immediately, they appeared at the French windows.

'Harry! Janet!' Elizabeth called in delight and quickly got up and hurried over to them. 'This is a surprise! I wasn't expecting you today. And so early as well. Come on, come and sit down.'

'So Mom,' began Harry as soon as they were all seated, 'have you heard the news?' He spoke excitedly and in a very loud voice for he was anxious that what he had to say should be heard by everyone in the room.

'What news is that?'

'You're not going to believe it, Mom, but that fellow Jackson has left £10,000 to Sophie in his will!'

'What?' asked Elizabeth, absolutely astounded.

'Yes, £10,000. Incredible, isn't it?' And seeing that Elizabeth was too stunned to speak Harry went on. 'We decided to come down and give you the news in person for we knew you'd be delighted to find out.'

'Did you hear that?' Elizabeth called over to the others.

'Hear what?' asked Penny – as if she hadn't.

'The Colonel has left Sophie £10,000! Imagine!'

'There is one snag however–' began Janet.

'It's nothing really,' interrupted Harry. 'But, for reasons best known to himself, he's stipulated that the money should be kept in trust for Sophie and used solely to further

her music career, as he calls it.' He threw his eyes to heaven. 'Music career, I ask you!'

'But if the money isn't used for that then she forfeits it,' explained Janet. 'And it goes to the St Vincent De Paul. And if–'

'It's a bit much really,' interrupted Harry once again, 'putting in such a ridiculous condition. But I gather from Mrs Reynolds that he was regarded as rather an eccentric sort of individual. Anyway, there's bound to be some way around it. I'm not going to have Sophie throw herself away on a music career, I can tell you. No, I intend having a chat with some of my friends in the legal profession, they'll know a way around it for sure.'

'You see,' Janet explained to Elizabeth, 'Harry is anxious that Sophie should study accountancy when she finishes school.'

'Oh, I thought it was Ned who was going to be the accountant,' said Elizabeth.

'And it was until I realised what a blockhead he is. And it seems that Chico and Harpo here,' Harry said, indicating the two younger boys, 'aren't likely to turn out much better. But I'm damned if I'm not going to have at least one of my family working in the firm.'

'But Dad–' began Sophie.

'Not now, girl,' snapped Harry.

'And Mom,' continued Janet, 'he's left her his piano as well.. Mrs Reynolds gave us a look at it before we came in to see you.'

'Yes,' said Harry, 'and it looks like it's worth a few bob. But it's an absolute monster of a thing. We'll have to sell it – there's no room for it in our house.'

'I know that things will be a bit squashed when I come to live with you, Harry, but surely you could manage to fit it in somewhere,' said Elizabeth, annoyed that the Colonel's gift was being treated so poorly. 'Maybe Sophie could put it in her bedroom?'

'Is Granny coming to live with us?' asked Tim, his interest sufficiently piqued by this news for him to postpone giving Benjy the Chinese Burn he'd been threatening. 'I thought you said that she was going to that place in Newbridge?'

'Tim,' said Harry, warningly.

But Tim blundered on.

'The old folks' home where Brian O'Leary's Gran lives.'

'Tim, we were just talking,' said Janet. 'Nothing has been finalised yet. That was just one option we were looking at.'

'Newbridge?' Elizabeth looked at her son enquiringly.

'Mom–' began Harry.

'Newbridge?' repeated Elizabeth.

'Mom, you know we'd love nothing better than to have you come live with us but we're just not sure it's a practical option given the size of our house. That's why we were thinking that somewhere like the place in Newbridge might be better. Somewhere where you'd have your own independence and space.'

'My own independence and space?'

'Mom, it's just one option. And with the roads being as good as they are, it wouldn't take much longer for us to get down to see you there than it takes us now. Of course, it would be perfect if we could find you somewhere nearer Dublin but, Mom, you wouldn't believe how expensive residential care is getting, especially near the city.'

'So, you've no room for me?'

'Mom, we're not saying that.'

'You're asking me to sell my bungalow here and move into some old nursing home over in Kildare?'

'Mom, listen–'

'It doesn't really seem like you've room for much. No room for Sophie's piano. No room for me.'

Harry glanced around the room. Everyone appeared to be engaged in their own conversations but, nevertheless, he lowered his voice a notch before going on.

'Mom, we've discussed all this,' he said sternly but so quietly that Ana and the others had to lean that bit closer in order to hear him. 'And if the service charges here keep on increasing I'm not sure I'll be able to go on paying them.'

'What are you saying?'

'I'm just saying that now that the service charges are set to increase, I'm not sure that I can afford to go on paying them.'

'I see.'

With a grim set to her face, Elizabeth sat completely still and stared straight ahead of her.

'Mom, surely you understand? It's just throwing away my money when most of yours remains tied up in the bungalow. If you were to sell and move into a nursing home I think it would make more sense financially. And in other ways,' he hastened to add.

Elizabeth remained stony-faced.

'Mom? Mom?'

Slowly Elizabeth turned to Harry.

'And it would be far more economical for you to subdivide that palace of yours into several apartments and confine yourselves to living in just the one room but you don't find me suggesting that to you. Or to foster out a couple of those young fellows there,' she said, waving her hand in their direction. 'You'd save a lot on grocery bills if you were to do that.'

'Mom, you're being silly.'

'You're talking about my home, Harry. You might see it in purely financial terms, but it's my home and the only one I have.'

'I know that, Mom, of course I do, but–'

'I've changed my mind, Harry. I'm not moving out and selling up just to satisfy you. Tell me, are you having business troubles or is it just plain greed that has you so anxious to get your hands on the money tied up in my bungalow? For that's what you're after, isn't it? Now you listen to me, Harry, you'd better stop your threats and just carry on paying those service charges or you'll get a nasty shock. Remember the bungalow is still mine to do with it what I want. It's not too late yet to change my will and there's nothing to say I have to give it to you. Isn't it just as well that I didn't listen and sign it over to you when I was buying it. You know, Harry, the funny thing is, I'd have happily sold it and given you every penny just so that I could come and live with you but I'm damned if I'm selling up just to move into some nursing home.'

Suddenly she got up.

'Come on, Sophie,' she said, taking hold of her granddaughter's arm. 'Let's go and have a look at this piano of yours. I'm sure I can find room for it in my living-room. Now, I know you used to come and practice on it in the Colonel's house,' she said to her as they crossed the room together, 'so there's no reason why you can't continue coming to Rathdowne, to my place. It would give us an opportunity to get to know one another and

I think it's about time we did, don't you?' She paused and turned around to her son and daughter-in-law. 'Harry, Janet, thanks so much for visiting. Now, I'm sure you'll need to head away soon so I won't hold you up any longer. After all, it's gone noon so no doubt you'll be getting worried about the evening traffic, that it'll be getting heavy soon. And of course the boys will want to be getting back. They always seem to be so busy. That fellow there,' she said pointing at Tim, 'probably has a football match to get back to. And no doubt that other fellow is starving so you might want to stop somewhere nice for lunch on your way home.' She turned to her friends, 'Ladies,' she said, 'would you like to come and listen to my granddaughter on the piano? Apparently she's a marvel, so Ana tells me.'

Ana, Ellen and Penny followed her and Sophie through the French windows.

'Laurence,' Elizabeth shouted out, spotting him coming out from the main house by a side door. 'Can you give us a hand? We're going to need some help moving the Colonel's piano over to my bungalow.'

'I'm not sure I'd be much good, Lizzy,' he called back, holding up his right arm to show her the cast on it. 'I'm not back at work yet. I just came down today to talk to Mrs Reynolds about taking some more time off.'

'Elizabeth,' said Ellen, 'he still looks a bit shook, he mightn't be up to it.'

'Nonsense,' said Elizabeth. 'Come on now, Laurence. One hand is better than none and you wouldn't want to be responsible for a bunch of old ladies dying of heart attacks, now would you?'

'There's not much fear of that. But I suppose I couldn't have it on my conscience.'

Somehow, between the six of them, they managed to lift up and carry the piano. Well, Elizabeth wasn't doing much lifting – she'd elected to take on a supervisory role and was busy issuing a stream of orders.

'Now, this way,' she directed as they manoeuvred it through the Colonel's front door. 'Alright, Ellen, easy does it. That's it, take it easy Ellen – stop, stop what are you doing! Come on, over the grass. It'll be shorter.'

'Elizabeth, I can't hold it. I'm going to drop my corner,' warned Ellen. 'I'm dropping it, Elizabeth, I'm dropping it.'

And she did, leaving the others with no choice but to leave it down completely.

'Ah Ellen!'

'I'm sorry, Elizabeth, I lost my grip.'

Sophie flopped down on the grass.

'We're never going to manage to get it over to your house, Gran.'

Suddenly Ana had an idea.

'We were looking for something to do.

Well, I have it – an open-air concert for all the residents and their visitors, this very afternoon, right on this spot. We have the piano. We have a singer in Laurence and a pianist in Sophie. And we have the audience. The fine weather is just perfect and what better place could there be than right here? With the backdrop of the lake and the trees, it's ideal.'

'Ana, you're a genius,' cried Elizabeth and hugged Ana much to her astonishment. 'That's a brilliant idea. We can bring out some chairs from the main house and set them up in rows just along here and ask everyone to come along. And we'll need refreshments of course.'

'Ladies,' began Laurence, 'I'm not sure I'm really up to singing today.'

'Rubbish!' Elizabeth dismissed his protest. 'What's there to be up to?' she demanded. 'We won't get a chance like this again, especially with all the changes happening around here.'

Ana couldn't help but notice that he did look very pale and weary and she regretted suggesting that he sing but there was no way Elizabeth was going to let him get out of it now.

Just then a carload of Penny's daughters came up the avenue and, seeing the group of people gathered around the piano, they slowed down.

'Mam,' one shouted out from the passenger's window, 'what's up?'

'Tell Olive to park the car,' Penny shouted. 'Then you're all to come back here. Tell her that I'll need her to show me how she makes that punch of hers.' And taking charge now, she began giving orders to everyone. 'Ellen, we'll want sandwiches, loads of them, so go up to the kitchen in the main house and take whatever you need before Mrs Reynolds realises that there's something going on. Lorna, love,' she said to her granddaughter who'd hopped out of the car before her mother had driven off to park it, 'will you go with the nice lady there and give her a hand with the sandwiches? Elizabeth, can you try and rustle up some desserts?'

'Excuse me,' began Elizabeth, annoyed that her supervisory role was being taken over, 'but I...'

Penny cut her off. Being the natural-born organiser that she was, she'd no intention of handing control back to Elizabeth.

'Sophie,' she ordered, 'go around to each of the bungalows and tell everyone that they're to be down here at two o' clock and, if they're expecting any visitors, tell them to bring them too, that there's a treat in store. Oh, and find out if any of them can sing or play an instrument. Ana, Laurence, you two go on up to the main house and start bringing down some chairs.'

'Aye, aye, Captain,' laughed Ana.

As the pair of them went back and forth, carrying out the chairs, it soon became obvious to Ana that Laurence was avoiding her. Each time she came into the sunroom he rushed off with whatever number of chairs he'd collected but, on the fourth such encounter, she managed to corner him.

'So Laurence, how are you?' she asked.

'Fine, Mrs Dunne.'

'Mrs Dunne?'

'Yes, fine, Mrs Dunne,' he repeated in the same reserved tone.

She noticed that he wasn't smiling his usual smile, that he wasn't even making eye contact with her.

'So it's back to Mrs Dunne again, is it?' she asked.

'Well, I wouldn't want you thinking that I was getting overly familiar. I wouldn't want you thinking that I was getting any ideas about you and me. So, as I said, I'm fine, Mrs Dunne. Thank you for asking.'

During the week he'd spent in hospital, Ana had visited him twice but on each occasion there had been other people present so she didn't get a chance to talk to him on his own. Both times she'd thought that he'd seemed a little subdued but had presumed that this was because of the Colonel's death. Now it seemed that that wasn't entirely the case.

'Laurence, I've already lost one friend in this place and so have you. What's the point in losing another? I know the whole thing must have been very upsetting for you especially since you were…'

'Especially since I was what? Especially since I was responsible for killing the Colonel, is that what you were going to say?'

'No, Laurence, of course not. You're putting words in my mouth.'

'Well, I do beg your pardon. Now, if you'll excuse me, Penny is waiting for these chairs.'

In the end few people bothered sitting but instead chose to wander around, chatting to one another and helping themselves to Ellen's sandwiches and to the punch and the home-made lemonade prepared by Penny and her daughters, whilst Sophie played and Laurence sang.

'Enjoying it?' asked Penny, coming over to where Ana was standing listening to the pair of them.

Ana nodded though she wasn't enjoying it near as much as she'd imagined she would when she'd first come up with the idea. Sophie was playing really well but Laurence was falling far below his usual standard. His voice seemed so much flatter than normal.

'Sophie is a beautiful pianist,' commented

Penny. 'Don't you think?'

Ana nodded.

'Your granddaughter's a right little performer, isn't she?' she remarked, now noticing that young Lorna was engaged in a lively performance of the cancan for Ellen and a rather bemused-looking Jack.

'Don't talk to me,' Penny sighed fondly. 'That one isn't happy unless she's the centre of attention. I'm telling you, her mother has her ruined, spoils her rotten she does. Mind you, I have to admit that I was as bad myself when the girls were young.'

They watched now as Lorna tugged at Jack's hand, trying to make him join in.

'Lorna,' shouted Penny. 'Leave the nice man alone. Lorna, stop now!'

Lorna scowled over at Penny, dropped Jack's hand, then wandered off, looking around to see what she might do next for entertainment.

'You know, Ana, I love my girls and their families to bits but the last thing in the world I'd want to do is move in with any of them. For the life of me I couldn't understand how Elizabeth was so anxious to go and live with Harry. Mine are bad but God, that Harry and his family are a nightmare. All the girls are forever on at me to come live with them but I know exactly what would happen if I did. Within a week they'd have me baby-sitting and doing jobs for them morning, noon and night. No, I prefer it this way. Now I can go and stay with them whenever I need a bit of pampering and then come back here before the novelty wears off for them and for me. Of course I'll be lonely when all of you lot go but nothing would induce me to leave here. Besides, I've a little project lined up to keep me occupied.'

'Oh yes?'

'I'm going to get Zanzibar Holdings.'

'How do you mean "get" exactly?' asked Ana.

'Well, as you know, there's no point in taking them to court for raising the service charges since they're legally entitled to but there are other ways of dealing with them.'

'Oh yes?'

'Yes. Blackmail for one.'

'Blackmail?'

'Yep. Blackmail.'

'What are you talking about? How are you going to blackmail them exactly?'

'You see, the shop I used to own is located very near *The Irish Times* offices so I know most of the journalists from coming in and out and I don't think I'd have a problem getting them interested in doing a story on what's happening here. You know, big rich nasty company versus defenceless old people. And *The Irish Times* would be just the start of it. I'm going to go to all of the other newspapers as well. And the radio stations. I'll start by ringing all their chat shows. But, before all that, I'll contact Zanzibar Holdings first and tell them what I intend doing. I don't think they'll be very pleased at the prospect of such bad publicity, especially when three of the bungalows here will be on the market soon but, if they still insist on raising the service charges well, it won't be long before they'll wish they'd never heard of me.'

'I can well believe it.'

'And, Ana, it's not that paying the increased charges would be a problem for me. The reason I slaved away in that shop for all those years was to be able to set the girls up and still have more than enough for my old age. But it just annoys me that Zanzibar think they can take advantage of us because we're old. And nothing, absolutely nothing, gets my back up more than being taken advantage of.' Just then she noticed that Lorna was inching her way along a branch while her mother stood directly underneath chatting, completely oblivious to the danger posed by her child to the two of them. 'Oh God,' Penny muttered before hurrying off. 'Olive, will you look at what your daughter's up to? Can you not keep an eye on her?'

There was a good crowd now, Ana saw, looking around her. Suddenly, becoming aware that the piano-playing and the singing had stopped, she glanced over and, when she saw that Ellen had taken up position beside the piano and looked poised to start singing as soon as Jack had settled himself on the piano stool, her eyes quickly scanned the crowd for Laurence. At first there was no sign of him but then she saw him straightening himself up having picked up his jumper from underneath the piano stool and she watched as he struggled to put it on over the cast. When he'd finally managed to get it on, she saw him turn to say a quick goodbye to those nearest him before walking off through the crowd, without so much as a glance in her direction.

'Are you okay, Mrs Dunne?' asked Sophie coming up alongside her.

'Fine,' Ana answered. Her eyes were still on Laurence as he made his way through the crowd. She wondered if he even knew that she was going to be leaving Rathdowne in the near future. 'Fine, Sophie,' she repeated, then smiled at her. 'What would be wrong with me?' she asked.

'I just thought you looked a bit down. But guess what, Mrs Dunne, you'll never believe what Gran is just after promising me?'

'What?' asked Ana.

'She promised that even if Dad succeeds in getting around the restrictions in the Colonel's will or if £10,000 won't cover everything, she'll help me out all she can so that I'll be able to study music.'

'Despite the fact that your dad doesn't want you to?'

'Yes, can you believe it? She said that if it's the last thing in the world she does, she's going to make sure I get to study music. I'm not really sure what her motives are, whether it's to get back at my dad or if she does genuinely want to help me.'

'Probably a bit of both.'

'And it's all due to you, Mrs Dunne. She told me what you said to her last week, after the Colonel's funeral. How can I ever thank you?'

'Well, by going up there for a start and getting Jack off the piano and shutting Ellen up. God, she's dreadful! They both are. But the way they're looking at one another so admiringly, you'd swear that he was Liberace and that she was Joan Sutherland. Go on, Sophie, please. Please, before they go on to another song.'

'Ana, are you alright?' asked Elizabeth coming over to her a few minutes later. 'You're looking very down.'

'I'm fine, Elizabeth – a little tired maybe. So, are you enjoying the concert?'

'Wonderful. Isn't Sophie just a genius on the piano? I really had no idea. It's no wonder the Colonel left her all that money. Isn't she just so talented? I expect she gets it from me, I was always quite musical, you know.' She paused and listened to Sophie play for a few moments, then turned back to Ana. 'Ana,' she began, looking slightly abashed, 'I don't normally find it easy to admit that I was wrong, but ... but well, I suppose I have been. You were right when you said I've such a lot to be thankful for and from now on I'm going to really get to know Sophie.' And, noticing Ana smile, she asked. 'What is it? What are you finding funny?'

'Nothing really, Elizabeth. I'm just glad for you, that's all. But tell me, are you very upset about having to stay on here?'

'Well, what can I do? I'll just have to make the most of it I suppose.'

They fell silent for a while and listened to Sophie.

'Tell me, Ana,' said Elizabeth as casually as she could after several minutes had lapsed, 'do you happen to know who that gentleman over there is?'

Ana looked to where Elizabeth indicated. The man was a stranger but there was something very familiar about him. She stared at him for a while trying to place him and then it dawned on her – it had to be Jack's brother Francis. He was the image of Jack, though a neater, slightly more refined-looking version.

'Why?' she asked, trying to stop herself

from laughing.

'Well, it's just that he appears to be on his own. I was thinking that perhaps someone should get him a drink.'

'You're probably right, Elizabeth. Listen, why don't you? We don't want him thinking we're an unsociable bunch.'

'No, indeed. I'll go over to him so.'

And Ana laughed out loud as she watched Elizabeth hurrying over, making a beeline for the unsuspecting Francis.

JANUARY 1999

CHAPTER 13

I shall wear the bottoms of my trousers rolled...
from *The love song of J Alfred Prufrock*
by TS Eliot

And I shall spend my pension on brandy and summer gloves...
from *Warning* by Jenny Joseph

'Yes, we have some lovely people living here,' Mrs Reynolds was saying to Ana as they turned the corner and came around to the back of the main house. 'And, if you do choose to buy the bungalow, I've no doubt but that you'll be very happy here, Mrs Dunne. And the fact that the ongoing service costs are quite high means that we have, how should I put it, a certain class of resident – if you follow my meaning.'

Ana only half-heard what Mrs Reynolds was saying for, now that the full extent of the gardens had come into view, she was staring down at them in awe. Adrian, on the other hand, was paying full attention being rather anxious to please his boss of whom he had a somewhat exaggerated fear. Walking along behind the other two, he was nodding in agreement with everything Mrs Reynolds was saying. Not that she noticed, or would have cared if she had.

'The gardens are wonderful, absolutely wonderful,' Ana remarked, interrupting Mrs Reynolds' spiel. 'Tell me, who looks after them?'

'Our gardener, Laurence Hynes. He's been working here now for–'

But she didn't get a chance to finish for the woman Ana had noticed hurrying along the path towards them had begun calling out as she drew near.

'Mrs Reynolds! Mrs Reynolds! Can I have a word, Mrs Reynolds?'

'Can it not wait, Elizabeth?' Mrs Reynolds asked crossly.

'Not really. You see there's something wrong with my fridge, it's making a very peculiar noise and I was just wondering if you could get someone to have a look at it for me. Oh look,' she said spotting a figure in the distance, 'there's Laurence now, maybe he'd oblige.'

'Laurence is the gardener, Elizabeth, not the electrician.'

'Of course. But I just thought–'

'I'll get on to someone for you, alright?'

'But I'm sure Laurence wouldn't–'

'Elizabeth, I'll get someone onto it.' Then, noticing that Elizabeth was now staring at Ana, obviously waiting to be introduced and, knowing that she wouldn't go away until she'd obliged her, Mrs Reynolds sighed but gave in. 'Elizabeth,' she said, 'this is Ana Dunne, she's thinking of buying number nine. Mrs Dunne, this is Elizabeth Daly, one of our residents.'

Elizabeth and Ana smiled at one another.

'Well, Mrs Dunne,' began Elizabeth, her eyes travelling slowly up and down Ana as she carefully registered every detail of her appearance, 'you can be sure that you'll be made very welcome if you do come to live here. New faces are always appreciated. I've been here now almost a year and I…'

'Elizabeth,' cut in Mrs Reynolds, 'there's a lot I need to show Mrs Dunne so we'd better keep moving.'

'Of course, of course. Don't let me hold you up.' But, barely pausing for breath, she continued. 'You've come on your own then, Mrs Dunne?'

'No, Adrian drove her down,' Mrs Reynolds told her. 'He's an old family friend.'

Elizabeth glanced over at Adrian as if she'd only now become aware of his presence. Then she looked at Ana once again and Ana watched the expression on her face change as the questions raced through her mind and then she noticed Elizabeth glance down at her left hand and knew that she was checking for a wedding ring.

'Oh really, wasn't that kind of him?' she

remarked eventually. 'Your husband couldn't come with you then? Or am I putting my foot in it? Have you had the same misfortune as myself of having outlived your better half? Tell me, do you have any–'

'Elizabeth,' interrupted Mrs Reynolds, 'you'll be able to quiz her all you like if, and when, she moves in. Now, if you don't mind, we need to move on.'

'Yes, of course. Well goodbye, Mrs Dunne, nice meeting you and I hope we'll see you again.'

Elizabeth began walking away but as she disappeared behind some hedges, her voice floated back to them.

'Laurence! Laurence! Have you got a moment?'

'One of the characters of the place,' explained Mrs Reynolds, a little wearily thought Ana. 'And we have quite a few of them as you'll soon discover if you move here – Old Mary, Ellen, and the Colonel as he's known. Mind you, you'll have to watch yourself with him, he has a bit of an eye for the ladies. Himself and Laurence are great buddies though what they have in common, God only knows. Now, where was I before we were interrupted? Oh yes, the service charges. Yes, well, they are comparatively high but that's because the range of services we provide here is so comprehensive. We have excellent laundry facilities to start with and then there's the…'

But Ana wasn't listening. Her mind was made up, the gardens had seen to that and, as Mrs Reynolds droned on and on, Ana considered the costs involved. Compared to property in Dublin the bungalow was very good value, almost identical to what she'd got for the house in Brighton. She could afford it, just about. The ongoing service charges that Mrs Reynolds was now talking about were going to be more of a problem but at least they could be paid on a monthly basis. Besides, if she didn't take the bungalow, there were very few other options open to her. Just two to be precise – either to go on living in that horrible flat in Dublin and wait until something suitable and affordable came on the market or to take up Adrian's offer of a room in his house. Though it was very kind of him she felt that if she was ever that desperate well, God help her, then she'd have really hit rock bottom.

She turned to Mrs Reynolds.

'Mrs Reynolds, I'm interested in buying the bungalow.'

'Oh my goodness, there's no beating about the bush with you, is there? Don't you even want to see inside the main house?'

'No, no, I've seen all I need to see. The bungalow is perfect and as for the grounds well, what can I say, they're just beautiful. When Adrian told me about this place I thought he must be exaggerating. I thought he was probably biased because he works here. But he wasn't – not in the slightest.'

As they travelled back to Dublin, Adrian took his eyes off the road for a second to glance over at Ana.

'I'm glad you're pleased, Ana,' he said.

'I am, very much so. It's perfect.'

'Good.' He reached over and touched her gently on the arm. 'But I just want you to know that the offer of a room in my house still stands. I don't want you to think that you have to go rushing into anything, that you have to go buying the bungalow in Rathdowne just because you're so anxious to get out of that flat of yours.'

The hairs on the back of Ana's neck rose at his touch; she wished he wouldn't do that. She was grateful for all he'd done for her since that day she'd collapsed in Bewley's, of course she was, but she just didn't like the way he'd become so proprietorial of late. And she really hated him touching her like that.

'I know that,' she answered. 'But you've done enough for me already, more than enough – between visiting me every day when I was in the hospital and then looking after everything when I came out. And I have you to thank for suggesting Rathdowne and for bringing me down here today. And it's prefect, really prefect.' She paused and gazed reflectively at the road ahead. 'You know, I do find it a little bit scary though. There's something terribly final about moving into this retirement village – like it's the end of everything. It just makes me feel so old.'

'Ana, Ana,' murmured Adrian, glancing over at her once again, 'what you've got to realise is that you are old.'

Ana sighed wearily.

'It's true, Ana. I'm afraid you've got to face up to the fact that your dancing days are over; that your dancing days are well and truly behind you.'

A month after Easter...

Ana kicked the suitcase lying on the floor. 'Damn you anyway,' she muttered, staring at it as if it was her worst enemy. 'Why won't you close for me?' She kicked it again. 'Right,' she said, eying it up meanly. 'See how you like this.' And, turning around, she slowly lowered her ample bottom down on top of it, pumped up and down several times then tried the zip again and, this time, she managed to pull it all the way around.

Not having the heart to get back up again, she stayed sitting there. It occurred to her that everything of worth which she possessed was contained in these two suitcases, the one underneath her plus the one standing before her, and in the mahogany box sitting on top of the second case. Not an awful lot to show for a lifetime she thought as she reached out for the box. As she brought it near, it slipped from her hands and fell to the floor – its contents spilling on impact. Getting down on her knees she began picking everything up – a purple evening shawl edged with silver tassels; a blue velvet jewellery box containing diamond – or glass rather – earrings and matching necklace; a child's pyjamas; a cork from a champagne bottle; a 21st birthday party invitation; Jack Kerouac's *On The Road*; her own book on Kenya; and letters from her father to her mother. Bundling everything into the box once again, she put it back on top of the case then, noticing a pressed daffodil still lying on the floor, she picked it up and sat back down on the other suitcase.

Absentmindedly, she fingered the flower as she sat there, thinking. She sighed loudly. This had to be one of the most depressing days in her life. To think that this was her third move in as many years. And why on earth, she asked herself now, had she picked her birthday of all days to move?

'Ana, can we come in?' Penny called from the front door.

'Yes, yes, come on in,' Ana shouted back and, before she'd time to get up, Penny, followed by Elizabeth and Ellen, came trooping in on top of her.

'So you're all packed then,' noted Penny, looking around the almost bare room.

'All packed, but for the furniture – a removals van is collecting that later,' Ana said as she got to her feet. 'I'd offer you tea or coffee but I'm afraid I've cleared out the kitchen.'

'We didn't come for tea,' said Elizabeth.

'No,' said Penny. 'Look, we'll come straight to the point. We want to know where you're going to live. You're being very evasive altogether and we're all very worried about you.'

'Well, you needn't worry, everything is sorted out now.'

'So where are you going then?' demanded Penny.

Ana took a deep breath. Up to now she'd deliberately not told them for she dreaded their reaction. Still, they were going to find out eventually. It might as well be from her and, anyway, she'd be gone soon.

'I'm going to live with Adrian Lloyd. He's offered me a room in his house.'

'Adrian Lloyd? Who's...?' began Penny, but then it clicked. 'Nurse Boo? You mean Nurse Boo? Ah Ana, you can't be serious. You can't be that desperate!'

'Would you mind not calling him that?'

'But–'

'Look, Penny, I know you don't like him, that none of you do, but that doesn't change the fact that he's been a very good friend to me.'

'But–'

'No buts. I don't want to hear another word. I'm going to go and stay with Adrian and that's all there is to it.'

'Well, rather you than me,' Ellen muttered under her breath.

'What did you say Ellen?' asked Ana.

'Nothing,' answered Ellen but then, after a few seconds' silence she quietly added, 'Though I know I wouldn't be able to rest easy at night.'

'What are you muttering about?' asked Ana crossly.

'Nothing, nothing,' Ellen answered, staring defiantly and, just as Ana was about to turn away, she muttered so softly as to be barely audible. 'Not if I was on my own in the house with him.'

'And just exactly what do you mean by that?' demanded Ana.

'Nothing. I was talking to myself. You said you didn't want to hear another word against him.'

'Look,' said Ana, beginning to lose her temper now, 'I know that none of you like him and I'd be the first to admit that he's a bit strange but there's no harm in him. You just don't know him, that's all.'

'No harm in him?' exploded Penny. 'How can you say that?'

'He's just odd.'

'Just odd? I don't believe I'm hearing this,' cried Penny, shaking her head in disbelief. 'I'm sure that nurse whose life he ruined would be inclined to put it a little more strongly.'

'What nurse? What are you on about?'

But the three women were staring at her now in astonishment.

'What?' demanded Ana, looking from one to the other.

'You don't know,' said Penny finally. 'You actually don't know.'

'Know what?' asked Ana irately.

'Ana, this is the first job he's had in years,' explained Penny. 'Only Mrs Reynolds would take on someone as dodgey as him. She probably got him cheap and figured that us oldies weren't likely to be in any danger from him.'

'What are you talking about? Why would anyone be in danger from Adrian?'

'Ana, he gave up nursing years ago after he was taken to court by one of his female colleagues for harassment,' Penny explained.

'And found guilty,' added Elizabeth.

'Harassment? Adrian?' Ana burst out laughing. 'That's ridiculous!'

'It's not, it happens to be true. One of the

staff, Catherine I think, happened to see his file on Mrs Reynolds' desk soon after he started working here and, well, you know what this place is like, it wasn't long before everyone knew who we had in our midst.'

'I can't believe you didn't know any of this,' said Elizabeth. 'I thought you knew Adrian since you were both children. And you must have read about it in the papers at the time. It got huge coverage.'

'It probably didn't make the English papers,' Penny pointed out.

'The poor girl,' Elizabeth went on. 'But she was very brave – she even came out after the trial and gave an interview about her whole ordeal.'

'Are you saying–' began Ana.

'Ana,' cut in Elizabeth, 'your friend Adrian Lloyd made her life hell. For years she couldn't step outside her front door but he'd be there, waiting for her.'

'I don't believe you,' said Ana.

'Absolute hell,' insisted Elizabeth. 'Pestering her non-stop. Writing to her, ringing her, following her – that sort of thing. And even when she moved job and house that didn't stop him.'

'It's not true, it can't be true,' protested Ana though not very confidently for she was beginning to recall now the aversion so many people – Julie, Eamon, everyone here at Rathdowne – had to him.

'And she wasn't the only one he harassed,' Penny told her. 'Two other women came forward subsequently and claimed that he'd carried on the same way with them.'

Ana shook her head in disbelief but at the same time asked herself how she could have been so stupid as not to realise that the hostility Adrian evoked in other people was too great to be accounted for by virtue of his odd manner alone.

'Apparently he even followed one of them to Germany when she went there on holiday one year,' said Elizabeth.

Slowly, little things began coming back to Ana. Like how puzzled she'd felt that time when he'd told her that he'd left nursing to go into research. And she remembered those anonymous letters she used to get all those years ago. Mark had always thought Adrian was behind them. Now she wondered if he'd been right.

'And you didn't know any of this?' asked Elizabeth incredulously.

Ana shook her head.

'You were probably living in England when it was all going on,' guessed Penny.

'But you'd think someone would have told you,' said Ellen.

Ana shrugged. 'Maybe people just presumed I knew.'

'Well, we certainly did,' Elizabeth told her.

'And you know yourself, Ana, you'd never

let anyone say a bad word against him.'

'But now that you do know, Ana, you're hardly still going to go and live with him, are you?' asked Penny.

Ana shrugged again.

'What else am I to do?'

'Don't worry, Ana, you can count on us,' Ellen told her. 'We'll help you sort something else out.'

At that moment there was a knock on the front door.

'That's not him now, is it?' asked Elizabeth in alarm.

Ana nodded.

'Probably,' she answered despondently. 'I'm expecting him to come about now.'

'You're not to go away with him, Ana, promise us now,' Penny insisted. 'And we'll be back as soon as he's gone to help you sort something out, alright?'

'I–'

'Promise,' demanded Penny.

'I – I–' Ana hesitated. 'I don't know, Penny. Will you stop badgering me? I have to think about things.'

Penny gave a sigh of exasperation.

'Come on, Penny,' urged Ellen. 'Let's go before he arrives in on top of us.'

'Ana!' came a call from the door, followed by another knock.

'Come on, Penny,' repeated Ellen.

All three women hurried off and as they

brushed past Adrian standing on the doorstep, holding a huge bunch of daffodils, each of them threw him a filthy look.

'These are for you, Ana,' said Adrian handing her the flowers when she came to the door. 'Six dozen in all. They're for your birthday.'

As soon as she'd taken them from him, he came in and headed straight into the living-room.

'You're the only person who's remembered what day it is,' she said quietly, more to herself than to him as she followed in after him.

'Daffodils were always your favourite, weren't they, Ana?'

She nodded and laid them on the coffee table, then sat down and he sat down opposite her. She wondered how on earth she was going to put what she'd just heard to him. Staring over at him she tried to think how she should start.

'Ana, are you alright? You look a bit strange.'

She shrugged.

'Adrian–' she began.

'Ana–' he began at exactly the same moment.

They both stopped.

'You go on,' he told her.

'No, no, you go on,' she insisted.

'Well,' said Adrian, 'I was just going to ask

you if you remember your ninth birthday. I was thinking about it on my way down in the car. Remember, it was that year the old woman you were so fond of was in hospital?'

'Not really.'

'Your parents forgot all about your birthday and you were so upset that you ran away.'

'Yes, I think I remember,' said Ana, but she looked uncertain.

'I came looking for you and found you down by the river. You were crying and I couldn't stop you so I ran back home and got my mother and she took the two of us into town, to the pictures. Do you remember? We ate so much that you actually got sick.'

Vaguely remembering the incident now, Ana nodded.

'God, how could you possibly remember that?' she asked him. 'It was so long ago.'

Adrian shrugged. 'Why wouldn't I?'

There was an awkward silence.

'What was it you were going to say, Ana?'

'Adrian,' she began after a few moments, 'is it true that you were taken to court for harassment by a colleague of yours some years ago?'

Adrian stared at her, but didn't answer.

'Adrian, tell me, is it true?'

He cast his eyes down to the floor then, almost imperceptibly, he nodded.

'And did you harass her?'

He didn't answer for a long while.

'I never meant to,' he finally said. 'At the time I was so obsessed that I didn't even realise I was harassing her. Of course, I can see now that my behaviour wasn't normal, but I couldn't see that back then. But I swear, Ana, I never caused her any real harm – well not any physical harm. During the trial her barrister insinuated that I'd ... I'd taken liberties with her but that wasn't the case at all. She made all that up. I think the barrister prompted her, to strengthen her case I imagine. But I never harmed her. Nor either of those two other women, for there were two others as well. But that was all a long, long time ago and I've never done anything like it since. I swear. I just wasn't myself back then.'

'But I don't understand. Why did you do it?'

He took a long time in answering.

'Because ... because they reminded me of you,' he finally told her.

'What?'

'Of course they weren't really like you but I convinced myself that they were.' Then he noticed the stunned look on Ana's face. 'Ana, you must have realised how I felt about you?'

'Of course I knew that you were always fond of me but...'

'Fond? Fond? Ana, I've been in love with

you ever since I can remember. All my life. When I was a boy I thought we were going to get married. We used to even talk about it, remember?'

'Yes but, Adrian, that was just kids' stuff.'

'No it wasn't, Ana, not to me. When I learned that you were getting married to that Mark Harrison my whole world just fell apart. To this day I still remember every detail of your wedding. It was the worst day of my life. After that I lost my head a bit and started sending you all those crazy letters, warning you about him and it wasn't long before I began pestering the first of those girls. Of course, looking back now I can see that I wasn't myself at all. Then, when Harrison died I thought I'd bide my time, give you some space to recover. After a while, I started going over to London, each time intending to call on you, to talk to you, but I could never pluck up the courage. I suppose it was just easier to bother those other women instead. But you know, Ana, I couldn't count the number of nights I stood across the road from your house in Burnhill, trying to summons up the nerve to ring your doorbell. I always hoped that you'd just come out and find me there and invite me in and that would be the beginning for us.'

'Adrian–'

'I saw your son a few times, coming in and out.'

'Adrian–'

'Please, let me finish, Ana. I need to tell you all this. The last time I went over to London hoping to see you, your neighbour told me that your son had died and that you'd gone away and she didn't know when you'd be home again. That's when I planted those daffodils in your back garden. You see, I remembered that as a child you were mad about daffodils and I wanted you to have something to cheer you up when you came home. You know, I often used to imagine how your face must have looked when you first saw them.'

'Adrian–'

'Then you married that Dunne fellow and I'd lost my chance again. You know, I'm glad all this has come up. You don't know how much I've wanted to tell you. Of course, if something were to happen between us now I'd be the happiest man in the world but that's not why I asked you to come and live with me. I don't really expect anything to happen. I just want to take care of you.'

He got up, crossed over and sat down close beside her.

'Ana–' he began.

'Look,' she interrupted, hurriedly getting to her feet, suddenly finding his proximity unbearable, 'I think I need to get out, to go for a walk. There's a lot to take in. I need to sort things out in my mind.'

'To sort things out?' He looked up at her in surprise. 'What things?You are going to come and stay with me, aren't you? Everything is ready.You wouldn't know my mother's room. I've had it done up for you. I swear you'll be happy there. Every evening we'll...'

'Adrian, I really need to–'

'Of course, of course, Ana, I understand,' he said quickly. 'Take all the time you need. I'll wait here until you're ready. But you don't know how much it means to have you finally coming to live with me in Mornington Close. You don't know how often I've imagined...'

'Adrian look–'

'Sorry, sorry, I'm sorry, Ana. I'm just a bit tense. Go on, you go for your walk. I'll be waiting right here for you.'

Ana walked as far as the lake and there she sat down on a bench. What should she do, she asked herself. Could she still go and live with Adrian after all she'd just learned? Regardless of the fact that he'd harassed those other women, she'd always felt completely safe with him; he'd never harmed her. Quite the contrary in fact. Growing up, he'd always been there for her and, lately, when she'd needed him, he'd been there as well – helping her after she'd come out of the hospital, finding the bungalow for her here in Rathdowne and, when that didn't work out, he'd come to the rescue once again and offered her a home. Who else would have done all that for her? Who else cared about her as much as he did? And, of everyone she knew, he was the only one who remembered that today was her birthday – a small point maybe, but significant somehow.

But would it be fair to go and live with him? Despite what he was saying now, would he end up expecting more than she was prepared to offer?

'Mrs Dunne,' called out Mrs Reynolds from where she was standing on the terrace at the rear of the main house. 'Mrs Dunne, you've got visitors. They're waiting for you in the sunroom.'

'Who?' Ana shouted back but Mrs Reynolds had hurried away leaving Ana no choice but to go and see, though she'd little mind to.

When she came into the sunroom she was surprised to see how busy it was. It seemed that nearly all the residents had found some reason to be here at this very moment although the actual reason soon became apparent. Mrs Reynolds had obviously taken the trouble to alert more than just Ana to these two unexpected visitors who were now being subjected to a range of looks, from furtive glances to outright stares, from everyone in the room. The strangers, both of them girls in their late teens, were sitting on two armchairs in the centre and what was striking about the pair of them was that they were both black.

'Mrs Dunne?' enquired one of the girls, standing up as Ana came into the room.

'Yes,' said Ana coming over to her, still wondering who they could be. 'Hello.'

'I know you don't know me,' the girl began, 'but my father Kaninu asked me to come and see you if we came to Ireland.'

Ana stared at her, momentarily at a loss for words.

'You remember my father Kaninu?' asked the girl, now puzzled by Ana's lack of response.

'Remember Kaninu?' stammered Ana, once she'd managed to recover from the shock. 'Of course I remember him. How could I forget? And you're his daughter?'

'Yes.'

'This is incredible,' said Ana, staring at the girl. 'I'm sorry, I'm just a little bit stunned. You've really taken me by surprise.' But then she laughed excitedly, reached out and gave the girl a big hug and, once she'd let her go, held her at a distance as she examined her. 'Yes,' she said finally. 'I think I can see a little of him in you, around the eyes maybe. But what are you doing here?'

The girl was about to answer, but Ana interrupted.

'I've forgotten my manners. Please, sit down.'

Once all three were seated, the girl began.

'My friend and I are studying in London but this weekend our university basketball team was travelling to play against UCD so we took the opportunity to travel with them. I hope you don't mind us visiting you unannounced but if we didn't come my father would be very angry. He made me promise before I left home that we would make every effort to come and see you. He always writes in his letters that we should remember that we have you to thank for the fact that we are studying at university.'

'I'm sure that your own hard work had more to do with it than anything.'

'That's what I tell him. But I do know that you started the school in our village and that you set up the college fund. You see my mother and father and many of the older people in our village still talk about you all the time.'

'Really?'

'Oh yes. How you set up the school and ran it for a while and how you helped our village so much in many ways. And my grandmother and grandfather used to talk about you all the time when they were alive, remembering the time you lived in the village. In fact, I think my grandmother was the one who decided I should be called after you.'

'So you're the little daughter they called

Anastasia. When you were born your father wrote and told me all about you.'

'And my friend's name is Anastasia too,' said Kaninu's daughter indicating the girl beside her.

'What?' asked Ana, and then she laughed. 'I don't believe it.'

'It's true.'

Ana looked at the friend who was nodding now and smiling at her.

'Hello, Anastasia,' said Ana.

'Hello, Mrs Dunne. I am pleased to meet you.'

'This is very strange,' said Ana, still smiling, still shaking her head in amusement. 'But both of you having the same name must cause a lot of confusion.'

'Very much so,' answered Kaninu's daughter. 'At our college in London but even more so at home in our village where six of the girls around our age are called Anastasia. You see, for a while it was the fashion and, as you probably know, it is not a Kenyan name so outsiders find it very puzzling. But it is not so bad because two of the girls are called Ana for short, including my friend, and other girl is called Ansty. Do you know, that in our village you are known as Grandmother Ansty?'

'No, I didn't,' said Ana.

'Would you mind if we called you that now?'

'Not at all, I quite like the sound of it.'

Ana couldn't stop smiling. The notion of a village far away in Kenya full of black Anastasias appealed to her very much.

Suddenly she became acutely aware of the silence in the room and of the interest she and her fellow Anastasias were generating. She looked over and caught Elizabeth staring over at them.

'Elizabeth,' she called out. 'I know you've always been keen to know about my family. Well, here are two of them now. Elizabeth, meet Anastasia and Anastasia, two of my granddaughters.'

The two girls got up and went over to Elizabeth to shake her hand and, as Ana watched, she couldn't help but smile to herself as she thought of what must be going on in Elizabeth's mind. No doubt she'd have dozens of questions for Ana after this but there was no way Ana was going to satisfy her curiosity. She quite liked the idea of leaving Elizabeth racked with curiosity following her departure.

The girls couldn't stay long, a college friend who'd driven them down from Dublin was waiting on them. But, since they were going to be around for a few days, they gave Ana a contact telephone number and she promised to ring them as soon as she was settled so that they could meet up again.

Once she'd waved them off, she turned and quickly began walking back to her bungalow.

Her mind was made up. She wasn't going to live with Adrian and it wasn't anything to do with all this harassment business, not really. Going to live with him she saw now, was simply throwing in the towel; it was just giving up. She was glad that the girls happened to call precisely when they had for their visit reminded her that she'd gone through far worse periods than this in her life and had managed to survive them. If she went to live with Adrian then her dancing days would be well and truly over, as he liked to say. Well, let him speak for himself. He was wrong about her. Not until she was six foot under would her dancing days be finished. There was still a lot of living to be done. God, what had she been thinking of?

She'd get a place of her own – somewhere, anywhere – and start over again, just as she'd always done. How, she asked herself, had she given up so completely?

'Ana,' she heard a voice call out and she looked around to see Laurence coming along the avenue on the Colonel's Honda 50. He pulled up alongside her and, noticing her glance at the bike, he grinned wryly.

'Don't mock it,' he said. 'With my van still out of action, it's the only way I have of getting about.'

'And you can drive it with your arm in plaster?'

'Just about.'

There was an awkward silence as they stared at one another. Laurence had finally come back to work at the start of the previous week but Ana had been careful to avoid him and he too had been avoiding her.

'Ana, I hear you're going to stay with Nurse Boo.'

'Yes.'

Why should she tell him otherwise? He'd made it perfectly clear that he'd no interest in being friends with her, not to mind anything more.

'I see.'

'I'd better keep going, Laurence, there's still a lot I need to do,' she lied.

'Before you go I need to tell you one thing. Please, it won't take very long. It's been on my mind and I really want to set things straight before you go.'

'I don't know, Laurence. I think we've–'

'Please, Ana.'

She sighed, then shrugged and, taking her shrug for an indication that she'd stay long enough to hear him out, he began.

'Ana, my ex-wife Sinéad, or Dawn as she's also known, and I have been divorced a long time. We got married in Las Vegas over thirty-six years ago and separated two years later. Since then she's gone through husbands number two, three and four and, according to my sons, is currently on the look out for number five – God help him whoever it turns out to be.'

'So?' demanded Ana. 'Why are you telling me this?'

'I just want you to know that you misunderstood me when I asked you out. Sinéad and myself are well and truly finished and asking you out wasn't something I did lightly. I'm not like that. Incredible as it might seem, in all the time I've lived apart from Sinéad you're the very first woman I have ever asked out. I just wanted you to know that.'

'I see.'

'And, Ana, I need to say one other thing. I like you an awful lot and even if you're not interested in me in the way I'd hoped I want to offer you a room in my house. I don't like to see you going to live with that Nurse Boo.'

Ana didn't say anything, she was wondering whether to tell him that she'd already changed her plans.

'Ana, he strikes me as a terrible fusspot and I think you'd go crazy living with him. I just can't see how it could work out. I'm not saying that I'm prefect but at least I'm fairly easy-going. Before our falling out I got the feeling that you enjoyed any time we spent together. I know I did, Ana. We got on well, didn't we? I think we'd have a bit of fun if you came to stay with me which I don't think would be the case at all with Adrian. He's an awful old misery. It would be the end of you, Ana.'

'Laurence–'

'You could stay for as long, or for as short a time as you want. And you'd have your own room of course.'

'That's very kind but–' began Ana.

'It's not kindness. I'd enjoy having you stay. So tell me, what do you think? I know it's come as a bit of a surprise but I really think it could work out.'

Ana looked at him for a long time without answering.

'I don't think so, Laurence.'

'Ana–'

'You haven't been exactly all that pleasant these last few weeks Laurence.'

'I know and I'm sorry. I just felt so terrible about everything that I couldn't think straight. It was bad enough that the Colonel was dead but that I should be the one responsible for killing him made it absolutely unbearable. I just couldn't…'

A thought suddenly struck Ana.

'Laurence, how did you know I was going to live with Adrian?'

'Lizzy phoned me at home, about half an hour ago, so I came straight down.'

'Elizabeth phoned you?' Ana stared at

him, amazed.

'Yes.'

'What on earth possessed her to do that? Why you of all people?'

Laurence shrugged.

'I don't know really but she sounded very strange, very un-Lizzy-like, going on about how everyone deserved a shot at happiness. But please, will you just think about what I'm saying to you, what I'm asking you?'

Ana stared at him for a few moments.

'Ana?' he repeated, looking at her anxiously.

She continued to stare. Then, finally, she answered.

'I'll come with you,' she began slowly, cautiously.

'That's grand,' he replied equally cautiously.

'But I'm only coming with you for your sake.'

'Of course.' He smiled.

'Up there in the mountains is no place for an old fellow on his own,' she told him.

'No place at all,' agreed Laurence.

'But...'

'Yes?'

'I have two conditions,' she warned.

'And they are?'

'First, as soon as I've told Adrian that I'm not going with him we'll head off straight away, on the Colonel's bike.'

'But it's a long way Ana. And what about all your things?'

'I can get them another day. It has to be straight away, I don't want to give myself time to think about what I'm doing. I know it's crazy, I just don't want to think how crazy. Besides, I've got a notion to feel what it would be like to head off up into the mountains on the Honda with the wind in my hair. The Colonel promised me that I could one day.'

'Alright. And the other condition?'

'I'm coming to that but, first, I have a question. Where do the dogs sleep?'

'What?' Laurence looked at her, baffled.

'Where do your dogs sleep? You don't have them in the bed at night with you, do you?'

'Indeed I do not. What kind do you think I am?'

'A mountainy Wicklow man and everyone knows what they're like. So they don't sleep with you. Well, that's good. Okay then, my second condition is that I don't have to stay in the spare room.'

'What?'

'I'm not sleeping in the spare room. If I have to then the deal is off.'

'So ... so what are you saying Ana?'

'I suppose I'm saying that I'll go with you but only if I don't have to sleep on my own. I've had my fill of that.'

Laurence looked at her for a few

moments, then a smile broke across his face.
'It's a deal. Hop up so.'

'Is that the Colonel's old Honda Laurence is driving?' asked Ellen, noticing the bike coming towards them on the path running past the sunroom.

'Looks like it,' said Penny, joining her at the French windows.

'And who's that he has up behind him?' Ellen asked, trying to make out the figure whose arms appeared to be wrapped unnecessarily tightly around Laurence's waist, given the slow speed they were travelling at.

As he drove past the window Laurence gave a beep at the two women standing there, staring open-mouthed, and Ana let go of Laurence's waist just long enough to give them a little wave. The bike backfired, then picked up speed and, in a cloud of smoke, Laurence and Ana disappeared out through the main gates.

'Elizabeth, Elizabeth, you'll never believe what we're just after seeing,' said Ellen rushing over to Elizabeth as she came into the sunroom.

'Let me guess,' said Elizabeth and smiled to herself.

This Large Print Book, for people who cannot read normal print, is published under the auspices of

THE ULVERSCROFT FOUNDATION

... we hope you have enjoyed this book. Please think for a moment about those who have worse eyesight than you ... and are unable to even read or enjoy Large Print without great difficulty.

You can help them by sending a donation, large or small, to:

**The Ulverscroft Foundation,
1, The Green, Bradgate Road,
Anstey, Leicestershire, LE7 7FU,
England.**

or request a copy of our brochure for more details.

The Foundation will use all donations to assist those people who are visually impaired and need special attention with medical research, diagnosis and treatment.

Thank you very much for your help.